THE BANKSTER

Ravi Subramanian, an alumnus of IIM Bangalore, has spent two decades working his way up the ladder of power in the amazingly exciting and adrenaline-pumping world of global banks in India. It is but natural that his stories are set against the backdrop of the financial services industry. He lives in Mumbai with his wife Dharini and daughter Anusha. In 2008, he won the Golden Quill Readers Choice award for his debut novel, *If God was a Banker*.

To know more about Ravi visit www.ravisubramanian.in or email him at info@ravisubramanian.in. To connect with him, log on to Facebook at www.facebook.com/authorravisubramanian or tweet to @subramanianravi.

THE BANKSTER

Ravi Subramanian

RUPA

First published in 2012 by
Rupa Publications India Pvt. Ltd.
7/16, Ansari Road, Daryaganj
New Delhi 110002

Sales centres:
Allahabad Bengaluru Chennai
Hyderabad Jaipur Kathmandu
Kolkata Mumbai

ISBN: 978-81-291-2048-9

10 9 8 7 6 5 4 3 2 1

Ravi Subramanian asserts the moral right to be identified
as the author of this work.

Typeset in 10/13 pts Requiem Text by SÜRYA, New Delhi

Printed and bound in India by
Thomson Press India Ltd.
18/35, Delhi-Mathura Road
Faridabad 121007

To all the banksters out there,
playing a game with customers' trust.

PROLOGUE

Angola, South Africa
Beginning of the 21st Century

The passenger in the back seat of the Range Rover shook out of his slumber as the vehicle hit yet another pothole. Roads in Angola were far from what he was used to back home. He strained his neck and looked back, out of the SUV. The escort car was following very closely. It was not safe to venture alone into these areas even for a local, let alone a foreigner. These trips gave him goose bumps, which became even more pronounced as he passed a few deserted diamond mines.

The rigour wasn't alien to him. He had been journeying here for two years now and could handle the roughness with aplomb. Every time he visited, the excitement was the same, the adrenalin rush similar and the anticipation overwhelming. Indeed, he seemed to be enjoying every bit. His small frame belied the intensity in his eyes. Curly hair, clean shaven, flawless skin. . .he would have made quite a few feminine hearts skip a beat, but for the cut above his right eyebrow, which extended across his forehead. Involuntarily, his hand drew to it, touching the deep gash gently, remembering that day a few years ago when he was caught in an ambush in Iraq. A land mine had gone off, blowing his escort team to smithereens. He had escaped with a superficial injury, but the incident was never far from his mind.

The Range Rover was passing through one of the many villages that dotted his route. A newspaper was lying in the seat packet in front of him. He pulled it out and glanced at the front page. 'It has been said that war is the price of peace. . .Angola and Sierra Leone have already paid too much. Let them live a better life,' screamed a local newspaper, headlining a statement made by Ambassador Juan Larrain, chairman of the monitoring mechanism on sanctions against UNITA (Union for Total Independence of Angola).

Strife-torn Angola was host to the longest and worst proxy battle the world had ever seen—a war that had lasted over three decades and had left half a million dead. UNITA was backed by United States and South Africa. It was fighting to end the regime of a Russia-backed socialist government—People's Movement for the Liberation of Angola (MPLA). The entire battle was to control Angola's diamond deposits. In its neighbouring diamond-rich nations—South Africa and Botswana—diamond deposits existed below the surface of the earth, requiring sophisticated mining equipment to dig up. Not so in Angola. Angola's diamond reserves were alluvial. Over the years, they were washed out of the soil and deposited on the vast and barren countryside, embedded in sand gravel and clay. Anyone with just sieves, pans and a shovel could extract diamonds. UNITA in those days controlled areas with 60–70 per cent of the country's diamond deposits, and this was the bone of contention between UNITA and MPLA.

Just a few hours ago, he had landed in the capital city of Luanda, flying in from Windhoek, in neighbouring Namibia. As he passed through immigration, the officer looked at him menacingly from top to toe, sending a shiver down his spine. Was his mission doomed even before it took off?

'Will you please step aside?' It was more of an order and he had to comply.

'Sure', he nodded and moved to his left. 'Is there a problem, Officer Grindle?' he asked casually. That was the name on the badge pinned on the officer's shirt. Over the years he had learnt that the more relaxed he appeared, the lesser was the probability of him being suspected of foul play.

'Not at all, just give us a couple of minutes. We need to check on something.' Grindle was courteous. Leaving him in the room, Grindle stepped out and walked towards a cabin, presumably of his superior. The walls of the waiting room were translucent; the person inside could see everything happening on the outside.

Within a few minutes, Grindle and his senior were walking towards him. The senior was furiously gesticulating at the immigration officer and had an irritated look on his otherwise deadpan face. They stopped outside the room from where the supervisor banished Grindle back to his desk at the immigration counter where a queue was beginning to build up—Grindle was one of the two officers manning the immigration counters.

The supervisor opened the door and walked in straight towards him. He offered him a handshake. 'Mr. . .' and he stopped. He had forgotten the name. The passport was in his hand. Embarrassed, he opened it, looked at the name and said, 'Aaaah. . .Mr Joseph Braganza,' and smiled. 'Welcome to Luanda.'

Joseph smiled, now extending his hand to shake the supervisor's hand and reciprocate his friendly gesture. 'Thank you.'

'Mr Braganza, my apologies, we had received intimation about your arrival from your company and we were requested to fast-track your exit. But this idiot, officer Grindle, is new here. Not everyone is aligned to us, you see. He does not understand the sensitivity involved, Mr Braganza. It's nice to see you in Angola.'

'Thank you. Now if you hand me my passport, I will get going. I have people waiting for me.'

'Sure, sure. Please accept my apologies. When will you be heading back to Namibia?'

'Tomorrow morning.'

'Aaaaaahh. . .short stay?'

Joseph nodded.

'Have a good time, sir,' said the supervisor, handing over the passport and simultaneously opening the door of the meeting room.

Joseph Braganza hastily exited and walked out of the airport. He did not have much time. It was a close shave for him this time around. Else, normally, the CIA contacts had always proven to be effective and he had never ever been stopped at immigration. This was the first time someone had questioned him. The first lesson that he had learnt while undergoing training as an agent was that there are no coincidences. It bothered him, but he decided to let it go, and be more watchful in the future.

A brief meeting at the airport hotel, where the ambassador of Zaire joined him, was followed by a quick exchange of pleasantries with his business associates based in Luanda, and then he had departed on this long journey—an eight-hour drive through the reverse pyramid-shaped mines, in the interiors of Angola. He was not alone in this mission. Three escort cars from the Embassy of the Republic of Zaire, two armoured vans carrying security personnel in battle fatigue and a similar number of private security personnel followed him. Relaxing in his bulletproof Range Rover, he reminisced how he had been instructed to make sure that he did not rely on the security cover provided by others, for anything was possible in Angola.

At a distance he could see the *garimpeiros*—Angola's artisanal miners—digging and sifting through endless mounds of sand and clay, as his cavalcade passed through yet another open diamond mine. A woman, carrying what looked like a baby a few months old, a girl barely out of her teens, a man on crutches, all feverishly digging using hands, shovels and everything else they could lay their hands on in their quest for riches and wealth.

An evil grin appeared on his face. 'Mad people,' he whispered as he turned his gaze to the other side. The sight was similar. 'Does it ever occur to them that they are not destined to enjoy the fruits of their labour,' he said to himself as he closed his eyes and slid into another one of his power naps.

When he opened his eyes, they were far away from any civilization, passing through a dense forest—a rarity in Angola. He could see the lights of the escort vehicles ahead as well as of the ones behind him.

'How much longer?'

'We should be there in half an hour,' the driver responded. Joseph was very particular. On each trip, he used the same driver. Driven by the fact that he knew the terrain, and was loyal—Joseph had bought his loyalty. Tipping was easy in the land of the poor.

'Hmm. . .' said Joseph and that was the end of the conversation. They travelled in silence till they reached the top of a mound and began descending. A few minutes into their descent, Joseph saw a light at a distance. It looked like a camp. A few burning lanterns and the rising smoke from a large campfire indicated they were indeed close to their destination.

Joseph immediately straightened up and adjusted his clothes. Subconsciously his fingers reached out to his hip. The gun was safe in the holster. He remembered what his father-in-law always said, 'No loose talk. Do what you are supposed to do and get out of there. No one is a friend in that camp.'

In another five minutes, the bushes started clearing up and the roads began to get wider. They could see a few gunmen in sandbagged bunkers guarding the sides of the road. No one stopped them. They were expected at the camp.

Both sides of the road were now lined with hutments with asbestos roofs, and sides draped with olive green camouflage. It was a large settlement. He had heard that over 25000 UNITA loyalists stayed in that camp. The MPLA knew about the camp, but couldn't do anything about it. Not only was the access treacherous, but any attack on the UNITA camp would have aggravated tensions between the Russian and the American establishments, which either side could ill-afford.

After driving through the camp, the motorcade stopped in front of a heavily guarded gate. A uniformed guard walked up and said something to the driver. Being locals, they spoke fluent Portuguese. Had Joseph heard them, he would have understood what they spoke; ever since he had started dealing with these guys, he had picked up the local language. It always helped.

The guard disappeared, the gates opened and they moved towards a big open ground converted into a makeshift ammunition dump. Large battle equipment, tanks, rocket launchers, sophisticated guns and battle-ready jeeps stood amidst heavy guard. A lone cottage stood at the other end of the ground. It was the largest one and looked like the most exclusive habitation in the entire camp. The driver turned towards it and drove on till he reached within fifty metres of the cottage. That was the perimeter; no outside vehicle was allowed beyond that limit. Guards stepped in front and stopped Joseph's car. The entire motorcade halted.

Joseph stepped out of the car. His whole body was aching on account of sitting in a car for eight continuous hours. He stretched, while the ambassador of Zaire and his security guards got out of their respective cars and surrounded Joseph. He started walking towards the entrance of the cottage.

'Good evening. Welcome to the UNITA camp. My name is Colonel Gato.' Joseph looked at him and felt tiny. Colonel Gato stood at an imposing six foot seven inches. Joseph had already been briefed on Colonel Gato and his allegiance to the Americans.

'Thank you,' said Joseph, extending his hand towards Gato. No one asked him his name and he didn't volunteer it either.

'If you are fine with it gentlemen, my men can go and inspect your vehicles while you come inside with me.' Both Joseph and the ambassador nodded.

'General Antonio Swabimbi would like to meet you,' said Gato as he walked them past the hallway to another heavily guarded part of the cottage. They crossed a large room with a posse of military guards—Joseph counted seventeen—into a small tunnel, which led them to an enclosure that had no exit door. Joseph was wondering where they were heading, when Gato bent and moved the carpet covering the floor, exposing a small latch. He tugged at it, revealing a secret passageway. A flight of stairs went into the earth and the three of them climbed down carefully.

For a moment, Joseph was awestruck. In front of him lay an exact replica of the cottage above, almost entirely below the ground, but far more robust than the one above. This was built to withstand attack from heavy artillery. The exquisite furniture and the glitzy fittings made it look almost like a five-star hotel.

'I will let the General know that you are here,' Gato said and walked away. He was back in no time and smiled at them. 'He will be here in a couple of minutes.' They settled down on one of the many comfortable couches in that room.

'Hello young man,' a voice boomed in the underground cottage.

Joseph turned, and found himself face-to-face with a tall man with dark curly hair, in military fatigue sans the cap. Instinctively, Joseph stood up.

'General Antonio Swabimbi,' introduced Col Gato. 'The leader of UNITA.'

Joseph fumbled for words and could only extend his hand. Words deserted him. He had visited this camp many times, but never met the big man himself.

'Words can't describe my gratitude for the service you and your great coalition is rendering towards us. The arms and ammunition you have brought for us all the way from Zaire will help us combat the government, which is hell-bent on selling out the nation to tyrants. They have become pawns in the hands of the Russians and the communists.' The General's eyes became red as he spoke passionately against the Russians. Joseph Braganza was a bit worried. Whenever passion overtook reason, he was uncomfortable. But he didn't say anything. A job had to be done. He was the best man for this errand, and his unit trusted no one else for this job.

General Swabimbi went on and on, only to be interrupted by a knock on the secret door. Col Gato nodded at a commando standing nearby, who climbed the flight of stairs and opened the door. Some words were exchanged and he immediately came down and whispered something in Col Gato's ears.

'What is it?' thundered Swabimbi.

'They have unloaded everything and it is in order. The payment can be made General.'

When Swabimbi heard this, he just waved his hand nonchalantly and Gato disappeared behind the curtains only to reappear within three minutes with a small box in his hand, which he handed over to the General.

The General looked at the ambassador of Zaire who stepped ahead, extended his arms and collected the box. Joseph, who was next to the General, took a step towards the ambassador and glanced into the box as the ambassador opened the lid. The ambassador let Joseph examine and evaluate the contents while he held the box in his hands.

Joseph dug into the box and pulled out a large stone.

'One of the largest and the finest that you will ever find,' said General Swabimbi.

'Hmm. . .' muttered Joseph, bringing the stone to eye level. He pulled out what looked like a magnifying glass from his cargo pants and examined it much more closely. He turned it upside down a few more times and put it back into the box. He repeated the same process for every stone in the box. In ten minutes he was done. The ambassador waited patiently all this while. The moment he was done, Joseph looked up and nodded. The ambassador accepted the box and headed towards the stairs leading up. General Swabimbi gave Joseph a warm hug even as he rushed to catch up with the ambassador.

Once outside, the ambassador walked up to his car and waited. Joseph caught up with him in no time.

'Let's go in my car. My driver knows his way around. It'll be safer.'

'Alright.'

The ambassador got into Joseph's Range Rover, while the armoured vehicles and the security guards followed them. Once safely out of the UNITA camp, Joseph looked at the ambassador and pointed towards the box.

'You know how much that would be worth?'

'All I know is that we have supplied the arms worth four and a quarter million dollars and that money needs to be paid to our supplier in the Middle East. Hope you won't forget the payment for our services.'

'I remember, ambassador, as always.'

Joseph took the box from the ambassador and pressed a button discreetly placed on the armrest of his seat. A small door slid open in the back of the seat ahead of him. He dropped the box inside the secret compartment.

'Is it safe there?' the ambassador asked.

'Hmm. . .' said Joseph, thinking of his near-miss brush-in with the immigration officials. What if they had figured out that he was travelling on a fake passport?

Early next morning, Joseph Braganza flew out of Luanda to Namibia and from there to an unknown destination in Europe.

The same evening, four and a quarter million dollars were transferred to Union Bank of Switzerland (UBS) in Zurich, into the account of an arms dealer. When the person authorizing the account credit pulled up the account on screen, the only information he could see was that the country of origin was Zaire.

Two hundred and fifty thousand dollars were transferred to another account in the same bank, an account in the name of Sese Mutombu, the Ambassador of Zaire—his commission for seeing the arms deal through.

The uncut diamonds, sent from an unidentifiable temporary address in Switzerland, were FedExed to an office in Luxemburg. The packet was handed over to David Kosinski, the Chief of Staff of the CEO.

David walked into the CEO's office, opened the safe with a code only he knew and dumped the box into the safe. Before closing the safe, he picked up a post-it from the table, flipped open his pen, and wrote a figure on the post-it before taping it on to the box.

'Diamonds worth nine million dollars,' he whispered to himself. 'That's a lot of money,' he said as he shut the door to the CEO's office silently behind his back and walked towards his own office. Just as the door was about to shut, he glanced back to see the photograph of the CEO's family kept on the table, facing the door. He noted how his CEO stood out in the family, and not just because of the large gash on his forehead. The door banged shut and David walked to his cabin.

'Where does Joseph Braganza get these diamonds from? Last time the diamonds were worth five million and this time it's nine million.' As he lowered himself into his chair, he said to himself, 'Not for me to ask. Not for me to know'. The only thing he knew was that on his next visit to Central Europe, a week from now, he would personally carry these diamonds to a safe hideout to be stored, till the time was appropriate for Joseph Braganza to dispose of them.

* * *

Interior Kerala
July 1979

It rained incessantly in the neighbourhood of the Periyar Tiger reserve in Kerala. The reserve and the adjoining areas of Ranni, Konni, Tenmala and parts of Punalur forests, all large elephant habitats, were reeling under the onslaught of rain and thunderstorm. Sparse in terms of human population, this area, better known for the Thekkady Elephant sanctuary, was the most compact of all the elephant habitats in South India.

It was amidst these jungles, two kilometres off the main road connecting Thekkady to Devikulam that Krishna and Sulochana Menon ran their home stay resort—a small quaint cottage set in a three-acre plantation was replete with all the luxuries money could buy.

Initially, post their return from the Middle East, where Krishna spent most of his life working with gold traders, the Menons made Thiruvananthapuram their home. But after their son, Arvind moved out to a boarding school in Ooty, the Menons felt lonely. They converted their large plantation into a resort and moved to Devikulam to manage it themselves. Over the years, the resort had come to have a sizable following and was quite popular, particularly with foreign tourists.

The three-acre plantation was also home to four captive elephants, which the Menons had acquired when they converted their plantation into a resort. Rides and a photo-op with the elephants were a big hit, especially with the foreign tourists.

One day, Appachen, the trained Mahout, caretaker of the four elephants in the Menons' resort, had come across a sick 65-year-old pachyderm, trapped under the fallen tree trunk. Appachen, being passionate about elephants took it upon himself to nurse him back to health; he even gave him the name 'Gopi'.

'Good job', Krishna said when Appachen told him about it. After giving him some money, Krishna and his wife left for Ooty to visit their son. It soon started to rain torrentially, trapping Appachen in his house for a week. The moment the rains stopped and the sky cleared up, Appachen rushed to Gopi's resting place, only to find that Gopi had passed away during that time. Appachen was a shattered man.

Two weeks later, on a Friday night, Arvind was woken up by a knock on his hostel room. It was a call from his mother.

'Amma, what happened?'

'I don't know what to do Arvind, please come home.'

'What's wrong Amma?' He could hear his mother crying at the other end as she answered.

'Don't worry, I'm coming there right now,' were his last words before he hung up.

The first bus out of Ooty was at 4.45 a.m. and it was noon before the bus stopped at a decrepit bus shelter on its way to Thekkady. Arvind was relieved to see a familiar Ambassador car standing there, waiting for him. The ride thereon was only two kilometres long, though it took close to fifteen minutes, given the slippery state of the muddy roads.

Sulochana was waiting for him when he reached the resort. Next to her was a smart, middle-aged man in black coat—their family lawyer.

'We were just leaving. Come let's go,' said Sulochana, and they got into the car. It took them thirty-five minutes to reach their destination, during which Sulochana briefed Arvind on what had happened.

On reaching a red brick building, the car stopped. They got out and rushed towards the entrance, where they were stopped by a man in uniform.

'Let them in,' boomed a voice from inside. As they entered, they saw a middle-aged pot-bellied man with a handle bar moustache seated behind a table. The top three buttons of his shirt were open, revealing a cleft of greying chest hair. The nameplate on his table read 'Shri K Moinuddin (Sub Inspector)'. Judging by the way the others were rallying around him, it didn't take Arvind long to figure out he was in charge of that police station. From his demeanour, it looked like he was waiting for them.

Seated next to him in a veshti and white shirt was a sinister-looking sidekick. 'Chief Wild Life Warden,' whispered Sulochana. Arvind knew that the chief warden was responsible for protection of the flora and the fauna in the forestland and yielded an enormous amount of authority. The chief warden looked at the three of them and nonchalantly lifted his right leg and kept it on the seat in front of him, his foot pointing in Arvind's direction. Arvind grimaced as he walked up to the Sub-Inspector.

'Why have you arrested my father? He hasn't done anything wrong.'

'Ask your mother. She knows everything.' Moinuddin was at his arrogant best. 'She was there when we picked him up.'

'Every single guy my father has worked with all these years knows how clean he is,' Arvind said, between clenched teeth.

'Hahahaha!' The inspector's laugh, accompanied by an unmistakable stench of liquor irritated Arvind even more. 'Pious man, your father,' he ridiculed, laughing even harder.

Then, as abruptly as he had started laughing, he stopped. There was a sudden silence. He glared at Arvind, got up from his chair and walked towards him, the inadvertent stumble confirming to Arvind that he was drunk. When he was close enough, he extended his left hand, caught Arvind by his collar, raised his right hand, pointed a finger towards him and screamed, 'He's not a good man. Your father is a smuggler. A rogue. Do you get it? That's why he is in jail now.'

'What nonsense!' Arvind was not one to be cowed down.

'Ask your mother, son,' the chief warden stood up this time. 'After killing an elephant, he has cut off the tusks and hidden them. And now he is refusing to tell us where he has kept them.'

'The elephant was old and sick. Our staff tried to revive it. They couldn't.'

'What about the tusks?' demanded the chief warden, 'Where has he hidden them? Or have you guys sold it and pocketed OUR money?' The stress on 'our' was not lost on Arvind.

'Appachen tells us the elephant's tusks were already cut off when it strayed into our neighbourhood. He gave it medication and tried to revive it, but the elephant didn't recover and died,' Arvind argued.

'Hmm. . . Isn't that what everyone says sir?' The chief warden said, looking at the Sub Inspector. Turning towards Arvind, he added, 'Look son. Just in case you are not aware, under Section 39 of the Wild Life Protection Act of 1972, any elephant captured or killed without approval of the competent authority or killed by mistake or found dead, or any animal article or ivory obtained from an elephant is deemed to be government property. Any person who comes in possession of such government property is under the legal obligation to inform the nearest police station within forty-eight hours.'

'So, what are you trying to prove here?'

'We got to know about it only three days after the elephant had died. When we exhumed the carcass, we didn't find its tusks. So son, unless you guys tell us where the ivory is, your father will rot here in jail.'

Arvind took the lawyer aside and asked, 'Is there a way out?'

'No. Ivory smuggling is a non-bailable offence, but. . .' he paused

'But what?'

'They haven't charged him yet. They haven't filed a First Information Report—the FIR. Moinuddin has so far only brought him in for questioning. We will only be in trouble if they book him for smuggling.'

'Then what do we do? He's a heart patient. If he doesn't get his medicines on time, he will have serious health issues.'

'Let's try talking to them,' was all that the advocate could say at that time.

Arvind walked up to the duo again. 'Can I meet my father?'

'No,' the Sub Inspector said firmly.

'Sir, please. It's important for you to hear his side of the story. Only then can you know the whole truth.'

'You will tell us. . .you. . .a kid. . .will tell us what the truth is? Why don't you just get out of the police station? You can go to a judge with your truth.' At the same time a door in the far right of the main hall opened and out walked a constable with a cruel smirk on his face. Trudging behind the constable was the frail frame of Appachen, his vest soaked in blood and his eyes swollen beyond recognition. Appachen looked at them pleadingly through tear-stained eyes, as he was led away. It sent shivers up their spines. Had the same fate befallen Krishna too? He would not be able to withstand it.

Arvind's demeanour completely changed after he saw Appachen's plight. He approached the cop again, this time with folded hands, literally pleading with him to let his father go.

'Once we get the tusks, we'll let your father go. Not before that.' Moinuddin was heartless. He and the chief warden got up to leave. Just as they crossed Arvind, Moinuddin tapped him on his shoulder. 'Go home. Wait for someone to come and talk to you.' The two of them then walked out of the police station, into a parked jeep and drove off, nearly knocking a constable down on the way.

Within the next three hours, a motorcade of three cars drove into the Menon's resort and came to a screeching halt in the portico. Arvind and Sulochana were waiting at the reception. They had been standing there ever since they got back from the police station.

A tall dark man, clad in a veshti and angavastram, stepped out of the lead car and stood in front of them. He looked familiar. When the person folded his hands in front of them and offered them his salutations, Arvind recognized him. This was the same pose he had seen on umpteen posters. The man in front of them was the local MLA, Madan Mohan.

What was he doing there? Even in the days of general elections in Devikulam, he had never ever visited them.

'I believe there is some problem here?' the MLA seemed concerned and asked Sulochana.

'No sir, no problem,' Arvind stammered. He didn't want the local MLA to blow the issue out of proportion.

'But Moinuddin was telling me a different story?'

'Moinuddin?' Arvind was momentarily surprised before he realised why the MLA was there. He was a part of the scam and wanted his pound of flesh. A deal was struck for twenty-five thousand rupees to exchange hands for the release of Arvind's father.

Krishna came back the same evening along with Appachen. The scars on Appachen's body healed over a period of time. But the deep wound it left in Arvind's mind refused to heal. That was the day he decided to leave India for good. Eight years after the incident, Arvind married the daughter of a Russian scientist and settled in Ukraine, where, a few years later, the world saw the worst ever nuclear disaster.

1

Greater Boston Global Bank
Head Office
Fort, Mumbai
February 2011

'Arre Vikram,' shouted Tanuja, waving her hand frantically as she sprinted casually across the passage between rows of workstations enroute to the conference room, trying to grab the attention of the Retail Banking Head of Greater Boston Global Bank (GB2). Vikram had just walked out of the core strategy meet the CEO had called in preparation for the high profile visit of seniors from the Global Headquarters (GHQ) of GB2. The flamboyant Vikram Bahl had been the Head of Branch banking, a role in which he spent about three years, before being promoted to head Retail Banking in the middle of 2010. He had stayed away from hiring his replacement in the branch banking business and managed it directly, despite having moved on to a more senior role. Many thought it was because of his hands-on approach to business, though many skeptics also said he was scared of skeletons tumbling out of the closet if someone else stepped into that role. In order to keep Guneet Chandra, the Head of Credit Cards and Vikram's professional rival happy, the cards business was not made to report to Vikram. It reported directly to the CEO of the bank, pending Guneet's elevation to the next level at an appropriate time.

'Kya hua? Anything interesting?' Tanuja asked when she caught up with him.

'Nothing yaar. Just the same old bakwas. These meetings are now beginning to get on my nerves. Indrani is just the same as Ronald McCain.'

'Who said things would change once Ronald moves and Indrani takes over?'

'Haan yaar. It's been close to a year that he moved back and Indrani became CEO. We were hoping that once an Indian takes over as CEO, things would improve. But it's still the same old crap, same old meetings, same old discussions. When will we get over this nonsense ya?'

'Okay okay. . . Dheere dheere. . . Keep your voice low. Someone might hear you.' Tanuja didn't want to get into trouble because of Vikram's antics. Being the head of HR she had to maintain decorum, which Vikram didn't quite care about, at least in her presence. The last thing she wanted was to be heard bitching about the CEO.

'Oh. Don't worry Tanuja. No one will hear us. And who wants to listen to whatever we say? They do their own thing anyway.'

'Well, aren't you in a good mood today,' Tanuja remarked sarcastically.

'What do I say? Had to go and see a property in Lokhandwala this morning. Indrani called for this meeting and screwed up my schedule.'

'What property?'

'Somebody brought a deal to me. Thought I would check it out and see if it's worth investing in.'

'Arre, how come you're looking for property without me?'

'Oh, ho. Let me see it first. If it is worth it, I will tell you na. Anyway what're you doing now? Come, let's go for chai.'

Tanuja glanced at her watch, and simultaneously opened the calendar on her BlackBerry to check her schedule for the remaining part of the day. Hurriedly, she typed out a message and in a matter of forty-five seconds she pressed 'send' and walked out of the bank premises with Vikram to a stall about two hundred metres away for a cup of cutting chai.

'Did you have a meeting?' asked Vikram, pointing to her BlackBerry.

'Haan, yaar. Nikhil wanted to see me.'

'Why?'

'Some issues with his performance rating that he wants to discuss with me.'

'What crap? Let him speak to Guneet Chandra first. Who is his boss? Guneet or you?'

'Of course Guneet... He tried to do that. But apparently Guneet couldn't convince him. Nikhil feels he deserves a rating better than the 3+ he's got. Now he wants to chew my brains about it.'

'When is he coming to meet you?'

'In the next fifteen minutes. I was just not in a mood to meet him. In any case what could I have done—only given him the satisfaction that he raised this issue with the head of HR. I would have given him some gyan and sent him away. But I've just told my secretary to tell him that I'm going to Delhi tomorrow and won't be back till the end of the week,' and she started laughing.

Vikram laughed too. 'You are now saved the trauma and harassment that Nikhil would have subjected you to,' he said, giving her a high five.

After the tea with Vikram, Tanuja was back at her desk in

forty minutes. Her secretary came in to tell her that Nikhil had come and left.

'Oh, something very critical came up. I couldn't skip it. So had to cancel it.' Her secretary nodded and left Tanuja's cabin, quietly closing the door behind her.

A few hours later the intercom on Tanuja's desk rang. Her secretary had left for the day and hence all the calls landed directly on her extension.

'Yes sir. . .ready to leave?'

'No, no. . .not yet. I suddenly remembered something. In the meeting today, Indrani talked about a directive from GHQ to start private banking in India.'

'I know. Indrani mentioned this to me yesterday,' Tanuja confirmed.

'You knew this? Why didn't you tell me?' She could sense some irritation in his voice.

'I didn't? Strange. It must've slipped my mind. But in any case, how does it matter? It's a different business; in fact it's going to be set up as a different company, a different legal entity.'

'That's exactly my point, Tanuja. It's going to be a different business. And that's why we need to be prepared.'

'Prepared? As in?' Tanuja asked, confused.

'Look Tanuja, private banking is a business targeted at the crème de la crème customers. It will compete with the top end of my branch banking business. They will end up targeting the same customers, that too with better services and more flexible products.'

'So?'

'We have to make sure they don't steal our thunder.' Tanuja didn't understand what Vikram meant.

Under Vikram, branch banking had become a very glamorous business. The stock market was on fire for the better part of the previous year, mutual funds were selling as if they were soon going out of fashion and gullible customers were very happy investing in mutual funds and other structured products, as advised by the extremely aggressive relationship managers in Vikram's branch network. A new private banking business set up on similar lines, albeit targeting only the high-end consumers, was sure to create turmoil. In the relationship management world, a private banking RM was seen as belonging to a superior breed as compared to the normal branch RM. It was but natural for Vikram to be worried that most of his RMs would want to move to private banking roles. Anybody in his place would have been worried that the arrival of Private Banking would create discontent and unrest in his team.

'Are you worried that your guys would want to move to them? If so, don't bother too much. We will mandate that no branch RM will move to the private banking jobs as and when they come up,' Tanuja tried to comfort Vikram.

'Arre, nahin yaar. That's not what I am worried about. On the contrary, I would want my guys to move to bigger and better roles. Let them take people from my team. Let them hire my RMs.'

'What!' Tanuja was surprised.

'Yes, of course. In fact if my RMs have good careers, I will be extremely happy.' Conviction was completely missing from what he said. There was silence at the other end. Then Tanuja burst out into a guffaw. 'Hahahaha.' She continued laughing for a while. 'Now I understand!'

'What?'

'Bahut kamina hai tu! You're too smart. . .just too smart.'

'Arre, why?'

'You want to fill in the new business with your own people. I know you too well, Vikram. If you pack the private banking team with RMs from your branch banking network who owe their allegiance to you, the business will be *de facto* in your control. And you, smart ass Vikram Bahl, will run that business remotely.'

'Hehe. . .no no.' Vikram was a bit embarrassed that Tanuja had called his bluff. 'That's not what I had in mind.'

'Sure. Sure. If that's not what you had in mind, then I am the Queen of England.'

'No Tanuja. That isn't my intention at all. But now that you say it, it might not be a bad idea. What's the harm in getting one of our own guys to head private banking? I will release one of my best cluster managers for the job.'

'Who? Rahul? Your brother-in-law?' Tanuja was the only one who knew that one of the senior-most cluster managers in Vikram's team was his wife's first cousin. It was one of the few closely held secrets at GB2.

'No yaar. That we will figure out later. But it will be someone from inside the team.'

'Not possible, Vikram. The mandate is that for the head of private banking, we have to get talent from outside the group. They want a fresh perspective for this role.'

'Is that so?'

'Hmm. Start hunting for the Head of private banking, Mr Bahl. . .and that too from outside GB2.'

'It won't be difficult. I'll send you a couple of guys. You speak to them directly. If you like them, I'll ask Yogesh Bhargav to send you their CVs. We can then put them up to Indrani to hire.'

'Good idea. The money Yogesh Bhargav will pass back to us if we hire through him will pay for our next Maldives holiday.'

'Not on the intercom, babes. . . Anyway, I'm done. Ready to leave?'

'Ten minutes. See you in the parking lot,' and Tanuja hung up.

As promised, in ten minutes Vikram and Tanuja drove out of the basement car park in a steel grey Mitsubishi Lancer. They were neighbours and would often come to work and leave together.

'I'm going to tell Abhishek to start preparing for the Maldives trip,' said Tanuja as they crossed Ambassador hotel and turned right into Marine drive. 'Tell Yogesh Bhargav we'll pay him only ten per cent of the actual commission due on this deal. We'll keep the rest.'

'He will quietly take what we give him. In any case, he is an old man with one foot in the grave. What will he do with more than that?' He looked at her and smiled. Tanuja smiled back. They crossed Haji Ali and were driving towards Parel where both of them stayed.

Vikram's phone rang. It was lying on the dashboard of the car. Vikram's hands were glued to the steering and the slow-moving traffic made it difficult for him to move his left hand away from the gear shaft. Tanuja picked it up. She saw the name flashing on the screen and looked at Vikram.

'Why is he calling you?'

'I don't know. Take the call and ask him.'

'It's okay. Let it be.' In any case, by then the phone stopped ringing.

In five minutes, Vikram turned left and drove into the compound of Marathon Towers in Parel. Tanuja stayed on the 18th floor of that building.

'Thanks Vikram. I'll talk to you tomorrow. Take care.'

'You too,' and Vikram pressed the button to roll up the window which he had opened to see off Tanuja. Before he could roll it up completely, Tanuja turned back. 'Oh, I completely forgot, Vikram. Tell me. . .are you going for Indrani's dinner tomorrow?'

'Nope.'

'Why? Chal na. Let's go. I won't need to then worry about getting a ride back home.'

'No Tanuja. Over a hundred and twenty people have been invited for this party. I saw the invitee list on Indrani's secretary's table. And you know na, I seldom go to parties that are for the masses. What's the point of going to an event where your presence will not be felt?' And he smiled, rolled up the window, turned the car and left.

As he exited Marathon Towers, he picked up his mobile. A casual glance told him there were no cops around. There was a missed call notification staring at him. He clicked on it and dialled the most recent missed call. It was picked up within one ring.

'Yes dude, tell me.'

'Vikram, sorry to disturb you so late. I called to update you.'

'Not a problem. I'm driving. By the way, I was with someone earlier, so couldn't talk when you called.'

'Vikram, I went to meet Tanuja today. Even waited for over half an hour. She didn't turn up.'

'What the fuck man?'

'Yes, Vikram, apparently she had something very critical which came up at the last minute. Something she couldn't avoid.'

'Bitch. Anyway, don't worry. You stay focused. And make sure you get an audience with her and give her your entire perspective. Tell her everything we discussed. I know she is off to Delhi day after tomorrow. You must land up at her office and meet her tomorrow at any cost.'

'Sure Vikram.'

'Don't worry, Nikhil. We'll make sure your rating gets changed. And if they don't, I'll pull you out of there. You relax. And sleep well tonight. I'm with you on this one.'

'Thanks Vikram.'

'How long are you in Mumbai? When are you going back to Pune?' Nikhil was based in Pune and he had come in to Mumbai only to discuss his performance appraisal.

'I'll be leaving after meeting Tanuja tomorrow.'

'Cool. Goodnight Nikhil. Talk to you tomorrow,' and Vikram hung up.

2

Nikhil met Tanuja the next day. Well aware of Tanuja's reluctance to meet him, he just landed up at her office and parked himself there till she got free. Nikhil was well prepared. All the data, performance reports and email exchanges between Guneet and him, even the comparative performances of his peers, he carried with him.

'Look at this, Tanuja,' Nikhil fired off a salvo. 'This guy has got a rating of "1" and hasn't even met sixty per cent of his sales targets.'

Tanuja suddenly perked up. 'How do you know the ratings? It's supposed to be confidential.'

Nikhil laughed, 'Tanuja, every organization is porous. Information does not stay within the four walls of any department. Everyone knows everyone else's salary, bonus, performance rating and that's not all. Let me tell you that even what goes into the personal files is not confidential.'

Tanuja looked shocked.

'Why are you looking so dismayed, Tanuja? As if you don't know? Can someone please tell me, that if this information was so confidential, how did Vikram call me up a week back and ask me why my rating was a "three" despite me meeting my numbers and delivering more than what the organization expected me to?'

'I. . .I. . .how would I know? You must askkk. . .Vikram. . .I guess.' Clearly, Tanuja was caught off guard.

'Look Tanuja, I have tabled the facts in front of you. The numbers speak for themselves. You tell me what to do.'

'Nikhil, this is a small issue.'

'Maybe for you, not for me. For me it's a culmination of a year's efforts. I can understand anybody else saying so, but how can you, as Head of HR, call it a small issue?'

'Stop being sarcastic, buddy. I understand. But you must realize, Nikhil, that this is a large organization. There's no point taking issues head-on. You will unnecessarily get into conflicts with powerful people. And in any case, I can't think of any individual in the bank whose rating has been changed in the last three years.'

'So you are telling me that I am wasting your time?'

'Not only my time, Nikhil. . .' Tanuja let the statement hang.

'Okay. Got it. Mine as well. Right. So you're saying, in essence, that you can't do anything about it.'

'Nikhil, we go back a long way. For the sake of that relationship, I will make an honest attempt and try to speak to Guneet again and get back to you. However, I am not too hopeful.'

'By when do you think you will be able to let me know?'

'I will try to get back to you by tomorrow evening, but don't raise your hopes.'

'Thanks.' And Nikhil left.

The moment the door closed behind Nikhil, Tanuja reached for the phone.

'Our friend had come. He was crying a lot. Kya karna hai?'

'We talked about this, Tanuja. The only reason I have given him a rating of "three" and not a "one", despite the numbers having been met, is because there have been lots of people management issues. He has been abusive to his people. He is extremely aggressive, so much so that I am a bit worried about the business he books in his region. If one goes by tangibles on his list of deliverables, I have to give him a "one", but performance appraisal is about behavioural aspects too, right? The "hows" rather than the "whats",' Guneet rationalized.

'Understood. Are you saying he's good for nothing?'

'No, I'm not saying that. If you look at his appraisal document carefully, I have written that he is an extremely talented individual. If he is a bit careful about the way he conducts both himself and his business, he can be a great asset. This rating is my way of giving him serious feedback. In fact, he has worked with me for five years now. I don't know why he has been behaving very strangely with me of late.' He paused, as if he was waiting for a reaction. When there was none, he continued, 'It's as if someone is playing him. I'm a bit concerned. Clearly, Tanuja, someone is instigating him.'

'I don't know about that; anyway, let that be. What do you want to do with this rating? Now that it has come up to me, I need to send him a formal response. What should I tell him?'

'I don't think we should change the rating. Keep it the way it is. I will make it up to him in his bonus and increments, but let the rating and the reasons thereof be documented. It's for his long-term benefit.'

'Whatever you say,' and Tanuja hung up. She called another number almost immediately.

The same evening she wrote to Nikhil, formally communicating to him that the organization's stance was that the rating of three, decided by his line manager was correct and HR would not be able to change it in any manner. She marked a cc on the mail to Guneet.

A few floors away, Vikram smiled as he looked at his laptop screen. He clicked open the mail which had brought the sinister smile upon his face:

Dear Nikhil,
This is with reference to our discussion this afternoon on your
performance appraisal and the subsequent rating. . .
Regards,
Tanuja.

Tanuja had blind copied him on that mail. At that very moment, his phone rang.

'Hi Nikhil. I'm extremely sorry I couldn't talk to you earlier when you called. Haven't had a minute to breathe all day. How was your meeting with Tanuja?'

'Good evening, Vikram. I met her. She was not helpful at all. In fact she has just responded formally.'

'Achcha. What's she saying?' Vikram asked him even as he read the mail.

'Wait, I will just send it to you. Sir, you please see it and tell me what to do. I am extremely upset.'

'Arre, it's okay, Nikhil. You're a rock star. Don't worry. Forward the mail to me. Let me read it. We will then work out what to do next.'

'Forwarded, sir, as we speak.'

'Okay. Wait.' His laptop beeped, indicating a new mail had come in. 'Wait. I think it's come'. Vikram didn't bother to open it. After pretending to read it, he came back on the phone.

'This is utter nonsense. Have you gone back to Tanuja on this?'

'Tanuja's mail has just come, Vikram. The moment I saw the mail, I called you.'

'Okay. Maybe you should just speak to her again. Or wait a minute, why don't you speak to Guneet's boss?'

'The CEO?'

'Yes.'

'No point, Vikram. These guys are a coterie. The CEO will

never show up Guneet for my sake. She will give me more reasons as to why she believes I'm a dud.'

'But you're not a dud!'

'I know, Vikram. There is no point taking on the system. I will now lay off on this.'

'No, I don't think you should. Why don't you do what I tell you to? It will help in the long run.'

The discussion went on for another thirty minutes. Nikhil was extremely flustered and Vikram was his newfound guru, his supporter. He knew Vikram was not particularly fond of Guneet but he didn't know that dislike was the sole reason Vikram was humouring him.

The same evening, Nikhil replied to Tanuja. As Tanuja read the message, she smiled. She couldn't help feeling proud of herself. Nikhil had been convinced. Issue handled. Or so she thought, till she came to the last line.

'However, while all that you shared with me was the organization's point of view, I do not think that it is a just appraisal. It's one-sided and does not take into account all the hard work I have put in in the last twelve months to make sure I come good on my deliverables.' What the hell was that? Tanuja suddenly sat up straight in her chair. *'Hence I wish to inform you of my inability to continue in this role. Please treat this as my formal resignation from the services of the organization. I request you to relieve me at the end of the mandatory three-month notice period.'* The mail was marked to Guneet as well.

It just took a few seconds to change Tanuja's mood. Suddenly, she was jittery. It was a known fact that the GB2 regional office did not take kindly to people quitting because they were unhappy with the appraisal process. She had encountered many individuals who had quit on such an account. But none of them had actually put it down in writing. Most of them would just quietly quit and move out.

She called Guneet. 'What should we do?'

'Nothing. Let him go. I think he is a good resource, but he is not more important than the organization. Remember I told you, someone is guiding him.'

'Hmm. . .but there will be repercussions, Guneet. He has been in the organization for twelve long years. After twelve years if he is quitting because he is unhappy with the performance rating, someone will ask uncomfortable questions.'

'Let them. I will answer for it.'

'That's not the point, Guneet. HR will look like a bunch of idiots.'

'Then you tell me what to do.'

'Let me think and get back to you. I don't have answers now. Anyway I have to leave for Indrani's dinner. You coming?'

'How can I not go? In these difficult days it is safer to have her on your side, right?'

Almost everyone from the senior management team of GB2 was at Indrani's house for dinner. The flux the banking industry was going through had made bankers so insecure that almost everyone who was invited had planned to be there.

Tanuja was standing in the corner on Indrani's terrace with the Compliance Head, and was talking to her on a new incentive scheme the bank was planning to implement. Someone tapped on her shoulder, making her turn.

'Arre. I thought you said you are not going to come.'

'Changed my mind at the last minute. I called your office, but your secretary told me that you had left.'

'Chalo, good you are here. Now I will have someone to drive me home after the party.'

'Why? Where is Abhishek? Why don't you ask him to pick you up?'

'Mr Consultant is travelling again.'

'Where to?'

'Europe.'

'McKinsey is keeping him very busy?' asked Vikram.

'How do I care? As long as you are there with me, I am happy with him travelling all the time, baby,' Tanuja said, winking at him.

Vikram was slightly embarrassed and hurriedly looked around to see if anybody had overheard the conversation. 'What are you drinking?'

'Wine. . .the usual,' and she picked up her glass, which she had kept on the table nearby.

'Hmm. . .nice. Let me get mine.' Vikram started towards the bar.

'By the way, there was lots of chaos today. Need to talk to you,' Tanuja said a bit loudly as Vikram walked, away from her.

'Now or later, on the drive back?'

'Okay, let's chat on our way back then.' Tanuja followed Vikram to the bar. Throughout the evening, Tanuja was with Vikram. A number of colleagues came and chatted her up. She was known to be close to Indrani and hence was rumoured to have Indrani's ears. Keeping Tanuja happy was akin to keeping Indrani happy.

Finally it was around 1.00 a.m. when the two of them said bye to Indrani and left. Vikram was at the wheel of his black CRV. The fact that he had to go to Indrani's house for the dinner had influenced his decision to bring the Honda CRV instead of his Lancer.

'You're looking good today.'

'Thanks Vikram,' giggled Tanuja, a little drunk.

'What were you saying about chaos at work?'

'Arre, you were talking about me. . . Why're you reminding me about the chaos. Stay focused, you idiot.'

'Haha. You really know how to get your way, don't you?' said Vikram as he drove into the parking lot of Marathon Towers. The drive had taken them only seven minutes.

He drove straight into Tanuja's parking lot and parked the CRV in the slot which was in a secluded corner of the basement.

'Thanks for dropping me, baby.'

Vikram just smiled. Tanuja leaned towards him to kiss him on the cheek. Her lips soon moved to his eyes, brushed past his mouth, his chin, the side of his neck, and eventually everywhere conceivable. It was just a matter of time that their clothes came off and the seats got pushed to recline fully backwards. The ease with which both of them manoeuvred themselves in that space made it clear that this was not the first time the CRV had played host to their sexual exploits.

'Nikhil has resigned,' said Tanuja, as she pulled up her trousers and buttoned them up.

'Yeah? I expected that.'

'Next week, Stella Jones is coming to review the appraisal process.'

'You told me that last week.'

'She has just taken over a month ago as the Asia Pacific HR Head and India is the first country she is visiting. I don't want this Nikhil issue to blow up and impact her perception of the India HR team.'

'You think it will?'

'Yes, it will. Guneet is adamant. He is quite happy to let Nikhil go, but won't change his rating.'

'Chutiya hai woh. He doesn't understand anything.'

'Hmm...but I don't know how to play this.' The romp in the car and the discussion had worn off the impact of the wine.

'Find Nikhil a job in some other team.'

'How? No one will hire him if they know his background.'

'Hmm...that's a problem. But you don't worry. Send him to me. In fact, I wanted to hire him two years ago, but he didn't want to move. You convince Guneet, and I will add Nikhil to my team. The position of the head of the Bandra cluster is open now. I would be more than happy to give it to him. You just make it sound like you have worked it out for him.'

'Will Nikhil be happy?'

'He better be. It's a big job. He will have to manage six branches of GB2, spread over the western suburbs of Mumbai. If he does well, he can get his promotion soon.'

'You're sure you want to do this?'

'Of course. I will do anything to make sure my dear HR Head doesn't get into trouble. You just manage Guneet.'

'You're a darling, Vikram.' She leaned over, held him with her right hand and kissed him on his lips even as she pushed the door open with her left hand and stepped out of the CRV.

3

Bandra, Mumbai
March 2011

The two-bedroom, thirty-first floor apartment overlooking the Arabian Sea, with a panoramic view of the Mahalakshmi Race Course, had caught Divya's fancy. The job of house hunting was left to her, for Nikhil was too immersed in his new role. In any case, the final decision was hers and Nikhil was smart enough to realize that.

For Nikhil and Divya, Mumbai was a far throw from Pune, where they had lived almost all their lives. Rentals were four times what one would normally pay in Pune, that too for an apartment one-fourth the size. Divya fondly remembered her apartment in Pune and longingly glanced one last time at the apartment and the lush green carpet of the racecourse through the large French windows in the living room, as she shut the door and walked out. She knew that this apartment, too, was beyond their means.

A week after landing in Mumbai, Nikhil was driving back from the Bandra Branch, which was the largest branch in Nikhil's cluster and housed Nikhil's office, to Taj Lands End Hotel, where he had been put up for a few days pending the shifting of his personal effects. His mobile phone rang. Pulling over to the side of the road, he stopped his car and answered.

'Good evening Vikram.'

'Hey Nikhil. How are you? Settling in well?'

'Yes, Vikram. It's a completely different experience. I am enjoying it.'

'I am sure, my friend. Had dinner?'

'Not yet. I'm on my way back to the hotel.'

'Oh, great. Anika is also somewhere in Bandra. I'm on my way to pick her up. Why don't we have dinner together? We can come over to the hotel if you are fine with it? I have never met Divya. Anika, too, will get a chance to meet the two of you. What say?'

Nikhil did not have much of a choice. Divya, not thrilled at this new development, understood that it was a part and parcel of corporate life and quietly toed the line.

Dinner was mostly a one-man show, where only Vikram spoke. He had an opinion about everything, and a contrarian approach to whatever anyone else said. Divya was getting frustrated. Thankfully Anika was also a bit tired after a long day and wanted to head back home. After ninety minutes of torturous conversation, the dinner was over. Divya and Nikhil walked Vikram down to the lobby of the hotel and waited with him on the porch till the CRV was brought in.

'Have you managed to find a house?'

'Not yet Vikram. Divya has seen some in the last few days but we haven't closed on any yet.

'Oh yes. . .the only issue we are facing is that apartments here are quite an apology, as compared to what we get in Pune. And my God, aren't they expensive!' Divya exclaimed.

'What is your budget?'

'About a lakh a month. The best we can afford is a two bedroom apartment,' said Nikhil.

'And to think, we were staying in a lavish four-bedroom palace in Pune,' added Divya.

'Hahahaha,' laughed Vikram. He put his right hand inside his pocket and pulled out a key. Dangling it in front of Divya, he looked at Nikhil, 'Go tomorrow morning and take a look. If you like it, we will talk.'

'What's this Vikram?'

'An apartment in Casa Grande, in Parel. I'm sure you would've heard of it. It's a nice four-bedroom apartment. The apartment number is on the keychain.'

'Whose apartment is it Vikram? And four bedrooms? I don't think we can afford it.'

'Take a look. I'll call you tomorrow.'

The CRV had arrived while Vikram was talking to Nikhil. He got into it with Anika and drove off, leaving Divya holding the keys.

Early next morning, pressured by the deadline prescribed by Vikram, Divya and Nikhil went to Parel. The apartment was a fabulous four-bedroom one. Nikhil estimated it to be a minimum of 2700 sq. ft., huge by Mumbai standards. The interiors were exquisite and tastefully done. It was clear that the owner had spent a lot of money on it.

'Let's go,' said Divya.

'Why? Didn't like it?'

'It's lovely. But do you think you can afford it?'

'I wish I could,' said Nikhil as they walked into the shiny steel elevator.

Back in office, Nikhil called Vikram. Vikram was talking to someone on his mobile. Nikhil stayed on the line. It was evident Vikram was talking to someone about a property deal.

'Oh. . .okay. Look, it cannot be in my name. The rental agreement with GB2 will be made in the company's name. Anika is the owner and director of that company. I am talking about the fourth shop. And make sure that the rental cheque comes only in the name of the company.' Then there was pause. 'I know we need only three shops for the branch. However, it's within my authority to approve a slightly larger area for the branch. Go ahead and do it. We'll talk later. And make sure that no one gets to know of this. If anyone does, you are history. . .' Another pause. 'Okay, call me if you need clarity on structuring this deal.'

'Hello. . . Hello. . . Hey Nikhil,' Vikram came on the line. He seemed to have forgotten that Nikhil was on the line and was a bit surprised when he realized that Nikhil was still on hold.

'Good morning Vikram.'

'Morning. . .morning. Tell me.'

'Vikram, we had gone to see the apartment this morning. It's lovely. But I don't think we will be able to afford it. It's too big, it won't fit into my budget.'

'Why?'

'It will be beyond our means.'

'You had a budget of a lakh right?'

'Yes sir.'

'Give me a minute.' He went off the line for a minute, leaving Nikhil to wonder what he was up to. He could hear some taps of a keyboard and then Vikram came back on the line.

'I have just sent you something. Take a look.'

'Email?'

'Yup.'

'Just a moment sir,' and Nikhil refreshed his inbox. An email from Vikram popped up on his screen.

Nikhil read through the contents. His eyes grew wider and wider. He was grinning from ear to ear. 'Thanks Vikram. This is so completely unexpected!'

'You're welcome my friend. Now tell me, can you afford to pay me a rent of two-and-a-half lakh a month for my apartment or not?'

'I don't know what to say Vikram. I am highly indebted to you. Whatever you say is fine by me.' Nikhil was too overawed to say anything else.

Back home that night, Nikhil and Divya got into an animated discussion. 'A second promotion in eighteen months is unheard of at this level. Wow! You're a star Nikhil.' Divya couldn't hide her excitement.

'I know Divya. I knew the job was graded higher than my personal grade, but I didn't expect them to give it to me so soon. I thought they would give it to me sometime towards the end of next year. But now this promotion, and the increase in salary, is so unexpected. Let's enjoy it while it lasts. I'm not complaining.'

'So now you don't have a choice but to take the house.'

'Yes,' nodded Nikhil. 'He has been so good to us; it will be difficult to say no to him. He said that he had increased my salary by eighteen lakhs per annum, to make sure that I am able to afford the rent, otherwise the normal increment with this promotion would be around two to three lakhs only.'

'We have one life. Let's enjoy it to the fullest.' said Divya. 'When are we shifting?'

Within two weeks they shifted into their new pad.

Having spent the day unpacking, both Nikhil and Divya were about to go to bed early one evening when their doorbell rang. Divya opened the door.

'Hi,' said the pretty young girl at the door.

'Hi,' said Divya with a blank look. In her assessment, the girl was at best in her late twenties.

'I am Sukanya, your next-door neighbour. We moved in about a week ago. I saw you shifting so I came in to check if you guys needed any help. Should I send some food? You must be tired.'

Sukanya was friendly and Divya had been yearning for company ever since she had moved to Mumbai. They hit it off well.

During the course of the conversation, Divya brought up the issue of the rent in Mumbai and how expensive real estate was in the island city as compared to Pune. The discussion veered towards the rentals in Casa Grande.

'Oh. We pay a lakh and sixty as rent. That's the best hubby's company could afford.'

The moment she said that, Divya looked at Nikhil. He too had a shocked look on his face. Neither said anything.

After Sukanya left that night, Divya walked up to Nikhil. He was lost in thoughts. 'What are you thinking?'

'Vikram took us for a ride.'

'As in?'

'He coerced us into taking a flat, which would have fetched him a rent of around a lakh and sixty, and charged us two and half lakhs a month. In the euphoria of the promotion, we, like suckers, agreed to it too. He hiked my salary so that the differential was taken care of. By doing this he ensured that I don't crib and keep my mouth shut. By increasing my salary, he's made a huge profit, can't you see that?'

'Hmm. . .' was all that Divya could say.

For the first time, Nikhil was exposed to the games business leaders play. He was angry, but he knew Divya was right. Wasn't he also the beneficiary of the largesse? Had he lost the right to complain?

4

Devikulam
March 11ᵗʰ, 2011

The entire world woke up to an event of tragic and monumental proportions on March 11th 2011—something that had never been seen or heard of in the past. The island nation of Japan was struck by a massive earthquake, measuring 9.0 on the Richter scale. Striking seventy kilometres to the east, off the coast of Tohoku Peninsula, it was the largest earthquake to have ever hit Japan and the fifth largest the world had ever seen since 1900— the time earthquake intensities started getting recorded. The impact of the earthquake was so devastating that it triggered off violent tsunami waves, which ran up to a height of over forty metres in Miyako and drove sea waves over ten kilometres inland. So intense was the earthquake that the entire earth shifted on its axis.

While the world was watching the dramatic visuals of the tsunami on their television screens, a disaster, with potentially greater repercussions, was just about to take place. The tsunami-propelled seawater overshot the thick walls at the Fukushima Nuclear Power Plant and entered the compound. Moments earlier, the earthquake had caused the disaster protection mechanism to automatically kick in, consequently shutting down the power to the installation. The emergency generators took over and were managing the electronic network and the supply of coolants to keep the nuclear reactors from overheating. However, once the water came gushing in with full force, it caused the generators to flood. The generators stopped functioning. This impacted the power supply to the nuclear reactors; the pumping of the coolant to the reactors got disrupted. In the absence of any coolant, the heat generated by the reactors rose at a rapid pace. The rising heat level of the reactors was worrisome, because if the temperatures approached the melting point of the nuclear rods, it could result in a core meltdown. It was a nuclear disaster waiting to happen.

The government swung into motion. Mass evacuations were carried out around the nuclear plant even as the administration and teams of scientists put their own life at stake to control the reactors and prevent radioactive leakages. However, multiple explosions hindered their plans to shut it down. Radioactive readings near the plant were beginning to get alarming. The Japanese government rated the situation as a Level Seven disaster—considered to be the highest possible level for a nuclear plant.

Eventually after significant collateral damage, the plant was brought under control. However, it was not before it had resulted in an enormous amount of radioactive leakage into the seawater, ground and atmosphere around the nuclear plant.

Water, food particles, air, everything was contaminated. About a tenth of the radioactivity released in the Russian air space at the time of the Chernobyl disaster was released in Japan as a result of the earthquake and the tsunami. While the issue was swiftly addressed, the long-term impact of the entire tragedy was something that even the strongest of souls shuddered to estimate. A nation in mourning led by a decisive government, quickly announced plans to decommission the Fukushima nuclear power plant.

While the world watched the spectacle unfold, one man was worried. The same issue had been bothering him for the last decade, but he had not been able to do anything about it. It seemed to be beyond him to fight for a cause. But now the Fukushima reactor proved that his concern, his anxiety, his main fear which until that moment had seemed to be a figment of his imagination, was now well within the realms of possibility.

He walked out of his house and stood there, hands on his hips, admiring the scenic beauty around him. A life bereft of natural splendour was unimaginable for him. An SUV was parked in the driveway. Not wanting to trouble anyone from his support staff, he quietly took the keys from the security guards and got into the driver's seat. The engine revved up, and the only noise in the entire neighbourhood was that of the SUV. He removed his foot from the brake pedal and allowed the SUV to kiss the road and roll out of the resort on to the muddy track towards the highway. Not much had changed in the three decades that he had been there.

After a ten-minute drive, made easier by the lack of traffic, he turned into another narrow lane. Unlike the pothole-ridden roads thus far, this narrow lane was well carpeted and smooth. The road was freshly laid, with barrels of tar lining its sides. The old man drove on for a kilometre before he stopped.

In front of him stood a towering iron gate. Men in military fatigue guarded the entrance and prevented anyone from going inside. He opened the door of the SUV and stepped out. Almost instantaneously, the men at the gate recognized him and smiled. He did not even bother to reciprocate their gesture. Standing in front of his SUV, he stared at the gate, and then at the huge wall which ran from the gate till the point where the land met the sky, and the big board right in front of him and above the gigantic gate. The board had been put up when the project had started, fourteen years ago. It hadn't been painted too many times; a fact reflected by the peeling paint on the letters, which made up the words 'Trikakulam Nuclear Power Plant—an Indo-Russian venture'. Despite the chipped paint, the board was still quite legible.

Krishna Menon just stood there, blankly staring at the facility in front of him. Worry lines appeared on his forehead as he thought about the consequences of a Japan-like earthquake striking the valley. The devastation that it would bring upon the region was unimaginable for him. Thoughts of his only son, on his deathbed, lying in isolation flashed in front of him. It had happened over twenty-five years ago, yet it seemed like it had happened yesterday. Arvind was in Ukraine with his wife, Laila, the daughter of a Russian nuclear scientist, when the Chernobyl Reactor had exploded, releasing large quantities of radioactive contamination into the atmosphere. The tragedy had not only killed his son but also his wife and her six-month-old foetus. Chernobyl was the only Level Seven nuclear disaster the world had seen prior to that day. Fukushima had brought back all the memories of that horror.

How long he stood there, lost in thought, he didn't know. Only when the vicious heat from the sun became unbearable did he trace his steps back to the SUV and quietly drove back to the resort. What would happen if an earthquake were to jolt the valley? Close to a million people stayed within a radius of twenty kilometres from the plant. If he didn't do anything for the people in the neighbourhood, who would? Something had to be done about it. But how? He hadn't found the answer yet.

5

The Bandra branch was in a landmark stand-alone building on the busy and crowded Turner Road. Spread over four floors, the ground and the first floor housed the branch. Nikhil's office was on the second floor.

A busy Monday, thought Nikhil, going over his calendar for the day, as he sneaked in through a side door meant only for staff. To reach his cabin he had to walk across the banking hall, to the lift at the other end. Two floors were not too much to walk up, but Nikhil never took the stairs.

There was a fair bit of commotion in the banking hall. Nikhil was surprised, for there was half an hour to go for the bank to throw its doors open to the public. Present in the banking hall were a bunch of youngsters, numbering close to a dozen, who through their constant chatter had succeeded in raising the noise levels in the branch. Nikhil looked at the Branch Customer Service Manager who was also the floor manager on duty and raised his eyebrows.

'Management trainees,' yelled the floor manager. It was loud enough for everyone to hear. The entire bunch turned and looked first at the floor manager and then at Nikhil. Some had seen him before but most of them hadn't.

'Oh, right,' said Nikhil and walked away from the crowd. He recalled the mail Tanuja had sent him a few days back, informing him that a batch of fourteen management trainees would be assigned to one of the branches in his cluster for three weeks. So this was the gang, he thought to himself as he turned the key and opened the door to his cabin. 'How did I miss it?' he wondered as he threw his bag on the sofa in the corner of his room.

He walked across to his table, tugged at the LAN cord sticking out from a socket and plugged it into his laptop. After a couple of minutes spent in logging-in and settling his table, he was about to download his mails when a knock on his door interrupted him. He looked up. It was his Branch Manager, Anand Shastri, along with his floor manager. Nikhil was a man of few words; he just raised his eyebrows.

'Good morning sir.'

'Morning Anand.'

'Sir, these management trainees are going to be here for three weeks. What should we do?'

'What do you mean?' He added nonchalantly, 'Manage them.'

'Sir, for three weeks? It's too long. The entire branch's processes will go for a toss. Can't we split them?'

'Split them?'

'As in, send two to the Juhu branch, two to Powai, some to Andheri and so on. It will make managing them easy without really disrupting my branch.'

'Anand, don't you think it's too late in the day to think about that? You knew a month ago that they were going to be assigned to us,' Nikhil chided, conveniently forgetting his own lapse of memory. It was a low priority task from his perspective, but a task that had to be completed nevertheless.

'I know, sir. . .but when we were told about this, we thought we would be able to manage them. Then last week, Vikram suddenly announced this insurance contest. We are in the last phase of that contest now. If I drag my team into managing these MTs, I will just not be able to pull through the contest.'

'In any case, you are lagging behind. Your branch sits at the bottom of the league tables, my friend. So how does it matter? Manage them. We need to keep our HR folks happy too. In any case, three weeks is not too much.'

'Sir, the insurance contest will really suffer.'

'Fuck off, man. Is this your new excuse for screwing up on the insurance contest? I know you too well.' And he smiled at Anand. 'Okay. . .wait!' Nikhil stared into his computer. 'Let me just look at the mail Tanuja sent me,' and he went silent as he scrolled through his inbox. In a few seconds he found it. 'Aah. . .here it is.'

'Okay, listen to me Anand. This does not say what we are supposed to do with the MTs. It only says that they need exposure to the branch. Attach each one of them to one officer in the branch. Let them shadow that officer. Rotate them end of week one and week two. Your guys just have to let them hang around. Don't waste too much time on them.'

'Good idea sir.'

'Your work will also not be hindered. Whatever they learn, they'll learn on the job. Let them learn by observation.'

'Yes sir. I will do that.'

Nikhil looked at Tanuja's mail again. 'And as per this mail, I am supposed to take them out for dinner after two weeks. Line up any day, the week after next. Let me know and I will pen it in my diary.'

Anand just nodded his head and turned to leave.

'And listen. . .' Nikhil said. Anand stopped.

'I don't care how you do it, but I need your team to start performing better in the insurance contest. You guys are really lagging. Is it that difficult to sell an insurance policy to customers these days?'

'We have been trying sir, but it's taking time.'

'Chipkao, yaar. Customers ko insurance chipkao. I am yet to meet a customer who knows what he wants. It's in your hands. You have to make them need what you want to sell. That's when you become a good salesman. You don't need me to tell you what to do during the contest. Only results matter, my friend. Do whatever you have to, but your branch has to be amongst the top ten branches on the league tables.'

After that conversation, Anand did not need any further license. Nikhil had said a lot that day without actually saying anything. Now it was up to him to interpret it the way Nikhil wanted him to. On his return to his branch a couple of floors below, Anand called for a meeting of all his branch sales and service officers. By the time they left his room, they were a bunch of transformed people.

As per Nikhil's suggestion, all the MTs were allocated to individual officers and started shadowing them to learn how the bank operated on a day-to-day basis. What they learnt, whether it was appropriate or not, no one cared.

That day Mrs Bhatnagar, a 50-year-old widow living on her husband's pension and a loyal GB2 customer for over two decades, was the first customer to enter the branch. Her loyalty could be gauged from the fact that, despite living off her husband's meagre pension, she did not move her money out of GB2 even when the rates of interest GB2 offered were the lowest in the market. Being someone who valued safety over returns, all her money was in fixed deposits. GB2 was the only bank she banked with.

Jasmeet met her at the door and walked her to the cabin. A customary cup of coffee—Mrs Bhatnagar loved the coffee served in GB2—and thirty minutes of conversation later, she walked out of the branch with a wide smile on her face. It was a normal reaction; she always felt good after talking to her own RMs in the bank. They took good care of her.

After Mrs Bhatnagar left, the traffic in the branch picked up considerably. The steady customer inflow made it a busy day for the Bandra branch, keeping all the RMs and the service executives on their toes.

By evening, everyone was tired, but Anand was a happy man. It was amazing how a five minute talk with the cluster manager could change the approach of the entire branch. The mood had changed. The branch was suddenly seized with enthusiasm. He could sense it when he met the team in the huddle that evening.

'If every day hereon, till the end of the contest which is three weeks from now, turns out to be like today, we will not only be in the top ten but we might end up being one of the top three branches in the country.' The entire branch went up in applause.

'Today's spot winner, the best performer of the day is. . .' and he paused for effect. The audience waited, holding their breath. '. . .Jasmeet Pahuja,' announced Anand. 'She has managed to close an insurance deal with a premium of rupees four lakh, one of the largest in the branch thus far. What makes it special is also the fact that this insurance has come to us from a customer who has never ever invested in anything but a fixed deposit.'

Everyone cheered and Jasmeet couldn't control her emotions. Her face went red and she couldn't stop grinning from ear to ear.

6

Mainland China, the premium Chinese cuisine destination in Bandra, was buzzing with activity at 8.30 that evening. Almost all the tables were taken. On one long table, in a private corner, Nikhil and Anand sat with the management trainees. Twelve of the fourteen MTs were in attendance—five men and seven women, all impeccably dressed, out to impress the branch management team that included Nikhil and Anand, who had come straight from work. Nikhil had invited Vikram too, but despite confirming his attendance he had ditched them at the last moment. *Typical of Vikram*, Nikhil thought when Vikram called him to say he couldn't make it.

At the head of the table was Nikhil, Anand to his right, and then the MTs. 'Third person to my right,' Anand nudged Nikhil and whispered into his ear. 'The girl in white.' Nikhil turned to look. That was the first time he saw Zinaida at close quarters. Anand had mentioned her on their way to the restaurant. Nikhil was curious to meet her. When he saw her, he just couldn't turn his gaze away. But he gathered himself quickly and looked towards the other side, hoping Zinaida hadn't caught him staring at her.

The dinner itself was quite a formal affair. The MTs were on their best behaviour. Nikhil interacted with everyone, even though he kept intermittently stealing a glance at Zinaida. Her fair skin complimented her lush brown hair streaked with coppery red. Her greenish brown eyes were so intensely deep, that she stood out in that entire batch of management trainees.

Post dinner, all of them walked out together towards the parking lot. As per protocol, Nikhil had to be seen off, being the senior most in the group.

It was windy that night. The road outside Mainland China was damp, the result of pre-monsoon showers. The monsoon had hit the coast of Kerala and was less than a week away from Mumbai. Strong winds were blowing, fuelled by the tunnelling effect of the portico of the restaurant. Zinaida was struggling to keep her hair in place and also manage her short skirt, which was flying because of the wind, exposing her silky thighs. Nikhil saw her struggle and stepped in front of her, which cut off the wind for a moment and helped Zinaida rearrange herself.

'Thanks,' she smiled at Nikhil.

'Not a problem. The wind here can be notorious.' He smiled back at her. 'So I hope you had a good time at the branch.'

'Yes sir. Learnt a lot.'

'Any feedback?'

'Only one, sir. In fact it's more of a compliment. We have a fabulous sales team in the branch.'

'Thank you. That's nice to hear.'

'Yes sir. Who else would be able to sell an insurance scheme to a 50-year-old lady, passing it off as a fixed deposit product?'

'Sorry?' Nikhil was horrified. 'Say that again?'

'Nikhil, your car has come,' Anand interrupted.

'It's okay. Ask them to park it on the side. I'll come in a moment.' He looked at Zinaida and asked her, 'What did you say young lady?'

'Did I say anything wrong sir?'

'No, no you didn't. I just want to hear that again.'

'I was with Jasmeet in my first week at your branch. And I saw her sell an insurance policy to a 50-year-old widow. She never told her that it was a Unit Linked Insurance Plan (ULIP) policy. The only thing she said was that she would get good returns and her investment was safe.'

'What did she tell her?'

'She just told her that it's like a deposit and that she would get a minimum return of twelve per cent, much higher than the eight per cent a fixed deposit gave her. Her control on the customer was amazing. The old lady didn't ask too many questions and just agreed to whatever Jasmeet told her. It was an amazing experience for me.'

Nikhil couldn't quite figure out if Zinaida was serious or sarcastic. Whatever the case, he was worried about the repercussions. He could have been in serious trouble if such a discussion had taken place in someone else's presence.

'Thanks for telling me, Zinaida. I will take care of this,' and he walked towards his car. Having barely taken a few steps he stopped, turned back and called out to Anand. 'Anand, come. I will drop you home.' Anand didn't have much of a choice.

Nikhil was livid and gave Anand an earful on the way back. The latter was left wondering what had happened till Nikhil replayed his conversation with Zinaida.

'But sir, this is normal stuff. Happens all the time. How else will numbers happen? There is no way we would have reached where we have in the insurance sales contest had this not happened. Jasmeet has over-achieved her target by 380 per cent and is in the running for the best sales RM.'

'I know Anand, all this is fine. My question is simple: Why can't we be careful in front of outsiders? These MT idiots have no understanding of what we need to do to achieve our revenue targets. The problem is, if they say something stupid like what Zinaida said, in front of Vikram or someone else, we'll be in serious trouble. We need to be careful so that people don't talk about such things. I know you will manage the one-in-hundred customer who comes back and complains. For them we will reverse the transaction and pay them back, but it's the others who will give us our profits. But that's not the point. These things are necessary to do. . .but never to be spoken about.'

'Yes sir.'

'Tell your team to be careful if any non-branch person is with them. Word must not get out.'

'Sir, can I say something?'

Nikhil nodded.

'Every branch in this country does this, sir, to meet their insurance targets. And that day you only said na. . .customers ko chipkao? Sir, humne chipka diya. . .And from being second last branch on the league table, we catapulted to the second position.'

Nikhil smiled. 'You haven't had this conversation with me, Anand. You haven't told me this and I haven't stopped you.' And he raised his hand, bringing the thumb and the index finger together and slid it across his face from one corner of the lips to the other. 'My lips are sealed.'

Anand smiled as he looked at Nikhil. The car crossed the toll plaza and on to the Bandra Worli Sea Link. For a moment there was silence in the car as it whizzed past the cables holding up the five-kilometre-long bridge. Anand didn't want to disturb Nikhil and was wondering what it was that Nikhil was thinking. Finally, as they reached the other end of the sea link and crossed over into Worli, Nikhil spoke, 'What do you think of Zinaida? Hot chick, na?' He was still looking outside the window.

Anand smiled. 'Heard she is close to Vikram.' Nikhil suddenly turned towards him. There was surprise in his voice when he asked curiously, 'Who told you?'

'Just heard some guys talking. I don't even know if it's true sir.'

'Hmm. . .she is cute.'

'She is apparently not a fresher. So I was pretty surprised as to how she made it to the MT programme. Guess they made an exception for her.'

'Helps if you know the big boss, doesn't it?' said Nikhil, still looking out as they drove onto the Worli sea face enroute to Parel.

Nikhil reached office early the next day. Vikram had asked for a conference call with the cluster managers and branch managers to announce the results of the insurance contest. Though most of the branches knew their standings in the league tables through informal channels, Vikram wanted to formally announce the winners himself. The call was at nine and Nikhil was already in his cabin at 8.30 a.m., looking at the previous month's Management Information System report and trying to pre-empt any question Vikram might ask. He liked to be prepared, especially at a time when his cluster had done well and when every single graph, on every parameter, was showing a positive trajectory from the time he had taken over. He felt proud of himself.

The call began at sharp nine. Vikram started with a lecture on sales effectiveness. He spoke about the contest, the need to drive results, about what the organization had achieved and went on and on for ten minutes. He loved to talk; it gave him a feeling of control. Not only did he love to speak, but he also got quite irritated if someone contradicted or interrupted him.

Finally he came to the contest results. Vikram had just started giving the preamble when Nikhil's phone rang. It was Anand. Putting the conference call on mute, Nikhil picked up the phone.

'Your call couldn't have come at a worse time. . .Vikram is about to announce the results of the contest on the call. . .someone had better died for you to be calling just now.'

'Sir. . .I was also on the call too. Had to log off because it was urgent. . .' Anand told him what had happened.

'What the fuck? Are you serious?'

'Yes boss.'

'When did this happen?'

'I don't have the details. I was only informed a minute ago.'

'Any idea how this happened?'

'No one saw it happen. There weren't any witnesses.'

'Alright, give me a minute, I will be down there. Let me inform Vikram first.'

'Okay boss.'

Nikhil cut Anand's line and returned to Vikram's conference call.

'Vikram, my apologies for interrupting the call. There is a small crisis here.'

'Crisis is never small, my friend. Had it been small, it wouldn't be a crisis.' And he started laughing. Vikram's laughter was dutifully followed by hesitant laughter by almost everyone on the call—everyone except Nikhil.

'Vikram, we have had an accident. Pranesh, our cashier, is dead. He lost his life in a hit-and-run accident on Eastern Express highway last night.'

'What?' It was a shocked Vikram this time. There was pin drop silence on the call; no one was laughing anymore. 'Are you serious? How and when did this happen?'

'No one knows, Vikram. It happened sometime last night. All I know is that his body was found by passers-by on a bushy stretch of road between Mulund and Thane. The impact was so great that the bike had rolled off the road into the bushes. The cops saw the ID card on his body and called us. That's all the information I have. I'm going down to the branch but I'll update you once I have more information. You'll have to excuse me.'

'No issues, Nikhil. You manage the issue at hand. That is more important. Call me once you've taken stock of the situation.'

'Yes Vikram.' Nikhil hung up. He ran down to the ground floor branch and straight to Anand's cabin. Two uniformed cops were there. The look on Anand's face was that of a pained man, partly on account of the grief of losing a colleague and largely on account of the stress of having to deal with the situation.

The Powai Police Station, under whose jurisdiction the accident had taken place, had deputed two smart-looking cops. Probably the fact that they were dealing with foreign bankers influenced the choice of who was assigned.

'Nikhil Suri. I'm the cluster manager.' Nikhil extended his hand even as he introduced himself.

'Myself Sub-Inspector Kailash Nath More from the Powai Thana.'

'How did this happen, sir?'

'Hit and run. Some big vehicle hit Mr Rao's motorcycle. We find body in morning.' It would have been easier if Inspector More spoke in Hindi, but he persisted with broken English.

'Do we know who, or rather what, hit him?'

'No. How we will know? It happen middle of night.' More suddenly took offence to the tone Nikhil used. The irritation in the policeman's voice was quite evident. Wasn't he supposed to be the one asking questions?

'Sorry sir, I'm extremely sorry. That was not what I meant,' Nikhil quickly corrected himself. Nikhil looked at Anand. 'Family? Have they been told?'

'No boss. He stays alone. We haven't spoken to his parents yet.'

'Do you know where he was going that time of the night?' It was More. He wanted to take charge of the conversation.

'Oh. Thane is where he stays. I think he would be going home at that time,' Anand responded.

'He travel everyday from Thane to Bandra?'

'Pranesh was earlier in the Thane branch. He got transferred a few months ago to the Bandra Branch. I had told him a couple of times to shift closer to Bandra, but I guess he was waiting for the lease on his house in Thane to get over.'

'That makes sense, sahib,' the constable spoke up, looking at the Sub-Inspector.

'Hmm. . .'

'Where is the body now, Mr More?' Nikhil forced his way into the discussion.

'It is in the government hospital waiting for the doctors to do post-mortem.'

'By when do you think they'll release the body sir?'

'What can we say? It can take two hours, it can also take twelve. Depend on when doctor comes.'

'What do I tell his parents? I am sure they will ask when I call them.'

This made More frown at Nikhil, then ignore him. He asked a few more questions and left. On his way out, he promised to call Anand the moment the post-mortem was over and they were ready to hand over the body.

After they left, Nikhil looked at Anand. 'Will you call his parents or do you want me to call?' Seeing Anand hesitate, he added, 'Alright, I'll call them. Give me the number. Ideally someone senior from HR should be calling them. But all of us know how our HR is.'

The call to Pranesh's parents was the most traumatic call Nikhil had ever made.

'Yes sir. Our people have been sent to the hospital to coordinate everything. . .Yes sir. . .No, no. . .you don't need to do anything sir, our Branch Manager in Vizag will make all the arrangements to get you to Mumbai. We will take care of it

sir. . .we are with you sir, in this hour of grief. . .Yes sir. . .I will
see you at the airport.' Nikhil hung up.

The next moment he pulled out his mobile and dialled a
number.

'Arre Venkat, what's up?'

'Nothing, you tell me. Hope all is well? After you logged off,
Vikram called off the call. He said we'll do it later.'

'Oh okay. . .listen buddy, Pranesh's parents are in Vizag. I
have already told his father that you, the branch manager of
Vizag, are on your way to see him. Can you go now? It's important,
my friend. I feel sad for his parents, they are quite old. And in
this age to be put through all this. . .'

'Oh ho! I am in Tirupati now, Nikhil. I would surely have
gone had I not come here for a branch review.'

'Oh, shit. . . What do we do now?' There was a pause on the
line. 'Okay, let's do this,' Nikhil suggested. 'You ask someone
from your branch in Vizag to go and meet his parents. Let him
say that he is the manager-in-charge, else I will look like an idiot.
Ask him to put them on a flight to Mumbai today.'

'That's definitely possible.'

'Okay, thanks. And let me know which flight they are coming
by and I will arrange for their pick-up and stay.'

'Will do.'

That night Nikhil, accompanied by Anand, went to the airport
to receive Pranesh's parents. Both of them waited in the car in
the parking lot, while the driver went to the arrival area to keep a
watch on flight arrivals. There was an uneasy calm in the car. For
long, no one spoke. Nikhil was wondering what and how to
speak to Pranesh's parents. He had limited experience in offering
condolences to anyone. Vikram had told him that he would
come to the airport with him but, as usual, had ditched at the last
moment.

Nikhil's phone rang. It was the driver. He held the instrument close to his ear and, without saying a word, disconnected.

'This air traffic congestion at the Mumbai airport is the worst. The flight's been delayed by another thirty minutes. Now I'll have to spend another half an hour staring at your dirty face.'

'Why boss? Would it have been better if that other babe were here?'

'Which one?'

'Zinaida! That girl who went all out to impress you yesterday. And from what I could make out, it worked.' Nikhil went red with embarrassment. 'Haha, very funny.'

Anand smiled. The silence returned. Nikhil fiddled with his BlackBerry for some time, and sent out a few messages, none of which were important. Then he returned to the unfinished conversation with Anand.

'Tell me Anand, why can't we get her as a relationship manager in our branch?'

'In the Bandra branch?'

'Right.'

'How boss? One thing is for sure. If she comes to the Bandra branch, branch mein raunak aa jaayegi.'

'Week after next, they will be allocated to various departments for their final postings. I know for sure she wanted to be in Retail Banking.'

'How do you know, sir?' Anand had a mischievous smile on his face.

Nikhil chose to ignore the taunt. 'She's fabulous looking. If we put her on the front line, no customer will be able to resist her charms. We will rock, month after month. If only we had more RMs as pretty as her.'

'Sir, unfortunately I don't have a single hot-looking RM in my branch.'

'You have to change your hiring policy, my friend. Hire smart, young women—even if they are thick-headed. You will do well in your life as a Branch Manager.'

'But sir, how will we get work done? Won't customers lose faith in us?'

'As if customers believe you today. Customers make their own decisions my friend. We bankers only execute those decisions. And if they get a sexy chick to meet them and help them complete their banking transactions, they will never move away from you. A Reliance mutual fund will give the same return if the customer invests through you or through HDFC bank or through ICICI Bank. However, a Zinaida meeting the customer once in three days will make it sweeter and more enjoyable for him as compared to any other bank. Spending twenty minutes with her every week is the next best thing to having sex with her, don't you agree?' Anand just nodded at this candid conversation. Though he remembered the conversation the day the MT's had landed, when Nikhil had said just the reverse—that customers will buy whatever one wants them to buy. After all, Nikhil was the boss and he had the right to contradict himself.

The conversation was cut short by another call from Nikhil's driver. 'The plane has landed, let's go,' said Nikhil, opening the door of the car. 'Painful work begins,' he said, as they walked towards the arrival area.

They drove Pranesh's parents to his Thane residence in Nikhil's car. It was an extremely traumatic experience for both of them. Pranesh's mom broke down on seeing Pranesh's body, and wept the whole night. He was their only son.

Sub-Inspector More landed up early next morning to meet Pranesh's parents. He brought with him a copy of the post-mortem report. It was unambiguous. Pranesh had died of injuries caused by the impact and because of uncontrolled internal bleeding. There was no trace of alcohol in his blood, so drunken driving was ruled out. He hinted to Nikhil and to Pranesh's parents that the police were likely to close the case, as they had no clue or witness who could lead them to the culprit. The only question SI More wanted to ask his parents was whether they suspected anyone and whether Pranesh had any enemies at work or outside. When they replied in the negative, More left. Anand, who was standing next to More when he was talking to Pranesh's parents, had a weird feeling Nikhil was trying to say something. Nikhil walked up to them a few times and then went back to talk to his team members, who had assembled there. This happened a couple of times, but Anand ignored it. He thought he was just imagining things.

Nikhil and Anand returned to their jobs the next day and took turns to meet the parents. A week later, Pranesh's parents left for Vizag, vowing never to return to the city which had snatched their son away from them. In a month, Pranesh was forgotten and it was business as usual for the Bandra branch. Vikram, who liked to project himself as a messiah, a true leader of people, didn't bother to meet Pranesh's parents even once.

7

Devikulam
June 2011

When Krishna Menon walked onto the makeshift wooden dais, in front of him were six thousand people. People from all walks of life had braved the pouring rain to participate in the agitation. There were even a few people from Singur, in West Bengal— people who had successfully taken part in the battle against the acquisition of their land by the state government of Bengal— who had also come to participate in this protest against what they called a unilateral decision by the government. It had taken Menon a lot of courage to organize such a large protest, albeit with the support of three large non government organizations (NGOs).

Krishna had been working for years to mobilize public support against the project. But for a long time, nothing moved. Despite being the face of the protest, he had struggled to achieve anything of significance. And this had a lot to do with his lack of political acumen. Despite having the desire, not having the requisite financial muscle had been a big deterrent in his ability to take his protest to the next level. Whatever he did with his limited resources had not been successful thus far.

All that changed the day he met Jayakumar at a congregation of Rotarians. That day, Krishna was standing in a group of five people enjoying his single malt when Jaya walked in. Diminutive and of frail build, clad in a kurta-pyjama, he wandered straight to the other end of the hall and mingled with a few locals. Krishna's gaze followed him as Jaya went from one person to the other, laughing and joking, at times holding serious conversations. There was something different about him. Something intriguing. His face conveyed an intensity Krishna had never seen before.

For over ten minutes Krishna tailed this intriguing gentleman, wondering who he was, and that was when he saw Ramadurai, the local political satrap walking towards him. Ramadurai's right hand was on Jaya's shoulder and he was dragging him towards Krishna.

'Meet Jayakumar,' said Ramadurai, as he came within a few feet of Krishna, 'A person of impeccable values and great commitment to the society at large.' Krishna smiled out of courtesy. A politician talking of impeccable values was a bit odd. Ignorant of Krishna's thoughts, Ramadurai continued, 'Jaya is the founder of CNRI.' Seeing the blank look on Krishna's face he turned to his right, looked at Jaya and asked, 'What's the full form?'

'Conservation of Natural Resources through Innovative use of Technology. We are an NGO based in Satara. It's about hundred kilometres from Pune.' He extended his right hand towards Krishna. His handshake was firm; to Krishna it communicated firmness in purpose.

'Oh, welcome to Devikulam.' Anyone with a little bit of knowledge of geography would know Satara was a semi-rural place in south-west Maharashtra and to Krishna, Jayakumar hardly looked like someone from that background.

'Jaya, this is Krishna Menon, one of the oldest members of the Devikulam Rotary club. He has a plantation on the outskirts and runs a very popular resort. Lots of foreigners come there. He is a very popular man.' And he looked at Jaya and added, 'Not just popular, he is also a very good human being.'

Krishna was embarrassed. He patted Ramadurai on his back and just smiled.

Jaya was very well-travelled and quite a voracious reader too. He could talk knowledgeably on any topic from the tsunami in Japan to Vladimir Putin's affair with a Russian gymnast half his age; from corruption in African cricket to the railway budget, Jaya was an expert on almost everything. Krishna immediately connected with him. His intellectual compatibility was quite stimulating.

Eventually that night, almost as if it was pre-planned, the two of them got down to discussing the nuclear Non Proliferation Treaty, the threat of the Pakistan's nuclear programme going rogue, the unabashed aggression shown by the Iranian president in defying the world with his own nuclear plans. It was not long before they meandered towards their own neighbourhood, the Trikakulam nuclear plant. Jaya was very worried, like Krishna, about the aftereffects of any natural calamity on the safety of the people in the vicinity.

'God forbid if any calamity hits this plant, it will render not only this neighbourhood, but entire town of Devikulam uninhabitable for hundreds of years, not to mention the loss of flora and fauna. It will spell a disaster of magnanimous proportions,' Jaya said.

'Yes, but what can we do? No one seems to be interested. I have been fighting a lone cause for years now. The plant is not too far away from being commissioned. There's little we can do at this stage, don't you think?'

'You can't give up, Mr Menon. If you have been fighting for so long, now is the time for your struggle to bear results.'

'Yes but I am beginning to think it's a lost cause. And more so,

I don't even have the resources to battle the strong reserves of the politicians.'

'What is it that you need? I can help you with that. People who work with CNRI will be interested in working with you on protecting the natural resources of your region—the same natural resources which will be rendered useless if what happened in Japan were to happen in Devikulam.'

Krishna's eyes lit up. Was that possible? Would someone help him with the required means, enable him to keep the battle going? He desperately wanted to stall the nuclear plant from going live. The research behind the choice of the plant's location was shrouded in secrecy. The government had not made it public. The relocation plans for people in the catchment were still to be announced. Krishna was not against it, but he wanted the government to come clean on the project and convince the people that everything had been thought through and taken care of.

'Is there a place where we can sit and talk in peace? This party is getting a bit too crowded.' When Jaya said this, Krishna led him out of the hall and drove him straight to his resort. Their discussion went into the wee hours of the morning. After all the frustrations and disappointments over his crusade, for Krishna this visitor seemed to have arrived from heaven.

By the time Jaya left, promising to contact him in the next few days, Krishna was fully rejuvenated. He was charged up and ready to kick-start and add fire to his protests against the nearly complete Trikakulam Nuclear Power Plant.

And today, when he stood on the dais, he reminisced over the past few months. The chance meeting with Jaya, the late night discussion at the resort, the promise of Jaya to help him raise funds, the quick-fire way in which Jaya had fulfilled those promises, the discussions with other like-minded NGOs that

Jaya had prompted to help him mobilise people and garner support in his battle against the commissioning of the nuclear plant.

He quietly walked up and took a vacant chair at the centre of the dais. Before sitting down, he looked at the person sitting on the right, folded his hands and paid his respects. Jaya looked at him, smiled and reciprocated his gesture. The friendship was sealed. In fact, the friendship had been sealed the day Jaya's emissary delivered thirty-two lakh rupees to Krishna Menon's resort. This was the first of many such instalments, meant to take care of the expenses incurred in educating villagers on the impact of the nuclear plant, mobilizing their support, transporting them to the protest rallies and managing politicians. Krishna's hands were massively strengthened by the contribution from Jaya's NGO.

By the time the rally ended, amidst a mammoth gathering of the people of Devikulam, a protest for a clean life was re-ignited—the war against the nuclear plant intensified.

8

Vikram forwarded the e-mail from Tanuja to all his cluster managers. It was a list of all the management trainees who had been allotted their respective branches. When Nikhil got the mail, he scanned the list from top to bottom, looking for one name. . .and there it was. . .at number eight, Zinaida Gomes—Bandra Cluster.

'Yaaaay!' he exulted softly. As per the mail, not only was Zinaida allocated to his cluster, she was posted to the Bandra Branch, right under his aegis. He had to share his excitement with Anand. Picking up the intercom, he dialled Anand's number.

'Yaar, she is going to be in our cluster!'

'Who, boss?'

'Zinaida, you dickhead. She has been allocated our cluster.'

'Wowwww. That's wonderful. Is she the only one, or there are others too, boss?'

Nikhil suddenly realized he was so thrilled about Zinaida's allocation he hadn't even bothered to scan the list for other names. 'Wait. . .wait.' After a long pause during which he reopened the email from Vikram, he replied, 'One more. . .some idiot from Rajasthan called Kalyan Rathore.'

'Great. So two of them.'

'Yes. And as per this list, both of them have been allocated to you. Let's plan Zinaida's role. I will talk to you in the evening.' Nikhil hung up. He suddenly realized he was too excited about Zinaida's assignment, a fact that he had revealed to his subordinate. Anand, when he hung up, wore a wicked smile. 'It's always nice if the boss likes someone from your team. You can use them to get things done,' he said to himself, as he stepped out of his cabin and headed to the restroom. He splashed some water on his face, combed his hair, tucked in his shirt and walked out of the branch. He was getting late for a call.

The meeting was in Taj Lands End, a favourite venue for all Bandra branch meetings, primarily on account of its proximity. It was a mere ten-minute drive from the branch and was the only five-star hotel in the vicinity. Anand was meeting the accounts officer of the US Embassy in India. Harshita Lele, his relationship manager who handled all the large value accounts of the branch, was keeping him company. Vidur Jagtiani, Nikhil's counterpart for the South Mumbai Cluster, had set up the meeting. He was to accompany them, but something had come up. *Everyone these days has started behaving like Vikram*, thought Anand, when Vidur's secretary called to convey that Vidur was stuck at work.

Three Americans were waiting for them; Harshita identified them the moment they walked into the lobby of Taj Lands End. She had met one of them earlier.

'Good afternoon, gentlemen,' said Anand, slipping out a visiting card from his shirt pocket and handing it over. 'I run the Bandra Branch of Greater Boston Global Bank.'

'Very good afternoon.' The American held his card with both his hands and handed it over with the slightest bow. Anand looked at the card that read 'Tim Cook, Director, Financial

Control'. 'Meet my team,' he continued and introduced the other two. They were inconsequential, a fact Anand figured out when neither of them made an attempt to hand over their visiting cards to him. Tim was the one driving the discussion.

'As you are aware, we currently have all our accounts with your bank in South Mumbai. In the next sixty days we will be shifting our consulate from Breach Candy to Bandra Kurla Complex (BKC). Have you seen our new building?'

'Yes sir, I have. It's a beautiful building,' Anand lied. The last time he had gone to BKC was over sixty days ago. *Does one have to perfect the art of lying if one has to become a branch manager?* Harshita wondered. She made a mental note ask to Anand on the way back.

'Oh, yes. It's a fabulous new office,' Tim responded with a broad smile. 'It will become very difficult for us to manage our banking transactions with your South Mumbai branch. That's why we asked Vidur to shift our accounts to a branch closer to BKC. He suggested we move to you,' Tim explained. Anand knew all of this, Vidur had already briefed him.

'We wanted to meet with the team which will manage our accounts once we move and that's why we asked for this meeting.'

'It will be a pleasure to serve you, sir.' Anand was quite happy with the move. The huge balances the consulate maintained with the South Mumbai branch would all move to his branch, giving a much-needed boost to his branch's profitability.

'Mr Cook, I wanted to introduce you to Harshita. You might have met her earlier. She used to be in the South Mumbai branch.'

Tim looked at Harshita as if trying to recollect when and where he had met her. 'I am sorry. Please put it down to my old age, else who would forget such a charming young lady?' Tim smiled at Harshita, who smiled back, partly in embarrassment.

'Once you shift to BKC, Mr Cook, Harshita will be your relationship manager. She will manage the transfer of accounts to this branch and, with her team of service managers, will take charge of every single transaction of yours. While she will be your single point of contact, should you need me, I will also be available to you and your team 24X7. Yours is an important account for us and we will make sure you experience a service level even superior to what you are used to in our South Mumbai branch.'

'Oh, that's going to be a bit difficult. The guys in your South Mumbai branch are absolutely brilliant.'

'They will be pleased to hear that, Mr Cook. I will surely let Vidur know.'

The formal conversation lasted for over twenty minutes, after which all of them left.

On the way back Anand looked at Harshita, 'Manage this account very carefully. It's a complex account. They will have multiple issues, remittances, forex transfers, salary payouts, visa fees etc. Just make sure you are very clear with them on what kind of transactions the banking regulations permit you to do and what you cannot. That way, you will save yourself a lot of fire fighting.'

'Anand. . .I have handled this account earlier, though only for a short duration. I have also handled accounts more complex than this one.'

'I know, Harshita. You are the best the Bandra branch has seen in a long time. But it's my job to forewarn you,' he said, as they drove into the basement of the branch building. Harshita just smiled. She knew there was no one to match her skills in her peer group. She was clearly the best they had.

'Boss just called,' Anand's secretary told him as soon as he set his foot inside his cabin.

'Oh, okay. Connect me to Nikhil. In any case, I have to tell him about this call with the embassy folks.'

'No, no. . .the big boss. Vikram called.'

'Vikram? Why?'

'Don't know. He said he wanted to talk to you on some lead.'

'Great. Get me his number then,' he said, as he walked into his room and started looking at his emails. When his intercom rang, he picked it up. 'Vikram on line one.'

'Hey, rockstar! How are you?'

'I am fine Vikram, thank you.'

'How is the mood in the branch now? Has everything settled down after the chaos post Pranesh's death?'

'Yes Vikram. That's a forgotten story now.'

'Good. I am confident you are taking good care of the branch and the people in the branch. They are lucky to have you as their leader.'

'Thanks Vikram.'

'Okay, listen, Anand. I met this guy at a party yesterday. He is looking for a loan of five crore against his property. Stays on Pali Hill. Get someone to meet him and see if something can be done. Take down his details. His name is Chandrasekhar and his mobile number is. . .'

'Sure Vikram, I'll get someone to meet him today itself.'

'Thanks Anand. Keep me posted.'

'Will do sir. . .I will also annotate the loan file and let the credit folks know you know him well, so they need to treat him with care.'

There was a long pause at the other end. 'No. . .I don't know him well. I just met him.'

'Alright sir, I'll keep you posted.' Anand hung up, wondering why was it that Vikram paused for so long before he said that he didn't know the prospect. Maybe Vikram was doing something else. After all, he was a busy man.

After the call, Anand called his mortgage RM and gave him the number, asking him to get in touch with the loan prospect.

'I've heard this name before,' said the RM. 'But can't remember where.'

'It's a common name, you idiot. Take Harshita with you when you go. If he needs a five crore loan, chances are he is a big man. He can give us some investments and insurance business, too. And moreover, it's Vikram sir's reference. So don't fuck it up.'

'Yes sir.'

'Best of luck,' said Anand as he got up from his chair and ran up two floors, skipping multiple steps at a time, to Nikhil's cabin to brief him on the meeting with the US embassy.

Zinaida, on her part, settled into her new branch extremely well. In no time she became everyone's darling. Being young, pretty and reasonably intelligent helped. The hotness quotient of the branch went up manifold with her arrival. Everyone, including Nikhil, was interested in her well-being. Nikhil believed every woman looks good at a particular age, and Zinaida was at that age. She was undoubtedly the most popular RM in the branch—not necessarily the most effective in terms of business volumes though. The latter was clearly Harshita's domain. And given her vintage and experience, beating her would take something special, even from a teasingly pretty RM. The latter was yet to learn the tricks of the trade.

In all this, poor Kalyan Rathore got left out. Even though he joined the branch at the same time, in a similar role as Zinaida's, he was completely lost.

The entry of the sexy Zinaida changed the dynamics at the Bandra branch. Unlike the other management trainees, she had worked in a bank earlier, though for a very short time; her learning curve was a lot steeper. When the high-value accounts were reallocated, Zinaida ended up getting some of the best accounts, much to Harshita's displeasure. But she didn't complain. She knew re-organizing and re-allocation of accounts was an integral part of an RM's life. It hurt at times when the relationships you built and nurtured got allocated to someone else. 'You win some, you lose some. . . As long as you win more than you lose, you are doing fine Harshita,' was how she consoled herself.

But it wasn't just the staff; over a period of time, even the customers started noticing her. And Zinaida, despite being a slow starter, kept improving. A larger percentage of customer leads she received started to convert into banking relationships. At the end of the quarter, when the branch RM league tables were put up, in terms of incentive earned in the Bandra cluster, she was second only to Harshita and the margin was ridiculously small. Beginner's luck, many would say.

'Yaar, yeh Zinaida kya cheez hai?' Vikram asked Tanuja one day when they were driving back home.

'Who? I don't know her.' Tanuja suddenly perked up when she heard the name.

'What is this, Tanuja? You are getting old. . .You haven't heard about the hot chick in the Bandra branch? And you call yourself the HR head.'

'Oh, that one. What about her?'

'She is supposed to be amazing. I have heard stories about her. The men in the Bandra branch seem to like her a lot,' he remarked snidely.

'You've met her?' Tanuja sounded irritated. She was extremely possessive about Vikram.

'I haven't, no, but I'm planning to go to the branch tomorrow. Will meet her then. Let's see kya cheez hai.'

'You run a branch network or do you choreograph a fashion show, Vikram?' Tanuja sulked. She made a face and turned away from him.

'Don't be jealous, babes. . . Irrespective of how she is, she can't be even half as attractive as you.'

The next morning, Vikram landed at the branch. He was visiting the branch after a good six months and it was a casual, unannounced visit. One of the things on top of Vikram's agenda was to meet Zinaida.

Even though it was a casual branch visit, Nikhil was ready with an updated presentation for all the branches in the cluster. Every week, Nikhil's secretary would key in the latest cluster numbers into the presentation and bring it up to date. Vikram was sufficiently impressed. Wasn't he the one who had poached Nikhil from Guneet and brought him to branch banking?

'Anand and Nikhil, this is brilliant! Looks like Bandra is on the right track and in the right hands.' He then turned and looked at Anand. 'I have seen too many branch managers go down because they won't get down in the mud with the fucking elephants. You are an inspiration for all the other branch managers. Well done, Anand. Come, let's do a tour of your branch.' Anand chest swelled a few inches with pride as he led Vikram down to his branch.

Vikram met all the employees—the tellers, the customer service executives, the RMs—everyone who was in the branch at that time.

'Anand, how many MTs do you have in your branch?' he asked, just before his tour ended.

'Two, Vikram'

'How are they faring?'

'The guy Kalyan is a bit slow, but the girl, Zinaida, is splendid.'

'Hmm. . .good. I would like to spend some time with them, one-on-one. Are they around?' All along, Vikram had been looking for Zinaida, but when he was unable to meet her, he had asked Anand directly.

'Kalyan is here, in the branch. Zinaida has gone out on a call. I will call her back.'

'Thanks, Anand. I need to make a few calls in the interim.'

'Sure Vikram. You can use this room. I will wait outside.' And Anand stepped outside to join Nikhil, who was talking to a few of the branch employees.

He dialled Zinaida and asked her to come back; Vikram was waiting. She was in the neighbourhood and rushed back, cutting short her customer meeting.

'Boss wants to meet you,' Anand said, as soon as he saw her.

'Give me five minutes; I just need to freshen up.'

'Take your time. He has been on a call for the last thirty minutes.' Nikhil was standing next to Anand, but didn't say a word.

Zinaida went into the washroom to freshen herself up. Vikram, meanwhile, finished his call and came out of his room. 'Call them. I am done.'

'Who would you want to meet first? Zinaida or Kalyan?'

'Anyone will do. . .You know, these youngsters are such an inspiration—new ideas, new thought processes. Just talking to these guys charges one up, doesn't it?' He didn't sound convincing at all.

'It surely does, Vikram.' What else could Anand have said?

'Ladies first,' Nikhil, quiet all this while, spoke when he saw Zinaida return from the washroom. 'Let Zinaida go first.'

A pleasant fragrance filled the air as Zinaida confidently strode towards them. Vikram looked at her and was awestruck. She was amazingly pretty. Not particularly a traditional Indian beauty, but hot. There was arrogance in her stride, as she crossed Nikhil and Anand and walked towards Vikram.

'Vikram, meet Zinaida,' Anand introduced them.

'Of course. I have heard a lot about you from these two gentlemen.'

'Something good, I hope.' Zinaida didn't show any nerves.

Normally MTs are quite overawed when they met a senior banker, but not Zinaida.

'Yes, of course. Come on in!' Vikram disappeared into Anand's room, followed by a sashaying Zinaida.

Nikhil and Anand looked at each other and smiled wickedly. Their eyes followed Zinaida's swaying posterior as she walked into the boss's cabin.

After five seconds, an excited Nikhil turned to Anand and asked, 'Did you see what I saw?'

'Yes, boss. How could I have missed it?' Anand had a mischievous gleam in his eyes.

'It was only two earlier. Right?'

'Yes sir. It was two when she came back from the call. I don't know when the third came off.'

'Hmm. . .looks like she opened the third button when she was freshening up. Lucky Vikram!' And both of them started laughing. 'Maybe the fourth will come off if ever Vikram's boss comes here. . .hahahaha!' This time their guffaws were heard by everyone around, who wondered what they were laughing at.

9

Bhavin Shah had been following up with Chandrasekhar for close to two months now. When Anand passed on the referral from Vikram to him, Bhavin had hoped to close the deal and win himself a good incentive in time for the Diwali break in October. However, the way it was going, it looked as if it would be well past Christmas before the deal got closed. Many a time he even contemplated dropping the deal, but given that it was a referral from Vikram, he couldn't do so. He knew that had he spent that much time following up on any other customer, he would have closed multiple deals by then. Harshita, who had accompanied Bhavin on a couple of visits to Chandrasekhar initially, had given up hope of selling any investment or insurance product to him and had quietly excused herself from further meetings.

But persistent effort always pays and Bhavin realized that when, one day, Chandrasekhar called in saying that all the required documents were ready. He offered to drop into the branch to complete the minor pendencies on the application.

Late evening on that Tuesday, Chandrasekhar walked into the Bandra branch to meet Bhavin. Almost all the staff had left for the day. Apart from being late in the evening, it was also the beginning of the month, a time most sales guys normally recover from the exhaustion of torrid month-ends—almost by default, everyone leaves early.

Bhavin was waiting for him in the branch lobby. Both of them sat down at Bhavin's desk. Thankfully, Chandrasekhar had come with all pending documents Bhavin had asked for and, in no time, the loan application was complete. It could now be submitted for processing. Bhavin was happy. He could now go back and tell Anand the deal was complete from his side.

On completing the loan application work, Chandrasekhar enquired about opening a normal banking account. Bhavin was clueless about account opening and deposit side of banking. He was only a loan specialist.

'Wait, sir. Let me see if someone from the branch team is available.' He scampered down to get someone from the RM team. It was around 8.30 p.m. and he was not really hopeful of finding someone. As he had anticipated, no one was there. He was about to return, dejected, when he saw Zinaida entering the office through the side door.

'Zinaida. . .Zinaida. . .' he called as he ran towards her. 'Thank God you came back. I need some help.'

'Tell me, Bhavin. I'd forgotten something so came back to take it from my drawer.'

'I have a customer with me who needs to open a new account. Can you help him? He is Vikram sir's reference.'

Zinaida looked at her watch, raised her eyebrows, considering, and finally nodded. 'Come, let's go,' she said. Bhavin followed her to the floor where Chandrasekhar was waiting.

'Sir, this is Zinaida. She will help you with your queries,' Bhavin said as he introduced Zinaida to Chandrasekhar, who nodded and acknowledged him. He looked at Zinaida from top to toe. He was visibly impressed. 'Hello, how are you?'

'I am good, sir. How can I help you?'

'There is a close business associate of mine. We do lots of business with him. He is a bullion trader—deals in gold.'

'Yes, sir,' Zinaida knew what a bullion trader did.

'He is also into logistics management. Currently he banks with a nationalized bank and is looking to move his account. Can you help him?'

'Of course, sir. But why does he want to move?'

'Some service issues. A month back, the branch manager changed and from that time onwards he's been having some problems. Till the earlier branch manager was there, he had no issues; in fact, he was quite happy.'

'I can understand, sir. But don't worry, we will take good care of him. If he can give me some time tomorrow, I will meet him and help him open the account.'

'Madam, he is going out of the country tomorrow evening. If you can meet him tonight, we can close the deal. While Bhavin was away looking for you, I called him. He is coming to Bandra for some work and will be here in twenty minutes.'

Zinaida looked at her watch. 'Sure sir. I hope he comes in twenty minutes because I have to meet someone for dinner at ten.'

'Yes, yes, no problem. I will call him again. When I last spoke to him, he was not too far from your branch.'

Zinaida looked at Bhavin. 'I am down in the branch at my workstation. Call me when he comes in.' Bhavin escorted her to the stairs. As she was climbing down, Zinaida looked up at him. 'If it's Vikram's reference, we better not screw up. You don't worry. I will put off my dinner and wait for this guy to come.'

In the promised twenty minutes, Asad Ansari walked into the branch and all of them made their way down to Zinaida's workstation.

'Hi. My name is Asad Ansari.' The customary introductions followed.

'What kind of an account is it?' asked Zinaida, after the pleasantries were over.

'It's a current account.'

Zinaida looked up, trying to conceal her irritation. That was the least she was expected to know. 'Yes Mr Ansari, I understand that. I was referring to whether or not you have any limits, any overdraft facility etc.'

'Oh, right. It's a normal current account. See, I brought the Bank of India statement for your reference. You can make out everything from this.'

The moment Zinaida saw the bank statement, her eyes lit up. The Bank of India account, in the name of Asia Logistics Pvt. Limited, showed an average balance of over two and a half crore in Indian rupees. She looked at the statement and passed it on to Bhavin, who was standing next to her.

Bhavin almost fell off his chair when he saw the statement. A few easy calculations told him that if she managed to shift that account to the Bandra Branch, it would mean an incremental profit of over twenty-five lakh for the branch, not accounting for the thousands of rupees profit the bank would make in fees and charges for transactions Asia Logistics would execute through their bank.

Bhavin was overcome by pangs of jealousy. The account had fallen straight into her lap. What a stroke of luck! It could have gone to any RM, but she was the one who came into the branch just when he needed help. But what bugged him the most was the fact that she would make a killing on incentives too.

'Sure sir. I will give you a list of documents we need to open an account. Once you give us those documents, we will proceed with all the other formalities that we need to fulfil to open your account.'

'Hmm. . .' Asad nodded.

'We need a Board resolution, authorizing you to open an account; we need a copy of the Certificate of Incorporation; Memorandum of Articles of Association; latest shareholding pattern certified by a Chartered Accountant; List of Directors, Pan card of the company, a Know Your Customer (KYC) of the Directors and a few photographs.' Zinaida rattled out the requirements. She knew them by heart. 'For the KYC, we need either a passport copy, driving license or pan card of the directors,' she added.

'I am carrying most of these with me, except the photographs of the directors. I can give them to you now.'

'Oh, wonderful. I will arrange for the forms.'

In a couple of minutes, Zinaida resurfaced with a few papers in her hand and within the next quarter of an hour, all the forms were filled up.

'Sir, we need a minimum of two directors to sign on the Account Opening Forms.'

'Oh. That will be a problem.'

'Why, sir? I can send someone to the other director's residence to get his signature.'

'No. That's not the issue. He is not available right now. Had he been available, I would have got the document signed and given it to you. What do we do now?'

'Mmm. . .' Zinaida started thinking of a possible way out.

'Okay. Allow me to suggest something.' Zinaida nodded and Asad Ansari continued. 'Why don't you keep a photocopy of the Account Opening Form and process everything on the basis of the photocopy. Give the original account opening form back to me and I will send the form to you tomorrow morning, after getting it signed by the other director.'

'That's fine, sir. In any case, before opening the account we have to make a mandatory visit to the company premises and file a visit report. I will personally visit the office tomorrow and will pick up the documents when I am there,' Zinaida was quick to point out.

'Tomorrow's a bad day for me, Zinaida. I am off to the Middle East on some work. Post that, I am in Russia for a week and then in China for three days. Will be back only after three weeks.'

'Is there anyone else I can meet when I am there?'

'No, Zinaida. I take care of banking relationships and also look after the financial affairs of the company. As you can see from our banking statement, there is a fair bit of inflow into the account. I cannot trust anyone with the money, right? So it's only me.'

'I will only need five minutes tomorrow, Mr Ansari. Any time of the day. At your convenience.' When Bhavin heard Zinaida getting desperate about the account opening, he wondered whether this was what high current account balances did to RMs!

'Oh, come on Zinaida. I don't want to trouble you. If you think it's too much of a problem, hold it till I come back. I will be back in three weeks and then we can chat and figure out when to meet and close out all the logistics.'

'It's okay, Mr Ansari, we do this for a living. It's not a trouble at all.' Even though she tried hard to smile, the disappointment in her voice overshadowed the optimism. It was not without reason. A quick back-of-the-envelope calculation had told Zinaida that three weeks would mean the end of the month. If she let Asad Ansari go, the two-and-a-half-crore lying in Bank of India would not get transferred to GB2 this month and she would have to look for alternate avenues to meet her targets. That was not the only reason. If she let the deal hang for three weeks, some other bank might jump into the fray and steal the account from her. She could see it slipping away from her hands.

Bhavin noticed her agony which made him silently laud her commitment.

'Okay. I'll tell you what we'll do. I'll send the form for processing. We'll defer the RM visit. I will take a sign-off from our Branch Manager. And we'll open the account but put a hold on debits into the account, pending the visit. Will that be fine?' It was a stupid suggestion and she knew it the moment she said it. Who would agree to open a bank account, keep funds in it and not be allowed to withdraw money pending a bank officer visit? But Asad's reaction was not as volatile as she expected.

Asad thought for a while. 'No, that's not acceptable. If you guys are going to be so tight about the entire thing, I am better off at Bank of India. I am coming to you guys for better service levels. If you guys are going to be as stuck up, then there is no point.' Zinaida was confused. It was her first big win—a current account worth two-and-a-half crore—and she desperately wanted it. There was silence all around. It was a stalemate, which was broken when Asad, probably softened by the look on Zinaida's face, took the initiative. 'Okay. Will it be possible for you to come very early in the morning?'

'How early?'

'7.45 a.m.?' He looked at her. 'I will come early to my office, only for you. Show you around the office and then go back home to pack for my business trip. The only catch is that I will not be able to give you the Account Opening Forms signed by the second director. I will send that to your office later in the day, because he only comes in by ten o'clock.'

'That should be fine, Mr Ansari. I will be there at 7.30 a.m.'

'No, no, 7.45 a.m. should be fine. You can get another fifteen minutes of beauty sleep.' Zinaida sensed the first hint of flirting, but it was fine. With an account worth two-and-a-half-crore at stake, flirting was the least of her worries.

'Thanks a ton. I will also send a few cheques to be banked, along with the Account Opening Form. You can send them for clearing once the account gets opened.'

'Thank you, sir. We will take care of your account.'

'I am sure you will. See you tomorrow.' Asad Ansari walked out of the bank, with Chandrasekhar in tow.

The next morning Asad met her at the reception, showed her around and spent some time explaining his business model to her. Bhavin accompanied Zinaida on this call. It was extremely early in the day, so none of the staff had come in, except for the guard who had opened the office. They even stepped out for a cup of coffee at a nearby Udupi restaurant. Asad waved out at a couple of people walking by. The guy at the Udipi counter, too, knew him. Bhavin inferred Asad was a regular and Zinaida concurred.

Once back, she filed the visit report. By then, Asad's errand boy had dropped in the original Account Opening Form signed by the second director, Aslam Shaikh. She attached her visit report, counter-signed by Anand, to the form and packed it off to the back office for opening the account. Asad had sent a cheque of twenty-five lakh rupees along with the form, which Zinaida kept with herself. She intended to deposit the cheque once the account was opened.

In the branch huddle that evening Anand singled out Zinaida for lavish praise, pointing out the current account of Asia Logistics and the twenty-five-lakh-rupee cheque. The applause that followed his announcement was loud, but for Harshita it was deafening. 'Let's not forget,' continued Anand, when the applause died down. 'There is an opportunity in every referral we get. It all depends on the passion we pursue a deal with. If we're happy that we have met our targets and don't go after any further deals with the same passion, someone else will come and walk away with what could have been ideally yours.' Everyone was confused. What was Anand trying to say? Harshita cringed. 'Asia Logistics could have been closed by someone who was initially allocated to meet the prospective mortgage customer, Chandrasekhar. But that RM—and I will not take names—did not demonstrate adequate passion, for the person had already met the month's targets. The deal subsequently fell into Zinaida's lap and she happily went after it and closed it.' Another applause followed. Anand looked at Harshita and looked the other way. It was a look of disgust.

Harshita was not at all happy with Zinaida's meteoric rise. To her, Zinaida was a challenger whom she didn't consider worthy of engaging in a duel with. *Maybe she is good*, she thought to herself, *but experience needs to be valued too. She can't use her charms and become the best RM overnight.* Even though Harshita still commanded greater respect in the RM community than anyone else, Zinaida was now beginning to bother her. She wished she looked a few years younger, maybe then she would have been more valued.

That evening, as Anand was walking out, she confronted him.

'Anand, need a minute of your time.'

'Yes Harshita.' Anand stopped and turned towards her.

Harshita looked around. There were still some people in the branch. 'Need to talk to you in private.'

'Come, let's go inside.' Anand pointed towards the conference room in the banking hall normally used by the branch staff to talk to irate customers.

'Anand. Is there a problem?'

'What are you talking about?'

'I have been noticing, Anand, that of late my performance is not being acknowledged, and accounts given to me have been taken away.'

'Okay. . .' Anand said warily. He wanted to continue, but held himself back.

'. . .and I am beginning to get the feeling that I don't belong here. I've never felt like this before.'

'Does this have something to do with what I said in the huddle today?'

'Maybe. But that for sure made me feel awkward.'

'Look, Harshita. You have been one of the best performing RMs. However, of late I am seeing a change in you. Whether it's because of repeated success, frustration at work, or any personal issue at home, I don't know. But a change nevertheless.'

'What kind of change are you referring to, Anand?'

'These days you tend to ignore a lot of instructions given to you. You take calls on your own. You don't consult with anyone. You are becoming a lone operator, and that is not good for the team.' Now Harshita was shocked. She hadn't expected Anand to say this. She just raised her eyebrows, as if asking for more.

'Now look at Zinaida. She is so friendly to the entire branch. Gets her work done so nicely. Always willing to learn.'

'Got it. Everyone says she is close to Vikram and that's why she gets this preferential treatment.'

'See, again. You're not even listening. It's not about Zinaida. It's about you. And for the record, I don't freaking care if anyone's dad plays golf with the president. All I care for is numbers, team spirit and having fun in the branch as long as we are here.' Harshita didn't like what she heard. Even though she was standing in front of Anand, she turned her face to the side. She didn't want him to see the little teardrop that had escaped the corner of her eye and was rolling down her cheek.

'In fact, Harshita, talking about today's huddle. Isn't it true that you could have opened the account for Mr Ansari? I asked Bhavin to take you on the call when he met Chandrasekhar for the first time. You were too busy to follow up after that.'

'No. . .that's not true. I went with Bhavin when he met Chandrasekhar the first time. I didn't get any comfort from that meeting. Maybe it was my gut, but I felt he was not a clean guy. And I asked Bhavin to drop the case. After that, it was only today I heard that the account he had referred was being opened and the loan application has gone for processing.'

'Do you know where the lead came from?'

'Yes. He told me it came from Vikram.'

'If it comes from the Head of Retail Banking, aren't you supposed to follow it up for closure? Am I an idiot, sitting here and chasing these transactions? Sometimes, Harshita, things have to be done because you are told to. You ignored Vikram's lead. That's what I meant when I said that you are taking your own calls. If I were you, I would have at least discussed it with the branch manager. You chose not to.'

'I am sorry, Anand. I thought Bhavin would have discussed with you.'

'Yes, he did. But I expected you to, given you are the senior of the two. Anyway, I think you have understood what I wanted to say. You still are one of the best we have. An integral part of my team. Fix these minor glitches and we are ready to roll.'

'Yes Anand.' Harshita was devastated by this conversation, but somehow controlled herself. The lone teardrop that had escaped her eyes dried out quickly. Anand stepped out and headed to his car. Harshita sat down in the conference room for a long time, staring blankly at the glass partition in front of her. Occasionally a colleague would pass by and wave a goodbye to her. How many of them went by and who they were, she had no idea. Finally, it was the security guard coming at ten p.m. to switch off the lights, seeing her and walking into the conference room that shook Harshita out of the trance.

Back home that night, she sobbed uncontrollably till she got tired and rolled over to sleep. Life was not the same in GB2 anymore. She hated Zinaida now. A younger and sexier RM, who had woven her charms around everyone in the branch, had upstaged her. She had to do something to change it. If anything, it made her more determined to win. The next day, while getting ready for work, she stared long and hard at the mirror. A few dark circles had cropped up, her face didn't look as fresh as it used to. Age was taking its toll, but she still looked good—thanks to her rigorous fitness regime. Her hair was speckled with grey, maybe because family and home didn't leave her too much time to pamper herself and work on her appearance. 'If I need to compete with younger girls, I need to look like one of them. I am going to streak my hair this evening,' she said at the breakfast table. Siddhartha, her husband, smiled when he heard that.

'You know, Harshita, if you want to do so, go ahead. But don't do it because you feel it will give you an edge at work. If people there admire you for your streaked hair and not for your work, then it's probably time to move on. And, for the record, you look as charming and attractive as you looked when I married you seven years ago.' He walked up to her and hugged her tightly. Harshita knew he was right. She dropped the plan.

Anand and the Bandra branch had another reason to celebrate in the first week of December. That morning, as part of his daily routine, Anand was checking the exceptional activity report—a report that listed out all the large-value transactions that had taken place in the branch. The report helped the Branch Manager keep a daily check on which customers brought in large sums of money into their account that day, and also who had withdrawn how much from their account.

Staring at him from the report was an inflow of USD 300,000 into the account of Asia Logistics. A credit of this size into a current account was big; more so, if the account was new. An excited Anand looked out of the cabin for his secretary. She was talking to Kalyan. 'Find Zinaida,' he yelled. Anand's secretary looked at Kalyan, who was standing next to her, and whispered, 'Ever wondered, sweety, how the chances of you getting summoned by your boss increase manifold if you are a hot-looking chick?'

'I will consider a sex change operation soon, I guess,' replied Kalyan, as he walked away.

'Zinaida, did you see your account's movements in today's exceptional activity report?' Anand queried the moment she sashayed into his room. She was wearing a short skirt and a tight top. It was not short enough to be called obscene, just enough to distract Anand. He struggled hard not to make it obvious to her that he was checking her out.

'Not yet, sir.'

'Here, take a look.' Zinaida took the printed report from Anand and examined it. A big smile came upon her face. 'Asad Ansari has brought in fifteen million rupees,' she said, disbelievingly.

'You should be happy! Call him and thank him for his business. He has been good to us.'

'Yes sir. I'll call him the moment I get back to my desk.' As Zinaida walked out, Anand could not take his eyes off her impressive derrière.

Back at her desk, she tried reaching Asad Ansari at the number she had. 'The number you have dialled is not reachable. . .' the pre-recorded message intoned. Not being able to get through, she sent him an SMS. 'Tried calling. . .USD three hundred thousand credited to your account. Thank you for using us. Please do call when u get this message. Rgds Zinaida Gomes.' She also forwarded the message to Anand, with the prefix: 'SMS sent to Asad Ansari since he is not reachable.'

That night Asad called. 'Hope it's not too late.'

'No, no Mr Ansari. It's perfectly fine. I was on my way home.'

'So late?'

'Yes sir. Had a customer meeting.'

'Did you get the deal?'

'Yes, I did, sir. Thanks to your wishes.'

'Who wouldn't like to deal with you, Zinaida? You are the sweetest RM I have ever dealt with.'

Was Asad flirting with her? She was not too sure, though she knew she was giving him the benefit of doubt. She liked it, though. It gave her a feeling of power, a sense of control over others.

'Mr Ansari, I was trying to reach you to thank you for operating your account. We have received the first remittance of USD three hundred thousand and it has been credited into your account. Do let me know if you want me to do something with it. . .'

'It's all yours, Zinaida. . .haha. . .'

'No, no. . .That's not what I meant. I wanted to check with you if you wanted me to transfer that to a fixed deposit or invest in some mutual funds.'

'Of course I understood what you were saying. I was kidding. . . And no, Zinaida. I will need those funds over the next three weeks. So let that be in my checking account. Don't transfer it to a fixed deposit. Don't know why I thought you would have been told that. Anyway, let it be there.'

'Oh, alright. No problem. Just call me or SMS me whenever you need anything and I will get it organized.'

'Sure, sweetheart.'

'Goodnight.' Ansari sounded drunk. But Zinaida had learnt to tolerate such flirtations; in fact, she had learnt to use them to her advantage a long, long time ago.

10

GB2, Mumbai
December 2011

Raymond Saldanah was not new to banking. After joining GB2 eight years ago, he was shunted around various units—NRI, operations, credit, branch banking and almost every single department in retail banking. It was not a surprise, then, that when a job in the compliance team came up, the pot-bellied Raymond was the perfect choice. He knew how every unit worked and also knew the loopholes. The games bankers played to circumvent compliance norms were not new to him. Raymond's looks were quite anti-compliance, soft and friendly. In his quest to look menacingly fit for a compliance role, Raymond even grew a moustache once he joined Juliana's team.

Despite his competence, Raymond got moved around so frequently for a reason. Raymond's candid approach had got him into trouble more than once. Anyone would have learnt from adverse experience, but not Raymond. Consequently, he never got along with his supervisors in most of his previous roles. Outspoken that he was, he would never mince words and bosses never like being told that they might be wrong. But Raymond didn't care and that always led to conflicts.

GB2 was known to have a great compliance culture all over the world. Every single process, every single product launch, every single branch was subject to compliance scrutiny and that made compliance very powerful and one of the most hated teams within the bank.

So when Raymond joined the 'horror chambers', as compliance was affectionately called, and took over as the Head of compliance for the bank's retail business, even the few friends he had started avoiding him. Conversations would stall in his presence. People measured every bit of what they said. It was not that everyone looked at him with jaundiced eyes, or treated him coldly. There were a few who also tried to get close to him. But the latter happened only when people needed favours from him—when they wanted him to clear a long-standing proposal, or approve an iffy process.

Raymond, however, had one trait which none of the others in the compliance team had. Raymond was pragmatic and had a business mindset. Often when approval requests would come to him, he would look at it with the business perspective in mind. If the impact of a particular change was significant, but the risks were limited in comparison, he would approve it. The 'material impact' yardstick was what was missing in the compliance team and Raymond and Malvika, his assistant, filled that gap to perfection.

That day, Raymond was loitering on the fifth floor Head Office of GB2, when someone called out to him. He turned to see Tanuja waving at him.

'Hi Tanuja.'

'Raymond. . .my friend. How's your compliance stint treating you?'

'Pretty okay, so far. Nothing much to complain about.'

'Like working with Juliana?'

'Haha. . .she is cold.'

'It's okay. In any case, you didn't get along with any of your bosses. If you don't like Juliana, no one will mind.'

'It's not like that, Tanuja,' Raymond was embarrassed.

'So all set for the branch banking gala night?'

'What gala night? When is it? I don't even know about it!'

'Arre. Didn't Vikram tell you?'

'When is it?'

'It's supposed to be today!'

'No. I didn't know.'

'I saw your name on the invitee list. How come you have not been told?' Then she started thinking. After a pause, she added, 'I think I know. Vikram would have sent the invite to Juliana, for all of you. And now that Juliana is out of the country, the mail would have got stuck in her mail box.'

'Possible. But you know na, I stay away from these parties.'

'I think you should come. It will be good. I'll tell Vikram to send you an invite separately, because I am sure your name was on the list,' she reiterated. 'These parties are fun as long as Vikram Bahl doesn't start speaking. Once he starts, he never stops. . .' laughed Tanuja, as she walked away from Raymond and he traced his steps back to his workstation. 'See you there tonight.' In the past, Raymond was a part of many of Vikram's parties, mainly because they were known for lots of alcohol, good music and great women. A refreshing change from the monotony at work. 'If he invites me, I will go,' he said to himself. Back at his desk, he looked around for Malvika, who occupied the next workstation. She was not there. He then picked up some reports lying on his table and started going through them. It was his daily routine. Even though Malvika was there to assist him, he never relied on her. More than anything, he relied on his own instinct and it always helped him.

That day after seeing the reports, he called Anand. They had a long discussion on certain suspicious cash withdrawals from accounts in the Bandra branch.

'But Anand, no compliant business would need to withdraw over a crore in cash over three days. There is something fishy here. I am also worried because it's a new account. Hope the customer is not using us as a conduit for bad transactions.'

'I know, Raymond. But I'm not worried. He's a good customer. Vikram too, knows him. In fact, three weeks ago, this customer mentioned to us upfront that he needed the money for some project work payments and that the money would be going out soon.'

'Hmm. . .'

'And Raymond, the day the money came in, the RM checked with the customer. We do our due diligence, you see, buddy.'

'I see what you are saying, Anand. I don't have any issue with that. Let's monitor this account for three months. Keep it on the suspicious transaction-monitoring list. We will take a call after three months.'

'I don't think that is required, but if you insist, I'll do it. But let me talk to the RM first.'

'Who is the RM?'

'Zinaida Gomes. Let me speak to her and get back to you. Will drop you a line by the end of the day.'

'Sure. Thanks.'

The next call Raymond made was to Harshita. The two of them shared a great rapport and went back a long way. At one point in time in her career, she had even reported to Raymond. Their closeness could be gauged by the fact that when Harshita's sister had finished college, Raymond had added Malvika to his team.

'Heard of Asia Logistics?' Raymond asked her.

'Who hasn't? It is THE account, sourced by THE RM of the Bandra branch,' came the sarcastic reply from Harshita. The stress on 'the' was not lost on Raymond.

'Why, Harshita? What happened? You sound peeved!'

Harshita was like a dam waiting to burst. The moment Raymond asked, she blurted out everything that had happened in the branch over the past few days. Harshita told him everything about the conflict and the fact that it was brought in by Chandrasekhar who was known to Vikram, which meant indirectly that the account had to be treated as a reference by Vikram.

'Now I understand. It kind of strengthens my resolve to dig deeper into this,' said Raymond.

'No ya. Leave it. You'll be hitting your head against the wall.'

They bitched for a few more minutes on how aggressive youngsters, with a penchant for making a fast buck, were ruining the impressive façade of the compliance-oriented business philosophy GB2 was known for.

'You hate her na?' asked Raymond.

'No I don't. I just hate the way in which she uses her charm to get her work done. And I hate the way the middle-aged men in the branch and outside are falling for her charm.'

'Let it not impact your confidence, Harshita. You are the best I have seen so far into my career.' This was the second time Harshita had heard this, in less than twenty-four hours. When she heard it from Siddhartha, she felt he was biased. Now, when Raymond said this, it was an endorsement of what Siddhartha had said the night before and it felt good.

'Yes, Raymond. Thanks for everything. How are things at home?'

'The same. No change.'

'Hmm. . .I can understand,' and then Raymond heard a noise in the background and then a 'thank you', which was obviously directed at someone else.

'You're not in office?'

'No, Raymond. Remember, tomorrow is Malvika's birthday? I had promised her an iPad long back. Just came out to buy it. I can't buy it in the evening because I have to go to the branch banking gala night.'

'Oh, okay.'

'You're coming for it na?'

'I don't know, let's see. Will chat later, and by the way, thanks for reminding me of Malvika's birthday,' and Raymond hung up.

In the interim, after the conversation with Raymond, Anand called Zinaida to his cabin and briefed her about the entire conversation.

'This is ridiculous, boss. There is nothing remotely suspicious about this transaction. Asad Ansari told us in advance about these cash withdrawals. He had some payments to make. I have visited his office and done our due diligence. What else does Raymond want us to do? He has lost it, boss.'

'Hmm, but Zinaida, a cash withdrawal of over a crore is quite unnatural na? What kind of business would need so much of cash over just a couple of days?'

'Boss, didn't Chandrasekhar tell us Asia Logistics is also into the bullion business? Cash is required when you deal with the yellow metal. And sir, if we allow Raymond to put this account on the watch list, then the customer will get to know of it. It will become a big issue.'

'How will he know? This list is never made public. It's internal to the bank.'

'Yes Anand, but our interrogation will go up significantly. Every time the customer deposits or withdraws money, he will be asked embarrassing questions about the source and utilization of funds. He will eventually get irritated and shift his account. He initiated the process of moving to us because he was not happy with the service levels at his previous bank.'

'Hmm. . .I can understand.'

'And Anand, we are topping league tables now. The average balances Asad Ansari has in his Asia Logistics account are partly responsible for that. If this account moves, we will drop down and it will be almost impossible to catch up.'

'Okay, that's a fair point. I will manage Raymond and see how this goes.'

'Thanks, boss.' As Zinaida left the room her lips turned up, morphing into a wicked smile. A small, albeit significant battle had been won. Asia Logistics had to be protected at any cost.

Anand sent a mail to Raymond that evening, stating he didn't quite agree with the view that Asia Logistics needed to be put on the suspicious transaction-monitoring list.

When Raymond read that mail, he was quite upset. He saw it not as an affront to his authority as a compliance officer, but more as a lack of ownership, of the need to be compliant with the laws and ethical business practices at the branch level. 'Why does business always take priority over compliance? Isn't there a need to do clean business?' he muttered, but there was not much he could do. Juliana, his boss, was away on a foreign trip and he had to wait for her to come and resolve this potential conflict. But could he wait that long? He was getting restless. At that very moment, his phone rang.

'Yes?'

'What time will you be home?'

'Why? And how does it matter?'

'Can't you answer any question in a straightforward manner? I thought my question was very simple. When are you going to come home?'

'I don't know.'

'What kind of an answer is that?'

'Oh, now I get it. You want to go out with that asshole. That's why you are checking.'

'You're a jerk,' came the exasperated response from his wife.

'Tell me. Tell me. Where are you meeting him? I will not stray in the vicinity.'

'Shut up, Raymond. I wanted to know because I am going to be late and Sharmin has to be picked up from her tuition at 8.30 p.m. If you will be back by then, it's fine. Else I'll make some other arrangement.'

'I will be back in time to pick up my daughter. You have fun.' He hung up abruptly. The relationship with his wife of ten years had deteriorated rapidly from the time he found out that she was more than close with her colleague at work. While he had no evidence of any kind of physical intimacy, a few SMSs he stumbled upon indicated to him it was more than a close friendship—a fact he could not digest. For Raymond, life at home was hurtling towards hell and that too at a furious pace. This was one of the reasons, in fact the key reason, he stayed back late at work almost every day.

After the call Raymond was even more infuriated. Almost everything around him made him lose his cool. Anand's mail was open on his laptop screen. An urge to reply to him took over. He looked at his watch. There was still some time to pick up his daughter. Adjusting his laptop, he started typing off a mail. . .to Nikhil, explaining why he thought the account of Asia Logistics should be formally notified for monitoring under the suspicious transaction-monitoring norm.

After drafting the mail, which was particularly nasty, he sat back, read through it and pressed the send button. Before he shut shop for the day, he took one last look at his mails. There was a mail from Vikram, inviting him to the gala celebration. We invite you to 'Play the Lead', the invitation said. Raymond smiled when he saw the title. Vikram never realized that in his peer group, he was the butt of criticism and ridicule for coming up with crazy names, which had absolutely no relation to the event in question. Vikram loved sycophancy and often during his events, one could see the branch managers holding aloft banners and posters with Vikram's pictures on them and screaming their guts out. He could well imagine what the scene would be like that evening. All branch managers and cluster heads, screaming 'We play the lead!!' 'We play the lead!!' and making a mockery of themselves. It would be good to attend it, especially when one wasn't in the branch banking team, because one could then sit back and enjoy the show.

But today, he couldn't have gone even if he wanted to. He had to head back home. He disconnected his laptop, put it into his bag, locked his desk and left for home. Back to hell. To his wife, whom he no longer loved.

Five minutes from home, his mobile beeped. It was a message from Harshita. 'Not coming?'

'No. Had to be back home. How is it there?' He replied.

'Same old tamasha.'

'Yeah? Who's making a fool of himself?'

'Almost everyone except the seniors.'

'How come?'

'They are here with their families. Indrani, Tanuja, Vikram and the Mumbai cluster managers have all come with their spouses.'

'All on their best behaviour then?'

'Everyone. I'm trying to see what they're wearing.'

'Who is the smartest?'

'Without a doubt, Abhishek, Tanuja's husband. Quite stylish. He's apparently a hot-shot consultant at McKinsey. That's what I overheard anyway. Anika is sad. Sonia is okay-okay.'

'Haha. Chal, I've reached home. Don't drink too much.'

'Goodnight,' said the SMS from Harshita, signalling the end of the conversation.

The next morning there were two messages for Raymond. One was a short three-line mail from Nikhil, which he saw on his BlackBerry: 'Raymond, have discussed this issue with Vikram and he seconds Anand's view that the Asia Logistics account need not be put on the suspicious transaction monitoring list. He has recommended that we revisit this after six months. Trust this closes the issue.'

The second was a SMS from Harshita, sent late in the night. 'The bitch got the Best RM Award. Fuck. And guess what, Tanuja's husband gave away the award. I don't know whether to be disappointed about the former or the latter. Life in branch banking sucks.'

11

It was the middle of the night in Israel. Joseph Braganza was fast asleep in his hotel room in Tel Aviv. He had just finished brokering and negotiating an arms deal for the Argentina government who were under renewed threat from the British over the Falkland Islands. A $150 million worth arms deal from Israel munitions had fetched him a cool $17 million. It was so much easier dealing with the Israelis. They were clear that they were interested in selling arms and ammunitions to anyone who wanted to buy them. Whether it was for a democratic or non-democratic process, it didn't matter to them. This unabashed sales focus had often embarrassed the United States of America, as Israel was seen as their ally.

When he heard the phone ring, he woke up with a start. It wasn't the regular phone. His principals required him to carry on his person twenty-four hours a day, a special scrambled phone on which they could reach him whenever they wanted to. Operatives like him had to follow that protocol. They could be called upon to act at a moment's notice.

He looked at the semi-naked woman lying next to him. He had picked her up at the upmarket bar in Hilton earlier. Sometime during the night—he had no clue when—she had put on some clothes. As far as he remembered, she was bereft of clothing when he was pounding her, earlier that night. Wasn't she awesome in bed? He smiled to himself, but only for a split second. There was no way that she could be there when he answered the call. She had to go.

With his left leg, he kicked her. She woke up in shock. By then Joseph had picked up her clothes and was standing by the door.

'Get out,' he said.

'What the fuck?'

'I said. . .Get the fuck out. NOW!!!' he screamed.

The girl snatched the clothes from him in frustration and started putting them on.

'Not here. Out!' he pointed towards the corridor. 'Move. Move!' He literally pushed her out and slammed the door shut. All this while, the phone kept ringing.

He walked inside, picked up the phone, selected a spot farthest from the door and pressed the connect button. The girl he had pushed out, naked, into the corridor would be loitering around the suite door. Joseph didn't want her to listen in.

The call was from somewhere in the United States of America, that was something he had gathered in his experience of over a decade working with these guys. As a covert Central Intelligence Agency (CIA) operative, all his dealings were over the phone or mail. He never, ever met them.

'Yes.'

'Calling from base. Identify yourself.'

'462389, Holiday in Paris.'

'Agent Solomon,' the caller said curtly, addressing him by his code name.

The discussion went on for fifteen minutes. Joseph's task was cut out. He was glad he had closed out the arms deal. He was free to attend to this business now.

'It will be done,' he said, towards the end of the call.

'The money has already been wired to your account with UBS Geneva.'

'Okay, thank you.'

'Will call you tomorrow to confirm. Good night.' It was the same voice for the last four years. Curt instructions, specific discussions, nothing else. They didn't even ask him if he would be able to deliver. He was expected to—there was no other choice.

He picked up his regular phone and dialled a number in Austria. Joseph Braganza hurriedly barked out instructions in German, which the man at the other end quietly listened to. A name of a bank, an amount and an account number were mentioned. 'Do this first thing in the morning.'

'Consider it done. You know where to send my money to,' the guy said in broken English.

'Done,' and Braganza hung up.

Getting up from his bed, he walked towards the bathroom. On his way he switched on the television. A news anchor on BBC was announcing that the United States of America had publically declared that it was siding with the British in the Falkland island dispute. Braganza smiled. He found it a strange and amusing contradiction of sorts that Israel, a staunch US ally, had gone ahead and sold the ammunition to Argentina, and what made the concoction even more interesting was the fact that he, Joseph Braganza, who had brokered this arms deal, was infact a covert CIA agent—one of many such agents who made up the clandestine network that CIA used to channelize and launder money for purposes that the United States could never have publically admitted to being involved in directly.

When inside the bathroom, he looked at himself in the mirror. Lean body, small frame, toned figure, not an inch of fat. He smiled as he remembered the escapades of the previous night.

Involuntarily his hand went up to his forehead as he touched the gash there. That was the only thing that spoilt his near-film star looks. How much he wished he had been careful the day his convoy was ambushed in Iraq!

12

The next quarter results were outstanding for the Bandra cluster. They topped GB2's branch network on almost every single parameter. Wealth management, insurance, deposit growth and even loan origination—they were winners across every single deliverable. Nikhil was a star cluster manager now. It had hardly been nine months since he had moved into his new role, still a novice. Now he was the toast of everyone. Within Nikhil's cluster, the Bandra Branch was the super star. Thirty-three per cent of the country insurance numbers came from this branch. The Bandra Branch also contributed to twenty per cent of the country's mortgage origination and this kind of contribution was unheard of in the past.

The day the numbers came out, the whole branch was in a jubilant mood. Everyone was thrilled, not only at the phenomenal performance at the branch, but also at the relative performance of the branch as compared to the other branches. There is more fun in winning when the margin of victory is staggering.

Amidst all this, Harshita was sitting at her workstation with a sullen face. A look of disgust and tears in her eyes told everyone a different story. Her sales numbers were abysmal. It was not that she had never had a bad month before. There were many, she was human too. But invariably, in the past, the branch performance tracked Harshita's performance. If Harshita failed, the branch failed. This was the first time that, despite Harshita's disastrous performance, the branch had achieved record numbers. This undermined her position as the leading member of the Bandra Branch's wealth management team.

As luck would have it, the top performer that quarter was a rookie. Zinaida Gomes delivered numbers Harshita was used to delivering and that hurt badly. Harshita's self-confidence had taken a tumble. In fact, it had nose-dived a few weeks ago itself when, in the presence of the entire bank, at the branch banking gala night, Vikram had announced that the RM of the year was Zinaida.

And now, when the final numbers of the last quarter of the calendar year were published, Zinaida had actually stolen the show. That day, Harshita walked to the washroom many times. And each time she would look at herself in the mirror and brood. Was age taking its toll? Had she become unattractive? Was she paling in comparison to the seductive Zinaida? Had customers started preferring to deal with Zinaida than with someone more stable and experienced like her? But then she would splash water on her face and remind herself of what Siddhartha had said to her during the conversation about streaking her hair. She was in banking and not in the business of entertaining clients. Looks didn't matter as much as trust, faith and dependability did. And on those counts Zinaida couldn't have beaten her. Even though she consoled and reassured herself, it really hurt to see someone earning a higher incentive than her at the Bandra Branch. How could she set things right? She thought hard and long, even called Siddhartha and spoke to him for close to an hour. Normally, Siddhartha would not have indulged her for so long while at work but he too realized what his wife was going through. The call to her husband helped her make up her mind on the future course of action. She got up and walked to Anand's secretary.

'Need to see Anand today.'

'Sweetheart, he is away for the day with Vikram and Nikhil. He'll only be back after lunch. Maybe you can meet him then. I'll let him know.'

'Please do. . .it's important.'

'Cool.'

Harshita didn't have to wait for long. Anand was quite sensitive about his responsibilities towards his people. At around three-thirty in the afternoon, Anand called her and she walked into his room.

'You wanted to see me, Harshita?' Anand had a smile on his face, probably because Vikram had said some nice things to him.

'Anand, I am not sure how you will react to this. I want to take an off for three weeks.'

'What? Three weeks? In January, the beginning of the year? Harshita, is everything okay?'

'I don't know, Anand. I feel like I'm just not living up to my own expectations. I want to take a break, think about what I need to do, how to get things back on track on the work front etc. I have started wondering if I have gone past my expiry date for this job. I need to find answers to some serious questions.'

'Harshita, it's okay. Everyone has a bad month.' Anand walked across and put his hand on her shoulders and made her sit.

'It's not about that, Anand.'

'I know. But it's fine. Look at it this way. The branch had a great month. So your poor performance didn't matter. We were able to absorb your off-day.'

'That's exactly the point, Anand. If my poor performance didn't matter to the branch, it means I don't matter. It only shows that the branch can do well without me. I don't want to sound selfish, but that's not a position I have ever been in. Nor do I ever want to be in such a position again.'

'Don't think so much Harshita.'

'Anand, I have not done anything different this month. I have worked the same way month after month, with the same commitment, the same dedication, yet my numbers are dropping. And that concerns me. Someone else is getting you your numbers, Anand, so you are fine with it, but for me it's not acceptable.'

'Okay, what do you want to do?' Anand was getting frustrated with this conversation. He wanted to get it over with and go home.

'I want to take a break for three weeks. I spoke to Siddhartha sometime back. He recommended we take a short vacation and come back recharged. I hope that will do me some good and after that I don't give you any reason to complain.'

'I will never complain, you know that. I have full faith in you. And if I ever say anything to you, it will be and has only been in your interest.'

Liar, thought Harshita, but didn't say anything. It was not too long ago that they'd had the dirty conversation about the branch's performance and her commitment and passion. Anand had probably forgotten it. But that had marked the beginning of her fall.

'Thanks Anand. You've been a great help,' Harshita said and almost as an afterthought, added, 'always.'

Anand smiled. 'Chill.'

'I'll send you a mail requesting a leave today,' and she turned and stepped out of his cabin.

As she walked out of Anand's room, she could sense a fair bit of commotion in the banking hall. The bank had just downed its shutters for the day, hence such a commotion was not routine. It didn't take her too much time to realize what the issue was. The mammoth numbers the branch delivered that quarter attracted the pests from the compliance and audit team. They landed up for a spot audit.

Doors were slammed shut. No one was allowed to enter or leave the branch. People had to drop whatever they were doing and move to a side, to allow the compliance folks to do their job.

Raymond walked in with two other junior blokes, who were trying their best to look menacingly important. They had left Malvika back in the head office because Harshita was in the branch and there would have been an obvious conflict of interest if she was in the auditing team. They went straight to the Branch Manager's room. Anand was surprised and stiffened up a bit when he saw them. He was standing by his desk, hands firmly planted on the two sides of his laptop kept on the table, eyes firmly fixed on the screen. In the same pose, he turned his head and looked at the three. 'Hey Raymond, what's going on?'

Raymond smiled. 'Nothing. Just a regular inspection. We should be done in about an hour. Can you please request your team to stand down? No one leaves the premises, no one destroys any paper, no one makes any notings. . .' After rattling off instructions, Raymond paused. Anand stood up, his face conveying a mix of shock and surprise. Raymond liked the pained look on his face and, with a sadistic glee, added, '. . .the regular stuff. You are familiar with the rigour, aren't you?'

Anand nodded. 'But why suddenly? Aren't you supposed to inform us?'

Raymond's already sadistic grin only got wider. 'You should know me better by now, Anand. Nikhil was informed in the morning. I am sure he told you.'

'No, he didn't.' He suddenly looked confused. 'But why?' After a pause, he added, 'Wait, let me call him.' Anand picked up his intercom and dialled Nikhil's number. Simultaneously he looked at Raymond and said, 'Are you trying to fuck me over because of the Asia Logistics issue?'

Raymond just smiled. Anand's question was not worth a response. 'Please go ahead and call him. I will do my job.' Raymond walked out of Anand's cabin, towards the banking hall. Nikhil picked up on the fourth ring. Anand's pleas of not being prepared fell on deaf ears. Nikhil would have none of it. He was clear: if there was to be an audit, it had to be a surprise one; else the purpose of an audit was defeated. 'Fucker,' muttered Anand as he slammed the phone down.

The audit lasted precisely ninety minutes. Everything was dealt with very efficiently. Raymond was not vindictive at all, as Anand initially thought he would be. He was quite rational, balanced and even overlooked minor discrepancies in adherence to the branch process manual. For the entire duration Anand was in the banking hall, talking to his people, joking with them, passing smart comments on the audit team—even likening them to Pakistan's ISI. Raymond didn't react to the needling and quietly went about his job.

Finally the audit ended and Anand breathed easy. The audit did not dig out anything of significance. January is the time foreign banks start working on employee salary increments and Anand didn't want an adverse audit to impact the perception of his stellar performance of the last six months.

From the looks of it, Raymond seemed quite satisfied with the outcome of the audit. He shook hands with Anand and thanked him for the courtesy—it was customary, he wasn't particularly keen to do that—and promised to send him the audit report within the week for his comments, before it was sent to the higher authorities. He walked out of the main door to his car parked outside the branch. He seldom drove to work. Only when he had to travel to some other branch would he drive, else he was quite used to the local trains. The moment he got into his car, the phone rang. It was his wife. He frowned, as usual and picked up the call. The moment Raymond said 'Hello', his wife started howling something into the phone.

'Okay. . .okay. . .I'm at the branch only. . .I'll get it. Don't worry.' The call abruptly disconnected. Raymond frowned again. His eyebrows curled, his moustache twitched and creases appeared on his forehead. He was irritated, it was evident. He hurled the phone on the dashboard. 'What the fuck?' he swore. For a few minutes he sat there, hands on his head, elbows on the steering wheel, looking stressed. He felt the back pocket of his trousers. The wallet was intact. He had his ATM card. He got out of the car and slowly walked up to the ATM installed just outside the branch.

The ATM lobby was empty. He glanced inside the branch. The staff was all huddled inside the conference room, presumably talking to Anand about the audit. He looked back at the ATM lobby. Three ATMs displaying various promotional messages smartly adorned the lobby. Wasn't GB2 a bank to die for? Almost everything they did was in impeccable style. He was proud to be working there.

He walked up to the closest ATM. His wife had asked for ten thousand rupees. 'Fuck,' he said, as the account balance came up on the screen. 'Over a decade of work experience and nothing in the bank to show for it,' he said to himself, letting out a deep sigh and turning back. Right next to the ATMs was a cheque deposit box. He saw the box and remembered he had been carrying a refund cheque in his wallet for the last two weeks, but hadn't managed to deposit it. Happy he had remembered when he was in the lobby itself, he pulled out the cheque, wrote his account number on the back and walked up to the box, and inserted the cheque into the slit on the top and let go.

When he dropped it, the cheque went into a free fall, dropped half-way into the box and stopped. Raymond was turning to leave when, from the corner of his eye, he saw half the cheque sticking out. Cursing the cheque, the cheque box and everything around it, he turned back and pulled the cheque out. Maybe he hadn't dropped it in properly. Maybe some other cheque was stuck, blocking the smooth flow of his cheque into the box. It was unlikely the box was full. These cheque deposit boxes were designed in such a manner that they never filled up; in case they did, it would be quite easy for someone with a sharp instrument to pull out the cheques on top and misuse them, though given the security ATM lobbies have, such incidents only had a theoretical possibility.

He tried to force the cheque in once again. Like the previous time, the cheque got stuck midway. Something was blocking its path. It was peculiar. He got down on his knees and peered inside. Inexplicably, it seemed to be full. There seemed to be lot of cheques inside the box. Straining his neck, he got his eyes in line with the slot and again tried to peer inside. As he pushed himself deeper to get a better sight, the wood of the box began to poke his cheek. He couldn't have gone any further. A couple of branch guys passed him. One of them stopped and asked him, 'Is there a problem Raymond? Can I help?'

'No, it's okay. I think I dropped a wrong piece of paper in this, just trying to see if I can get it out. Don't worry.' He called out to the guard. 'Do you have a torch?'

The guard nodded and produced a torch from his kit in no time. Raymond took it from him and pointed the beam of light straight into the slit in the box. He pulled up, blinked his eyes a few times and went back to examining the box. It was a bit hazy; he couldn't make out what was inside. As he moved his gaze away from the box for the second time, his phone rang. He looked at the screen, lifted his head, looked around and into the branch before he picked up the phone.

'Hello?'

'Raymond.'

'Tell me.'

The conversation went on for the next three minutes, after which he picked the box and walked back into the branch. This time, he did not go to Anand's cabin. Without even waiting for the lift, he walked up two floors, straight into Nikhil's cabin. Nikhil was packing up to leave.

Seeing Raymond walk into his office, he smiled. 'What Raymond, planning to lose some weight? This kind of weight-lifting is not good, dude.'

'Nikhil, I want this box opened right now,' said Raymond, completely ignoring Nikhil's poor attempt at cracking a joke.

'What's wrong?' The firmness in Raymond's voice made Nikhil realize that this was not a casual visit. 'You sound pissed.'

'I am pissed, Nikhil. Very, very pissed.' He went on to tell him everything he knew.

'Relax. We will find out. Don't worry.'

Nikhil called Anand and asked for the duplicate keys to the cheque deposit box. 'It will be better if you come up with the keys, Anand,' he said, before banging the phone down. In no time Anand came up. Someone from his team had seen Raymond take up the box to Nikhil and warned Anand; he was ready with the keys even before Nikhil called.

When they opened the box, all of them were shocked. Inside the box, were twenty-eight hurriedly-stuffed blank investment slips signed by customers. Most banks instruct their relationship managers and wealth managers not to take blank instruction slips from customers. These slips are normally signed when customers ask the bank to invest, or redeem, their money into mutual funds. RMs, in the quest for quick returns, might use these blank but signed forms and transferred customer funds into mutual funds without explicit customer instruction, or even swap them across mutual funds without checking with the customer. The bank earns its revenue from the mutual fund company and the RM meets their targets. Eventually, nothing is hidden from the customer and when he does find out, either the RM silences him with some other sops or the matter snowballs into a major customer service and compliance issue. To prevent any of this and ensure greater transparency, most banks ban their RMs from holding blank customer mandates. In GB2, like in most other banks, this was a sackable offence.

Raymond was livid. 'See. Didn't I tell you?' Nikhil looked at Anand, who had no answer.

'There's no point asking Anand. He clearly doesn't know about this. This has been done by someone from his team. When they saw the Audit team coming in, they quietly and stealthily stuffed all these papers into the cheque deposit box so that no one would get to know. We normally don't check the ATM lobby as it's covered by a separate audit. This issue would have remained undetected were it not for my own cheque, which I wanted to deposit.'

'Whose accounts are these, Anand?' Nikhil, too, sounded pained. 'I wonder what else is hidden beneath the carpets in your branch.'

'I will find out, Nikhil. Give me some time.'

'Not required, Nikhil. I will tell you whose accounts these are.'

'What?' Nikhil looked at Raymond and suspiciously asked him, 'How do you know?'

'It's my job to know, Nikhil. Just ask Anand to confirm if all these are Zinaida's accounts.'

'Zinaida?' Nikhil wore a grim look as he nodded to Anand, who went out of the room. Within ten minutes, he was back. This time the look on his face was enough for Raymond to declare victory. 'I rest my case. I will send you my report tomorrow, but be assured, it's going to be a difficult one for you to respond to,' Raymond threatened, as he started walking out of Nikhil's room. Hardly had he stepped out of Nikhil's room when he turned back and walked towards Nikhil's table where the cheque deposit box was kept, dipped into his shirt pocket, pulled out something and dropped it amongst the large mess of cheques and documents on Nikhil's table. 'Oops, before I forget. Let me drop this real cheque into this box. Isn't that what the box is meant for?' he said, smiled and walked out of the room, leaving Nikhil and Anand looking at each other. He removed his phone from his pocket and redialled the most recent number on his call log.

'Thanks Harshita,' he said, as he walked out towards his car.

'Not a problem, Raymond. I saw it happen, so I thought I should let you know. But I guess you had seen it before I could tell you the story.'

'Oh no. If you had not told me, I would have assumed some customers had dropped some papers by mistake and might not have insisted on the box being opened. Thanks for your help.'

'Always a pleasure, Raymond,' and she disconnected. The moment she disconnected, she felt a tap on her shoulder.

'Who were you talking to, Harshita? To Raymond? What a bitch you are!'

'It's none of your business, Zinaida,' an agitated Harshita retorted, as she turned away from her and walked to her cubicle. From the corner of her eye, she could see Zinaida walk up to Anand, who was heading towards his cabin with the cheque deposit box in hand. Anand looked angry—and rightfully so—but Zinaida's charm was enough to cool him down. She could see them having a long and animated conversation. Finally, when Zinaida lifted her hand and pointed towards Harshita's cubicle, she knew it was time to leave. It would have been difficult for her to face Anand and Nikhil after having squealed to Raymond. While she knew what she had done was right, her conscience was pricking her for not being a team player. In any case, she would be back only after three weeks. Hopefully by then, everything would have settled down. It was holiday time. A week hence, visa formalities permitting, she would be off on her European sojourn.

13

Devikulam
First Week of January 2012

A princely sum of $3 billion had already been spent on the Trikakulam Nuclear Power Plant by the government of India. There was lot at stake from a political as well as a financial standpoint. The plant was ready to go live in another sixty days.

It was now or never for Krishna. If they didn't manage to do anything in the next two months, their protest would be futile. Apart from Krishna and Jaya, the core protest team had now expanded to include some powerful and influential people. Two other NGOs, an independent MLA, a satrap of the local opposition party, Madan Mohan, had joined in. Krishna was initially opposed to politicians joining the battle, but Jaya convinced him otherwise. 'They are a necessary evil. It's better to have them on your side. This will bring in the media, the people and also lend us significant financial clout,' Jaya explained.

Taking inspiration from Mahatma Gandhi and his effective non-violent means of protest, a massive rally coinciding with Mahatma Gandhi's death anniversary was planned. Monday, the 30th of January, was the day the battle against Trikakulam was to enter the home run.

Work for this protest began weeks in advance. Posters were printed, communication meetings organized, vehicles hired, announcements made in almost every street corner, street plays organized, local colleges and high schools galvanized, media brought, advertisements imploring people to come in and be a part of this protest inserted, everything that could be physically and financially done was done.

One morning, Krishna woke up to an unexpected full-page advert in the local edition of *The Hindu* newspaper. Apparently inserted by the Central government, which had taken all the credit for the commissioning of TNPP fourteen years ago, the advertisement listed that TNPP was one of the major initiatives taken by the Centre for the betterment of the lives of people in the region. The ad surprised Krishna because such propaganda was normally seen only if the days of the ballot were approaching and they were at least a couple of years away from elections of any kind. This clearly was the beginning of an attempt to sway public opinion in favour of TNPP. The government was rattled by their call for a rally.

'The advertisement is quite damning. I only hope our people are not swayed by it. We need to counter it,' said Jaya that day, sipping freshly brewed coffee at Krishna's resort.

'But how? We know the Russians reactors are not as safe as the ad claims them to be. And have you heard of this Global Seismological Research and Mining Association (GSRMA), whose report the advertisement refers to and claims that the region is very low-risk as far as earthquakes are concerned? The earthquake zoning of India, on the contrary, puts Devikulam in Zone 3.'

'Moderate risk of a quake,' agreed Jaya.

'Yes. How do we make sure people do not get influenced? They are gullible and that's what the government is playing upon.'

'I have an idea,' Jaya suddenly got up. 'Come, let's go.' He led Krishna up the stairs to the business centre within the resort. As he opened the door and walked in, the business centre in charge welcomed them. 'We need some privacy. Can you give us fifteen minutes?' The executive looked at Krishna, who nodded. Within no time, the executive disappeared, leaving them alone in the room.

'Can you log on to the Internet?'

'All the computers are connected to the Internet.'

'Great,' Jaya sat down on one computer. Krishna stood beside him.

'Come. Sit down next to me,' said Jaya, as he clicked on the Skype logo and the login screen appeared.

'Your Skype ID and password?' he asked Krishna. Jaya was aware Krishna spoke with his clients on Skype. Krishna quietly reached over and logged into Skype using his ID and password.

Once that was done, Jaya keyed in a strange sounding ID—stopnuclearproliferation—and pressed the video call button. In no time, the call got connected and someone came on line. Krishna didn't recognize him. He had never seen that guy before. The line was quite clear, as evidenced by the clarity of the picture and sound.

'Hello Dr Kohl, how are you?' exclaimed Jaya. Seeing the blank look on Krishna's face, he introduced the stranger to him. 'Krishna, meet Dr Heldrich Kohl.'

'Hello, Dr Kohl,' said Krishna. And turned and looked at Jaya, wondering who Dr Kohl was.

'Dr Kohl is an expert on issues that could crop up on account of seismological imbalance. He has also done a research paper on how security measures at the plant could be compromised in case of an inherent terrorist strike. His expertise can help us counter the claims made in today's advertisement.' Krishna smiled. So Dr Kohl was a friend who was going to help them.

'I am a close friend of Mr Yayakumar, have known him for a long time. What say, Yaya?' The manner in which he said 'Jaya' was quite hilarious. Krishna realized only later during the conversation that Kohl was born to a German father and a Dutch mother, leading to a very strong Dutch influence in his English. The Dutch are known to pronounce all J's as Y's. That's why Jayakumar became Yayakumar when Kohl spoke.

It was an interesting call. Dr Kohl was very forthcoming and shared all information he could. Krishna was quite surprised at his knowledge of the intricacies of TNPP. He even queried Dr Kohl about it, to which Kohl said that as a research scientist, he was tuned into various nuclear sites across the world which were, in any case, few and far in between. It seemed like a reasonable explanation and Krishna didn't query him much after that.

Krishna invited him to his resort, if Dr Kohl were to ever visit India. Kohl didn't respond to the offer. Probably he didn't understand the English Krishna spoke, or so thought Krishna as they hung up after a forty-minute call.

Later, at around six in the evening, another scientist from France, Louis Bourgeu, came on a call with Jaya and Krishna. The latter was surprised on two counts. One was the ease with which Jaya could connect him to the international scientists. But what shocked him even more was the fact that the entire international community was tuned in to the developments at TNPP. Both Kohl and Bourgeu seemed aware of everything, including the full-page advertisement of that day. The access to the best brains in the business made him feel powerful.

What began that day as a one-off Skype call became a routine. Nuclear scientists from various western countries would give tips and advise the two of them, helping them counter-balance the government aggression. By the time the day of the protest drew near, the two of them, with assistance from scientist friends all over, had worked out an eleven point agenda—a document which contained all their objections to the TNPP and its after-effects.

As a consequence of the eleven point charter, the government promptly set up a review committee which worked with the citizens' team and eventually submitted a three-hundred page report to the government, surprisingly within two weeks, which, backed by the global scientists, rubbished almost everything Krishna and Jaya were saying.

And finally when the Prime Minister came on national TV and defended TNPP stating, 'It's the safest nuclear plant in the world', it was clear: the battle lines had been drawn.

There was no option but to go ahead as planned with the strike on January 30th—a protest Jaya and Krishna had been planning for weeks.

14

A furious Raymond published the audit report in the next two days. Ideally he would have waited for a week to do it, but he was very agitated. He wanted to get it out of the way and bring the guilty to book.

The report scathingly reprimanded the Bandra branch. It rubbished Zinaida and the team of relationship managers. Raising serious questions about the internal control team in the branch and the checks they did, it just stopped short of questioning Anand's leadership in the branch. The report was also marked to Vikram.

When he saw the report, Nikhil was livid. This was one of his first reports as a cluster head and it was a C-minus report. He knew every word in the report was true. There was no one but the branch team to blame. And there was one name that stood out in the report—Zinaida.

Nikhil forwarded the report to Anand with only one comment. 'Take a look. We need to respond carefully. It might be difficult for us to protect her. Please send me a draft response by tomorrow.' Anand quietly drafted a soft response and sent it to Nikhil, who relayed it to Raymond without making any changes.

That evening, Raymond got a call from Juliana's secretary. '*Femme Fatale* wants to see you in her cabin. Can you come?'

'Five minutes.'

Within the promised time Raymond was knocking on the door to Juliana's cabin. He was sure she had seen the report and called him to discuss the next course of action. He was right—almost.

'Raymond,' she began. 'I saw the report you sent to Vikram's team.'

'The Bandra branch one.'

'Yes, Raymond. The same one.'

'They tried to cheat us, Juliana. We have a problem there. They have responded to the audit queries and have accepted their wrongdoing. We will now be circulating their responses to the core team.'

'I have seen it, Raymond.' This statement shocked Raymond. He had not sent it to her. How had she managed to get it?

'You've seen it? But I didn't send their responses to you.'

Juliana didn't bother to answer. 'I want you to retract the report.'

'What? Sorry. . .what, Juliana? You want me to withdraw the report?'

'You heard me,' Juliana nodded.

'But why? The branch team has accepted everything they did. They have agreed to the report.'

'Raymond. Do I have to explain every decision of mine? Do I have to tell you that external parties see audit reports like these?' Seeing the blank look on Raymond's face, she elaborated. 'RBI, the board, etc see these reports and can use it to castigate the bank. You have to be careful of what to put in an audit report and what to take up outside the formal audit report. In this report, particularly, I noticed you have been extremely ruthless and harsh on the branch and even on certain youngsters who are just kick-starting their careers. This is not good. I don't want brashness in my team. Make sure that, henceforth, these reports are more constructive in nature.'

Clearly this was not the Juliana he knew. This demeanour, the stance she was taking was quite strange. In the past, she always pushed him to highlight any issues he might have found in the formal audit report. It was abnormal, to say the least.

'Juliana, the branch people tried to hide things from us. They clandestinely hid documents which could have landed them in trouble. I suspect the intent of the people in the branch. I don't think we should be lenient towards them.'

'Raymond. Don't you get it? You have always landed in trouble by not listening to your supervisors. People warned me when I hired you in my team. But I liked you and wanted to give you a chance. Please don't make me wonder if I was wrong at that time. Withdraw the report. And redraft it without the cheque deposit box issue. I would like to validate the report before it goes out to the branch. That's all I called you for. Thank you.'

Raymond stood there like an idiot, wondering why all this was happening. Where had he gone wrong? Hadn't he been nice to the branch team till such time they tried to cheat him? He felt as though his feet were glued to the floor in shock. He didn't like a word of what Juliana had just told him. But she was his boss and called the shots.

'We are done. And now if you excuse me, I have to make a few calls, Raymond.' With her curt response, he was brought back to reality.

'Thanks, Juliana,' was all he could say before exiting Juliana's room. Angry and bitter, he went back to his desk. He sat down, staring blankly at his laptop screen for a few minutes. Is this the way an organization pays one back for all they have done in the past? He had given them ten years of his life. In the bargain his personal life was screwed, his wife was on the verge of leaving him. He had no savings. And now his dignity was being targeted. Today, despite his past, he was humiliated for no fault of his.

He picked up the phone and dialled a number. 'I need to come and see you for ten minutes. Can I come now?'

'Give me fifteen minutes and then come down.'

'Cool,' and he hung up.

Within ten minutes, he was outside Tanuja's cabin and shown in by her secretary. He was hoping that in a professional organization like GB2, HR would intervene and set right all the issues he was facing.

'What happened, Raymond? You don't sound too good. Don't tell me there's an issue with your boss again.'

'In fact, Tanuja, there is an issue,' and he narrated the entire sequence of events.

'Tu bhi na. . .paagal hai.' When Tanuja said this, Raymond raised his eyebrows. 'Why do you want to take pangas with everyone? Do your work quietly and go back home. Enjoy life. Why do you want to get involved with multiple people and fuck up your life and career?'

'What? Tanuja, do you even realize what Juliana told me to do today? She asked me to withdraw a report in which I had raised serious issues. She wants me to shove it under the carpet.'

'Arre bhai. It's not like that. She wants you to take it up with the branch and resolve it informally. Why do you want to make a song and dance about it? What do you gain? Nothing, na. Look Raymond, in one's career, it pays to be loyal to individuals. It pays to be aligned to powerful people. There is no point fucking around with powerful people because if they start fucking around with you, you will soon be dead,' and after a pause, added, 'professionally dead.'

'Who are you talking about? Juliana?'

'No. Why do you want to get into Vikram's bad books? See, even Juliana wants to keep him humoured. Indrani likes him. Why would you want to take him on by screwing his branches and his favourite RM?'

'Favourite RM?'

'Yeah. Don't you know Zinaida is his favourite RM?'

'No I didn't know that, but how does that matter? And what should I do if his people are running riot in the branches?'

'You think he doesn't know?'

'I'm not sure he knows.'

'He's not a dickhead, Raymond. I'm sure he has enough control over his people. And secondly, boss, in this bank there are a lot of people who would want to be Zinaida's saviour. Don't even try to kill her career in this bank. Even before you realize, you will be history. Just in case you didn't know this, she was the only MT in her batch that was not hired from MBA campus. She was hired from the market and she is not even a management graduate. That should tell you something about her contacts. Just be careful.'

'This is ridiculous!'

'Look, Raymond. You are smart. I've told you what I wanted to. What do you want to do? If you go against Juliana or, more importantly, Vikram, you might become a hero. . .or maybe you will be out of the bank in fifteen days and I might have no control over it. It's your call now.'

Raymond didn't say anything. He was lost in deep thought, when Tanuja spoke again. 'Chal, I have another meeting. Kuch problem ho toh phone karna. Thoda chill kar yaar. Why do you stress yourself so much?'

Raymond got up and left the room, completely disgruntled and frustrated.

'Raymond came to see me. Just left,' said Tanuja on the phone.

'What did you tell him?'

'Told him not to fuck around with anyone, particularly you,' and then started giggling before adding, 'That's *my* birthright honey. . .only mine.'

'Hahahaha, of course,' Vikram guffawed, before he hung up.

Within the next forty-eight hours Anand got a mail from Raymond with a cc marked to Nikhil and Vikram, which just had two lines in it.

> *Dear Anand,*
> *The Audit report sent to you two days ago is withdrawn due to some internal inconsistencies. We will repeat the audit at a future date.*
> *Regards,*
> *Raymond.*

Though Anand was happy with the retraction of the report, he was left wondering what had happened over the last forty-eight hours to change the course of action.

15

Inorbit mall in Malad was teeming with hundreds of people that Saturday. It seemed as if all of Mumbai had descended on one of the oldest shopping paradises in the suburbs. The Mumbai winter, hardly cold enough to be called winter, was in decline and almost all the shops had a sale on, because of which the footfalls were staggering.

The person at the billing counter at the Spencer store inside the mall had the look of a very harassed man. Steve (that's what the badge pinned to his chest said) looked up from his desk and saw a long queue of people waiting to be served. Over the last fifteen minutes, it was the sixth time he had lifted his head up to take stock and each time it was bigger. Hurriedly, he stole a look at his wrist watch—there was still time for his shift to end. 'Goddamn,' he cursed under his breath and went back to billing. Each shift of his was four and a half hour long. Another three hours to go before someone else would relieve him of his cash duties. A thousand thoughts weighed heavily on his mind as he scanned the bar code on one item after the other. It was a monotonous job. After all the work they did, most customers didn't even bother to say thank you. The lady on the other side of his counter signed on the charge slip and handed it back to him. Steve collected the charge slip, opened the cash tray, slipped the charge slip into a pre-designated section and pushed the tray back in. Time for the next customer to be billed.

He started scanning the barcodes on the items the next customer bought—a steam press, two kilogrammes cashew, expensive imported chocolates, four bottles of wine and a lot of other stuff. 'Bill amount is rupees twenty-eight thousand, six hundred and forty-eight, sir', he said and looked up. One glance at the customer, a quick look at the queue and he looked back at the screen in front of him. Something was not right. 'Maybe he's just an errand boy,' he muttered to himself as he punched in 'Cash' as the mode of payment. 'Rupees twenty-eight thousand, six hundred and forty-eight, sir. . .' and as an afterthought he added, 'Do you want a carry bag, sir? We charge for it.'

The customer just nodded. He brought his hand up, dipped into his shirt pocket and whipped out a credit card.

'Oh, you're paying by card?' He noticed the card came out of the shirt pocket. Normally, card users carry it in their wallet. His antenna went up almost instantaneously.

'Yes.'

'I am so sorry, I thought you were going to pay by cash. Please give me a minute, I have to change it on the system.' Steve then got busy. Changing the mode of payment on his billing system, he also buzzed his supervisor to come to his counter. Such changes had to be explicitly authorized by the supervisor. In this case, he wanted his supervisor to also take a look at the customer.

In no time, Steve's supervisor was at the counter. Steve whispered something to him. The supervisor heard him out and discretely evaluated the customer from head to toe.

'Is this your card sir?'

'Mine. My card.' The customer couldn't speak proper English.

'What's your full name, sir?' The supervisor asked him again.

'On the card. It written.'

'I can read that sir, but I am asking you,' this time the supervisor was firm. The customer mumbled his name.

'Is this your card, sir? Where do you stay?'

'Why? Why should I tell you?' the customer demanded. He clamped up and became tense and edgy. This was signal enough for the supervisor; something was definitely out of place.

'Do you mind stepping this side for a moment, sir?' requested the supervisor. But the customer knew it was not a request, it was a clear instruction.

'Why? What problem?'

'Sir, please step aside, you are blocking the queue.' By this time, two burly security personnel had also stepped up next to the customer. They didn't hold him, but they left no ambiguity in his mind that if he tried to scoot, they would not hesitate.

Steve and the supervisor, followed by two guards, led the customer to the waiting room. Steve excused himself and made a few calls. In no time, Shankar and Unmukt, two officers from the fraud control team at GB2 who had dashed to the store on getting the call from Steve, joined them.

After an hour of interrogation, a call went out to the local police station and the cops were called in. By the time the saga ended, a handcuffed Lyndon was led out of the store by the cops, for attempting to use a credit card that was not his.

'People have become very careless with their credit cards these days,' Shankar looked at Unmukt and said. 'Lyndon has been using this guy's card and our man doesn't even know that his card has been stolen.'

'It's okay,' Unmukt replied. 'Let's call the customer and tell him his stolen card has been recovered. Hopefully then he'll realize that his card was stolen.'

'What kind of people have cards and don't even realize it's been stolen?'

'Rich, very rich ones, who have many cards and are also quite careless about their money and accessories,' Unmukt replied patiently.

'But, you know. We also run a screwed-up process. . .' Shankar mused. Unmukt looked at him. 'As in?'

'It could also be this guy reported the card lost or stolen and our team fucked up and missed hot-listing the card.'

'Possible. Very possible. I won't put it past our team to have committed such a screw-up.' They smiled at each other as one of them pressed the button on his car key to lock his car. They walked out of the parking towards their office building.

'Let's finish fast. The party would have begun,' Shankar said, as they settled down at their workstations next to each other.

Shankar hurriedly logged into the cards system using his ID and blocked the card—that was the process.

'Shankar,' Unmukt called out to him. 'The card is with the cops, the fraudster is in their custody. It is a Saturday, so no courts will be open and Lyndon will be safely in lock-up till Monday. Why can't we just leave for the party and come back and handle this Monday morning? There is no financial implication in any case.' The rest of the fraud control team was in Madh Island, celebrating a great year gone by.

'Not a bad idea. Let's quickly send a case report and leave.'

Both of them drafted a short note to their supervisor, giving him the details of the case, and quickly logged off from their laptops. They were getting late for the Madh Island jamboree.

16

Vienna
29th January 2012

Harshita's trip to Austria and Switzerland was one of the most exciting vacations that she had ever taken. Frustration at work was so high it was festering negativity in her—it threatened to destroy her pleasing personality, her work and, possibly even her marriage. It was her quest to maintain sanity that made her walk up to Anand and ask him for permission to take some time off. Thankfully her visa had come on time.

It was not difficult to decide on Vienna. Harshita was a student of history, keenly interested in music and architecture and in Vienna one would find remarkable architecture, loads of artistic treasures and museums. What skewed the decision in Vienna's favour was the city's tryst with music. No other city in the world could boast of such diversity in its music and of being the home to scores of great musicians.

Architecturally, Vienna was a delight. Majestic buildings dating back centuries dotted the impressive Ringstrasse—a five-kilometre horseshoe-shaped boulevard, which began and ended at the Danube canal. Together with the canal, Ringstrasse completely encircled the city. No visit to Vienna was complete without spending a day walking up and down the Ringstrasse.

A walk down the exquisitely delightful gardens of Schonbrunn palace was like a dream come true for Harshita. This was the first time she and Siddhartha were on vacation in over five years and she wanted it to last forever.

The sight-seeing bus of the Panorama Tours and Travels drove into the gates of Hofburg Palace and stopped. The tour guide started off in French, which neither Harshita nor Siddhartha could understand. Thankfully, she repeated everything in English. Though German was spoken all over Austria, their guided tour had a mix of English and French speaking tourists, which explained the tour guide's diction. The entire history of the centuries-old Hofburg Palace was communicated in all of four minutes. 'So much for compression of facts,' said Siddhartha, smiling at Harshita.

'We will be here for the next thirty minutes,' the guide said into the microphone. 'Please be back in time people, else you will have to walk out through these gates and take a cab back to your hotels.'

Harshita looked at the overbuilt and bulky Siddhartha. 'Only thirty minutes. What the hell?'

'It's okay. Let's get down and see. If we like it, we will let the coach go and explore on our own.' That made Harshita smile. 'Okay, let's go!' She picked up her bag, her camera and with a wide grin walked out of the coach. Siddhartha had to puff and pant to keep pace with her.

The moment they got off the coach, Harshita's phone rang. She looked at the screen, smiled, but didn't pick it up. International roaming was too expensive. If there was anything important, the caller would SMS or email her. She dropped the phone deep inside her handbag. The next thirty minutes were pure bliss. Siddhartha and Harshita visited every corner of the Hofburg Palace, clicked hundreds of pictures to show off to friends and family back home, and also a few interesting ones to be put up on Facebook. By the time they were done, their thirty minutes were almost up. They were a good five-minute walk from the bus. Harshita ran and Siddhartha followed suit. Luckily the bus was just pulling out of its parking place when Harshita saw it and flagged it down. Hurriedly she got in and waited for Siddhartha to come. As she settled into her seat, she could hear a muffled noise. It was her phone ringing. She dug into her bag and pulled it out. It was the same caller.

'Who is it?' By then, Siddhartha was lowering himself into the seat next to her.

She just turned the phone towards him so he could see who the caller was.

'Oh, okay. Why don't you take the call?'

'Mad or what? You know na, how expensive international roaming is? From Day One I have been staying away from all unimportant calls. The only calls I will pick up are mom's and dad's, both yours and mine.' She was about to put the phone back, when she stopped.

'Oh my God!' she exclaimed. The shiver in her voice startled Siddhartha, who cut short his last few moments of admiring the Hofburg Palace through the bus window and turned to look at his wife. 'What happened?'

Harshita had a shocked look on her face and the screen of her phone was turned towards him. On the screen was a notification: '14 missed calls'. And next to it was one number. 'Something seems to be wrong. I think you should call him back,' advised Siddhartha on seeing the screen.

'Wait. I don't want to call him now. Let me check my mail when we get Wi-Fi next and then, if need be, I will call him. He would surely have sent me an email if it was so important. Else I will Skype him from the hotel in the evening. Wi-Fi in the room is free.'

'You and your obsession with free stuff,' smiled Siddhartha, looking out, back to admiring the streets of Vienna.

'The coach will now stop at the *Parlament*,' announced the obese guide who had a sexy voice. 'The Austrian Parliament building is where the two houses of the Austrian parliament sit. Dating back to the late nineteenth century, this imposing structure has a span of over 13,500 sq metres. Built in Greek style, this is one of the largest buildings on the Ringstrasse. Please do not forget to take pictures at the Athena fountain, at the entrance of the *Parlament*. The fountain, ladies and gentlemen, was not part of the initial design but a late addition. You have twenty minutes here. The coach will pick you up from the parking lot outside the Café Coffee Day outlet fifty metres down the Ringstrasse to your right.' She bent down and pointed in the front, straight out of the windscreen of the bus. 'Can you see the purple signboard in front of us? That's the Café Coffee Day outlet.'

Despite her belligerence, Harshita couldn't ignore the fourteen missed calls; they distracted her. She worried about what could have caused all those calls. She was lost in thought; the only time she really paid any attention to what the tour guide was saying was when she heard Café Coffee Day. 'CCD? In Vienna?' Harshita looked surprised. Back in Mumbai, Siddhartha and she would go on late night coffee dates. CCD was one of their favourite places. Even in the days Siddhartha was dating her, the Carter Road CCD outlet was their regular haunt.

She strained her neck to look out of the window in the direction the guide pointed and a little ahead saw the CCD logo.

'Coffee? After this? Let's finish this fast.' So excited was she about having coffee at CCD that she didn't leave Siddhartha with much of a choice. The weather was close to two degrees centigrade and the chill had made the prospect of a coffee, that too at CCD, very appealing to him.

By the time they were done with exploring the *Parlament*, there were four more missed calls from the same number. This Harshita got to know when she took out her phone as the two of them were settling down on a plush sofa in a cosy corner of CCD.

'Two Macchiatos please,' Siddhartha said loudly, forgetting for a minute that he was in Vienna and not in India. People there take offence to anyone screaming out their order. Thankfully for them, the person at the counter was an Indian.

'Yippee!' a yell from Harshita made Siddhartha turn towards her.

'Don't look at me like that. I yelled because Wi-Fi is free for thirty minutes for everyone who comes here. And it says that if your bill amount comes to more than fifteen euros, on a weekend, it's free for twelve hours. Today is Sunday Sid. . .free Wi-Fi for twelve hours. . .wooooo. . .I am so thrilled.'

'You and your fetish for free stuff!! I have no intention to sit here till the shop shuts down,' said Siddhartha and went back to the menu card. Not only was he feeling hungry, he also had to run up a bill of fifteen euros, to make sure that his wife got unhindered access to free Wi-Fi.

Harshita started fiddling with her iPhone trying to connect to Wi-Fi so that she could download and check her mail. After struggling with it for a few minutes, she was able to connect—a success that she announced not only to Siddhartha but also to others in the coffee shop with an excited shout.

'Wow, it's fast. Twenty-six mails,' she announced to Siddhartha, who didn't seem very interested. She had left her personal mail ID with some of her colleagues, just in case they wanted to get in touch with her for something urgent. 'It's fast ya. All my mails got downloaded in forty-five seconds flat. That's real fast. Considering that it's free Wi-Fi, CCD rocks.' And she started reading through the mails one by one.

'Call back. It's very urgent. Tried calling you so many times today.' She read out one of the mails. 'I think you should call him back. Something seems to be really wrong,' Siddhartha advised.

'Will call,' she replied and at the same time typed back a response to that particular mail: 'Get on Skype. Calling in ten minutes.' She was confident that the mail would be seen on the BlackBerry. It was 5.00 p.m. in Vienna, and hence in India it would be well past dinnertime. Skype was a definite possibility.

'We only have one more place to visit in this guided tour. Can we ditch it? We will see it tomorrow. What say?'

'No problem. I'm tired too. Can do with some rest. And now that we have found this Indian coffee shop. . .you go ahead and finish whatever you have to do, while I enjoy my coffee.' He raised his hand to catch the steward's eye, and when the steward did look towards them, he just raised his index finger and pointed towards his cup. The steward understood that Siddhartha was asking for a repeat and went back towards the counter to get him more coffee.

Harshita didn't have to struggle too much to connect on Skype. The call was picked up within the first few rings, indicating that the receiver had seen her mail and was ready. Internet speed was good resulting in good video quality. 'Hiii. . .' began Harshita, and then suddenly changed track. 'Why are you looking like this? What happened?'

The call went on for twenty minutes. Harshita called the steward and asked for something to write on. After a minor confusion, the steward brought her a small piece of paper on which she took down some notes.

'Okay, great. I will get back to you. Let's connect on this at 4.00 p.m. tomorrow. Vienna time. By that time you will hopefully be back home. I will find out the details and let you know.'

'Thanks, Harshita. Hope I haven't screwed up your holiday, but this was important.'

'No problems, sweety. Take care.' She hung up only to see Siddhartha staring at her with raised eyebrows.

'Oh Sid. You know na, what a darling he is,' she cajoled. Siddhartha smiled; he knew the two were really great friends. He had no reason to doubt either of them. The raised eyebrows were because of something else. There was something about the call that gave him a bad feeling. Even though he heard only one side of the conversation—Harshita had put on her headphones—he was very uncomfortable. Something was wrong. But he just let it be. They were on a vacation, and there was no point spoiling the mood by worrying about unnecessary things. In any case he could always ask her what the call was about, later. And ask he did, as they were strolling back from CCD to their hotel, a couple of miles away. 'Is everything alright? Why were you getting so worked up while talking to him? Is there a problem?'

'No. Not much. It's just that he wanted some help on some issue that's come up. He wanted me to check on something. I told him that I will confirm by tomorrow evening.'

'Confirm what?'

Seeing him edgy and inquisitive, Harshita narrated the entire story to him. 'That's all that he wanted to know. Happy sweetheart? Now the only problem is how to give him the information he needs by tomorrow evening.'

'We have time na? It's only six. We can do it tonight and revert to him by tomorrow. You can mail it to him tonight, in time for him to see when he gets to work tomorrow.'

'No. He doesn't want me to mail him. He said that he would prefer to do it on a call.'

'Great that gives us more time. But we have a packed day tomorrow. We have a half-day trip to Hitler's Eagles nest, for which we will have to leave at 7.30 a.m.' said Siddhartha, reminding her of their tour schedule.

'Oh yes. We'll be back only by two. So I'll have to complete it tonight itself.'

'Great. Let's quickly go and grab a drink. It looks like a long night to me. Let's just pray it doesn't snow.'

'Yesss,' said Harshita as she clutched his arm tightly and they walked back towards the hotel.

A little distance away, on Wiener Strasse, at the Wien Police Headquarters, the President of Police, Gerhard Purtsi was strolling up and down his cabin. Hands in his pockets, a smile on lips, and a relaxed look on his face; he belied the normal impression one would have of a tough cop. In attendance were all the department and zone heads of Vienna Police. It was a great occasion for them, and that's why all of them were smiling on a Sunday evening despite being at work.

'We have just crossed a very important milestone', began Gerhard, in his deep voice. 'In the whole of last year, eighteen murders were reported in Vienna, and I am glad to inform you that as of this morning, we have solved the 18th murder and that gives us a hundred per cent strike rate for the year. I can't remember a single year in the history of Vienna Police when we have had such a strike rate.'

The entire team went up in applause. 'It's not me alone, but each one of you who has made this happen. I have called for a media briefing tomorrow. The briefing will be followed by our celebrations at The Imperial Grand at Karntner Ring. Please be there. It's our moment of glory. Let's bask in it.'

The entire room cheered, also in anticipation. The Imperial Grand was one of Vienna's oldest and finest hotels. 'Thanks gentlemen.' Gerhard went on, 'Tomorrow is our day. Let's make it special.'

The last comment brought a smile on the faces of everyone present as they turned to leave. But before they could leave the room, the President thundered again, 'And before you forget gentlemen, if I were you, I would get a good night's sleep tonight, because after the media briefing tomorrow, you are bound to get pounded by calls from the media.' The entire top brass of the police force was in a great mood that evening.

The next morning, the first working day of the week, the ballroom at the Imperial Grand filled up very rapidly. Over a hundred reporters from the local and world media were jostling for space in the large ballroom with imposing chandeliers. Looking strikingly commanding in his uniform, Purtsi walked in. A well-defined swagger in his walk was reflective of a job well done. Some television channels cornered him for sound bytes, and he readily obliged without giving out the reason for the briefing.

Purtsi was about to take his position at the head of the table, when his deputy Johann Schroeder walked up to him. Schroeder, the perennial prince in-waiting—the longest serving deputy in the history of the Vienna Police—was a lot more popular than the snobbish Purtsi, more so for his trademark handle bar moustache.

Schroeder whispered something into Purtsi's ear. He then walked up to the podium and started speaking, 'Friends, something urgent has come up which needs the President's attention. I would request you to be patient. He will be back with you in fifteen minutes,' and both Schroeder and Purtsi walked out of the room.

'This better be good,' threatened Purtsi the moment they were out of earshot of the prying media.

'I wish it was, Gerhard,' said Schroeder with a stern look on his face. 'Unfortunately, it isn't.'

'What's the problem?'

Schroeder narrated the entire sequence of incidents to Gerhard whose facial expressions first depicted curiosity, then shock and finally anger. 'What the hell?'

'Does the media know? Can we hold this back for some time?'

'That wouldn't be advisable sir. We will have to take it head-on.'

'I think you are right. Let's go. We will face it.'

'And Gerhard, here is the press statement that we have hurriedly put together, just in case the media asks too many questions.'

'Thanks,' was all that Gerhard could say as he accepted the paper and walked back to the media briefing.

There was sudden commotion in the briefing hall as Gerhard, followed by Schroeder, strode in. Everyone rushed to take their seats and cameramen moved towards their cameras to record the proceedings. Finally when everything settled down, Gerhard began to speak.

'Friends I am extremely glad to inform you that as of today we have resolved all the homicide cases which took place in our capital city over the last year. This brings the investigation success rate to hundred per cent. I do not remember a single year when all murders were resolved in the same year. It is almost as if we are in Colombo,' he smiled, 'I'm sure you would have watched that popular US criminal series. . .the one starring Peter Falk,' and he smiled again. Gerhard went on for the next ten minutes, outlining everything that his unit had done to make Vienna a crime-free city. He even compared the crime rates in Vienna with the neighbouring Czech Republic, labouring to explain how the crime graph in Vienna was far superior to the neighbouring countries. Not only was the crime graph better, even the rate of resolution was far superior. The police in Vienna was far more effective in controlling crime than anywhere else in the region.

The media was in awe, but something was holding them back from going gaga over the Vienna police and Gerhard could sense that. After the speech, the floor was thrown open to the media for questions.

'Mr Purtsi. Congratulations on a stellar year in office. You have continued the good work done by your predecessors and maintained a very low crime rate. Kudos to your team for that. I just have one question. I believe there has been a serious incident last night involving foreigners and tourists. Can you please tell us more about it?'

Gerhard turned left and looked at Schroeder, a visible act of nervousness. It was only for a fraction of a second, but the media caught on to it. They sensed that something was wrong.

'Yes, I would like to confirm that there has been an incident last night involving two tourists. Even though all indications are it is a hit and run case, we haven't ruled out homicide.'

There was an immediate chatter that ran through the room. Some of the reporters who hadn't heard about what was being discussed wanted to know more. In no time, it had become loud enough for Schroeder to step in and ask the media to focus on the main agenda of the press briefing and put forth their questions to Gerhard.

'Can you tell us more about this incident?' someone screamed even before Schroeder could complete his statement.

'Okay. We will give you all the details we have at this point in time.' Schroeder took over the media briefing from the President as he had more information on the incident.

'Last night, it is suspected, sometime between 02:45 hours and 03.15 hours, at a blind spot just off Ringstrasse two people were run over by a garbage disposal van. According to the driver of the van, who has been taken into custody, the two were lying in the middle of the road, possibly drunk, when the van turned into the alley. He was at a reasonable speed and it was almost impossible for him to stop in time and he ran over them. The road conditions were wet and slippery on account of overnight sleet. We are verifying the facts of the case and have some vital clues, which will help us resolve it soon. An autopsy is being performed. We will brief the media once we know the results.'

'Where were the two tourists from?'

'The tourists were from India. Nothing was recovered from their person and hence there was some delay in identifying them. We had to run a match against the immigration database, post which we were able to establish their identities. They have been identified as an Indian couple, visiting Vienna on a tourist visa—Mrs and Mr Lele. Harshita Lele and Siddhartha Lele. The Indian embassy has been informed and they are working with their counterparts in India to get in touch with the family of the deceased and inform them about this tragic occurrence. As always, the Vienna police is committed to solving this in the quickest possible time. We will keep the media informed as and when we have more information.'

'Was the truck over speeding?'

'Like all other utility vans in Vienna, this one too was fitted with a speed governor, which was found to be working fine, and hence the question of over speeding does not arise.'

'What were the tourists doing at 2.30 a.m.? Everything including the bars and pubs are shut by then?'

'Unfortunately I don't have an answer for that. We are piecing together the story from the information we have. Once we have the complete picture, we will let you know.'

This one issue hijacked the rest of the media briefing. Death of tourists in a friendly city like Vienna was a serious issue for the media and the police was unable to allay all their concerns. It was probably just the awkward timing of the incident. The

President of Police, Gerhard Purtsi, was caught in no-man's land. The media wanted answers and it was a bit too close to the time of occurrence of the event. 'Give me some time, I will be able to give you further details soon,' was what he ended the media conference with. He was a bit pained though, that no one really bothered to see that the overall crime rate in Vienna had dropped.

17

That afternoon, Tanuja was in office going through a PowerPoint presentation to be urgently sent across to the GB2 regional headquarters in Singapore when she got a call. It was from a representative of the Ministry of External Affairs (MEA), informing her about the unfortunate death of Harshita and Siddhartha in Vienna. They called her because they didn't know the contact details of either of their families.

'We will send someone to personally convey this. In fact, I will go myself,' Tanuja volunteered.

'That will be good, madam. You have my telephone number. Please call me and let me know once you have spoken to them.'

'Sure.'

The moment the MEA person disconnected, Tanuja called out to her secretary. 'Melinda, get me Vikram!' He too was shocked when he heard what Tanuja told him.

'I think we must go personally. Let's not leave it to the branch to handle,' Vikram agreed. 'Have you told her sister?' he asked.

'Sister?'

'Yes, she works with us. In Raymond's team.'

'Oh. Didn't know that.' Tanuja was surprised. 'Let me try to get in touch with her.'

Within five minutes, Tanuja called back, 'She's just got onto a flight from Calcutta. Won't be here for the next three hours. Even Raymond is not traceable. We might have to go. You coming?' and after a couple of seconds added, 'we don't even know where her parents stay.'

'That's okay, I'll come. Have already told Nikhil to find out. Apparently they stay somewhere in Juhu. Nikhil said he will come with us. Let's pick him up on the way.'

'Sounds good. If more people go, it'll be easier to manage.'

'Done. Ten minutes, at the main entrance. Not in the basement. See you there.'

'Great.' Tanuja's hand was shaking as she kept the phone down. Picking up her bag, she gave instructions to her secretary and walked out of her cabin. The secretary immediately picked up the phone to call her driver to ask him to bring the car up to the main entrance of the building.

The head of security smiled at Tanuja as she reached the entrance. Being closer to her office, Tanuja had reached there ahead of Vikram. The security guards were busy checking the bags of customers waiting to enter the branch. Tanuja had blanked out. She was pointlessly looking at the metal detector, when a tap on her shoulder broke her reverie.

'Hey Tanuja.'

'Hey. What brings you here?'

'Nothing. Just came in to meet Raymond.'

'Raymond?' Tanuja was surprised.

'Yes Tanuja. Had some work.'

What work could he have with Raymond? Tanuja wondered. However, she recovered quickly. 'How are you doing? Long time.'

'Been good. The media keeps you busy, much busier than banks, I guess.'

'Haha. . . By the way, did your favourite, McCain, call you up before he left from India?'

'No. He was not particularly fond of me. And you know that.'

'Yeah. . .but towards the end of his tenure, he became a big fan of yours,' Tanuja smiled.

'Never told me that. Chal. I'm getting late for the meeting, I'll run. Keep in touch.'

'See you. And if you see Raymond, tell him to call me. Have been trying to get in touch with him.'

'Cool. Take care.' Hardly had he disappeared into the waiting elevator that Vikram arrived on the scene. 'Has the car come?'

'Not yet, Vikram. Sad na, this Harshita thing?'

'Hmm.'

'Aah. . .there.' Tanuja pointed to her black Honda Accord as the driver brought it round to pick them up.

In the car, Tanuja looked at Vikram. 'I should tell Indrani na?'

'I think you should.'

'Okay, great.' And she dialled the CEO's number. In no time she was rattling off all the details to Indrani, who rightfully expressed her deepest anguish but politely declined the offer to meet the parents that day. She was to attend a conclave addressed by the finance minister.

'Bitch she is.'

'Why, what happened?'

'Madam has to go to a party where the finance minister is speaking and hence she can't meet Harshita's parents. She says if she visits Juhu today, she will be late for the conclave and the after-party.'

'Arre, she is the CEO. She can't be coming to meet parents of all employees who die?'

'If I die, Vikram, I expect her to visit my parents and offer condolences.'

'Mad woman, she will come for your funeral. Harshita is too junior for her to even be moved by it.'

'What's seniority got to do with it? Isn't Harshita human, too? Isn't she an employee of this bank?'

'Let it be, yaar. Why should we spoil our mood over it?'

'Hmm...yeh bhi sahi hai. Let it be. Forget it. Achcha, guess who I met today?'

Vikram shook his head. 'Who?'

'Karan Panjabi.'

'Really?' There was a tinge of surprise in his voice and almost as an afterthought, he said, 'Where?'

'I met him in the bank lobby. You just missed him. He left a couple of seconds before you came in.'

'Why was he in the bank?'

'I asked him. He said he had come in to meet Raymond.'

'Strange. Why would he meet Raymond? What's cooking?'

'I don't know. I asked him, though. He didn't say.'

'Hmm...They were good friends even when Karan was with the bank. In fact, Karan was the only boss Raymond got along with.'

'Hmm.' And Tanuja started looking out of the window, staring blankly at the buildings go by.

'Achcha, listen. Now that Harshita is history...'

'That's rude, Vikram.'

'Haha. Anyway, now that we are faced with this unprecedented and tragic situation, we need to put our sorrow behind us and look at what we need to do at the Bandra Branch, to take care of her accounts.'

'Vikram, don't be so cold. Your senior RM has just died. Can we discuss the succession plan later? And in any case, I don't need to be party to that discussion; it's in your remit.'

'I know, baby. But the entire world knows that you run Retail Banking and not me.' He winked at her and lifted her left hand, which was intertwined with his right, and brought it up to his lips and kissed it.

'Vikram, not here. Are you mad,' she whispered. She was worried the driver would see. Drivers are known to gossip about everything said or discussed in the car. In fact, when Vikram called her 'baby' earlier, she wanted to stop him, but her mind was far too slow to react.

'Haha,' Vikram laughed.

Both were silent for a while as the car drove on to the sea link and entered the reclamation area of Bandra.

'Achcha, tell me. What do you think of Zinaida?' This time it was Tanuja.

'About what?'

'About her big and shapely mouth. About her ability to give you a great blow job. About her sexy figure. Her ability to be an awesome fuck,' she said tartly. 'Obviously I am asking you about her work. What else will I ask you about?'

'Haha. . .anything!' And he lifted his eyebrows, moving his head to indicate the driver was listening in and so she should watch her language.

Tanuja just looked the other way.

'Do you think she will be able to do Harshita's role? Will she be able to manage? Should we give it to her?'

'Ask Nikhil. Ask Anand. How would I know? All I know is that she is hot.' Vikram was a bit peeved at Tanuja's sarcasm.

Tanuja made a face.

'Kidding ya. She is good, but she has been in the system for less than a year.'

'Yes, I know. But she has done very well. Might as well give her the job and see how she performs. Unless we throw these youngsters into the water, how will we know they can swim or not? It will also serve as a shot in the arm for the entire batch of MTs.'

'Your call. You run the Retail Banking, don't you?'

'I think we should bite the bullet and give it to her. As HR I don't have any issues.'

'Yes sweetheart. I just have to make sure there are no other sensitivities involved. And we also have to be mindful about the audit issues that have been raised in Bandra on account of her indiscretion.'

'Yes Vikram. That's more of a training issue. If we take care of that, isn't she an excellent resource?'

'Undoubtedly.'

'I have, in any case, a replacement candidate in mind to take Zinaida's job when we move her up. I'll ask Yogesh Bhargav to formally send the CV.'

Vikram smiled. He just squeezed Tanuja's hand to show his concurrence. They were about to reach the Bandra branch. Nikhil, Anand and the branch Customer Service Manager were waiting for them on the road outside the branch. When they saw Vikram and Tanuja, Anand and Nikhil hopped into the car.

'Let's follow that car,' said Nikhil, pointing to a blue Hyundai i10 in front. 'Kalpesh knows their residence.' Kalpesh was the Branch Service Manager and had been to Harshita's parents' house a few times. No one had any clue where Siddhartha's parents lived, but that was not too much of a concern. In any case, Harshita's parents would know.

18

On Monday morning, Unmukt reached office before Shankar. By then, Hemant had already replied to the case report they mailed him on Saturday.

> *'Guys, is this the way a case report is filed? Half the details are missing! All I can make out is the card number and the fact that you guys went to Inorbit mall on receiving a call from the store. The person in possession of the card turned out to be holding someone else's card and was arrested. I can't see anything on who the customer is, what his background is, is this a good card / bad card. . .and, most importantly, your analysis. . .disappointed. Remember, Madh Island parties are secondary. If you have a job to do, that comes first. Please resend with complete details. Want it in the next couple of hours.'*

It was an extremely caustic mail. He was on to the fact that they hurried things up because they did not want to miss the team party at Madh Island. By that time Shankar too was in and Unmukt told him about the mail.

'Okay,' Shankar sighed, pulling out his laptop and keeping the bag by the side of his workstation. 'What a start to a Monday morning!'

This time around, the two rookie officers of the fraud control team logged into the cards system and got into the details.

'Arre, he is a staff of our bank!' exclaimed Shankar.

'Of course not. The card number does not pertain to a staff card series.'

'Yes, Unmukt. It's not. . .for some strange reason, it doesn't reflect as a staff card, but the cardholder's work address is that of Bandra Branch!' He read out the address. 'Pranesh Rao, Banking Assistant, GB2, Turner Road, Bandra West, Mumbai.' He turned towards Unmukt, 'Know him?'

'No.'

'Let's call the branch and tell them about it.'

'Cool. I'll get myself a coffee. Need it very badly. Why don't you call and let them know?' Unmukt disappeared towards the pantry.

By the time Unmukt returned, a lot had changed. Shankar looked shell-shocked. He saw Unmukt and tried to say something. Words failed him. His lips were moving, but no words came out. He started coughing uncontrollably.

'Shankar. Are you alright? What happened?' Unmukt picked up a glass of water lying on Shankar's table and gave it to him. 'Settle down. Settle down. Drink some water.'

Shankar drank some water, wiped the sweat off his forehead and looked at Unmukt. 'Remember the guy who died in a road accident on the Eastern Express Highway some time back?'

'Yes.'

'Pranesh is the same guy. This is the same guy who died. See!' He moved his monitor to face Unmukt. The intranet page carrying an orbituary for Pranesh was open. 'See. This is the guy.'

'What the fuck?' Unmukt exclaimed, looking at the screen and intermittently at Shankar. He forgot to bat his eyelids.

'How the hell is his card with Lyndon?'

'Don't know!' He typed some commands on the computer and brought up some details on the screen. 'Look at his transactions.'

Both of them stared at the screen for a while. 'Scroll down,' Unmukt said, telling Shankar to go to the next screen.

'F5,' said Shankar, simultaneously pressing the F5 button on the keyboard.

'Hmm. . .' Both went quiet. They were looking at the transactions in Pranesh's account.

'Pranesh was a heavy user of this card. Two days before he died, he had paid the entire outstanding for the month. Nothing strange about that, since he had paid up his bill on the due date. It's an auto-debit to his joint savings account with some woman—the name sounds like it's his mom. Even on the day of his death there were three transactions on this card. And then. . .' Shankar stopped and looked at Unmukt.

'There was a lull. No transactions for a long, long time. Which can only be in case the card got stolen after he died and. . .'

'Whoever stole the card lay low till temptation got the better of him and he started using it.'

'Yes, Shankar. And since Pranesh was dead, no one complained about the lost card. And our cards team, like idiots, assumed he only had a staff card and hot-listed that when HR informed the cards team about his death. No one blocked this card. And when Lyndon started using this card a few days back, the transactions got authorized.'

'Correct. But the question is, how did Lyndon get the card?'

Almost simultaneously both of them banged the table. 'Oh fuck. . .yes!'

'The only way Lyndon could have got the card was if he was on site when Pranesh met with the accident. And seeing him injured or dead, he quietly relieved him of some of his possessions and went his way.'

'Let's go.' Grabbing his car keys, mobile phone and wallet, he strode towards the lift.

While driving to the Malad west police station, Hemant called the Asst. Commissioner of Police (ACP) of that sub-division from his mobile. He briefed him about the entire incident. The ACP promised to reach the Malad West Police Station in thirty minutes. It was quite normal for the collections and fraud control unit of banks to have cops on their payroll. It helped them when they wanted to get something done or whenever they got into trouble. But this ACP was not one of those. Hemant had helped him crack a few cases and hence the ACP was obligated to Hemant.

By the time they entered the police station, the ACP was already there.

'We have run a background check,' the ACP announced after they settled into the chair opposite him. 'This guy is a bits and pieces guy. Runs all kinds of errands. Drives auto rickshaws at times. Has a family. Wife ran away a year ago. No children. Lives in the chawl near the fisherman's colony in Khar Dhanda, on the outskirts of Bandra. He doesn't have a criminal history, nor is he a regular charge-sheeter. And here, take this,' he handed a bunch of papers to Hemant, 'I've pulled out all the case details of your employee's accident. Seems a regular accident only.'

'Can't be, ACP,' retorted Hemant. 'No one can be so cold-blooded that he would steal a credit card off a dead man. He has to be a seasoned criminal, a heartless person to have done such a deed.'

'Or a dying man,' added Unmukt, only to get a glare from Hemant. The latter never liked to be interrupted. He had his own ego, which had to be massaged at all times. He was the boss and he liked to show it.

'I have a gut feeling that this guy killed Pranesh. For what. . .I don't know. Only he can tell us.'

'Or. . .' mused Shankar.

'Or? Or what? What could be the other option?'

'If Lyndon was the guy responsible for the accident.'

'Oh shit! Yes. Why didn't I think of it? Shanks, it could g
messy. I think we should bounce this up.' Shankar nodde
his concurrence.

The two of them immediately got up and walked straight to
the room of Hemant Aldangadi, the Head of the Fraud Control
Unit for GB2. Hemant was a very perceptive guy whose intuition
was his strength. He invariably went by gut feeling, which was
seldom wrong.

Shankar narrated the entire story to Hemant, from the time
they got a call from Spencer's to the cops coming in and taking
away Lyndon. The cursory check they did on the system on
Saturday and Monday morning and what all they found out.

'Lyndon is not a thief. He is a murderer!' exclaimed a horrified
Hemant.

'We can't be a hundred per cent sure, though it seems to be a
strong possibility,' Unmukt responded smartly.

'Possibility my foot!' the small five-foot-one frame of Hemant
seemed like a demon when he shouted at the top of his voice. 'If
he crashed into Pranesh and killed him and subsequently got
tempted and stole the card, he is a murderer. If he was not
involved in the accident, but found him critically wounded and
didn't do anything about saving him, but stole his card and ran
away, he is still a murderer in my eyes.' Shankar and Unmukt
nodded their heads in unison. They had so much to learn from
Hemant.

'It's not about a stolen card any more. It's about the murder of
a colleague. He can't get away with it. Which police station did
they take him to?' Hemant asked, looking at Shankar.

'Malad West.'

'Hmm. . .' the ACP smiled. It was so difficult to find cops who smile during an intense discussion. 'Your gut has often proven to be true.'

'Not often, ACP. Always.'

'Yes. That's what I meant. Always. Your gut has always proven to be true. So I will back it. Let me ask for a location report on his mobile phone. Maybe that should help.'

In India, anything is possible with a little bit of jugaad. The cops, and even Hemant, knew someone inside the cell phone company. Verbal information flow was fine, permissions were required only if something was to be given in writing. In this case, all they needed was a verbal confirmation of the location of Lyndon's cell phone on that fateful night, and that was possible with a little bit of jugaad.

'Let me talk to the fucker,' said the ACP as he got up and walked towards the lockup.

'Will you have a problem if I am with you when you are interrogating him?'

'No, Hemant. But you can't touch him. I will be in deep shit, if word gets out that a civilian beat up a suspect in the lock-up.'

'I am not that naïve, ACP. Let's go.'

Lyndon was not the normal hard-nosed criminal one would have imagined. Frail, unshaven and a man in fear, Lyndon was looking at them, hoping they would set him free.

'So you are saying you found this card on the road.'

'Yes, s-s-s-sir.' There was a stammer in Lyndon's voice.

'Where did you find this card?'

'Close to my house, sir. On Khar Dhanda road, somewhere near Cotton Cottage.'

'When was this?'

'Many months back, sir. I think sometime in May or June last year.' Hemant remembered Pranesh died in early June.

'What time of the day was it?'

'Late at night, sir. Around 11.00 p.m. I was standing by my bike, smoking, when I saw this card on the road.'

Hemant looked at the papers. 'At 10.50 p.m. on 7th June, the card holder filled petrol in his bike and paid using this card. That was the last transaction, for a long, long time, before you started reusing this card last week.'

A smile came on Lyndon's face. 'Yes yes. . .maybe he dropped it after that. That's how I found it,' He was relieved he had the time right.

'Asshole!' screamed Hemant. 'He filled petrol on the Eastern Express Highway and you claim to have found it on Khar Dhanda road, twenty kilometres away, at 11.00 p.m. Chutiya samjha hai kya? Out with the truth! Otherwise you won't get out of this place alive!' Hemant knew that there was the small statistical probability that someone stole the card off Pranesh and later lost it or wilfully threw it away, which was later found by Lyndon, in which case Lyndon could be telling the truth. The mobile records of Lyndon and his whereabouts on that fateful night would be the key to prove his involvement in the crime.

'I am speaking the truth, sir. Believe me.'

Thuddddd. . .a slap landed on his left cheek. Even before he could react, another one landed on his right. Blood started oozing out of his nostrils. 'Aww, I didn't know criminals were so delicate,' thundered the ACP. 'Can't even take two slaps. It couldn't have been after that, because on 7th June Pranesh died. Three hours after the last transaction on his card, he died.' Another slap landed on Lyndon's jaw. 'Imagine how Pranesh would have cried when he was killed.'

The interrogation went on for the next forty-five minutes. It only abated when a constable walked in with a sheet of paper and handed it over to the DGP. The DGP read it and looked at Hemant. 'I always knew that you were right,' was all he said before he handed the paper to him.

19

Finally, the day of the protest dawned. Krishna had worked tirelessly to make sure it was a massive rally. Over twenty-five thousand people were expected to turn out. So anxious was Krishna that he spent the entire night tossing in bed, waiting for the sun to rise on a day that would define the direction their movement would take. He was up and ready much earlier than other days. Once dressed and raring to go, the four walls of his bedroom were not enough to contain him. He walked out to the reception area, where he asked for a strong cup of coffee and waited for Jaya to arrive. The sun was just about breaking through when he had stepped out into the reception area. He had time to kill. They were expected at the venue only at 9.00 a.m.

Everything was under control. Jaya's team was at the venue coordinating logistics. Madan Mohan's men were organizing transport for the protestors. The leading opposition party had also thrown its hat into the ring by announcing support for Krishna Menon's cause. All indications were it would be a successful event. However, Krishna was restless, a bit worried. So lost in thought he was that he didn't notice a champagne-coloured Toyota Corolla speed into the porch and stop. The screech of the tires disturbed him and he looked up. A foreigner dressed in jeans, a crumpled white linen shirt and a cap on his head, stepped out of the car. His unshaven three-day-old stubble accentuated his already unkempt look.

Where have I seen him? thought Krishna. The foreigner looked extremely familiar. It was not common for any guest to just drive in. They were normally picked up from the airport or the railway station, particularly foreigners. He stood there, keenly watching the foreigner who walked up to the reception and waited patiently to be attended to. When the receptionist looked up, he said, 'I want to meet Krishna Menon.'

Krishna heard every word of it because he was seated on a couch right next to the reception. Stepping up closer to the foreigner, he enquired, 'Can I help you? I am Krishna Menon.'

'Hey Krishna, how are you man?'

Krishna did reciprocate, but with a blank look. 'I'm sorry,' he stammered. 'I am not able to place you. Have you been here before?' When the foreigner showed so much familiarity, Krishna assumed he was a guest at the resort in the past.

'Oh, no, no, Krishna. You don't recognize me?' Krishna was both apologetic as well as a bit confused. Was he supposed to have recognized the gentleman?

'Hey! When did you arrive?' Both of them turned. It was Jaya. The foreigner smiled.

'When did you arrive, Dr Heldrich?' Jaya asked again.

'Oh, just now.'

Krishna was stunned. Heldrich? The man in front of him was Dr Heldrich Kohl? The only time he had seen him was on a video conference and now the renowned American nuclear scientist of German origin was standing in front of him. 'Hope you had a safe flight?' Jaya continued.

'Oh yes. It was lovely. I spent the weekend in Kovalam. Lovely beach. And here I am.'

'How come you are here today?' Krishna was still confused. He was feeling like an idiot for not recognizing him.

Even before Heldrich could respond, Jaya volunteered, 'Heldrich was planning a holiday. So I recommended he come to India and watch how protests are held in India. Hahaha.'

Krishna still looked confused. He didn't know what to say. 'That's really nice of you. Would you want to freshen up?'

'It's fine, Krishna. We can leave now, if you folks are ready to leave, too.' He then glanced at his watch and added, 'We will be very early, though.'

'Let's eat some breakfast and then leave,' Krishna recommended. That was met with immediate endorsement from everyone.

After breakfast, the three of them made their way to the protest site outside TNPP. A huge crowd was gathered there. Being a quasi-political rally, there was enough paramilitary presence to maintain law and order. The government seemed to have pulled out all stops to make sure that everything would go off peacefully. In some pockets the cops seemed to be outnumbering the protesters.

Closer to the dais, a space was earmarked for dignitaries to alight. Heldrich, however, got off earlier. Since he was not a part of the organizers or the official invitees, he couldn't have taken up the dais. A CNRI employee was assigned to shadow Heldrich and ensure his safety. They didn't want him to get lost in the sea of humanity that had erupted.

The rally began. Madan Mohan, who was there with his supporters with the sole intention of extracting political mileage, started the proceedings. Jaya spoke after him and made a very passionate appeal to people on why he was against the TNPP. His speech was met with roars of acceptance.

Krishna spoke next. His was the more balanced of the lot. He spoke about the ill-effects of nuclear radiation, about the problems a natural disaster-led calamity would cause in the region. And then he stopped. He stopped because he could sense some commotion at the far end of the ground, in the direction of the road they had come from. A number of cops had congregated there. They had picked up someone and were leading him to a police van. Krishna looked at Jaya and then towards the epicentre of the commotion. It soon became clear to Krishna what was going on. He brought his hand up, covered the microphone with his right palm, looked at Jaya and said, with loads of concern in his voice, 'They are taking Heldrich away. But why?'

Jaya had a blank look on his face. But when the gravity of what Krishna said dawned on him, he stiffened up, stress lines appeared on his forehead and he jumped. He quickly got up from his seat and rushed in that direction. A couple of other folks from CNRI followed him. By the time they reached there, Heldrich was already carted away by the cops in a van. Heldrich had not committed any offence; he was the only foreigner on site.

The CNRI personnel shadowing Heldrich came and whispered something into Jaya's ears. This infuriated Jaya. He stood there on the spot and hurled abuses at the men in uniform, who were haplessly standing there and watching. In a mob when one man is the aggressor, the rest can't be spectators; else it wouldn't be called a mob. Everyone else follows the aggressor. Here too, that's what happened. The rest of the crowd followed Jaya. Soon the bickering became unbearable and someone hurled a stone at the police. That was the catalyst. All hell broke loose. Chappals, stones, chairs, anything and everything the mob could lay its hand on became a missile.

Krishna was aghast. This was not what he had in mind when he started this protest. But a vast majority outnumbered him. The crowd now turned violent and was heading menacingly towards the main gate of the nuclear plant. Apart from forty

Indian scientists, an equal number of Russian scientists engaged in commissioning the reactor were holed up inside the plant. Since morning, the protestors had blocked the main gate and prevented vehicles from going in or coming out, but now they were heading towards it, their demeanour suggesting they would forcibly tear down the main gate. Krishna kept appealing for calm over the microphone, but no one heard him.

The army and the riot police, who were assisting the local police, took guard outside the main gates, the former two known for being dispassionate in their execution of duties. They were there, for a job had to be done. The nuclear installation could not be compromised. It had to be protected at any cost. They took up their positions. The protestors didn't stop. With makeshift missiles in hand they marched ahead. They were possessed, possibly irrationally. Jaya was leading the march. What had initially begun as a supporting role for him, had now turned into a full-fledged lead role. The riot police kept their calm. They were trained in dealing with such a situation. They swiped out their megaphones and made the mandatory announcements. The crowd was warned not to try anything ambitious else they would have to pay for it. Often these warnings worked. But not today. The water jets and tear gas were brought into action. Even that didn't work. It was beginning to get messier. When the mob got closer, the riot police fired in the air. This was meant to be a final warning to prevent them from getting any closer. But when even that went unheeded, the cops didn't have a choice. They fired at the mob. Rubber bullets were used and they fired at knee level to make sure that they didn't kill anyone.

This, finally, had to have the necessary impact. Five rounds were fired in different directions. When it comes to life or death, it's surprising how fear gets the better of almost everyone. The protestors panicked. Almost instantaneously, they turned and ran, some faster than the others. The aged stumbled and fell. The women and the few children there got no mercy. People pushed them in their quest to get away. The fear of the next bullet was overwhelming. And then it was all over. The fury with which it all started and the pace with which it all ended were the same.

And when the dust settled down, the impact became clearer. Forty-six injured, twelve of them severely, and three dead—all on account of the stampede. Trikakulam Nuclear Power Plant lived to see another day.

All this devastated Krishna. 'Was this necessary?' he yelled at Jaya when he got within hearing distance. Krishna's idea of a protest was more in the Gandhian mould. Violence, bloodshed, pain was never what he had envisaged.

'Let's get out of here first. Else, we'll also be bundled up with the rest,' implored Jaya.

'What about Heldrich?'

'We will figure out what to do later. Let's go!' Jaya was getting paranoid.

Krishna thought for a minute and said, 'Why will we get bundled up? We haven't done anything wrong. I have to go to the police station. To free Heldrich. Else he will be stuck. He doesn't have anyone to help him.' Jaya knew if they went to the police station, they could be arrested. Weren't they the architects of the entire protest? And Jaya was particularly worried because he was the prime cause of the protest turning violent. It could all boomerang on him.

However, if Krishna were to go to the police station all alone, the situation would get worse for Jaya. He just followed Krishna as he headed to his car. For one last time, Krishna surveyed the destruction around him. Chappals, torn shreds of cloth, personal belongings and bags were strewn all over the ground. His heart bled. Struggling to hold back his tears, he got into his car.

20

The story of Harshita's death spread like wild fire. Within an hour of Tanuja being informed, the news was up on the intranet and in no time the entire organization knew about it. Harshita was very popular in GB2. Very lovable and committed, she was someone who knew her strengths and her limitations and that's what made her special. Her death came as a shock to everyone. The Bandra branch went into a complete state of mourning.

Harshita's parents were stunned into silence when Tanuja and Vikram told them about it. They didn't know how to react. Tears deserted them. Tanuja, Vikram and the entire GB2 team was trying to console them when Vikram's phone rang. It was from Indrani's office.

Vikram stepped outside to take the call. 'Good afternoon, Indrani.'

'Vikram, Jacqueline here.' Jacqueline was Indrani's secretary. 'You busy?'

'We're at Harshita's house. Meeting her parents. Anything urgent?'

'No nothing very urgent. Raymond has been calling. He wants to meet Indrani to talk to her about something in your business.

Indrani asked me to check with you and Juliana if there is anything urgent. I checked with her. She doesn't know of anything that might need Indrani's time. So checking with you.'

'Nothing that I'm aware of.'

'Okay, then I'll tell Indrani accordingly.'

'You know what Jacqueline? Tell Raymond to speak to one of us and not to approach Indrani directly. Don't encourage him. He doesn't need to go to Indrani for anything. He is a bit of a weird guy. Put him off for a few days. In any case, once I'm back from Harshita's house later today, I'll speak to Juliana and fix it.'

'Sounds good. Heard about Harshita. What a thing to happen on her vacation! Feel sad for her. She was a great person.'

'Fate,' said Vikram and hung up. The cries from inside the house had become louder and were disturbing him.

In the interim, Tanuja called the MEA official back and informed him that Harshita's and Siddhartha's parents had been told about the calamity. When the MEA official told her that they, in consort with the Austrian authorities were making arrangements to bring back the mortal remains of the couple, Tanuja patched in the administration in charge at GB2 with the MEA official to make sure that GB2 also extended all possible help in this regard.

After an hour, leaving behind Anand to oversee arrangements, the other three left for work. By that time a number of family friends and colleagues of the couple had also arrived, and there were enough people to take care of the aged parents.

On the way back, Tanuja once again brought up the issue of succession. 'Let's close on Zinaida to take over Harshita's job. It will send a strong message to the fresh batch of management trainees.'

'Let's wait till Anand comes back.' Nikhil stepped into the conversation. 'There may be some sensitivity with regard to other people in the team. As far as I know, there are more senior people who have been in line for a promotion. If we give the job to Zinaida, we might have issues to deal with. And there is no hurry boss. Let the dust settle on Harshita's death. People in the branch are in any case traumatized by this.'

'Nikhil, a true leader is one who acts in the interest of the business and at a time when it is good for business and not necessarily at the time when it's the easiest from a decision making perspective. Learn from your boss.' When Tanuja said this, Vikram's chest swelled a few inches with pride. 'Zinaida has delivered despite being a junior resource. We must back her.'

'But Vikram. . .' Nikhil wanted to continue but was cut short by an indignant Vikram. 'Nikhil, I think Tanuja is right. If your Bandra team is doing well today, you know it is because of the energy she brings into her role. For the last three months she has been your best performing RM. If you don't reward her who will you reward?'

'I agree Vikram, but there are others who have been around for longer.'

'Nikhil, by having these conversations with me, don't make me wonder if I did the right thing by bringing you here.' That was the end of the discussion.

The same evening, Tanuja issued the letter promoting Zinaida to the post of a Senior Relationship Manager. What would normally have happened after 12–18 months in a role, for Zinaida, it happened within eight months. Apart from performance, the justification given to Anand was that she had prior experience before joining GB2. Yogesh Bhargav sent in a new CV for the RM to be hired to replace Zinaida in her old role. Everything was sealed and life moved on for GB2 in general and the Bandra branch in particular. Not even forty-eight hours had passed since the event in Vienna.

Raymond called Jacqueline again that evening. 'Jacqueline I desperately need to see Indrani. It's important.'

'Sweetheart, Indrani is in a photo shoot. It's a *Business Today* cover photo shoot. I can't disturb her.'

'Will she be free after that?'

'Not sure. At 6.00 p.m. she has a CSR activity planned with some differently-abled kids and after that she will be at Taj Lands End where she is attending an event where the Finance Minister himself is speaking.'

'Can you block some time for me tomorrow morning?'

'Raymond, why don't you speak to Juliana or Vikram and let them handle it with Indrani.'

'Oh. So that is the issue. You will not let me speak to Indrani till I have Juliana's or Vikram's blessings.'

'No. It's not that. It's just that Indrani is too tied up and hence it might be easier for you to go to the two of them.'

'Thanks Jacqueline. I got the message,' and Raymond hung up. Jacqueline was not going to allow him to meet Indrani without the concurrence of Juliana or Vikram. Juliana didn't care about what he had to tell Indrani and if he told Vikram, he would manipulate the situation in his favour. He didn't trust either of them.

Barely did he get off Jacqueline's call when his mobile started ringing. The frown on his face was a trademark reserved for his wife. If only he could erase the last few years of his life. His wife was at it again. This time she wanted him to call up his mom in Ernakulum and ask her to put on hold her travel plans to Mumbai. She had been harassing him about this for the last one week, without realizing how difficult it was for a son to ask his parents not to come to their son's home. But his wife was adamant leaving him with no choice. He felt he was hitting a new low in his life. A career going nowhere, a boss who didn't listen to him, a business leader who manipulated things to such an extent that he was rendered toothless, five role changes in four years, a wife who was seeing someone else, and no friends to show for. Even the one who he considered a friend and was reasonably close to had gone away from him—dead in an alleged accident in Vienna. Was this life worth living? He would ask this question in various forms every single day of his life, and the answer was, give it one more day. It will change.

That particular morning had started in a great fashion for him, lulling him into a false sense of comfort. Little did he know that it would end like this. On his way to work that Monday morning, he was fiddling with his phone, when he saw that there was a small red circle on top of the Skype logo, indicating that he had a missed call. He touched the Skype logo and it opened up on his screen. There was a message from someone dear to him. He opened the message to listen to it.

'Hi Raymond. How are you? Wanted to just let you know that we are now back in the hotel. I completely forgot that tomorrow we are going to Eagles Nest—Hitler's hideout. It's on the Austria-Germany border. I'll only be back late in the afternoon. Sid recommended that we finish your work today itself. I'll go and check out the place in a while. In any case, I'll call and update you around 6.00 a.m. Vienna time or else late in the evening. Talk to you then. Ciao. . .and by the way, Sid also says hi to you.' It had brought a smile on his face.

He had been looking forward to Harshita's call in the evening all day, but then he heard the news of her death in an accident, which had shattered him completely. He had called Malvika, who had requested that he should not come to offer his condolences in person. She sounded too distraught and broken. After all she had lost her only sister, and her best friend.

21

The Devikulam police station had turned into a virtual fortress. The constables manning the gates recognized the two of them as the ones leading the charge and making the speeches. They walked straight into the station in-charge's cabin, virtually unstopped. Heldrich was sitting there. Next to him were two uniformed policemen. There was also a third guy who looked a bit different. Tall, middle-aged, sculpted cheek bones, and a properly trimmed moustache, he was wearing a tailored suit. His accent was impeccable and he was trying to speak with Heldrich. The latter was struggling to answer him back seemingly because he was a German. Krishna was surprised because back at the resort and earlier on the Skype call, Heldrich had spoken reasonably good English. It seemed as if he didn't want to answer too many questions and so was putting up a façade.

'Why have you held him here? He hasn't done anything wrong,' Krishna announced to everyone in the room.

'What was he doing in Devikulam?' one of the uniformed guys asked him.

'He was in India holidaying and simply came along with us to the rally.' When Krishna said this, the suited guy looked at him.

His Oakley glasses glinted, a poor attempt at giving himself a menacing look; he appeared to be irritated and angry. 'This gentleman here was in town holidaying?'

'Yes sir,' Krishna replied innocently.

'And how long has he been in town?'

'Only for a week. After spending a week in Kovalam, he came to visit us.'

'Do I look like a fool Mr Menon?'

'Sorry?'

'How do you know this gentleman here and why did he come here? I want to know the truth.' Suddenly his tone became aggressive.

'He has a legal visa to visit this country and I am sure with a visa, unless one is a Pakistani, one can visit any part of the country that he pleases.'

'Let's not get into technicalities Mr Menon. It would be better if you answer my question.'

'We had spoken to him a few weeks back on prospective issues which could arise in case nuclear reactors are built on hilly areas in terrain with seismic imbalance. We sought expert advice from him. That's how we know him. And now that he was on a holiday here, he visited us today and we invited him to come along.'

'And where was he when you spoke to him?'

'Germany. We held a video conference with him?'

'Is that right?' the guy in the suit asked sarcastically. 'And who is this "we"?' The cynical stress on the word 'we' was unmistakable.

'Jayakumar and myself,' he said pointing towards Jaya who was standing just behind him.

'Hmm. . .maybe then you could explain this,' and he threw Heldrich's passport towards Krishna.

'What about this?' Krishna picked it up and looked at the officer. It was clear by now that the gentleman was a senior officer who was there to oversee things. Krishna, by virtue of being in that area for long, knew most of the senior cops around, but he had never seen this person before.

'Heldrich Kohl,' said the officer, 'Eminent American nuclear scientist of German origin. He holds a dual citizenship and has helped commission a number of nuclear plants in his home country and in the US, France and UK. He's one of the most knowledgeable scientists on nuclear reactors in the world today. He travels to India on his German passport, lands up at the site of India's latest nuclear plant, participates in a protest, as you insist, from the fringes.' And he stopped. He looked at Jaya and Krishna and continued, 'and you say he is here on a holiday in Kovalam. You expect me to believe it Mr Menon?'

'Yes of course. Why don't you ask him?' and Krishna looked at Dr Heldrich. 'Why don't you tell him Dr Heldrich? Why don't you tell him?'

'He has nothing to say. And if you carefully look at that,' and he pointed towards the passport in Krishna's hand. 'If you look at that you will know. Dr Heldrich has been in India for the last three months. If you spoke with him three weeks back, he was very much in India then. Right here, in the vicinity of Trikakulam Nuclear Power Plant. Like you and this gentleman next to you, he was covertly lobbying with parties interested in making sure that India does not commission a world-class advanced nuclear facility, feeding negative information so that there is public outrage and the reactor doesn't go live.'

'What?' Krishna was dumbstruck. He looked at Jaya. Jaya was looking in the other direction, avoiding eye contact with Krishna. So this was a ploy! A ploy Jaya used to get him on board with their plans. Heldrich was working with Jaya and they chose to piggy-back on his reputation to further their cause.

'Dr Heldrich, the CBI has been trying to get information about you and your activities for some time now. Unfortunately, we couldn't lay our hands on you earlier. . .' The officer's phone rang, interrupting him. He walked to the other room and took the call.

When he came back inside three minutes later, there was a dirty smirk on his face. He looked at Dr Heldrich and said, 'You are coming with me. To Chennai from where you will be put on a plane to Frankfurt tonight. Immigration authorities in Chennai will have your deportation papers ready. If you resist, you will be booked for carrying out prohibited anti-national activities in the region. Where do you want to pick up your bags from?'

Dr Heldrich Kohl got up and looked at Jaya. There was not a hint of remorse on his face. Turning to his right, he faced the officer and thundered, 'Let's go,' and he walked out of the cabin.

'You cheated me,' Krishna said once they had stepped out of the cabin and were not within the earshot of anyone.

'No I did not Krishna. Heldrich was just helping us. And I had no clue that he was in India or what his agenda was, for that matter.'

'It doesn't look that way. An individual trying to help us with his own knowledge to fight a righteous and just battle is one thing. A country using the two of us, more so me, to fight a battle against my own nation is a very, very different thing altogether. You knew that Dr Heldrich was here to shut down the facility. Jaya, I do not want the nuclear plant to shut down. I just want the Centre to satisfy all the impacted people that this is a safe reactor. People need to be relocated to safer destinations; their lives need to be taken care of. That's all I want. Forget our means Jaya, our objectives are not aligned. There is no convergence in what we want. In what was an internal matter of a nation, you let a third party with vested interests in. The difference Jaya, is that you worked with people who did not want India to build this nuclear reactor. I worked with my conscience. There is a wide chasm between the two.' And he walked out. Jaya followed him, without uttering a word.

On their way out, as they reached their car, they saw Madan Mohan head towards them. The local MLA had disappeared from the protest site, at the first sight of trouble. It was a touchy issue and he didn't want to get impacted by anything negative that was linked to it.

'Four people are now dead. Twenty-six are critical. I am just coming from the hospital.'

Krishna just clutched his head in his hands and sat down on the seat of his car. The door was open and his legs were hanging outside the car. Jaya came up to him.

'Don't worry Krishna, we will do something.'

'What can we do? We can't bring them back from the dead. Can we? Big mistake.'

'We will do our best Krishna. We will rehabilitate their families. We will take care of their children. We will set aside ten lakhs in a corpus for each of the families. We are morally bound to take care of them.'

'It's only money that counts eh?'

'No. But for these families that have lived in poverty all their lives, money does mean something. And ten lakhs is something they will never ever see in this lifetime.'

'Where will the money come from?'

'Leave that to me. Tomorrow morning we will go and visit the families. There you can announce the grant from all of us for families who lost their near and dear ones in this battle for the survival of the human race,' Jaya was extremely good at histrionics. He paused and put his hand on Krishna's shoulder and continued, 'Though, as you said, we cannot resurrect them, we can atleast try and soften the blow. You go home now. I will pick you up tomorrow morning.'

That was when Krishna realized that he needed Jaya to fight this battle. He needed the money that Jaya had the ability to mobilise. He needed his energy to fight. But it came with associated baggage. Henceforth, he had to be a lot more vigilant and not be naïve and expose himself to manipulations.

It was a long night for Krishna. Sleep deserted him. The thought of the four families that had lost a dear one was very traumatic for him.

22

Sitting in the first class compartment of a Mumbai local train, Raymond was lost in his thoughts. Whenever there was turbulence in his mind, or stress at work, he would call Harshita. Talking to her would help him calm down. The value of a five to seven minute chat with Harshita everyday was becoming clearer now. The day just gone by had been particularly bad for him. The only thing that he had done that day was to try and get in touch with Indrani. It pinched his conscience that he hadn't done any other work. So obsessed was he about getting an audience with Indrani, that he had not even checked his voicemail at work. Feeling guilty, he dialled into his office voicemail. Since he was accessing it from outside, he was required to key in a password—it would not have been required had he been dialling from his extension. He diligently keyed it in.

'You have one new message, to read press 1.' He pressed a button as instructed by the IVR, and listened to the message. All of a sudden he perked up. It was a strange message. When it ended, he replayed it all over again. A strange fear set in.

He called the only person who he could think of.

'Hi Raymond.'

'Hi,' there was a strange shiver in his voice. 'I wanted to tell you something. There seems to be a serious problem.' Raymond felt ill. His whole body was shaking and he was sweating profusely. He took hold of himself and narrated everything he knew. Even though the compartment was quite noisy, it being a first class compartment, he was able to move to one corner and talk without running the risk of someone else overhearing the conversation.

'I don't know who you're talking about. But let me find out. Give me some time. And Raymond, you don't sound good. You need some rest.' The person at the other end said after Raymond finished.

'Yes. It's been a bad day overall.'

'Where are you now?'

'I'm in a train, reaching Ghatkopar in a bit.'

'Get off the train and call me. I'll try and find more information by then. I can't hear you clearly Raymond. Let's chat about this once you. . .' and the call dropped. 'Damn these cellphone signals!' Raymond exclaimed. He tried calling the same number once the mobile signal stabilized, but no one picked up. Each time it went into voicemail. He tried a few more times before he gave up. He was really scared.

The message in his voicemail and the subsequent call had cluttered his mind. Thoughts of Harshita, the bank, the issues with the retail bank, Jacqueline's snub and his painful wife drifted in and out of his mind as he aimlessly fidgeted with his phone.

The more he thought about it the more of a wreck he became. He had to talk to someone. The train was entering the Ghatkopar station. Desperately wanting to speak to someone he could confide in, and who would advise him selflessly, he picked up his phone and dialled another number. Even as the dialled number was ringing, he walked to the exit and got off the train.

The moment the call was picked up, Raymond broke down. He started sobbing. All this while, he had managed to hold himself, but at some point or the other, the dam had to burst. 'I. . .I. . .got-t-t a call sometime back. . .' In between his sobs he tried to get across his story to the person at the other end. It was proving to be difficult.

'I can't hear you Raymond, where are you?'

'Outside the Ghatkopar railway station.'

'Stay there, I'm coming to get you. We'll talk when I'm there.'

Back in Vienna, Johann Schroeder was overseeing the post-mortem and other investigations into the death of the two Indians. The media briefing was a bit of an anti climax and he was not happy about it, neither was Gerhard Purtsi. Both were hoping that this would turn out to be a genuine case of an accident. Otherwise it would spoil an impeccable record that Vienna had built up over two decades. No tourist had ever met such a fate in Vienna. It was considered an extremely safe place for foreigners.

However, there was one thing which kept troubling Schroeder. The initial reports that had come to him had suggested that nothing had been found on their person. No passport, no bags, not even a mobile phone. It was extremely unnatural for tourists to roam around without any of these. The only saving grace was that the jewellery Harshita was wearing, which was quite expensive by any yardstick, was safe. Robbery as a motive of murder was ruled out. Just in case it was a murder and not an accident, what could have been the motivation? Schroeder had no answers. He was confident he would find them in time.

23

The Thane Creek, a part of the estuary of the Ulhas River, has the Thane City at the head of the creek and opens into the Mumbai Harbour. Home to the migratory flamingos, it is also notified by the Bombay Natural History Society as an important bird area. A six-lane carriageway across this creek connects the city of Mumbai to the Indian mainland at Vashi, also referred to as Navi Mumbai. This carriageway, built not too long ago, was thrown open to traffic in 1997.

Adjacent to this six-lane carriageway was an old dilapidated three-lane bridge, which was commissioned in 1972. Within two years of being built, the bridge had started showing signs of stress. Cracks had appeared on the bottom of the pre-stressed girders. This led to the bridge being sparingly used and a new one being constructed. Today, the old bridge is bereft of vehicular traffic, has a pipeline running through it and is often used to shoot films and at times clandestinely, by drag bikers. The entire traffic to and from the island city of Mumbai now flows on the new Vashi bridge.

Driving on the new Vashi bridge from Mumbai to Navi Mumbai can be an interesting experience—sandwiched between the old road bridge fifty metres to the left and the railway bridge a similar distance to the right—an astounding view of three mammoth piles of girder and concrete, built to withstand extremely volatile and corrosive environmental conditions that prevail in the creek.

That night, Ramnath Balram Naik had gone fishing with three of his partners in the creek. It was a normal fishing boat with a small motor engine, which was enough to keep it going at a reasonable speed. Naik belonged to a fishing family from Panvel, where his family was one of a thousand others that depended on fishing and related businesses for livelihood. There was a time when he would fish in the Panvel creek, adjacent to the Thane creek, but of late, with the government announcing plans to build an international airport at Panvel, half of the creek where they used to carry out fishing activities had been levelled with sand, rendering it useless for fishing. They now had to go deep into the Thane creek to catch good quality crab, which they would then sell on the Panvel-Goa highway.

Ramnath Naik, along with his team of three helpers, had left after an early dinner that evening. The fishing trawler crossed the railway bridge, then the new road bridge and finally the old dilapidated bridge before they entered the creek. The tide was low. It was just about time for the tide to turn and water level to start rising. Naik knew that in a high tide situation, he would easily go past the rail bridge and the new road bridge but would struggle to go under the old road carriageway, which was significantly lower in level than the two newer ones. But he didn't have to worry about that because he was crossing the bridge just as the tide was setting in. By midnight the tide would have risen to its maximum only to drop back by early morning, allowing him a window to cross the old carriageway safely on his way back.

Around the same time that night Indrani was attending the panel discussion at Taj Lands End, about twenty kilometres from where Naik was leaving on his fishing jaunt. Financial sector reforms, microfinance ordinance, rising interest rates, new banking licenses, the finance minister spoke about all of these issues. For Indrani, this was an opportunity to show allegiance to the finance minister and consequently she applauded him the most. Secretly she harnessed dreams of a gubernatorial posting at some point in time, after drawing curtains on her banking career. Getting closer to the people in power would help.

Sharing the table with her were the CEOs of some of the large private banks in the country. While the FM's speech was on, one of them tapped her on the shoulder and pointed to her phone, lying face up on the satin cloth covering the round table. The screen was flashing; thankfully it was on silent mode. So engrossed was she in the proceedings that she hadn't noticed it. She picked up the phone and brought it closer to her so that she could see who had called. Raymond's name was flashing on the screen. She didn't pick it up. Raymond tried calling her quite a few times. When the calls didn't stop, she quietly lifted the phone from the table and dumped it into her handbag. She could do without any frivolous distractions. Her future depended on the person on stage—the Finance Minister.

Once the event ended and she was in the safe confines of the back seat of her Mercedes, she took out her phone. There were quite a few missed calls and messages. The most missed calls were from two numbers. One was Raymond, who had called her some eleven times before giving up. The second was from a number she did not recognize. She had seven missed calls from the other number. She looked at her watch. The smaller hand of the watch was just about touching the twelve mark. Too late to return anyone's call. She would do that the next morning.

Naik enjoyed a satisfying round of fishing that night. It turned out to be a lucky night for him too. The biggest catch for him was a sixteen kilogramme crab. Though this was not the biggest that he had ever caught—that privilege went to a twenty-five kilogramme crab that he had once caught on a moonlit night on the Panvel creek—however, the one he caught today would surely fetch him a good price. By the time he decided to turn back and head home it was six in the morning. After all the hard work, he was hungry and so were the others. They decided to stop by at the jetty closer to the Vashi bridge for some breakfast. The good catch had worked up their appetite. By then the tide had receded, after hitting a high somewhere around midnight.

Turning the boat to the left, they headed to the nearest jetty, which was now in sight. The early morning mist had still not settled, leading to limited visibility. They could hear the rumblings of a local train crossing the Vashi rail bridge heading into Mankhurd ferrying hundreds of early morning office-goers. As they neared the shore, the rumble in the bottom of Naik's stomach grew louder. He had worked up his hunger in anticipation of a well-deserved breakfast.

He could now see the pipeline on top of the old bridge. A film crew was shooting an early morning fight sequence adjacent to the pipeline. A huge vanity bus—the kind film stars normally use—was parked on one side. *One day, I will also act in a film,* he said to himself and he smiled, suddenly remembering his age—at fifty, he was hardly fit to be a movie star.

A few props erected for the shooting came into his sight. It looked as if a market scene was being shot. Going by the decorative torans put up, it could also have been a festival shot. As he got closer, he could see a number of people running up and down, with what looked like megaphones, trying to scream some instructions, all of them sounding important. He was a bit too far to make out what those instructions were. The entire thing seemed so fascinating, so upmarket for him. 'Let's go closer,' he said to his team. Watching a film shooting always provided an opportunity to meet or atleast see the stars and his team readily agreed. They altered their trajectory just a bit and headed towards the bridge. They didn't have to go too far from where they would have hit land and so it was not too much of an effort. Breakfast would be delayed by twenty minutes. But when one gets the opportunity to see the stars in person, breakfast doesn't matter.

They stopped when they were about a fifty metres from the bridge. Just the right position to look up at the bridge from the water below and yet manage to catch a glimpse of what was going on. He was extremely tempted to dock and go up and see what was happening there, but that would have made a mess of the entire effort that the three of them had put in last night. They would reach home late, effectively leaving them with no time to clean their catch before getting to the highway in time to sell them off.

He strained his neck to see what was going on up there. Unfortunately what he saw was not enough to satiate his curiosity. All he could see was what he could see ten minutes ago; with the difference that everything seemed closer now. The detailing didn't improve. The stars didn't appear. He was disappointed.

'Fuck it,' he told his team in chaste Marathi, the local lingo. 'Turn left. Let's atleast get a good breakfast.' His team readily obliged.

The boat turned left and headed towards the jetty, where breakfast would be waiting. They passed a pillar of the bridge, dirty green and corroded. The level reached by the high tide was marked by an overgrowth of green fungus, partly because of the continued dampness and partly because the water in the creek was extremely dirty. Scaffolding had been erected next to the pillars and covered the underside of the deck of the bridge;

probably some kind of restoration work was going on. The bridge offered a good view of the creek and the Vashi municipality was keen to promote it as a leisure destination.

Naik counted. Five more pillars and they would hit the shore. He was leaning on one side and looking at the dirty water below, and the vast expanse of the creek beyond the three bridges and their pillars, wondering how far the pillars were below the water. They passed the second last pillar. One more to go and then the shore was just twenty metres away. He was staring blankly into the wilderness. Leaning on the side of the boat, he was mentally calculating how much today's catch would fetch him when he spotted something hanging from the bridge. It was as if he had forgotten to blink. His eyes were wide open and his mind went numb. He couldn't do the math, probably because he was tired after working all night.

And then suddenly he shook himself awake. Was he dreaming? Something shocking had passed right in front of his eyes, and he hadn't noticed it. He rubbed his eyes, pinched himself and looked back. Was it a prop used for the film being shot on top of the bridge? Was it something else? Was it real?

'Stop the boaaaaaatttttttttt!' he screamed; a scream so loud that two of his workers came running to him. The colour had drained from Naik's face. He had never seen anything like this. He couldn't speak. Despite the chill, drops of sweat appeared all over his face. This could not be true.

But it was. And when he realized it, he quietly took out his antique Nokia cell phone and dialled the police control room.

It took the cops about two hours to remove Raymond Saldanah's body, which was hanging by a rope from the scaffolding below the old Vashi bridge. It appeared he had climbed down on to the scaffolding, walked to a place between two pillars, tied one end of the rope to the scaffolding, tied the other end around his neck and jumped. He was wearing a jacket and his GB2 Identity card was still dangling from his neck. A suicide note was found in his right coat pocket—an undated note that said that no one should be blamed for his death.

It was a case that left the cops flummoxed. Why would he choose such a location for committing suicide? If he really wanted to, there were easier ways to do so. Why didn't he choose those?

Raymond's body was sent for post-mortem. The Vashi police started their inquest assuming that this was a regular suicide by someone who was depressed, had a struggling personal and professional life and did not see any value in living his life to the fullest. The suicide note sealed the possibility of a debate.

This time around it was not Tanuja, but Juliana who received the first call. Someone from Raymond's immediate family had called her, and she called Tanuja.

'Are you in your cabin?'

'No Juliana, I am yet to leave. Abhishek just got back last evening, so I'm running a bit late. Just leaving in ten minutes. Tell me.'

'Tanuja, Raymond Saldanah committed suicide last night.'

'What the fuck? When? Where? How?'

'They found his body hanging below the Vashi bridge.'

'How do they know it's suicide?'

'A suicide note was found on the body.' And Juliana told Tanuja everything that she knew about the case. This was another shocker. Two days in a row. First Harshita and now Raymond.

'He was probably depressed about Harshita's death. They were too close to be just friends or good colleagues.'

'Who can say? Call me if you hear something,' and that was the end of the conversation.

'It's all fate. I don't know why all this is happening. Satya narayan ki pooja karvate hain. Kisi ki nazar lag gayi hai,' was all Vikram could say when Tanuja called him to tell him about Raymond's death.

24

Sitting on seat 4A, in the first row of business class on an Air India flight from Chennai to Frankfurt, Dr Kohl wondered when and where things had started to go wrong. Was it a mistake to have been at the site of the protest? In hindsight, it probably was. He was sent there on a mission. A mission to stop TNPP from being commissioned. His core objective was to work covertly, behind the scenes, with key influencers and drum up mass support and whip up hysteria against the project. Providing on-site information and feedback to everyone in the European and American nuclear fraternity. Now that he was caught and identified, he had put the entire coterie of people backing him, in danger of being exposed. The rush of blood, the momentary lapse in concentration was making him feel miserable about the whole thing. But was he to be blamed for the way things turned out to be? No one had expected the protest to take the turn it did.

He was worried. It was just a matter of time his 'lapse' would hit the front pages of newspapers and would escalate into a diplomatic row. His home nation would not take kindly to his deportation and that was because other than pure speculation and circumstantial evidence there was not much to link him to the current conflict. If some evidence did show up, which was unlikely, all his country would do would be to turn around and deny any involvement. Their stated position would be that Dr Heldrich Kohl was on a vacation in India, on a genuine visa and had visited the TNPP site out of genuine interest. Being at the wrong place at the wrong time was not a crime in the country he came from.

The airhostesses started making some announcements and Dr Kohl shut his eyes. It was going to be a long flight back home.

25

The phone on Jacqueline's desk rang for the third time that morning. Each of the earlier two times, it stopped ringing just as Jacqueline reached her desk to pick it up. She was standing away from her work area and discussing Raymond's death with a few of her colleagues who had walked in. This time around Jacqueline managed to pick it up in time.

'Hey Jacks, is Indrani in?'

'Hey sweetheart, how are you? Long time.'

'Yes Jacks, it's been a long time. Will come and see you. But tell me na, is Indrani in yet?'

'No, she's not. In fact, she's coming in late today!'

'Why? What happened?'

'She had gone for the FM event last night and got really late. She's catching up on beauty sleep I guess.' And she chuckled.

'Oh okay. So she will be home now?'

'I guess so.'

'Same place na? Breach Candy?'

'Yup. Why? Are you planning to go there?'

'I think I will go and see her.'

'Why?' Jacqueline was curious.

'Will tell you when I meet you love. Got to go. Please don't mention it to her, even if she calls you.' And even before Jacqueline could say anything, the caller hung up.

At her Breach Candy apartment, Indrani was reading her newspaper and sipping her steaming shot of caffeine. A stunner in her early days in banking, she looked quite charming even now. She was scanning the newspaper to see if they covered the finance minister's speech, and more importantly to see if they had carried any photograph of her at the event, when her doorbell rang. Her chihuahua jumped and ran to the door, barking in excitement. It took it some time to reach the door of the sprawling apartment spread over an area in excess of 8,000 square feet on two floors. A divine luxury in Mumbai, but as the CEO of a global bank, she deserved every inch of it. Her maid beat the dog to the door, and promptly opened it. Indrani, being the restless soul that she was, had quietly walked up behind the maid, curious to see who was at the door.

'Good morning Indrani.'

'Oh. Good morning. Since when did the press come calling unannounced!' Indrani was surprised to see him there.

'I am so sorry Indrani, I had to come in this fashion. But it was important.'

'If it is about a quote on last evening's event with the finance minister, my team will mail you my quotes and thoughts on it as well by noon.'

'No Indrani it is not about that.'

'Then what is so urgent you can't wait till I get to work?'

'Two of your employees have been murdered Indrani. And no one seems to be bothered. If no one does anything about it, there will be more.'

'What nonsense?' Indrani was shocked at the mere suggestion, but quickly recovered. 'Harshita died in a road accident in Vienna.

Did I hear you say two employees? The last time I checked, her husband was not working for GB2, just in case you didn't know.'

'I am not talking about her husband Indrani.'

Indrani raised her eyebrows in a manner that conveyed a question. Who else was he referring to?

'Raymond, Indrani! Raymond Saldanah.'

'What happened to Raymond?' When Indrani asked him, it became clear to Karan that no one had mentioned this to Indrani yet. They were probably waiting for her to come into office.

'His body was found this morning, hanging from the old Vashi bridge.'

'What the hell? What are you saying Karan?'

'Yes Indrani. Every bit of what I said is true. This morning, a few fishermen found his body hanging from the scaffolding below the old road bridge. . .the one over the Thane creek. A suicide note was found in his pocket.'

'Why would he commit suicide?'

'He didn't.'

'Can you please stop being dramatic and tell me what it is that you have come here for,' said Indrani, suddenly feeling a chill. All this was becoming a bit eerie.

'He didn't commit suicide. He was murdered. In cold blood Indrani. He was murdered in cold blood.'

'Oh my God!' Indrani exclaimed. 'What the hell is going on?'

'Can I now come inside Indrani? Or do you want me to speak to your team for quotes and impressions.' Karan could afford the sarcasm. It was over four years since he left GB2 and joined *The Times of India* group.

Indrani, who was in a state of shock, just moved away from the door allowing Karan Panjabi to walk into her living room.

26

The death of the four people in the anti-TNPP protests blew up into a big issue in the Kerala assembly that day. The newspapers, both national and vernacular, covered the protest in detail. Photographs of Krishna and Jaya addressing the rally along with Madan Mohan made it to all the newspapers. Quite strangely the press hadn't caught on to the deportation of Dr Heldrich Kohl. Since it happened quite late and that too at the Chennai airport, the press seemed to have missed it completely. The government too was silent on it. Though there was a fleeting reference to a few foreign tourists present at the spot, no one caught on to the fact that it could be a part of a much larger plan.

When Krishna woke up that day, he was not at ease. His mind was like a centrifuge, churning at a furious pace, at times making him sick. Unable to make up his mind on the future course of action, he decided to just go with the flow.

Jaya sent his trusted aides to various banks from where they withdrew forty lakhs to be paid to those who died in the stampede. The money was accumulated by afternoon and the two of them, with a band of supporters, went together to meet the families of the dead and offer their condolences and more importantly, compensation for their extreme sacrifice towards the cause. The money that Jaya offered them was in addition to what the state government had offered as ex-gratia to the next of the kin. The latter was a measly two lakh rupees only.

Standing at the doorstep of the house of one of the deceased, Jaya addressed the assembled gathering and vowed not to let TNPP be commissioned. 'Over my dead body... We shall not let the life of four martyrs go waste,' he thundered.

Krishna quietly accompanied him on all the visits, but hardly spoke. Jaya was the one who managed the press.

As expected, the daggers were quickly drawn out over the issue of the presence of the German-born nuclear scientist. As a precursor to a full-fledged CBI probe, two investigating officers were dispatched to meet and interrogate Jayakumar and Krishna. They reached Devikulam by noon on the 31st of January and almost immediately summoned Krishna and Jaya.

The two of them were at the residence of the fourth deceased when an inspector from the local police station walked up and informed Krishna about the summons. Krishna got extremely nervous. After the elephant tusk issue ages ago, he had never had any run-in with the police. All his protests against TNPP were peaceful and had always been held with prior approvals of the authorities concerned. It was only after the entry of Jaya that the canvas had got smudged. Violence, protests, money power, had all made it a tamasha rather than an issue which endangered the lives of people. Political style rallies, money in lieu of support, buying allegiance etc., all this was something Krishna had never resorted to. He knew that it would land him in trouble one day. That's why he was a tad nervous. Jaya on the contrary, was supremely confident. He seemed to be a pro at managing the regulators and law enforcers.

The CBI had a lot of questions. The two of them were quizzed for over three hours on the role of the foreign scientist.

Jaya denied any knowledge of why he was in India. He claimed he had absolutely no idea or information about the scientist's agenda. Yes he agreed to have spoken to him, but more to seek information on the ills that would befall the region in case TNPP went live. Jaya argued that in any case, he didn't have classified information about the plant and hence could not have passed on any confidential information to the foreigner. Jaya's confidence stemmed from the fact that no documentary evidence linking him to the deported scientist could be found.

Krishna sat through the entire discussion quietly listening to what was being asked and spoke only when specifically asked to. Most of the time he was left wondering what he had gotten himself into.

27

Johann Schroeder walked into Gerhard Purtsi's room with the post-mortem report of Harshita and Siddhartha Lele, a worried look on his face.

The report confirmed their worst fears. What the dumper driver told them was true. The Indian couple was on the road, long before the garbage dumper ran over them at the intersection of Odeongasse and Zirkusgasse. This particular intersection, a couple of miles away from the Hofburg Palace, gets very lonely at night, with little or no traffic. Hence speeding was very common. The one who had killed the two had left them there hoping someone would run over them and it would appear as an accident. And the Vienna police, among the smartest in Europe, had nearly been taken in by this charade.

The post-mortem report put the hour of death at around 1.30 a.m. Vienna time, whereas the dumper ran over them around 3.00 a.m. If they were killed, who had killed them? If robbery was not the motive, what was?

'It's come Gerhard.' A grim-looking Schroeder announced as he walked into Purtsi's room. When Purtsi gave him a blank look, he waved the clutch of papers in his hand and added, 'the post-mortem report.'

'What caused their death?'

'Overdose of drugs.'

'Drug overdose? What drug?' Gerhard showed no emotion on his face.

Johann Schroeder pulled out a piece of paper and referred to it. 'The initial autopsy report says that this is on account of an overdose of sedative chloral hydrate, that became significantly more lethal and toxic in combination with other prescription drugs in their system, specifically Lorazepam, Oxazepam, Diazepam. The male was also found to have consumed Benadryl and Topamax, an anticonvulsant that aggravated the sedative impact of chloral hydrate. Although the individual levels of benzodiapines in their system would not have been sufficient to cause death, their combination with a high dose of chloral hydrate possibly led to their death.'

'Oh my God! Where did they get their hands on all this?'

'We are trying to figure it out sir.'

'Does this mean that we are also dealing with a drug cartel here?'

'Can't say for sure, because some of these are prescription drugs. But. . .'

'But what Johann?'

'The post-mortem report points to minor indentations, divots, at a few places on the bodies of the Indians, that are not natural for drug injections, if you are a regular. Which means that they had been held forcibly and the drugs were injected into their bloodstreams. It's definitely not an accident Gerhard. It's clearly cold-blooded murder.'

'That doesn't sound good. What else do we know about the Leles Johann?'

'They were seen drinking at the hotel pub shortly before twelve. The hotel CCTV confirms that they left the hotel together at around midnight. We don't have any information on where they went afterwards.'

'Any other clues?'

'No Gerhard, no more clues. We're at it.'

'We will have a problem Johann. If this gets out, the media will hound us. We have to make sure we have answers for them.'

'Yes Gerhard. Unfortunately there is nothing for us to work on. There are absolutely no clues. It seems to be the handiwork of professionals.'

'I don't care Johann. Round up a few people. Present a few suspects, the regular stuff that we do. We need to push back till we have something to show for in this case.'

'Will do Gerhard. If something goes out of hand, am counting on you to bail me out.'

'Yes of course. As usual my friend, we need to keep our pride intact. Don't we?'

28

Karan Panjabi's reputation preceded him. Indrani, who was cagey about meeting him, had softened when she heard about Raymond's death. She knew Karan from the days that he was in GB2. Karan had quit GB2 and moved to Citibank after an acrimonious showdown with Deepak Sarup which was the outcome of a point of no return reached in a clash of personal egos. After a short stint in Citibank, Karan moved on to *The Times of India* group and was with them as their finance editor. He had sensationally shot to fame when he had exposed the underbelly of banking and had helped uncover a rampant money-laundering racket run by some insiders within GB2. His run-in with the then CEO of GB2, Ronald McCain, was part of folklore in GB2. However, once Ronald saw the real side of Karan, he developed a huge amount of respect for him.

'Indrani, Raymond was a close personal friend. I hired him into my branch. I brought him into GB2. It pains me to see what became of him. The suicide note. . .' and he became silent.

'What about it?'

'It's an old one. Raymond had been carrying a suicide note in his jacket for long Indrani. I caught him once when I borrowed his oversized jacket, as I spilt coffee on mine just before a crucial meeting. This was when I was in branch banking, years ago. I had found a note in his inside coat pocket and confronted him. He told me about the times he had felt like giving up everything because of his personal issues and frustrations in life. The note was a result of those occasional fits of imbalance he would suffer from. However, he had changed over the years. Become a lot tougher. So it's unlikely that he would have taken the extreme step. When I met him yesterday, I jokingly asked him if he was still carrying the suicide note. He smiled and patted the inside pocket of his coat.'

'Which means he still had it!'

'Yes Indrani, we can't make any kind of assumptions based on the suicide note. It would have been found on him even if he had been killed.'

Indrani kept quiet.

'Raymond called me last night Indrani. He said that he had tried to reach you too. But you were busy.'

'Yesterday was a bad day Karan.'

'It can't be worse than losing your own life Indrani.' When Karan said this, Indrani felt miserable. Could she have saved his life had she spoken to him? Maybe yes. . .maybe not.

'Raymond knew something no one else did,' Karan continued. 'He apparently tried to bring up the issue a few times in the past, but every time he did, he was shot down. Raymond believed that whatever he was trying to bring up to you could have been the cause of Harshita's death. He wanted to tell you about it. He had lost faith in the senior management. Obviously someone figured out what he was up to and silenced him forever.'

'What did he know that cost us these lives?'

'I'll have to figure that out Indrani. When he called me, we spoke for a brief while. After which it was becoming a bit difficult to speak openly. He was in a crowded place and so was I. The poor mobile signal near the Ghatkopar station too didn't make things any easier. He wanted to meet in person so he could tell me everything that he knew. When I reached the place he had asked me to come to, there was no sign of him. I waited for a long time. Tried calling him multiple times, but to no avail. This morning, I got to know that he had committed suicide. If he had to commit suicide, he would atleast have waited till I knew what he wanted the world to know.'

'Hmm,' Indrani was lost in deep thought. She was worried. What was going on?

'Last night Indrani, when Raymond was killed, his laptop and his phone disappeared. I know for sure that if we go through the backup of all his mails and data on the server, we will be able to get to something.'

'Why would you get involved in this? If it is such a big issue.'

'Indrani, Raymond was my friend. A dear friend. I want his killers to be brought to book.' He paused and added, 'Out of everyone else in the world Indrani, he chose me to confide in. I can't let his faith in me down.'

'And why would I let the media into this mess? You will only complicate things for me. We have a capable enough team to investigate this. If we do find anything amiss, we will ourselves get the law enforcers involved.'

'Indrani, please don't make the mistake we made last time. Ronald McCain refused to listen to me when I met him to warn him of the consequences of his actions. He chose not to listen to me and the organization was hauled over coals for what later transpired. I have worked for GB2 for seven years of my life. I would never have quit GB2. You know that. Now that I have, I can assure you that not a word of what I find out will go out to the press. I will not carry any expose or article on this issue...But...'

'But what?'

'Once we get to the bottom of this, you will allow me a day's lead over the other media. I will carry this story first.'

'How can I trust you? You only have your interest in mind.'

'Indrani, remember I came to you myself. If I so wished, I could have made sure that tomorrow morning's newspaper would carry the transcripts of Raymond's call with me. That could have been the lead story and would have created enough sensation and consequent problems for GB2 to handle. But I don't want to do that. I owe my career to this bank.'

Indrani thought about it for a moment. She was caught in a tight spot. If she went ahead and internally investigated what Karan was saying, she ran the risk of the truth being brushed under the carpet. She could in fact have ignored what Karan was saying. Raymond's death would have passed off as a suicide. Things would have gone on as they normally do. But carrying a rot within could only have disastrous consequences, albeit at a later date. And therein she ran a risk of the media sensationalizing the case, given the revelations Karan could have made on the basis of his dialogue with Raymond. She was caught between a rock and a hard place.

However, when she thought about it, what Karan was saying made sense. He could have gone ahead and published the details of Raymond's conversation with him, which could have proved to be damaging. But he didn't. That showed that he was genuinely interested in working with GB2 in resolving this issue. 'And Indrani,' Karan interrupted her thought process, 'I'm not sure we know who to trust and who not to in your management team. It's possible that there are only one or maybe two black sheep, but they are dangerous. Most importantly, we don't know who they are. And not knowing who they are is going to seriously impact your ability to investigate this internally.' This clinched the deal.

'Okay agreed. Meet me in my office in the next one hour.'

'Thanks Indrani. Please do not speak about this to anyone. It's preferable that we do not tell people what we are up to.'

'Thanks Karan,' said Indrani as he turned to leave.

'Anything for you Indrani.' Before Indrani could shut the door, he turned back, 'and one last request Indrani'. She nodded. 'Do you mind if I get Kavya to work with me on this? Since we don't know who is on our side and who is not, we need someone who we can be sure about. And Kavya is one person I am willing to bet my last shirt on.' Karan and Kavya had been in a relationship for a long time. They fell apart after a three-year courtship, only to be reunited when Karan was busy exposing the huge money laundering scam that had engulfed GB2, nearly consuming Deepak Sarup in it. 'And she is good with systems and data extraction.'

'Sure. You can work out of my boardroom for the next two days. Am not too sure we will be able to hold things back beyond two days. There will be too many questions'.

'Yes Indrani. We will give it our best shot over the next forty-eight hours. If we get to the bottom of it, then great. If not, then we will let the pros come in and handle. I'll meet you in your office in an hour. I will brief Kavya too.' And Karan left.

Within an hour, Karan was in Indrani's fifth floor office. Indrani had already briefed Jacqueline, so she was expecting him. Karan went in straight into her office, without completing any formalities at the entrance. Normally, he would have had to write his name down as a visitor in the register placed at the entrance. And then it would be there for everyone to see. Thankfully no one saw him enter Indrani's office.

Kavya too joined them within five minutes. It was relatively easy for her to be smuggled in. She had a reasonably low profile in the bank and no one really knew her in the head office.

Indrani who had reached by then led them to an attached boardroom. The boardroom had two doors—one that opened into the lift lobby to enable visitors to walk in, the other opened, into Indrani's room. 'Folks, this is your office for the next two days. I understand we are working on a hypothesis and all our efforts will be towards proving that hypothesis. You believe that the two were murdered; cops believe one was an accident and the other was a suicide. This effort is only to protect us and get to the bottom of it, so that recurrence of such calamities may be avoided. Remember, whatever findings we have at the end of two days, I will have to report. So whatever help you need, whosoever you need to be pulled out, just ask. Jacqueline here has access to my mailbox; she can send and receive mails from my ID. Use her. There is no one else I trust more than Jacqueline. She will be my conscience keeper in this. And most importantly, she will validate the need, in case you ask for any sensitive data.'

'We'll do our best Indrani.'

'If anyone asks you what you are doing here, the response to that is that you are doing a front page story on GB2 in your Sunday edition and that's why you are here, to complete your research. Try not to interact directly with people unless you really have to. Maybe once you finish this investigation, you can genuinely consider doing a front-page story on the management team at GB2. We will talk about it later though.' Karan, for the first time that day, smiled. 'Sure Indrani.'

'I'm around in the next room.' She looked at Jacqueline. 'Cancel all my appointments for the next two days. This is more important. I wish I had cancelled yesterday's appointment. Maybe then, Raymond would have still been alive.'

The phone on Jacqueline's desk rang and she ran to pick it up. 'Yes Tanuja. She's in a meeting right now.'

'I need to meet her. It's urgent.'

'She is really tied up now, Tanuja. She has also asked me to cancel all of today's and tomorrow's appointments.'

'Does she know about Raymond's suicide? Has Juliana mentioned it to her?'

'She is aware of it, yes.'

'Alright then, that's what I wanted to brief her on. The press might be coming in to talk to us. We need to be prepared.'

'Let me check with her.'

'Sure. I'll wait.'

Jacqueline walked back into the conference room. 'Tanuja is on the line. She wants to come up and brief you on the Raymond issue. Can she come up now?'

'Ask her to come in ten minutes. I will be done with these guys by then.'

After giving them instructions Indrani left. Karan looked at Kavya. 'So. . .'

'So?' Kavya replied.

'How are you?'

'Quite the same. Not much has changed since last evening, when you left our dinner midway and never came back.'

'In fact I came back after an hour and a half. You had left by then.'

'I couldn't sit in the restaurant, all alone, waiting for you to come back.'

'I called you after that and explained, didn't I?'

'Yes of course you did Karan. But it's okay. After what I heard this morning, I would have got upset if you had not tried to do anything to help Raymond out.'

Karan smiled. 'Where do we begin Kavya? Too much to do and too little time. I am a bit confused. Let's think for a minute before we begin.'

'Tea? Coffee?' Jacqueline came in and asked.

'Anything will do Jacqueline,' Kavya responded. For the next five minutes he put his head down, didn't speak to anyone and kept scribbling in his pad. Finally when he lifted his head, he looked at Kavya and said, 'Okay Kavya, let's start. Here's where we begin. . .'

29

Jayakumar and Krishna's visit to the CBI office was a hush-hush affair. After a grilling three-hour interrogation, Krishna and Jaya were allowed to go with clear instructions that they were not to leave Devikulam. While being led to the interrogation room, both Jaya and Krishna had to surrender their phones. By the time they returned, there were a number of missed calls on Jaya's phone. Jaya looked at them, but didn't bother returning any of those calls. Picking up his phone and other belongings, he walked straight into the waiting Toyota Innova.

'Phone,' he screamed, the moment he got into the car. The driver, not wanting to be at the receiving end of his anger, hurriedly pulled out an instrument from the glove compartment and handed it over to him. It was an old Nokia instrument. Jayakumar scrolled through the contact list and hurriedly dialled a number.

'What the hell is this?' he demanded, as the person on the other end picked up. 'Why am I being treated like a criminal?'

Krishna looked at Jayakumar, phone glued to his ear, his face red in anger. He had never seen Jaya like this before. The guy at the other end was trying to say something which was muffled, so Krishna couldn't understand.

'What? Lie low? Why the hell should I lie low? Look Mahadevan, I'm warning you, if you don't figure a way out to get these guys off our back, you know what I can do?'

The guy at the other end started offering some explanation that was clearly unacceptable to Jayakumar.

'Mr Nair, I have been extremely accommodating. Everything that you had asked for has been given. I have conceded to all your demands and have patiently waited long enough.' And then he paused, listening to the person at the other end. 'Not my problem,' Jaya yelled in response. 'I know there are multiple people involved in seeing this through, but my patience is now running out. You release the purchase order for the trucks and I will back off from this agitation. The way I convinced people to back this protest, I will convince them to back off too. The way I bought the protest, I can buy peace too. But that will only happen if you keep your side of the bargain.'

Mahadevan's reply apparently didn't cut curry with Jaya. 'I want this issue resolved in the next forty-eight hours Mr Nair and I want the CBI off my back. Remember, the country has spent three billion dollars—fifteen thousand crore on the nuclear plant. It will be unfortunate if that investment were to rot. It doesn't take too much to get one person to kill himself at the gates of the nuclear plant every day till such time that the government calls off the project. There are enough people in this country willing to die, if someone promises their families two square meals a day. And these people are now with me.'

Krishna Menon was furious when he heard this conversation. It was a curious mix of anger juxtaposed with fear. If Jayakumar had such an approach towards Mahadevan Nair, who he knew through newspaper reports was the Secretary in the Ministry of Defence, wonder what his approach would be towards a simpleton like him. He wanted to let go of everything and head back to his resort. What was born of a genuine feeling of discontent and care for the people living in the surroundings, arising out of his own personal tragedy, had turned into a completely different battle. This was not his cup of tea.

Jayakumar disconnected the line and looked towards Krishna. 'Bastards', he said with a scornful look on his face. 'Let them fuck with me again, I will show them what I can do. You don't worry Krishna, leave this to me. I will get you out of the CBI wrangle.'

'Yes Jaya', was all Krishna could manage. He was too scared to ask him any further questions. That evening he told his wife about the entire conversation which Jaya had with Mahadevan Nair. 'He is using me.' He said with an air of desperation.

'Why blame him? You are allowing yourself to be used. While I have nothing against the protest and I am with you in this cause, you got carried away by the fact that this was making you famous in your neighbourhood. You started believing that you have the power to change the world. Nothing changes. Remember that. The people who came running after you were fighting their own battle—through you. They will scoot the moment someone throws a few morsels at them. Dogs like Jaya will make use of that and mould everything as per their own needs.'

'I know Sulochana. But I had good intentions.'

'Jaya thinks he has them too. Your perspectives are different, that's it. And Krishna, nothing in this world comes free. You needed Jaya to pump in money to help you fight this battle, and Jaya had the resources to do so. He needed a handle on the government, which you provided him. Both of you gained in your respective agendas. Why complain?'

30

'From what Raymond told me when I met him yesterday morning Kavya, he had serious issues with regard to the account of one Asia Logistics. Our starting point has to be that account.'

'What did he tell you about the account?'

'Not much. Before he could tell me everything about it, he heard about the death of Harshita and that disturbed him. We had to cut short our meeting. In retrospect, I wish I hadn't left him in that state.'

'Hmm. . .what about the call last night?' Kavya queried.

'Nothing much. He started sobbing. There was too much noise in the background. I couldn't hear a thing. I could make out that it was about the same account. But nothing beyond that. Anyway, you ask for the entire transaction history. It's a relatively new account and so should be easy to get.' Karan was getting into the groove. The last few years in the media business had been very exciting for him, but this was different. He was trying to investigate and get to the bottom of what killed his friend. There was an unmistakable emotional angle to this entire affair.

'Also try and see if you can extract the following data for me. This will be very useful.' He handed her a list. 'Lastly Kavya, I also want to see the list of accounts managed by Harshita Lele in Bandra. For starters, this should do.'

'Sir,' said Kavya nodding and gently bowing her head. Karan smiled at her. The next couple of days were going to be interesting for both of them.

In Mumbai, oblivious of what was going on in Indrani's mind and in her office, Vikram was in his cabin responding to mails. Juliana had said that she would be going to Raymond's house only in the afternoon. The body was still in the morgue, in the custody of the cops and they had said that they would release it towards late afternoon after the post-mortem. The admin team of GB2 was working on securing an early release so that the last rites could be performed.

Indrani had instructed Tanuja to work with the public affairs team to prepare a media release, just in case Tanuja's apprehension came true and the media did come calling.

A knock on his cabin door made Vikram look up from his laptop.

'Hey Zinaida. Good to see you.' Seeing her hesitate, he added, 'Come on in.'

'Good morning Vikram.'

Vikram looked at his watch and smiled, 'Just about.' Laughing at his own joke, he said, 'What brings you to this side of town?'

'Vikram I had come to meet a customer. The customer stays in Bandra, but has his office in Colaba. Since I was in this side of town, I thought I would drop in and convey my thanks to you in person. I'm really grateful to you, that you thought it fit to give me this role. Though the circumstances under which I got this role were not particularly happy, nevertheless it atleast told me what you think of me.'

'No no not at all. There's no need to thank me. In fact, Anand and Nikhil have been singing great praises of you. They were the ones who wanted me to give the role to you.'

'No Vikram. Nikhil told me of your discussion with him and Tanuja. I will try to live up to the faith that you have reposed in me.' She walked up to Vikram and when she was very close to him, she gave him a big hug and said, 'Thanks boss.'

Vikram felt his whole body shiver when she hugged him. It had been a while since someone had given him such a tight, sensual hug. He too reciprocated. At that very instant his cabin door flew open.

'Oops. I am so sorry.'

'It's okay Tanuja. You can come in.' Vikram quickly withdrew his hands and released Zinaida.

'I guess I came in at a wrong time,' said Tanuja. She had gone red in her face, more out of anger than embarrassment.

'Thanks Vikram, I will come back later. Bye Tanuja,' and Zinaida disappeared. She didn't want to get caught between two seniors.

Tanuja glared at Zinaida as she left. She was furious.

'Arre, she just came in to thank me and gave me a hug. What can I do about it?'

'You were not exactly behaving like Vishwamitra, Vikram. Your grasp seemed to be tighter than hers.'

'Oh, come on Tanuja. Stop being so jealous and possessive. Atleast I won't do these things in my cabin in office.'

'Oh then where will my lover boy do these things? In the car? In the loo? In the basement? Where exactly have you done it with her?'

'Oh shut up baby.'

'Hmm. . .We will talk about this Vikram. You haven't heard the end of it.'

'Cheer up baby. You should know me by now.'

'I was on this floor. So I thought I will step by and say a quick hello. But I came in at a wrong time I guess.' Tanuja was visibly upset.

'Arre no yaar. Stop being so suspicious.'

Tanuja ignored the comment. 'Anyway, I am with Soumya. We are drafting a press note for Indrani. Let me know if you need anything.' Soumya was the Head of Public Affairs at GB2. She managed the relationship with the press.

'What I need, I know I won't be able to take from you here.'

'You can take it from Zinaida, but not me? It's okay. I will speak to you once we're done with work,' and she left, banging his cabin door behind her. Vikram just smiled.

From Vikram's cabin, Tanuja went straight to Soumya's room. It didn't take them long to draft the press briefing. They showed it to Indrani, who didn't have too much to say on it, and the issue was sealed. The briefing, after being vetted, was sent out to all the business leaders, just in case they got queries from the local media. All this was happening on the fifth floor of the GB2 HQ, oblivious of what was going on inside the boardroom.

The Account Opening Form (AOF) of Asia Logistics was the first document to hit Jacqueline's mailbox. She promptly printed out the scanned copy and walked in with the AOF and the transaction history and handed it over to Karan.

All KYC documents were in place. Even the RM concerned had visited the office and done a site visit report. That too was in order.

'The AOFs seem perfect,' he said when he handed over the documents to Kavya. 'Just perform a sanity check. I couldn't see anything fishy here.'

Kavya went through the entire account opening form. Nothing was out of place. It was a form signed by two directors. And both of them were authorized to operate the account. The company had signed up for e-statements, which were sent to the email ID of one of the directors. She went through all the documents one by one, carefully so as not to miss anything.

'Karan, tell me one thing. . .'

'Hmm?'

'Under what circumstances do organizations give a HOLD instruction?'

'What hold instructions?'

'Arre idiot, HOLD instructions. . .for holding back all correspondence at the bank branch, and not mailing it to the customer.'

'Oh, understood. HOLD instructions are given when the account holder does not want the bank to send him any correspondence—statements, advices, cheque books, transaction receipts etc. They give the bank a 'HOLD' instruction, on the basis of which the bank sends all the correspondence it would normally send to the customer, to the branch where the customer has his account. The customer then arranges to pick it up from the local branch of the bank at his convenience. In case of company accounts, it's normally done if the company is shifting offices, in which case any correspondence sent to the company's given address is likely to get lost. But banks don't encourage this too much. Not only does this put pressure on the branches to manage customer correspondence as these customers pick up their correspondence from the bank branch, it also gives rise to a lot of frauds. But why do you ask?'

'Well, because Asia Logistics has given GB2 a HOLD instruction. Anyway what are you going through?'

'Transaction history of their current account.'

'Okay, sorry for the interruption.'

'No problem. . .but wait. Did you say that this company has given a "correspondence on HOLD" instruction from day one?'

'Yes.'

'Are you sure? I haven't seen many companies give a "correspondence on HOLD" instruction from day one.'

'Yes Karan. All their correspondence is on HOLD. It goes to the Bandra branch, from where it gets picked up by their errand boys.'

'Kavya, but in my entire banking career I haven't ever accepted a HOLD instruction from a new account.'

'Why?'

'Because in the case of a new account, it could also mean that the company does not exist at the address that it has given in the AOF. So it does not want any correspondence to go there.'

'Understood. Could it also mean the company exists at the address listed but someone opened an account in the company's name giving fraudulent documents and so they don't want the correspondence to go there?'

'Yes of course. It could be either of the two.' He suddenly jumped from his chair, 'Oh shit. . .Kavya. . .we will have to check this out. This could be the fraud we are looking for.'

Kavya's eyes lit up. Was this the big moment they were waiting for? No chance. It could not come so soon. They had just begun the investigation.

'I will have to check this out.' Karan was suddenly excited at what Kavya had discovered.

'Wait, Karan. Don't get so hyper. Zinaida has visited the office. There is a visit report on file.'

'Who Zinaida?'

'An RM in Bandra. She has visited the office of Asia Logistics and filed her report. It's on file.'

'I saw that. However, the HOLD instruction seems fishy. It's a first for me. Never seen a new account with a HOLD instruction. I need to check it out quickly. I'll go now.'

'Now? As in, right now?'

'Yes. I don't have a choice. It has to be you or me. You stay here. Run the reports I have asked you for and I'll go to the address, check it out and come back. The office is in South Mumbai so it won't take too much time.' He made a grab of the papers, which included all the AOFs and ran out of Indrani's room. 'Get the other reports fast. I'll be back in forty-five minutes.'

He was waiting at the lift lobby on the floor, hoping he would not run into anyone he knew. A tap on his shoulder made him turn around. As it turned out, he was not that lucky. 'Hi Karan.' It was Tanuja. 'What brings you here?'

'Oh Tanuja. How are you? Just the regular shit. Work. We're doing a lead story on GB2 and we wanted to spend a day with Indrani to write about her. I'm just heading out because there's an emergency at office. Will be back in an hour or so.'

'Once you are done with that, come down to my room for coffee. Let's catch up. It's been a while.'

'I'm not sure about today but I'll definitely catch you tomorrow. Need to talk to you about Indrani's style of functioning. How is she as a leader? It will be helpful in the story we are writing about GB2.'

'Any time. Just buzz me. You have my mobile number.' Tanuja said, before she got off on her floor. Karan nodded as the lift door closed behind her.

31

Karan flagged a passing taxi and headed towards Colaba. When he reached the Gateway of India, he passed a fifty-rupee note to the taxi driver and got off. Quite a steep payment for a short distance, but he didn't have time to stop and negotiate or even wait for the cab driver to return the change.

The address of Asia Logistics as mentioned in the AOF was of a location behind the Taj Mahal Hotel. Swiftly, and with long strides he walked past the Gateway of India on his left, and reached the by-lanes behind the Taj. He was looking for a building called Connoisseur. It didn't take him much time to locate it. A run down building, it housed small and medium sized offices. Most of the businesses there were of freight agents. Walking in, he reached the lift lobby. There were three creaky old lifts which ferried passengers up and down. Displayed on a large wall in the lift lobby, on the right of the three lifts, were the nameplates of all the companies housed there. Karan stood there, hunting for the name. . .and there it was. . .ninth floor. . .Asia Logistics Private Limited, Office No. 906. The address matched the one he had on the Account Opening Form. *So far so good,* thought Karan.

A silent prayer escaped his lips as he stepped into the dilapidated lift hoping that it would safely take him to the 9th floor. Thankfully, God heard his prayer. Moving aside to allow an old lady to pass through, he followed her out of the lift and surveyed the exterior to figure out where the office of Asia Logistics was. He nearly tripped on a tile laminate which had come loose. Thankfully he had the wall to hold on to for support and didn't fall, although the papers in his hand spilled on to the floor. He hurriedly picked them up. There was no time to lose.

He walked a few steps. A hastily stuck, partly torn paper on the wall announced the fact that the corridor ahead was home to offices 906 to 910. He marched on. Another fifteen metres and he was in front of a glass door. On it was inscribed in large letters, 'Global Telesys'. He looked towards his left, opposite the main door of Global Telesys. He was staring at a freshly painted wall. He didn't have time to wonder what benefit the fresh coat of paint would provide if the surroundings were so shabby.

He pushed the glass door open and walked in. A cute-looking girl wearing a flimsy, revealing top with a deep, never-ending neckline sat at the reception desk. Karan followed the neckline down till he reached the point where it dipped into her cleavage. He let out a sigh and looked up.

'Can I help you?' the girl said, smiling at him.

'Hello. I am looking for this address,' and he handed her a slip of paper with the address of Asia Logistics.

The receptionist looked at the address and read it out loud, '906, Connoisseur, Taj Lane, Colaba. You want to know where to find this place?'

'Yes.'

'You are standing there.'

'This is 906?'

'Yes sir, who do you want to meet?'

'But the sign says Global Telesys.'

'Yes sir. That's the name of our company.'

'You mean office number 906 is the address of Global Telesys? Is there any other wing in this building? A-Wing? B-Wing?'

'No sir. This is the only building and you are standing in office 906 which is Global Telesys.' The irritation in her voice was evident. She didn't like being asked the same question repeatedly.

'But the name of the company I have is Asia Logistics.' There was panic in Karan's voice.

'Oh Asia Logistics. Why didn't you say that earlier? They were here before us.'

Karan suddenly felt a bit relieved. So Asia Logistics was operating from there. The address on the account opening form was correct. It was not a fraudulent account. Maybe they were shifting and that's why they had given the HOLD instruction.

'Oh thanks ma'am. Any idea where they have moved? By the way, the board at the entrance of the building still shows 906 as the office of Asia Logistics.'

'They have moved to the sixth floor,' she said, pointing downwards.

'In the same building?'

'Yeah. And we have been asking the building administration to change the name plates. . .but they are far too lazy to do it.'

'Oh no issues. Even reminders don't work?' Karan said playfully.

'Nothing works on these guys. In fact, we've had it easy; we've been hounding them for only the past three months. These guys, Asia Logistics, have been chasing them for over eight months now.'

'Yeah?'

'Yup. Ever since they vacated this office and moved downstairs.'

'Oh. Hope it gets changed soon then. I am sure there are many like me who come up asking for the wrong office. Thanks anyway.' Karan opened the door but the moment he stepped out, it struck him. *Eight months?* He froze. *Did the receptionist say eight months?* He looked at the documents in his hand. The account had been opened approximately three months back. Retracing his steps, he walked back into the office of Global Telesys.

'Did you say eight months?'

'Pardon me?'

'You said Asia Logistics moved out of this office eight months ago.'

'Yes they did.'

'And you moved in around three months ago?'

'That's correct.'

'Was this office occupied in the intervening five months?'

'No it was not occupied. It was put up for rent, but no one had taken it up. It was vacant, to the best of my knowledge.'

'Thanks. Sorry for bothering you.' And he rushed to the 6th floor. He wanted to meet the guys at Asia Logistics. Something was amiss. He ran down three floors, at times skipping multiple steps and finally landed at the door of Asia Logistics.

It was a small office with twenty-odd employees. Even though the employees were few, they were very well organized. Everyone had nametags and ID cards, the entry to the main area was controlled with access cards, and there was even neat seating provided for visitors. All in all, it seemed like a good organization.

The lady at the reception was a thin girl who looked as though she might be from south-India but sported a nametag that read 'Misha Bose'. Karan wondered how the name and appearance were completely divergent. But it was not the time for that discussion. He walked up to her and said, 'Misha, I need to see the person in-charge here.'

'What's this regarding?'

'I am here to investigate a fraud.' Typically all front-office personnel change their approach the moment the word fraud is dropped upon them. They suddenly become a lot more helpful, and Misha was no exception. She went in and when she returned she had a fat, pot-bellied, nerdy-looking guy with her. She pointed towards Karan and the nerdy guy approached him. He looked at Karan through his thick glasses and asked him, 'Yes, what can I do for you?'

'Sir my name is Karan Panjabi and I am here on behalf of GB2. Are you the in-charge here sir?'

'I am Tripat Gill, the branch in-charge. Tell me.'

'Mr Gill, I want you to confirm if these Account Opening Forms have been filled and signed by your directors.' And he handed over the complete set of forms to the nerd.

Tripat Gill studied the forms for precisely ten seconds and handed them back.

'No.'

'No?'

'Hmm. . .no. . . We don't have a director named Asad Ansari.'

'Are you sure?'

'One hundred per cent.' Tripat was supremely confident about his claim.

'Maybe if you see their photographs, you might recollect something.' And he opened the page which had the photographs and turned the papers towards the branch in charge.

'Oh this guy!' Tripat Gill was shocked when he saw the photo. He looked at Misha, 'See what this guy has done? Didn't I tell you the day I first saw him, that he is a fraud?' Misha walked up to them to check out the photograph. It seemed to shock her too.

'What happened? You know him?' Karan queried.

'Yes. He was my ex-boyfriend. He used to come to the ninth floor office quite often. In fact, when we moved to the sixth floor, he was considering taking the ninth floor office for some business of his, but that never worked out.'

'Hmm. . .do you know where he lives?'

'No. I haven't seen him in the last three months. Even when I was dating him, he never took me to his house.'

Karan spoke to them for a few minutes more and rushed back to Ground Zero—the conference room adjacent to Indrani's office.

'Bastard, fraudulent account. The company exists, but the guys who opened the account have opened it without the knowledge of the actual company. The real Asia Logistics does not even know that there exists an account in their name in GB2.' He gave Kavya a run-down of all that he had seen and heard.

'Which means the money which is coming in is being used for clandestine purposes. It's a clear case of money laundering,' said Kavya. 'But Karan, there is a visit report of a RM on file. How did the RM miss it?'

'Let's ask her.'

'Wait, I don't think that will be necessary.' And she quickly glanced through the report. 'She visited the site early in the morning. And if one links it up with what you are saying, Zinaida went there before Global Telesys moved in. If the name plates in the lobby were there even today, they would surely have been there when she would have visited the office. She would have fallen for it. If you see her report, she has mentioned that no employees were seen because it was so early in the morning. The visit was stage-managed for her. GB2 got taken in by the amount of money involved and took the bait.'

'Hmm. . .that can be the only explanation. So it looks like we are on the right track. We would not have figured this out hadn't you noticed that Asia Logistics has a HOLD instruction. Don't know how I missed it.'

'It's okay boss. You have been out of touch with banking for a long time now.' And Kavya winked at him.

'That reminds me, where you able to get the details of all those accounts wherein a large quantum of money has come into the account and has been withdrawn in the form of cash within a few days? Can I see the list Kavya?'

'Yes yes. I got that Karan. There are sixty-eight such accounts across the country. In the last three months, about two hundred crore rupees have come in from overseas into these accounts and almost everything has been withdrawn in cash. In fact twenty-one of these sixty-eight accounts have already been closed—and that too within three to four months of their being opened.'

'Hmm. . .that means that these accounts were possibly set up with the objective of getting tainted money from overseas and once the money was siphoned out, these accounts were closed.'

'And you know what. While you were away, I was struggling to run this query. So I asked Amit how to run it.'

'Who Amit?'

'Works in the data mining team?'

'You asked him for help? Didn't we tell Indrani that we wouldn't?'

'Yes. But I had to get the job done. And guess what, he told me that two days back he had run this query and given the same data to Raymond.'

'Shit. You shouldn't have told him. Now he will know.'

'Don't worry, he's going out of town tonight and will be back next week. We will be done by then.'

'Okay cool. Hope he doesn't open his mouth.' He walked to the corner of the room. Raising his right hand, he twisted the venetian blinds and allowed light to filter into the boardroom. Standing there, he stared out blankly at the road below and the parked cars on the sides. The traffic, the crowd, the hawkers. . .nothing made an impact on him. 'If Asia Logistics was fraudulently set up, it's understandable. Nothing earth-shattering about it. The banking system is full of such benami accounts. Despite the banks trying to weed them out, they do exist. What baffles me Kavya, is why were all these guys killed? Why was Raymond killed? Why was Harshita killed? If the bank had been vigilant, they could also have found out that Asia Logistics was a bad account. But could that have stopped the murders?'

'Is it possible that they were killed because they found out?'

'Which means we're next in line,' he winked at Kavya. 'If we don't see each other tomorrow, remember baby that I love you.'

'Very funny.'

32

Raymond's funeral was a very muted affair. Not many people attended. From GB2, Tanuja, Vikram, Juliana and a few others who were dutifully obliged to attend, were present. Indrani didn't attend this funeral too. For once, it was not her obsession with self-promotion that held her back. She didn't want to leave Karan and Kavya behind, managing things alone.

The post-mortem report had estimated the time of death at around 2.00 a.m. It also put the reason for Raymond's death as one caused due to strangulation and the resultant cut-off of oxygen supply to the brain. There was no other injury, external or internal, which showed any fight or violence of any kind. No one was interested in pursuing the case. Raymond's wife had given up on him, his parents were incapacitated and old, and in no position to take on anyone, GB2 was an organization that did not want to involve itself in any controversy and as far as friends are concerned, Raymond didn't have many. Most importantly, the suicide note found on Raymond made it an open and shut case.

'Jacqueline!' called out Karan. He was logging into his laptop for the first time after coming back from the Asia Logistics office. 'I am sending you something via email. Can you please print it out for me?'

'What is it?' asked Kavya, curiously.

'The draft post-mortem report and the staff photographer's pictures from the site.'

'Post-mortem report? Whose?'

'Raymond's.'

'So soon?'

'This is the draft report which is first prepared and released after some bureaucratic procedures. The media has contacts, so we get stuff out before the formal report is published.'

'Wow. Will print it out for you,' and Jacqueline got busy with her computer.

'Show me the pictures,' Kavya butted in. 'Can I see?'

'Yes you can. But they are quite graphic. Extremely inhuman and repulsive.'

'That's fine. I will manage.' And Kavya walked up to Karan, who brought the images on the screen for her to see.

Meanwhile, Jacqueline demonstrated why she was reputed to be the most efficient secretary. In a jiffy she had printed out the post-mortem report and the pictures and had handed them over to Karan, who was visibly impressed. 'I work for the CEO you see,' Jacqueline smiled at him and walked out.

Karan started reading the post-mortem report. Intermittently he would hold up the pictures and intensely scrutinize them and almost immediately revert to the post-mortem report. It was as if he was comparing the two. He even asked for his laptop for a few minutes and checked something before going back to the report. Kavya had by then seen the pictures and was waiting for the next round of instructions from Karan.

'Rubbish,' said Karan when he finally finished reading the report.

'What happened?'

'This post-mortem report is bullshit. Absolute crap. It's been done by someone who just wanted to get it over with. Probably the cops didn't want another case on their hands, so they were happy to call it a suicide. I can bet my ass on it, it's not.'

'Don't do that sweetheart. Your ass is far too cute. In fact, it's the only thing cute about you.'

'Shut up Kavya.'

'Fine, fine. Why do you say that the report is rubbish?'

'It's very simple,' said Karan and fiddled with his laptop.

You saw the picture of Raymond hanging by a long rope right? He was hanging between the two pillars, right in the middle of the horizontal scaffolding. Right?'

'Yes.'

Karan brought up the picture on his screen. 'See this?' He pointed to the rod on which the rope was hanging from and then to the scaffolding. 'The entire underside of the bridge is covered by scaffolding.'

'Hmm,' Kavya nodded her head.

'If you look carefully, there are two sections of the scaffolding. One which covers the piers. . .'

'You mean the pillars which hold up the bridge.'

'Yes idiot. That's what a pier is. One section of the scaffolding covers the piers. Then there is a separate segment of the scaffolding that is underneath the bridgedeck and runs horizontally along the belly of the bridge covering the entire span between the two piers. It's quite a long section—the piers are about twenty metres apart.'

'Yes.'

'And our friend was found hanging from the centre of this horizontal scaffolding, in other words, he was at least ten metres from each of the piers, irrespective of which side you look at.'

'Correct.'

'Now, if he has managed to tie the rope on the horizontal scaffolding, he couldn't have done it standing on or taking support from the scaffolding on any of the pillars. Which means that the only way Raymond could have got to where the rope is tied to the scaffolding, is if he somehow got on the horizontal scaffolding—below the deck—from the bridge, and carefully walked like a trapeze artist, to the centre of the horizontal span, where he tied one end of the rope, put the noose on the other end around his neck and jumped.'

'I'm listening. It's so gross.'

'And Kavya, the body is hanging from a long rope. From the looks of it, the rope is about three metres or so.'

'Yes? The length of the rope looks like it's twice his height atleast. But what does it prove?'

'Hold on. Hold on. Let me complete. I am also thinking aloud. I'm not drawing conclusions. Assume for a minute that Raymond did commit suicide. He would have jumped from here. . .' and he pointed to a place at the centre of the scaffolding on the underbelly of the bridge, between the two piers.

'Okay?' Kavya was getting more and more intrigued.

'And in case he did jump from there, he would have had to jump atleast three metres, because that's the length of the rope. And assuming that one drops three metres while hanging themselves, the jerk would be intense, more so in the case of Raymond, because he is of a heavy frame. In such a case, getting away with all the cervical vertebrae intact is almost impossible.'

'Cervical vertebrae?'

'The human neck, Kavya, is comprised of seven cervical vertebrae that lie in front of the spinal cord and help provide support, structure and stability to the neck. In case of a big jerk, the cervical vertebra gets damaged.' And he touched her neck to point out the part he was referring to.

'Hmm.'

'The post-mortem reports no other injury or in other words Raymond's cervical vertebrae were intact. Simply put, it means that Raymond did not fall three metres while hanging. He was killed and later hung slowly from the scaffolding.'

'Oh wow. How did you learn all this?'

'I'm training to be a crime investigator Kavya. TOI is putting me through intense investigative training. You know that, why are you asking me?'

'Alright, calm down. But what if, because of some weird reason—put it down to statistical inconsistencies—his cervical vertebrae stayed intact despite the fall?'

'I know what you are saying. But this is not the only thing in favour of my hypothesis. Look at these.' And Karan turned the screen of the laptop towards her.

'What are these?'

'Wait wait, before that, let's go back to the point that I was making earlier.' And he brought up the picture of Raymond hanging from the horizontal scaffolding. 'The distance between the point where Raymond is hanging from and the two piers on either side is atleast ten to twelve metres. Right?'

Kavya nodded quietly. She was hooked, listening closely to what Karan was saying.

'It means that the only way Raymond could have reached the point to tie the knot was by walking on the scaffolding underneath the deck.'

'You told me this earlier too, remember?'

'Yes. I remember. I am just reiterating my point. Now look at this,' and he clicked on his laptop and brought up a few images on his screen. He zoomed in on one and turned the screen towards Kavya. She couldn't make out what the picture was about. 'What's this?'

'This is a picture of the scaffolding leading to the place where Raymond was found hanging from. Wait till I zoom in'. Karan clicked on a section of the picture and zoomed in further.

'Pretty neat for a scaffolding, except for the dust that has settled on it. Clean by Mumbai standards. Probably because it's new.'

'Hmm. . .yes. Covered by dust though. If Raymond walked on these and reached the place where he tied the rope, there should be footprints, right? Can you see any footprints?'

Kavya looked at the picture again and said, 'No. No footprints.'

'See these?' Karan brought up multiple pictures and zoomed in to all of them and looked at the close-ups one by one. 'Our staff photographer has covered the scaffolding from all angles. If there are no footprints on the scaffolding, how did Raymond get to where he was hanging from?'

'Oh yes! Obviously he couldn't have floated there.' Kavya was extremely intrigued by Karan's disclosures.

'He could have, Kavya.'

'What?'

'Yes Kavya, he could have. He could have floated there on a boat and could have been hung there by someone who killed him.'

'You mean to say, someone brought him there by boat and killed him by hanging him there?'

'No, I'm not saying that. I am saying he was already dead by the time he was brought there. He was just strung up, to make it look like a suicide.'

'How can you be so sure?'

'Wait,' said Karan, getting busy with his laptop again. He pulled up a website; from a distance it looked like the same website that he was looking at a little earlier when he was reading the post-mortem report. 'Come here,' he summoned Kavya, eyes focused on the picture on screen.

'I'm right behind you.' Kavya said.

'Oh, right. Look at this picture. It was taken by our guy at 8.52 a.m.' It was a close-up of a hanging Raymond. The time stamp on the picture was intact. Kavya felt nauseous. Involuntarily her hand went up and covered her mouth. Karan went on. 'Look closely at the trousers. Don't they look clean?'

'Yes they do. So what? He was on his way back from office.' Kavya looked at the picture. She felt sorry for Raymond. He looked so still, in stark contrast to the water that was flowing about two to three feet below his shoes. *No one should meet such an end,* she thought.

'Sweetheart, the post-mortem says that he died around 2.00 a.m., which means he jumped from the scaffolding with the noose around his neck around the same time.'

'Hmm.'

Karan pressed a couple of buttons and toggled to a website showing the tide levels at various points in time. 'See, this is the table which shows last night's tide levels.' Kavya looked at the screen. She didn't understand anything.

Bombay, India
18.9167°N, 72.8333°E

Time	Height of Tide
12.00 Midnight	1.80 metres
01.00	2.60 metres
02.00	3.24 metres
03.00	3.81 metres
04.00	4.02 metres
05.00	3.70 metres
06.00	3.12 metres
07.00	2.40 metres
08.00	1.95 metres
09.00	1.68 metres

On seeing her bewildered expression, Karan volunteered, 'Last night at 2.00 a.m., the tide was 3.24 metres high. That was the time when Raymond would have jumped and hanged himself, assuming for a minute that he committed suicide. This picture is taken closer to 9 a.m., when the tide is at its lowest, at 1.68 metres. This also means that the water level at the time Raymond died should be atleast a metre and a half higher than what our picture shows.'

'Why?'

'The difference in tide levels at these two times is 1.56 metres. The water level in the creek tracks quite close to the tide levels and so the difference in water levels in the Vashi creek at these two times would also be on similar lines.'

Kavya's eyes widened. 'Which means, Karan, that if he did hang at 2.00 a.m., and if the water at that time was indeed a metre and a half higher than what this picture shows us, then water would have been up to his neck level. . .if not his neck, then atleast somewhere between his hip and chest. Definitely not lower.'

'Bang on Kavya, proud of you. But if you see this picture, it doesn't look as if the water even touched him. His clothes seem so clean. And Kavya, that is just not possible if he had jumped at 2.00 a.m.'

'That means that the post-mortem is wrong about the time of death.'

'Post-mortems are not often wrong about the time of death. They often mess up the cause of death.'

'Then what could it mean?'

'It can only mean, sweetheart, that he was killed somewhere else at around 2.00 a.m., brought to the spot sometime in the morning, when it was still dark enough to camouflage the heinous act, and made to hang from a rope tied for this specific purpose on the scaffolding, making it look like a suicide. And in the morning, given that the tide would have been low, his feet stayed untouched by the dirty creek water. . .'

'. . .which is why they are clean and not muddied.'

'Yes. That's what I can make out.'

'Oh my God!'

'Had he genuinely hung from that spot, his cervical vertebrae would have broken, and there would have been footprints on the scaffolding and some green dirty water and weed stains on his trousers—the Vashi creek is really, really muddy, mind you. In Raymond's case none of the above has come into play. It can only mean dear, that he was killed and it was made to look like a suicide. Unfortunately no one is interested in finding out the truth, because there are no stakeholders for Raymond.'

'Fabulous analysis.' When they heard this, both of them turned around. Indrani was standing in the doorway; she had overheard every bit of the conversation. 'Karan, this morning I was worried, wondering if I did the right thing by placing the reputation of the bank in your hands. But after hearing this conversation, I am convinced that I haven't made any mistake here. Well done.'

'Thanks Indrani.'

'Just remember we are running short of time. We need to get to the bottom of this quickly. The more I listen to you guys, the more worried I get.'

'Don't worry Indrani. We will figure this out by tomorrow.' Karan had no clue how he was going to crack this by the next day. But he was confident that something would show itself up.

'Okay guys. Let me know if you want anything from me.'

'Sure Indrani.'

'And mind you Karan', Indrani said just before she stepped out of the boardroom, back into her own terrain, 'Raymond has stakeholders. Once we have put this behind us, I will take it up with whoever I have to, to make sure that Raymond's killers, if what you are saying is right, don't go unpunished.'

Karan looked up. He had a nervous smile on his face. 'Thanks Indrani.' The CEO of GB2 smiled back before shutting the door. It was now just the two of them in the room.

'Okay, now that we are sure that Raymond was killed, and that Asia Logistics was a benami account, there has to be something linking the two. My gut says that our hypothesis has to be true. And Kavya, if there is something linking the two of them, it has to show up in the statement.' He picked up the transaction summary of Asia Logistics' current account and started going through it.

'What a fucking bastard he is!' He exclaimed, partly out of anger and partly out of frustration.

'Language, Karan!'

'Hmm. . . This guy has brought in ten crores in the last three months—all through overseas remittances and has withdrawn about eight crores in cash from all over the country.'

'I saw that Karan.'

'And the withdrawals have been made from all over the country—largely through branches in Kolkata, Mumbai, Chennai, Cochin and Delhi.'

'Cochin?' Kavya asked, surprised that she hadn't noticed this when she had seen the transactions.

'Yes. There have been large withdrawals from Cochin. I'm surprised no one noticed.'

'The branch is supposed to report large cash withdrawals to head office and even report suspicious transactions to the Reserve Bank. Wonder how no one highlighted it?' Kavya showed off her knowledge of banking processes and then after a moment's thought added, 'Maybe they did. All their reporting on suspicious transactions would go to Raymond right? Raymond is not here

to tell us about it.' Karan's eyes were firmly fixed on the transaction sheet.

'When was the last withdrawal from the Cochin branch?' Kavya asked him.

'Let me see. . .Today!'

'Today?' Kavya was surprised.

'Yes Kavya, today. There has been a cash withdrawal at around ten o'clock this morning. This transaction dump has been taken off the system at 11.04 a.m. and the last transaction in the account has been before that. . .and that too, from Cochin. In fact there has been a strange lull in this account. For the last ten days there have been heavy withdrawals. Prior to that there has been no cash withdrawal from Cochin in over a month.' He was quiet for a couple of minutes. Kavya could make out that he was doing some calculations. 'Over three crores of cash withdrawn from Cochin in the last two months. Very strange.'

'What do we do?'

'Call the Branch Manager Kavya. Tell him you are calling from the compliance team. Out station branches normally don't know the junior blokes in the Head Office teams. So they will believe you and will not realize that you are lying. Ask them how they allowed someone to withdraw over three crores in cash over the last two months. Why was it not reported?'

'Arre. . .you just said that it's possible that they have reported it, and Raymond is not here to tell you about it. If we ask someone else in the compliance team about it, they will tell us. Why go through this façade?'

'We don't have time to go through all that. In case they have reported these cash withdrawals as suspicious, they will say so. In case they haven't, but they know something about this, they will tell us. Even if they don't know anything, atleast we will know that they fucked up.'

'I'm calling them right now. In case they reported anything suspicious, I will ask them to forward the details to Jacqueline's ID.'

'Super.'

Karan went back to the transactions in the account for clues. There was something that was wrong in the statement. But it was eluding him. He removed his shoes, pulled a chair next to him and put his feet up on it. Hands supporting his head from behind, he stretched a bit, eyes wandering all over the room, but staring at nothing. The projector, the screen, the Bose speakers, the cherry wood panelling, the anti-fire sprinklers, the brightly lit fluorescent bulb, the smoke detectors, the security cameras, the square cut panelled roof. . .Suddenly he straightened up. 'Security cameras!' he exclaimed. His eyes were wide open. He was now staring at one thing and only one thing.'Why didn't I think of it earlier?'

He quickly ran to Jacqueline's desk. Kavya was already making the call. Seeing him approach, she put the call on hold. 'All okay?'

'Yes Yes. All okay.' He had hardly dashed for twenty metres, but he was panting as if he had run a marathon. The excitement was getting to him. 'The security cameras,' he said pointing to the one in Jacqueline's room.

'What about them?' Jacqueline suddenly jumped in. 'They are working.'

'No no. Not these Jacqueline. There will surely be security cameras installed at the cash counters in Cochin. Ask them to stream the images that the security camera captured around the time the cash was withdrawn from Asia Logistics. We can see who withdrew the cash from the bank. That might give us some clues.'

'Oh. Cool. Good stuff.' Kavya was proud that she was in love with this man, who was proving to be more of a private investigator than a banker. Karan returned to the boardroom, leaving Kavya to make the call in peace.

In five minutes, Kavya was back in the conference room.
'They don't have it.'

'What?'

'They don't have the videos that the camera captured.'

'What crap? They are supposed to retain them for some time.
It's a requirement as per global norms. At least, it used to be so
when I was the Branch Manager. Unless things have changed now.'

'Yes Karan,' Kavya replied, patiently. 'The video is streamed
centrally these days. Branches don't store the videos. The Central
Security Team in Mumbai will have them. Jacqueline is talking
to them to get it. We should have it in about 20-30 minutes.'

'Oh wow. You are wonderful Kavya.'

'Thanks Karan. I know that.'

'And what about the reporting of the high value cash
transactions? What did they have to say on that?'

'I asked them. Told them that I am calling from Indrani's
office. Didn't lie to them that I am in compliance.'

'In fact, calling from Indrani's office must have given you a
greater leverage,' Karan smiled.

'Yes. And you know what? They gave me a very strange
response. The branch manager told me that they didn't raise a
suspicious transaction report when the Asia Logistics guys
withdrew huge amounts of cash because they were told that the
account was opened with Vikram's reference.'

'And who told them that?'

'Zinaida, the RM who opened the account. It was also
corroborated by the branch manager, Anand Shastri.'

'Does this mean the entire money laundering scheme is being
run with the connivance of such senior employees? Is Vikram
involved? Oh shit.'

'Hold on hold on. Let's not jump to conclusions. I am getting
scared here. Hope I don't lose my job after the dust settles on
this.'

'Unless Zinaida and Anand lied. But why would they?' Karan completely ignored the other concern raised by Kavya.

A mail popped up on Kavya's screen. It was from Jacqueline. 'Here, the details of the sixty-eight accounts have come.'

'Okay, move. Let me see. These are accounts where huge sums of money have come in from overseas and all of it has been taken out through cash withdrawals. Right?'

'Yes. Yes. Yes. . .for the umpteenth time. . .YES! Transactions of all these accounts, scanned copies of account opening forms and everything else that you might need.' Kavya frowned. 'Wish I had that much cash to withdraw from my account.'

'Hehe, I am sure one day you will Kavya.' And Karan hugged her. Kavya pushed him away. 'Security cameras dumbo.'

They got down to reviewing the documentation related to the sixty-eight accounts. As in the case of Asia Logistics, in all these accounts, the documentation was perfect. Account opening forms filled up perfectly, KYC in place, visit report by RMs in place. Everything done as per procedure. . .but there was one fact which was intriguingly common across all these accounts—they had a HOLD instruction for all communication from the bank.

Karan scrolled to the list of RMs managing these accounts, 'Let's see the RM list. I wonder if any of them were around when I was with GB2. Hmm. . .Ram Sharma. . .don't know him. . .Gulqbal. . .don't know him. . .Ramesh Yadav. . .don't know him. . .Abhijeet Bhandekar. . .never heard of him. . .Zinaida Gomes. . .we just heard of her,' and he looked up and smiled at Kavya. 'There is no common thread in the names or branches of these RMs. They are spread all over,' Karan said, thinking aloud.

'You think there is merit in looking at these RMs in detail? Their backgrounds, their performance appraisals etc?' Kavya asked.

'I don't know. But there's no harm in it. Ask for their personal files from HR. Let's see if there is anything common in their backgrounds.'

'I'll tell Jacqueline.'

In no time, a representative from HR came up with some fifty files.

'Why so many? We needed the files pertaining to only thirteen RMs na?' Karan was surprised to see so many files being piled into the room.

Yes, but if I had asked for just thirteen files from HR, they might have suspected something. So I added some other names to the list and asked for all their files. No one will know who we are looking at.'

'Smart,' said Karan, impressed.

'Learning from you sir,' Kavya just smiled.

Karan picked out the files of the thirteen RMs and walked to a corner of the room. He wanted to go through them and evaluate for himself whether they were working as a consortium. Any trends there would give him some clues.

Kavya was collating some of the other reports that Karan had asked her to put together. Out of sheer curiosity, for one last time, she picked up the transaction sheet pertaining to Asia Logistics and cursorily glanced through it. 'Karan, isn't something wrong here?'

Karan looked up at Kavya with raised eyebrows.

'How likely is it that a non-Muslim religious foundation transfers funds to Asia Logistics, a firm held by Muslims—Asad Ansari and the other guy, whose name I keep forgetting?'

'Very unlikely, why? But anything is possible, given the fraudulent nature of the Asia Logistics account.'

'Almost all the amount that has come into the account of Asia Logistics is via a boutique bank in Liechtenstein. And that too from an account of UJF which stands for the Union of Jews Foundation.'

'I saw that. The statement mentions that the remittance has come in from UJF. How do you know it's the Union of Jews Foundation? It could be anything.'

'I know. The statement of Asia Logistics doesn't mention it. But look at this account in Delhi, which is one of the sixty-eight suspected accounts. The credits into this account are from the account of the Union of Jews Foundation, and have come in through the same bank in Liechtenstein. I am just co-relating it with the Asia Logistics account—Liechtenstein, remittances, money laundering etc. there is too much in common. In this background, UJF can't be anything but the Union of Jews Foundation. While making the data entry for their respective accounts, the person who does the data entry for Mumbai accounts would have been lazy and entered the abbreviation UJF in the account of Asia Logistics.'

'Yes Kavya. You are right. This is the Union of Jews Foundation. Why would the UJF transfer money to these accounts?' and after a pause added, 'Unless it's a scam. And the fact that it is coming from a bank in Liechtenstein does raise a few eyebrows.'

'As in?'

'You know what Liechtenstein is popular for. This tiny country sandwiched between Austria and Switzerland owes much of its wealth to its reputation as a tax haven. I've heard that drug lords from Columbia, Mexico and other countries have often used Liechtenstein as a base to launder money, till one day they were exposed.'

'Hmm. . .'

'Even now it's a known haven for launderers and tax evaders. Anyway, now that you point it out and we know that money has come from the Union of Jews Foundation, we have only one hope of finding out where they are located.'

'Google?' Kavya asked innocently.

'Arre no re. The Foreign Inward Remittance Certificate (FIRC). It should have the address of the remitter. A FIRC is normally given to all bank customers who get inward remittances into their account from overseas. The FIRC has all the details of the transaction, including the name and address of the remitter. Why don't you call remittances and ask them for a copy of the FIRC?'

'I don't think that will be necessary. A copy of the FIRC goes to the customer too. Since all these accounts have correspondence on HOLD, the remittance certificate would in all probability have been sent to the branches instead of the customer. I'll call the Bandra branch and ask them to fax the latest Inward Remittance certificate. If they don't have it, I'll call the remittances department.'

'Sounds great to me.'

The FIRC was in the Bandra Branch. It took them just five minutes to locate it and fax it across to Jacqueline.

'There you go,' she said as she walked in and handed over the certificate to Karan.

'What the bloody hell?' Karan saw the name and address of the remitter and nearly fell off his chair. He looked really shocked. 'Is this what killed Harshita?' And he stared at Kavya who was staring back at him, puzzled. Dazed, he looked back at the sheet of paper and said, 'It probably did!'

33

Schottenring, an area situated between the historic city centre and Alsergrund in downtown Vienna, is well known for the stock exchange. It also houses the Office of the President of Vienna Police.

Sitting in his office in Schottenring, Johann Schroeder was ecstatic when Richard Anderson came to meet him. When the latter had first come to the office of Vienna's President of Police, he was shooed away. No one allowed him to see the president or his deputy. He had somehow managed to get the email ID of Schroeder and had sent him a mail requesting for a meeting, mentioning the agenda. So compelling was the reason for his request that Schroeder had called off a few meetings to accommodate him. That explained why Richard Anderson was sitting in front of him that morning.

The Deputy to the President of Police stared calmly at Richard, who looked rather meek in his presence. Richard, who was of Indian origin, was a young guy in his mid-twenties who aspired to be a body-builder, but had nothing done about his aspirations, as evidenced by his waistline.

'So you sell coffee?'

'No sir. I don't sell coffee, I work in a café.' Anderson was a bit irritated at this comment from Schroeder. It took a lot of courage to say it the way he said it.

'It's one and the same thing,' Schroeder retorted. 'So tell me what happened.'

'Sir, it was quite late in the night. The last customer had left. And there was hardly any traffic on Ringstrasse. There were three of us in the café at that time. Two of my colleagues and I.'

'What time was it?'

'Around 1.15 or 1.30 a.m.'

'What were you doing in the café at that hour?'

'The café closes at 1.00 a.m. After that it takes us about an hour to close our accounts, upload data for the day to our central server in Bengaluru in India, clear up everything in the café and get it back in shape for opening in time for breakfast the next day. And being on Ringstrasse, we get a good crowd in the morning, so we open early.'

'Okay, keep going.'

'We were just about finishing our routine when we heard someone banging on the grill. It was a couple. They seemed to be in duress. Very hassled. Panting as if they had been running. I recognized them as the same couple that had come to the store a few hours back, in the evening. A cute Indian couple. They had spent over an hour at my store browsing the Internet and talking to a few friends over a cup of coffee.'

'That's fine. Tell me what happened,' Schroeder said, gruffly.

'By the time we could get the key from inside and open the grill, they had left. We saw a Lamborghini parked in the parking lot outside the café and three guys pointing towards our outlet. And then one of them came running towards the café. Thankfully he didn't come towards us but went running in the direction that the couple had disappeared to.'

'Hmm. . .' Johann's eyes were focused on Richard Anderson and didn't leave him even for a second. This was making Richard sweat a bit. He was wondering if he had made the right decision in coming to Johann Schroeder.

'That was the last I saw of them. Within a few minutes the Lamborghini drove off, and two more burly men headed off in the same direction as the first one. They were relatively relaxed.'

'Were any images captured on the CCTV camera?'

'We have security cameras outside the café, to capture movements at night. But. . .'

'But what?'

'The video is too dark. The lights outside the café were not on. And so the figures are unrecognizable.'

'Okay.' Johann was getting a bit irritated. 'So?' He was wondering why Richard was there and what it was that he had to offer.

Richard fumbled a bit and pulled out a pen drive from the right pocket of his trousers. 'This has the video from the security cameras. I am not sure this will be of much help, but I wanted to hand it over to you sir.'

'Thanks, I will ask someone to look into it. Is there anything else you want to tell me?'

'Sir, I'm not sure if this is of help, but I also brought along the bill that they had rung up that day. Just in case you asked for it.' He reached into his bag kept by the side of the antique wooden chair he was sitting on and pulled out the bill.

Schroeder, stretched his right hand out and took the thin piece of thermal paper from Richard's hand. He looked at it carefully. 'Two Espresso Macchiatos, one plain and one with hazelnut flavour, a double choco muffin, a chicken sandwich, a bottle of clear water, two more Espresso Macchiatos.' He read out the bill sarcastically. What use would it be to him to know that the killed Indians had a basic espresso with milk foam six to seven hours before they died? He wanted to throw Richard out for having wasted his time, but he was not the regular, arrogant cop. He was the human face of the Vienna police. When he had agreed to meet Richard, he did harness hopes of being able to solve the case. No longer. 'Thanks Richard. I'm glad that, as a responsible resident of Vienna, you came forward to help with whatever information you had. Thank you.' Richard knew it was an indication that their conversation was over.

Johann got up and forced a smile on his face. Richard had taken the effort to tell him all he knew. There was no point being critical of him. He held out his right hand to shake Richard's hand, and with his left he brought up the café bill to his eye level. *Your two cups of Macchiato have cost me twenty minutes of my critical time, Mr Lele*, he thought, as he stared at the bill. Richard turned and started walking towards the door. Schroeder settled into his chair, wondering how and what they were going to do to resolve the case.

He tossed the bill nonchalantly on to the reams of paper on his table and casually watched it float and finally settle on his table a few feet away from him. As it flew down and came to rest in front of him, something caught his eye. Immediately his right hand reached out and picked up the paper. He stared at it, but couldn't make out anything. Switching on the table lamp, he held the cheque against the lamplight. And then he shouted for Anderson, who by then had stepped out into the corridor. Richard turned and headed back into the room.

'There seems to be something here.'

'Pardon me?'

'Look, there is something here.'

Richard stared at it but couldn't make out anything. 'Alright, wait here. I will be back.' Johann stepped out of his cabin, walked up to his assistant's table and asked her to bring a pencil and a parer to his room. In no time he had a new pencil and a battery-operated pencil sharpener on his desk. 'Sit down', he thundered when he saw that Richard was still standing. 'Tell me, what do you do with the bills once the customer pays?'

'Sir, the moment we pick it up from the customer, it is taken to the cash counter where it is placed in the tray below the counter and it stays there till end of day, when all the accumulated bills are taken to our back office. At the back office, the entire bundle is placed in a box and sent for storing. Occasionally someone tallies these to see if any bill is missing. Even if it is, it doesn't matter, because we have our system records to go by.'

All this while, Johann was sharpening the pencil. Richard was bewildered at what he was doing, because he had shaved almost half the pencil off, without really making use of it. The lead particles and the wood shavings were soiling his table, but that didn't seem to bother him. Once he reached two-thirds into the pencil, Johann stopped. He carefully picked up the wooden shavings and threw them away, stopping to make sure that the black lead particles attached to the wooden shavings stayed on his tabletop.

Putting aside his laptop and all the other accessories in front of him, he carefully laid out the Café Coffee Day bill on his table. With the air of an expert, he collected all the lead particles into a heap on the right side of the bill. Richard Anderson was wondering what Schroeder was up to.

Schroeder scooped the lead particles into his hand and scattered them over one corner of the bill. With his right hand, he carefully and softly spread the lead dust all over the bill. 'I was in forensics before I moved in here, son. So relax,' he said looking at a confused Richard and for the first time that day, he was smiling. He lifted the bill and jerked his hand softly to shake off the remnants of the lead particles from the paper and placed the bill back on the table. He blew on it and the last vestiges of the lead disappeared from the bill. He now picked it up and held it against the light as both Schroeder and Richard peered at it.

'Wow', Richard exclaimed. 'What is that?' Something was scribbled on the bill which could now clearly be seen.

Schroeder ignored the question. 'Now think clearly and tell me the sequence of events when they came for coffee in the afternoon.'

'Sir I told you everything I knew. After ordering coffee, the lady got onto Skype. She was speaking to someone, I think from India, because at times they spoke in Hindi, the local language spoken by most Indians. And then she asked me for a piece of paper. I thought she was asking for a bill and took it to her. She told me that she wanted a blank piece of paper. In the rush to give her the paper, I just pulled a blank tab of thermal paper from the scroll on the bill printer and took it to her. She wrote down something on it, I think it was an address. She said something like, she was going to check out something. After finishing the call, both of them left.'

'Hmm. . .that explains it.'

'What sir?'

'You see this?' And Johann held up the bill. Richard stared at it as if his life depended on it. He could vaguely see something scribbled on the paper. 'Strange. How come I didn't see this earlier?'

'Because it was not visible to you. In fact it would not have been. . .to anyone. When she asked you for a paper to scribble on, you first gave her the bill and then a blank paper. She kept the blank paper on top of the bill and wrote down something. Given that your bill printer uses a thermal paper, which is extremely thin, whatever she wrote on the blank paper left an impression on the bill. The tip of the pen you gave her to write with was obviously hard enough to have left an impression on the bill below. The impressions were not clearly visible to the naked eye. But when held against light, the impressions appeared darker than the rest of the paper. When I spread out black pencil dust on the paper, it gave texture to the impression and whatever was written became visible immediately.' Schroeder spoke at the speed of light. He now seemed like a man on a mission.

'Oh wow.' Schroeder had made it sound so simple.

Schroeder quickly called the chief of police of Central Vienna district, 'I want you and a team of four cars outside my office in the next five minutes. We are going on a search operation. Move out, now. We don't have much time,' he barked over the phone.

He looked at Richard. 'Thanks Richard. You have been very helpful. Hope something comes out of it now.'

The Chief of Central Vienna Police was outside Schroeder's office with four cars, each containing a team of three trained officers in tow, within the committed five minutes. Schroeder joined them in a jiffy. 'Let's go!' he ordered. 'We have a solid lead. If we get this one, we crack the Lele deaths.'

'What's the lead sir?'

'We have the address where the Leles might have gone that night.' And he told him the entire story. 'The address has been scribbled onto their bill. Vienna Police might just be able to maintain its stellar record.'

34

That afternoon, Hemant, accompanied by the ACP, walked into Indrani's office. Jacqueline asked them to wait in the visitor's room while she spoke with Indrani, who at that time was with Karan. Karan was briefing her about what they had found thus far.

'Karan, would you like to join me?' asked Indrani. Over the last few hours Indrani herself was beginning to wonder why she trusted Karan so much, and that too over her own teams. For her own interests, she wished that Karan would be able to solve this issue.

Within a couple of minutes, Indrani, with Karan in tow, walked into the visitors' room. Never having met Karan, Hemant assumed he was an executive assistant to Indrani.

'Indrani, we happened to stumble across something today.' And Hemant narrated the entire issue of the credit card fraud at the mall. 'Now we come to the most critical part.'

'Yes?' Indrani was all ears. She glanced at Karan, who was busy taking notes. The journalistic streak in him was intact.

'The credit card that we picked up belonged to Pranesh Rao, the teller with the Bandra Branch who died sometime mid-last year.'

'Really?' Indrani's eyes widened and her eyebrows almost disappeared into her hair, anxiety writ all over her face. Somehow, the way things had been going over the last couple of days, she knew that something worse was to come.

'And Lyndon, the guy we picked up, has confessed to. . .'

'Confessed to what, Hemant?'

'Confessed to having killed Pranesh.'

'What?' Indrani nearly fell off her chair. 'Killed Pranesh? Oh my God. I thought it was a road accident.'

'Indrani. It was not a normal road accident. He was killed. Knocked down intentionally by a speeding truck. The merciless guys who knocked him down stopped to check if he was dead before they moved on. Lyndon was one of the guys. When they got off the truck to check if he was dead, Lyndon stole his credit card. They didn't steal the wallet, else it would look like a crime committed for robbery and not a hit and run case.'

'Oh my God,' Indrani's hands had involuntarily moved up to her mouth as she exclaimed. There was fear in her eyes and horror in her voice. She looked at Karan and in a trembling voice, said, 'What the hell is going on?'

The ACP answered. 'Apparently they were lying in wait for Pranesh to pass through the lonely stretch before knocking him down. In fact, that's what helped us nail him. Lyndon's cell phone GPS showed that he was in the area for three hours before the incident. And he moved out swiftly once the act was done. When we confronted him with the GPS records, he couldn't say much. He broke down and confessed. He has given up the names of all his accomplices. Search teams have been sent to pick them up. But our experience in such cases has been that these guys are just the hired muscle. The brain behind all this is surely someone else. Secondly, there is no way for us to get to know the motive, and only once we have the motive can we get to the bottom of this.'

'Indrani, may I?' intervened Karan. Indrani just nodded.

'Maybe he was killed because he knew too much about something.'

'About what?' The ACP asked.

'Don't know. That's what we are trying to find out. I am not too sure if you know, but a compliance officer of the bank was found dead this morning. Also, a Relationship Manager was mysteriously found dead in what was presumably a road accident in Vienna. This could be a part of one big scam. We don't know yet. But soon we will find out.'

The ACP looked at Karan suspiciously. 'He is helping me sort out a few things internal to the bank,' Indrani volunteered.

'Sure,' said the ACP as he got up. Looking at Hemant he said, 'Maybe you can give them the details. I will have to head back. Have to report this new development before I leave for home.' The ACP shook hands with them and left. Indrani turned and looked at Hemant. 'Now that you know what's going on, please help Karan and Kavya through this.' Hemant looked at her blankly. Karan took his arm and led him inside the conference room. It was time for a quick debriefing.

35

Early evening, after Sulochana's sermon to Krishna, she left him alone to reminisce on his easy chair, and went to the nearby temple—a routine that she had followed every single day since they had moved to Devikulam. Krishna sat there for a long time wondering what had gone wrong. He had set out to do some good for the people in the neighbourhood. The ill fate that had befallen him over two decades ago should not come upon anyone else in Devikulam. That was all he wanted. Was that a crime?

Jayakumar's ascendency in the protest-related matters had caused him a fair bit of grief. Not because he was now beginning to hog the limelight, something which even Sulochana thought was the reason for the rift, but because the agenda Jayakumar had was completely divergent from his. While Krishna wanted the well-being of people in the neighbourhood, Jayakumar wanted favours. The latter had a political agenda, which if met, would not only signal the end of Jaya's role in the protest, but the protest itself.

It could also not be ignored that the protest had really gathered steam and got noticed both by the local and national media only after Jaya's NGO had backed the protest. Whether it was the aftermath of the Fukushima disaster that got the press to notice TNPP or it was the financial muscle of CNRI, he wasn't too sure.

But after hearing multiple conversations that Jaya had had with people across, he was shattered. He had to distance the protest from Jaya's agenda before it was too late.

He picked up his phone—an old Nokia handset. He stared at it for a long time while confusing and contrary thoughts churned through his mind at a feverish pace. Should he or shouldn't he? Finally, he decided to go ahead and make the call. Selecting a contact on the phone, he dialled the number.

'Times Today, Mumbai,' someone picked up the telephone at the office of the most popular TV News channel in the country.

'Can I speak to Mohit Sengupta?'

'Who should I say is calling?'

'Krishna Menon. I am calling from Devikulam and it is regarding the protest against the Trikakulam Nuclear Power Plant.'

36

Hemant's debriefing took about fifteen minutes. When he walked in, Hemant had wondered as to why Indrani had preferred an outsider to investigate what was internal to the bank, and not handed it over to the fraud control team. When he heard the entire story, however, his doubts vanished.

Kavya was patiently waiting for Karan to finish. The moment he was through, she butted in, 'Karan, the CCTV feed for the Cochin branch has come in. Do you want to see it now?'

'Do we have an option Kavya?'

'I would love to have one, but unfortunately I don't.' The banter between Karan and Kavya was flirtatious but for Hemant, who had no clue about their relationship, it was a bit strange.

'Hemant, I had asked for the Cochin CCTV footage to figure out who had withdrawn money from the account of Asia Logistics from the branch in Cochin this morning.' Hemant nodded.

The video started playing on Kavya's laptop. The security camera was placed high up on the ceiling, behind the cash queue and facing the cashier. So when a customer walked towards the cashier his back was towards the cashier. The idea was to encapsulate every single thing happening at the cash counter. If ever a customer made a suspicious move, the security camera would capture it.

Like most other branches, GB2 opened its branches at 9.00 a.m. As per the transaction report, the cash withdrawal from the Asia Logistics account had occurred at 10.06 a.m. Kavya kept forwarding the CCTV footage till the overlaid clock in the video showed a time of 9.57 a.m. and then she played back at normal speed. The cash counter was empty.

9.58 a.m.: The first customer, a lady walks in. She walks up to the counter, hands over some documents and leaves.

'Looks like a normal transaction,' Karan observed.

9.58 a.m.: Three customers walk up to yellow line before the cash counter, waiting for their turn. Their backs are clearly visible. But their faces are turned towards the counter. The cashier is not at the counter.

'Probably gone for a comfort break,' Karan whispered, and suddenly wondered why he was whispering. It was not as if the people in the branch would hear them.

9:59 a.m.: The cashier returns to his station and one customer walks up to the counter. The other two patiently wait for their turn.

10.00 a.m.: The cashier again gets up from his station, probably to check on something to do with the cheque. Returns in thirty seconds. He hands over the cheque to the customer, who turns it around and signs it. The cashier hands him the cash and the customer turns. His face is now clearly visible.

'Is he the guy?' Karan was excited. 'No Karan, our transaction took place at 10.06. Its only 10.02 now,' Kavya pointed out.

10.02 a.m.: The next customer walks up to the teller counter. The cashier is busy doing something on his computer and doesn't even look at the customer. The customer keeps a cheque on the counter, which the cashier picks up. He says something to the customer. The customer answers back.

'Why don't they build security cameras which capture the audio too? Will make life so easy for us. Who the hell knows what they are saying?' Hemant, like a true fraud control guy, wanted to know everything. 'Life's never perfect, dude.' Hemant just smiled and returned to the video feed.

10.03 a.m.: After a brief chat, the cashier gets up and moves away. He has the cheque in his hand.

'Probably getting it authorized by his supervisor,' Kavya looked at both Hemant and Karan. 'Hmm,' both of them nodded simultaneously.

10.04 a.m.: The cashier returns. Goes though the normal routine of making the customer sign on the back of the cheque. Pulls out cash from a drawer below the counter and passes on bundles of cash to the customer, who puts it in his bag

10.05 a.m.: The customer leaves and the next one walks up to the counter.

'Aaaaah there is our guy,' said Karan. 'Fraud bastard!' exclaimed Kavya. Hemant remained silent.

10.06 a.m.: The customer patiently waits for the cashier to look up from his system and take his cheque. The cashier smiles at him. Accepts the cheque. Looks at the back of the cheque. It's already signed. He pulls out bundles from a cash trunk kept next to his table and hands over cash to the customer.

10.07 a.m.: The customer picks up the cash. Counts the bundles. Puts them in his bag and turns.

'Freeze it there!' shouted Karan.

'That's our man.' Kavya had a grin on her face, as if the issue had been resolved.

'Can we zoom in on his face?' At Karan's request, Kavya took a screen shot and zoomed into the image. It was a bit hazy, but the face could still be seen.

'Who the hell is he?'

'I don't know. We will have to figure that out.'And then he looked at Hemant. 'Is there any way we can figure out who this guy is?'

'Not too sure Karan. But I just saw something. I'm not too sure if you guys noticed it too.'

'What would that be?'

'The cashier smiled at this customer. He didn't smile at the previous two.'

'What does that prove?' asked Karan

'It shows that the customer who the cashier smiled at might be a regular in the Cochin branch,' Hemant argued. He was not convinced that this customer was a fraud. 'We have seen multiple cash withdrawals from the Asia Logistics account from Cochin. So it's possible that this customer is a regular.'

'Yes. That's true. But the cashier smiled and acknowledged this guy. He was also very prompt in giving him the cash. He even gave him multiple bundles without any supervisor authorization. It shows us that the cashier knows him very well. So to me, unless the cashier too is involved in this transaction, there is no way this guy is a fraud.'

'But the transaction has taken place at 10.06 a.m. as per the reports. And this is the guy in the Cochin branch at 10.06.' Kavya had a frown on her face as she explained this to Hemant.

'Can I see the transaction history of the account?' Hemant stretched out his right hand towards Kavya, who promptly handed it over to him. Hemant took a minute to read it.

'Hold on guys,' he exclaimed with a grin on his face and looked up at the two of them. 'The transaction report shows that the cash withdrawal was at 10.06 a.m. That means 10.06 a.m. is the time when the transaction was entered into the system and authorized.'

'Keep talking. . .keep talking. Don't stop', Karan prodded.

'Karan, it means that the transaction happened before 10.06 a.m., but was posted into the system at 10.06 a.m. See this video again,' and he played it again on Kavya's laptop. He also started giving a running commentary.

'When the second customer leaves, it's 10.05 a.m. The third customer walks up to the counter, it's still 10.05 a.m. The cashier is still doing something on the computer. The clock is ticking. It's 10.06 a.m. now. The cashier is still at it. Let's see when he looks up. . . Aahh. . .and now our friend looks up. It's well past 10.06 a.m., very close to 10.07 a.m. All this while our cashier was posting the large value cheque given to him by the second customer. The customer we are looking for, whose entry reflects at 10.06 a.m. is not the third but the second customer.'

'Not bad Hemant. I am glad we have a fraud control guy in our team', complimented Kavya, and that almost instantaneously made Karan jealous. They quickly rewound the tape and looked at the video image of the second customer.

'Wow!' exclaimed Hemant when Kavya froze the frame and took a screen shot of the second customer. 'I haven't seen a better CCTV image in ages.'

'Kavya, can you please print out copies of this picture. Let's see if we can figure out who this guy is?

'Why don't we ask the Cochin branch?' Kavya recommended.

'Let's do that. Hemant, will you please take charge of this?'

'Sure Karan.'

Karan picked up one of the pictures printed out by Kavya and gave it a long and hard stare, as if memorizing the pixel positions in the picture. 'Who are you my friend? Who are you? If I get to you, I will get to the bottom of this mystery. Come on, come on. Show yourself up.'

'Karan,' Kavya interrupted his soliloquy. 'What did you say?'

'Nothing sweetheart, was just wondering who this guy is.'

'We will figure that out. Hemant is on it. By the way, do you want to look at the personal files of the RMs or shall I return them? HR came asking for it. They have to lock it up in a fireproof safe before they leave for the day.'

'Tell them that there is a bigger fire burning here, bigger than anything they've ever seen. Don't return any files. Let them be here.' Karan never liked his thought process to be disturbed.

'Yes, my lord and master,' Kavya retorted, sarcastically.

37

Johann Schroeder and his team made a dash towards Mohrengasse, a block away from Hotel Nestroy, a popular hotel on Rottensterngasse. Mohrengasse was a fairly peaceful street, with some classy residential buildings. Just off the upmarket and posh Mohrengasse was a long stretch of a narrow lane called Odeongasse. A stretch which symbolized the urban microcosm, in Vienna's Leopoldstadt district, was where Schroeder and his team were headed. An overcrowded locality, it was the probably the only part of Vienna which was an unpleasant mix of tiny apartments and offices. It was also, to a certain extent, the underbelly of most of the city's limited criminal activities.

Schroeder's car screeched to a halt in front of a building. Adjacent to that building was a low rise—a three-storied building called Jewish Towers. A scowl formed on Schroeder's face when he saw the name. The four cars stopped in a pattern they were used to. One stopped ahead, one behind Schroeder's car, and one went around the building to the back as a cover in case anyone tried to escape from behind. They seemed to know their job very well. A back-up team was stationed at Hotel Nestroy, just in case help was required.

Schroeder got down from the car and walked towards Jewish Towers. No one stopped them. They entered from the ground floor and walked straight to the lift. Next to the lift was a staircase. Schroeder decided to use the staircase, as he had to go up to the second floor. The building seemed unoccupied.

Under normal circumstances, Schroeder would have left it to his team to manage, but this was a high profile case and he had to make sure that it was quickly resolved. The Austrian police had been acknowledged as the best in Europe, and Johann Schroeder wanted to keep it that way. It was the only way for him to succeed Gerhard Purtsi when the latter retired from his current role in six months.

The stairwell was not lit well, but it was good enough for the team to carry out the operation. Stealthily, they climbed up to the second floor. The door to the unit they were looking for was locked. Outside was a board that said: Union of Jews Foundation. The entire floor was deserted. It was quite strange because the building itself was a mix of private residences and a few office units. In fact, from the look of it, some residence units were being used as an office. The local laws in Vienna permitted such usage.

'Open it,' said Schroeder, looking at one of the officers. An officer got to work and in no time the door was thrown open and they entered the office.

'There is no one here!' cried Schroeder.

'Yes sir.'

'Looks like it's been cleared up very recently,' Schroeder commented as he looked around the room.

'It looks pretty clean to me sir,' the Chief agreed. 'Maybe we should watch it and see if someone comes along.'

'Frederick, look here,' said Schroeder to him, pointing towards something on the floor. It looked like a patch on the carpet.

Schroeder walked close to it, bent down and looked at it himself. 'See this patch?' Frederick nodded. Schroeder looked around, surveying all the tables in the room. 'You will find one such patch below most of the tables in this room, a patch where the carpet seems trodden and weighed down.'

Frederick went closer. There was indeed a patch below most of the tables wherein the carpet was crushed. 'It's as if something was kept on the carpet for a long time.'

'Yes Frederick. This is where their computers were. The weight of the CPU has crushed the carpet, leaving a patch below all the tables. They have shifted out every single CPU in this room. Monitors are there on every table, so are the connecting wires, but where are the CPUs?'

'They have taken them and evacuated,' said Frederick.

'Yes, and it looks like they evacuated in a hurry. They have taken everything with them. They didn't have time to remove just the hard disk, so they took out the entire computer unit,' said Schroeder. He looked around. There was nothing else in the room. No paper, no files. . .nothing. Johann looked at the others in the room and said, 'Pack up guys, you won't find anything here.' He knew the search was going to be futile. 'Send a forensic team to check for any traces.'

As he was heading outside, he stopped at the reception, a couple of feet from the main door. A six-inch high glass screen separated him and the receptionist's desk. He bent over the frosted glass partition and picked up the phone lying on the desk and pressed the redial button. This was the litmus test of any forensic operation. The tone persisted. All phones were wiped clean. All the contacts, all the incoming call details and the outgoing numbers were erased. He was beginning to get worried. Chasing the telephone route would be futile. The calls would have been routed through a complex maze of exchanges and it would be virtually impossible for them to trace the actual number called. What he was seeing here was an organized crime syndicate. If there was nothing to hide, why was everything wiped clean?

A worried Schroeder bent over the glass again to place the telephone instrument back. As he stretched himself over the glass counter, something caught his eye. He walked around the glass to the receptionist's side, bent down and picked it up. 'So we were right. She was here, but why?' He pocketed what he had picked up and quietly walked back into his waiting car and drove back to his office.

Once in his room, he opened his top drawer and pulled out the Café Coffee Day bill that Richard had brought to him and spread it out on the glass on top of his table. The address was very clear. The lead particles were still stuck to the paper. Had they got the address slightly earlier, they could have reached on time. Ruing this fact, he pulled out the piece of paper he had picked up from beneath the reception and spread it out alongside the other one. It was the same handwriting. The same text. In fact Richard had brought him the copy—the paper that had the impression. The original, on which Harshita had actually written down the address, was what he had picked up from the Union of Jews Foundation's office. It would have fallen out of Harshita's hands when she was being chased or maybe being killed. In the process of clearing out, this had been missed. Every criminal leaves behind a clue. This piece of paper was all they had.

38

'Is there anything else you need Karan? I might be leaving in the next half an hour.' When Jacqueline walked in and said this, it suddenly struck Karan that the day was coming to a close. So involved was he with what was going on at GB2 that he had not even told Andy, his boss, that he wouldn't be coming in for the day. Andy would be furious. 'It's fine. When I tell him that I was away for a cause, he will understand,' he said to himself.

'We might be needing a few things Jacks. Is it possible for you stay back with us? Just in case. I'm sorry about it, but we are hard-pressed for time and I really don't know what might come up. We only have time till tomorrow evening.'

'No problem Karan. I will be at my desk. Let me know whenever you need me.'

'Once everyone has left Jacqueline, we would like to inspect Raymond's desk to see if there is something we can find which can be of relevance to this case.'

'I will organize that. Duplicate keys etc.'

'Thanks Jacks.' Jacqueline just smiled and disappeared.

'Sweet lady,' this time Karan said this purposely to irritate Kavya.

Hemant walked in just as Kavya shot Karan a dirty look. 'No luck on the Cochin Guy. The branch does not know who he is.

He came with the cheque, they apparently checked with the Bandra branch, who told them that this customer was a Vikram Bahl reference. So they quietly paid up even though it was a high value transaction.'

'We know that Hemant. What we want to know is whether they know the person who withdrew the funds or not?'

'No they don't.'

'Hmm. . .dead end again.' When Kavya said this, Karan got really worked up. 'Guys we have twenty-four hours to go. I am sure we can arrive at a theory, even if we can't conclusively prove what we are investigating. As of now we don't have even that.'

'Yes baba,' Kavya was irked by this aggressive outburst from Karan. 'I was just stating a fact. Was I talking about giving up?'

Karan smiled. 'I am sorry. I guess it's just the end-of-day syndrome.' Kavya smiled in return. This was what she liked about Karan. He was always quick to apologize and make up.

'Maybe we should speak to Nikhil and see what he has to say on this account. Now that we know that Asia Logistics was a front account for organized fraud, let's find out what went wrong? How did such an account get opened? Maybe we will also get insights into the death. . .or rather, murder of the cashier. I think it is worth the fifteen minutes. What say?'

'Agreed. Let's call him. Ask Jacqueline to tell him that Indrani wants to meet him.'

'Cool,' and Hemant disappeared.

'I have gone through two personnel files of the relationship managers. Another half an hour and I should be through all of them.' Karan was quick to bring them back on course.

'Sure.'

Indrani came in once in the next ten minutes and seeing them working away seriously, she disappeared.

'Kavya,' called out Karan after a prolonged period of silence. 'I have seen six personnel files and there's already a pattern emerging.'

Hemant too walked into the conversation.

Karan continued, 'In all the six files, I have seen something strange. In fact, a couple of things are strange.'

'As in?'

'Like every other large organization, GB2 also performs a formal, third party verification on its employees. They hire an external agency to do the background checks and to validate the information provided by the employees in their résumés. And this is done around the time that they are hired into the organization. As far as I know, GB2 used to do its verification through an external agency called Matrix.'

'Matrix Business Services, yes we use them. You're referring to the Chennai based company right?' Hemant knew them. In his role in fraud management, he often dealt with them.

'Yes, the same blokes.'

'The bank still uses them. We interact with them almost everyday.'

'Great. They are the best in the business. Anyway, I had earlier casually perused a few files from the fifty files that Kavya had managed to get from HR. All the files that I saw from the general lot had the background checks done by Matrix. Till here, it's all fine. The problem is that the six personnel files of the RMs under cloud that I have just gone through don't have the verification report.'

'Doing a verification is a mandatory requirement for HR. It's a Group HR directive—prescribed by Global Head Quarters in Boston,' added Hemant. He was a veteran in the bank and hence knew its processes inside out.

'Then how come these tainted RMs don't have a verification report on file?' Hemant shrugged his shoulders in response.

Karan thought for a moment, 'Hmm. . .There can only be two possibilities. There was a report, but it was negative which is why it was pulled out and hidden. Or, there was no report at all.'

'But you have only seen six files. Maybe it's there in the rest,' Kavya interjected.

'My guess is that if this is not there in the six that I have gone through, it is unlikely that it will be there in the remaining seven.'

'Okay. Let me check with Matrix. I know PC Balasubramanian, the CEO who sits in Chennai. If he has done the verifications, I will ask him to send the reports for all these guys. If he has not done it, then it's obvious: someone has pulled the names out before sending the names of new employees for background checks.' Hemant volunteered. 'That would be great,' Karan smiled.

Hemant was about to walk out of the room when Karan stopped him. 'Wait. Listen to the balance part of my observation and then go.'

'You're making it sound very dramatic Karan,' Kavya said, sounding amused.

'Yes Kavya. It's indeed dramatic. And that's what I want to verify.'

'I'm all ears.'

'The first six RMs that I have seen have all been referred by one individual,' and he paused. 'I want you to glance through the other files quickly and see if what I have observed is true.'

Kavya didn't wait for him to tell her anything else. She pulled out the other files and started hurriedly going through them.

'I am taking a five-minute break,' announced Karan when he saw Kavya busy with the files and Hemant trying to call Bala of Matrix. He desperately wanted the break to recharge his sapping energy cells.

Jacqueline walked in, struggling to balance bottles of coke and a few McDonalds burgers. 'I got a mix of both veg and non-veg. I can see it's going to be a long night.'

'I'm lovin' it', quipped Karan and jumped out of his seat. He took the tray from Jacqueline's hand and kept it on the table on one side of the room.

'SRK slaps ex-friend Farah Khan's husband,' Karan read out a headline on the front page of *The Times of India* that lay on the table. 'What an asshole he is!' he said with intensity only an Indian can display about films. Right next to it was another headline—'Jadeja. IPL's next million dollar baby?' He had an irritated look as he scanned through the article. 'I always hated the guy. If guys like him start making a million dollars in one season, I want my kid to play in the IPL and not test cricket,' he said to himself. After reading the article he looked at Hemant and lamented, 'Looks like cricket and films have taken over the front page of our newspapers.'

'Maybe. I guess commercial needs drive the media these days,' said Hemant. 'By the way, Nikhil is on his way here. I got Jacqueline to call him.'

'Great. Thanks.' He was still reading the article showering lavish praise on Ravindra Jadeja. 'See what closeness to Mahendra Singh Dhoni can do for you?' Karan said, still lost in that article. Hemant was not interested.

'Bala was with someone. He said he will call in five minutes.'

'Bala?'

'P C Balasubramanian, the CEO of Matrix.'

'Oh, right.'

At that very instant, Hemant's phone rang. He looked at the other two.'Bala,' he whispered before picking it up.

'Hemant. . .it's been far too long.'

'Hey junior Rajini,' Hemant always called Bala junior Rajini, thanks to his appearance. Bala looked like a pint-sized version of the South Indian superstar Rajinikant. 'Bala, I need some help.'

'When you called me at this hour, I knew you needed help. Tell me.'

'I am sending you a list of thirteen names. I need to know if you have done the verification for these guys, and if so, I need the verification reports.'

'Sorry, Hemant, but I can't give it to you.'

'Bala, I need it desperately.'

'I can only give it to authorized personnel from GB2. I have a business to run, a reputation to protect. Unless GB2 gives me specific instructions, you won't get it out of me.'

'Authorised personnel?'

'Yes, there are only certain people in HR who are authorised to deal with us.'

'Is Indrani one of them?'

'Indrani? The CEO?'

'Yes.'

'Are you kidding Hemant? If Indrani says something how can I not do it? She is my karta dharta, my all-in-all.'

'Great! You will get a mail from Indrani in the next five minutes with these names. I need the reports tonight.'

'What? Tonight? Hemant, it's already well past seven.'

'Bala, it's an emergency. We need it. I know you can do it. There's no one I have met who is more resourceful than you.'

'I will wait for instructions from Indrani, and then I will do my best.'

'Thanks Bala.'

Hemant looked at Karan. 'Now please stop reading the newspaper and send him the message from Indrani's ID asap. Bala will send all the information we need, tonight. I know him well enough.'

Kavya saw Karan looking dejected. He had just taken a breather. 'I will send it,' she volunteered and got up.

'Just kidding Kavya. I will do it. Don't bother,' and Hemant smiled. 'Thanks,' added Karan, who followed it up with an instruction. 'And please guys, let me read one article in the newspaper in peace. And that too in my own newspaper.' He desperately needed a break. Kavya would take about ten minutes to finish her analysis. She had to go through all the personnel files.

The other big story on the front page was the Times of India starting off their Cochin edition. February 1st was the day the Cochin launch had been planned. He was a part of the core project team, which had been put together for the launch. His chest swelled up a few inches with pride. From the time he led the GB2 fraud investigation a few years back, life had not been the same for him. He turned the page. A few Mumbai stories on page three—rapes, murders, corruption, drugs. . .the usual. He moved on. By the time he reached page eleven, he was just skimming subconsciously through the pages. However, something on the page caught his attention. He folded the newspaper around the article and began reading it. His eyes widened; he knew what he had just seen would have a huge bearing on their resolving the case.

39

The phone at Krishna Menon's residence rang a good ten times before it got picked up that evening.

'Mr Menon?'

'Speaking.'

'Mr Menon I'm calling from Times Today. Mr Sengupta would like to talk to you. Can I connect you now?' and without waiting for his response, the lady transferred the line to Mohit Sengupta.

'Mr Menon, how are you?'

'I am fine, thank you.'

'It's a pleasure to talk to you sir. I only heard about your call a few minutes ago. Tell me sir. . .'

'Yes Mr Sengupta. I called up a while ago. Something has been seriously bothering me for the last few days. And I wanted to discuss it with you.'

For the next ten minutes Krishna spoke and Mohit Sengupta heard him out. For once, the latter was quiet and didn't interrupt. Once Menon was done, he took over. There was palpable excitement in his voice, an energy, which was lacking at the start of the call.

'I have a suggestion Mr Menon. One of the most popular shows on our channel is *The Big News Debate*. If you are fine with it, we can get you on the show to talk about this. There will be other panellists too who will speak on the same issue, but it will be largely your show. You will get an opportunity and an audience to say whatever you want to. And we can do that tonight.'

'But won't it be too late to catch today's debate? It's already seven'

'No sir. It can be managed. In fact, it's a live show. We go on air at 9.00 p.m. sharp. Luckily I have an Outdoor Broadcast (OB) van stationed in Devikulam, which had been sent there to cover the anti-TNPP protests. That van can hook you up from your home. Does this sound acceptable to you sir?'

'Yes sounds good. I will be able to structure my thoughts by then.' Krishna was elated at this quick and positive response from Times Today.

'Thanks. My team will be in touch. I will hook you up at 8.55 p.m. and we will go live at 9.00 p.m.'

The moment he hung up, Mohit went into a frenzy. He had a big story, which he wanted to break. The best part about it was that he had exclusive access to this scoop. His research team went berserk trying to put together a briefing note for the programme. Panellists had to be gathered, questions had to be readied, background work had to be done and they were going live in two hours. How the two hours passed, no one at Times Today knew.

At 8.58 p.m., Mohit was in the anchor's chair, all the panellists were wired and connected, waiting, ready to go live. The opening montage began playing, indicating that the programme had started. The teleprompter for Mohit flickered a bit and came on.

'Good evening friends. We are back again tonight on your favourite channel Times Today with your favourite show, *The*

Big News Debate. Today, we bring you an exclusive. You will see and hear this for the first time on your own channel. This is breaking news, and as usual, Times Today will be the first to bring it to you. The controversial Indo-Russian project—the Trikakulam Nuclear Power Plant seems to be headed for yet another controversy now. This time it's the team protesting against the TNPP which is courting trouble. Times Today brings to you an exclusive story about the rift in the core team leading the protests against the commissioning of the TNPP. You are hearing it for the first time on your own channel Times Today.' In true Mohit Sengupta manner, he raised his pitch and introduced the panellists. 'On our panel tonight is Mr Krishna Menon, the individual with guts of steel who has been battling the TNPP for over a decade. A resort owner in Devikulam, Mr Menon has been at the forefront ever since the government decided to commission a nuclear plant in his neighbourhood. Mr Menon tragically lost his elder son in the nuclear disaster in Chernobyl, twenty-five years ago. Thank you, Mr Menon, for joining us on the show.

Apart from Mr Menon we also have Mr Jayakumar, the president of CNRI—Conservation of Natural Resources through Innovative use of Technology, an NGO that works in rural India in the field of conservation of natural resources. His NGO has been actively involved with Mr Menon in the protests against TNPP. Out third guest tonight is Mr Moinuddin, retired DGP of Devikulam district. We also have on our panel, Mr Madan Mohan, social worker and MLA from Devikulam. Mr Madan Mohan is currently an independent MLA from the region and like most of the residents of the Devikulam catchment is a staunch critic of the TNPP. We are happy to have you on this debate gentlemen.'

A chorus of 'thank yous' erupted from all the four guests.

'We will begin by asking Mr Jayakumar, sir why are you hell-bent on stalling the nuclear plant? What will you gain by it? The viewers want to know from you today—what is your motivation? Power cuts in the four southern states will be a thing of the past. The whole country will benefit from the energy that the plant is expected to generate. Won't it? It is slated to be the most state-of-the-art facility built with Russian collaboration. That's not all. The government has spent close to three billion dollars on it already. Would you want that to go down the drain Mr Jayakumar?'

'Mohit, no amount of money is more precious than the lives of thousands of innocent individuals. All of us have seen what has happened in Japan. We do not want a repeat of that.' He went on to give the reasons for the protest against the plant.

Hardly had he completed his first point, when Mohit interrupted, 'I can see Mr Menon shaking his head. Mr Menon wants to say something. Mr Menon. Mr Menon, can you hear me. . . Please go ahead.'

'Mohit, if you look at it from the perspective of the people of the catchment area, all the reasons for the protest against the TNPP are valid. No one can counter those. We have been asking for clarity from the government on various things, which include the site evaluation report. But that has not been forthcoming. So what Mr Jayakumar has been saying about the anti-TNPP protests, all that is true. But I would like to make one thing clear. We are not against the nuclear plant. That's a misconception. We are against the project being shrouded in secrecy. We want transparency. We want the people to be convinced that their interests and lives have been protected.'

'Okay. Mr Menon says that there have been no candid discussions or disclosures about the nuclear plant. Fair point. But Mr Menon, we have been hearing about rifts and ideological clashes between you and Mr Jayakumar. The fact is that you have been involved with the protests for over a decade now, but it is also a fact that your movement has got the necessary impetus and thrust only in the last few months, which coincidentally is the time when Mr Jayakumar stepped in to support you. Tell us today, Mr Menon, is there a rift in the team?'

'Mohit. . .' Jayakumar began, but was interrupted even before he could say anything meaningful. 'We will come to you Mr Jayakumar, but first we will let Mr Menon answer.'

'Yes.' When Menon said this, everyone fell silent. 'There are irreconcilable differences which have cropped up within the team.'

'So what we are hearing about a rift is true. There is indeed a rift, which threatens to jeopardise your movement. This is big breaking news on your channel viewers. No one else has heard of this before and we, your own channel, bring it to you live and exclusive as the story breaks. Mr Menon, go ahead.'

'Yes there is a fissure. I have now decided that if Mr Jayakumar is in the movement, I will not be a part of it.'

'And why would that be?'

'Because I am not convinced about the validity of the force driving the mission at his end.'

'Mr Menon, you are playing with words. What is the true story? Our viewers are waiting to hear from you.'

'There are multiple reasons. First and foremost, I have a serious issue with the motivation behind Jayakumar joining the movement. The source of funds driving the movement is also suspect. I have a suspicion that dirty money is flowing into this movement to embarrass the government into submission.'

'That is a very big accusation Mr Menon. I hope you know what you are saying. On national television, you are accusing a senior member of your team of corruption. What is the basis of this accusation? Do you have any evidence in support of this claim?'

'This is rubbish!' Amidst the raised voice of Mohit Sengupta, another voice was heard. 'Absolute nonsense.' It was Jayakumar, shouting at the top of his voice.

'Hold on Mr Jayakumar, you will get a chance to rebut. Go on Mr Menon.'

'This afternoon, I was party to a conversation wherein my honourable colleague Mr Jayakumar was speaking to the Defence Secretary, threatening him with aggravation of the protest if the defence deal with Israel does not go through. He said he would continue the protests if the order for military trucks wasn't released. I do not want to build this protest on a foundation laid on blackmail and corruption.'

'This is a huge exposé on your own channel Times Today. The very people who are driving the anti-TNPP protest are linking it to the Israel defence deal. This is turning out to be a lot murkier than what we had initially thought it to be. Mr Jayakumar this is a very big accusation, how do you respond to this?'

'I don't even think this is worth responding to. This is absolute rubbish and a figment of imagination of a senile old man. I don't even want to comment. I'm ready to disclose my telephone bills publically for anyone to see. I have devoted my entire working life for the upliftment of society. I am pained, that after decades of selflessly serving the public, I have to even sit here and defend this accusation.'

'So are you denying that the conversation that Mr Menon is referring to ever happened?'

'Yes, I deny it totally. It never happened.'

'Mr Menon, this is your word against Mr Jayakumar's. Two renowned and respected individuals, both involved in a public cause, seemingly for the benefit of the people. Do you have any concrete evidence, any document in support of what you are saying?'

'No, I can just talk about today's conversation, which prompted me to go public.'

'Before we go into a break on this discussion tonight, wherein we have broken an exclusive story about the rift in the TNPP protest team, let's get some views from our other panellists. Mr Moinuddin, ex-DGP of Devikulam joins us from Devikulam. Mr Moinuddin.'

'Mr Mohit, thank you for having me on this show. I think Mr Krishna Menon is making a crazy accusation right now. In my view, he is quite upset that he is losing ground to Mr Jayakumar in the battle against TNPP. Mr Jayakumar is emerging as the public face of the protest, and that too at a time when the global media is focusing their attention on Devikulam. This is upsetting my dear friend, Mr Krishna Menon. And he is levelling unsubstantiated accusations to settle scores. In fact, what *locus standi* does Mr Krishna Menon have to talk about corruption when he has been arrested on charges of smuggling elephant tusks, years ago?'

'That was just an unjust accusation!' Menon cried, indignantly. 'I was never arrested. And that was years ago. It was a misunderstanding, which was settled. Mohit, Mohit. . .I can explain it.'

'Oh yes. We have it here,' said Mohit Sengupta as he picked up a piece of paper from his table prepared by his research team and waved it at the camera for the audience to see. 'The Tusker Gate controversy. Mr Menon would you like to say something on this? In the late seventies, you were arrested in Devikulam for smuggling elephant tusks. In fact, the accusation is that you killed an elephant to graft its tusks.'

'This is untrue. The elephant died of natural causes.'

'That is not what my research says Mr Menon. Let's go across to Mr Madan Mohan. What's your view on this discussion

Mr Madan Mohan? You have been an MLA from Devikulam for the three terms, the only independent MLA to have been re-elected twice. What do you have to say about the new direction this protest is taking?'

'I have worked with both Mr Jayakumar and Mr Menon. I am yet to see Mr Jayakumar do anything illegal. All his dealings have been in public interest and he has been a true and committed individual. This is the first time I am hearing anything like this. While I don't believe what Mr Menon is stating, I would be shattered if this were to be found true.'

'And your dealings with Mr Menon?'

'My first interaction with Mr Menon was when his family came to me to help them in the ivory smuggling case.'

'Oh so you are validating the fact that the Tusker Gate controversy in fact took place. . .The ivory smuggling issue which Mr Menon so vehemently denied, indeed happened. Mr Menon, this is an interesting direction that this discussion is taking. What is emerging is that personal vendetta is driving this accusation rather than real issues. Is the accuser fast becoming the accused? We have a lot more to discuss on the other side of the break. Don't go away, we will be right back.'

The commercial break gave Menon some time to think. He figured out that the others had come together to fix him on national television. If he fought them, he would be dragged through the mud even further. The people on the other side were powerful people who had a strong public standing. It was foolish of him to have gone to the media. Despite being one of the best news channels, Times Today could also not see through their façade.

Krishna Menon got up from his chair, removed the microphone pinned on his shirt, flung it at the crew and walked into his house without saying a word. It was pointless. He had tried to harness support, but it had just turned upside down and he had become the accused instead.

Jayakumar emerged as the unexpected hero from the show, despite starting off as a victim. By the time the show ended the world at large viewed Krishna Menon as the villain and Jayakumar as the saviour.

Meanwhile, Krishna Menon walked back into his room, shut the door and sat down on the long wooden easy chair and put his feet up on the table. Sulochana asked him how the interview was, and he didn't respond. He just didn't speak. An hour passed. Sulochana came a few times, even brought him his dinner, but hastily exited when she saw the mood Krishna was in.

Krishna was in deep thought. Something dramatic had to be done. Else the political pests would usurp the entire movement.

40

Back at GB2 a lot had transpired even as Mohit Sengupta was busy conducting his Big News Debate. Karan had tried to call up some of his colleagues in *The Times of India* in connection to the page eleven article, but was unable to speak to them. He finally sent them an SMS, hoping that they would call him back.

Kavya had by then finished reviewing all the personnel files. 'Karan, we have a problem. All the RMs in question have been sourced for the bank by Yogesh Bhargav, the placement consultant.'

'It was the same in the six files that I saw. So there seems to be a confirmed trend here.'

'Yes, but this is the lesser of the two problems.'

'Yes?' said Karan, suddenly excited.

'All these RMs have been personally recommended by Vikram for hiring.'

'Bang on', agreed Karan. 'That was exactly what I noticed in the files that I saw. All these guys have been hired on his say-so.'

'Yes, in each one of these personnel files is a mail from Vikram, asking for these guys to be hired. He has personally vouched for them. It's only on the basis of that mail that these guys have been hired as RMs.'

'Two questions come to my mind,' said Hemant. 'First, why would the Head of Retail Banking refer and push such junior level RMs? And second, if they were all known to Vikram, why pay Yogesh Bhargav a recruitment fee for these guys?'

'We will leave the second point out of this discussion, otherwise we will be opening up a Pandora's box,' suggested Karan.

'Agreed.'

'Karan,' it was Kavya this time. 'This could mean that Vikram is compromised.'

'Yes, but we have to be very careful. We have to make sure that we do not accuse someone at that level unless we are very sure. But to me, he looks like the guy behind it all. Even the Cochin guys said so. Right?'

There was a knock on the door. It was Nikhil.

'Hi Nikhil.'

'Hey Karan. Good to see you. What brings you here? Hope all is well?'

'Yes buddy. All is well. Come on in.' Karan then looked at Kavya and Hemant. 'Can you give us some time together? We need to chat.' He did not want to talk to Nikhil in front of the other two.

'Sure', said Hemant. 'I'll talk to Bala and follow up on the reports.' Kavya followed him out of the room.

Karan and Nikhil got chatting. After about fifteen minutes, they stepped out of the room, picked up a cup of coffee and then stepped back in the room again. It was an hour by the time they finished.

Once Nikhil left, Karan sat down to take stock with Hemant and Kavya. They had perused every bit of data that they had. Only two things remained: The identity of the person who withdrew cash from the Cochin branch and the verification reports from Matrix.

Hemant, in the interim, had discretely got the addresses of a few of the sixty-eight suspected benami accounts verified, and as anyone would have expected, they were all found to be fabricated.

Thankfully Karan's office called back. He picked up his phone in a single ring. 'Bhaskar, good you called back. I was in fact trying to reach you earlier to check with you as to who has put out the report on the anti-TNPP, protest. It's on Page 11 in this morning's paper.'

Bhaskar was his colleague and a senior. The two of them worked very well as a team. In fact, Karan was often seen as Bhaskar's protégé. The latter had played a key role in Karan's rise to fame over the past couple of years. Karan had not sought his assistance this time around, and the only reason for that was that Bhaskar would not have shared the same concern for GB2 that Karan did and hence may have wanted to sensationalize the news in the interest of the newspaper. Something which Karan had promised Indrani, would not happen.

'Let me check and call you.'

Within three minutes, Bhaskar called back, 'Don't know. But I got you the number of the guy who is at the centre of all the action. He is the guy leading the protest—Krishna Menon. Try your luck with him if you need any information.'

'Okay, thanks.'

'Karan,' Bhaskar added, 'Just be a bit sensitive when you chat with him.'

'Why, what happened?'

'The guy was on TV. Mohit Sengupta screwed him over on the Big News Debate.'

'As in?'

Bhaskar told him the entire story—about CNRI, about Krishna's accusations, about the way tables were turned and how he had walked off from the TV show in a huff. 'Poor guy,' said Karan and hung up.

41

Krishna was woken up from his restless slumber by the ringing of his mobile phone. He opened his eyes and glanced at his watch. It was pushing 10.30 p.m. The disgrace that had been lumped on him after the TV show was still hurting.

He picked up the phone. 'Yes?'

'Is this Mr Krishna Menon?'

'Speaking.'

'Mr Menon, I'm calling from Mumbai. Hope you are doing fine. I just needed a minute of your time sir.'

'Tell me.'

'Sir, the papers here have carried a picture of yours addressing a rally—the protest rally against TNPP. . .'

'Look. If you are calling for any information regarding the protests, or today's TV show, please note that I have decided to withdraw from the protests. I am not party to that movement anymore.'

'Oh that's tragic. But why sir?' Karan knew, thanks to Bhaskar. He was just expressing his concern and sympathy.

'I have my reasons. How can I help you?' Krishna was in no mood to go through it all over again.

'Sir I called to ask you about that gentleman behind you while you were addressing the rally yesterday. Who is that person Mr Menon?'

'There were many of them. Who you are referring to?'

'The one in the striped shirt.'

'The one wearing the red striped shirt?' Menon seemed to recollect something.

'I'm not too sure about the colour sir. The picture I saw in today's newspaper is a black and white one. But wait. . .let me see.' After a brief pause, Karan came back on line, 'Sir there is only one gentleman in the striped shirt and he is the one I am referring to.'

'He is Shivakumar, brother of Mr Jayakumar. He assists him at CNRI and is always around him.'

'Jayakumar?'

'Yes Jayakumar, my erstwhile partner. He also runs an NGO called CNRI.' Karan recalled his discussion with Bhaskar and figured out that Jayakumar was the person responsible for all of Krishna Menon's woes. Bhaskar had told him about Jayakumar and the arms deal accusation that Krishna Menon had levelled on him.

'Oh. Is Shivakumar working with you in the protest against the TNPP sir?'

. 'Yes, he is always around Jayakumar. Very resourceful and helps him in a lot of things. Is there an issue?'

'No sir. He was somewhere else this morning, and we are trying to trace him.'

'Okay. But where are you calling from?'

'I'm calling from Greater Boston Global Bank, Mumbai. I will call you sir, in case I need any further help. Thank you,' and Karan hung up.

After hanging up. Karan sat back on his chair and replayed the entire conversation in his mind. When Krishna had told him that the guy in the newspaper was Jayakumar's brother, Karan had panicked. *Foreign money coming in to fund NGOs running an anti-nuclear protest in India? How much murkier could it get?* Precisely at that point, his phone rang. It was Bhaskar.

'Karan, have you spoken to Krishna Menon?'

'Yes I have. Just got off the call with him.'

'Okay great. Just wanted to check. I wasn't too sure about the number when I gave it to you.'

'Bhaskar, you know what? Everyone including you condemned Krishna Menon for what he said on the show. Probably even painted him as the villain. Have you considered the fact that he might be telling the truth?'

'How can you say that? He has a history which you can't ignore.'

'I will tell you something if you promise to have the story cleared by me tonight and also promise me that GB2 will not feature in the story.'

'Done. Tell me.'

'Jayakumar and his brother Shivakumar are getting funded by certain agencies outside India, to disrupt India's nuclear plans. The funds are being routed through an organization called Union of Jews Foundation. We don't know who's behind it; for that matter we don't even know whether Union of Jews Foundation is a genuine organization or a façade. The funds are coming in through multiple benami accounts held with various banks. We can't say for sure if these guys have a larger agenda in trying to disrupt the TNPP, but one thing is for sure—Krishna is right.'

'How can you be sure?'

'This morning Shivakumar withdrew large sums of money from a suspected fraudulent GB2 account, from their Cochin branch. This account is under the scanner for receiving dirty money and is one of the benami accounts I just told you about.

He has been caught on camera withdrawing cash from that account. The CCTV grab matches with the image of Shivakumar in *The Times of India*, on page eleven.'

'Oh shit. If what you are saying is true, this is a big one. It will be front page news. Nobody who saw him on The Big News Debate believed what Krishna Menon said.'

'Hmm. I can imagine. But look, I have given my word to Indrani. So GB2 can't be in the news, atleast tomorrow.'

'Okay let me see what I can do. By the way, this puts the presence of the German-American scientist at the TNPP site along with the other protestors, in perspective. Germany and USA are two nations that bitterly oppose India's nuclear plan, and this is not a secret. From what you are saying, it appears that CNRI is just a front. They have a bigger agenda. Money coming to these benami accounts could be from these nations and is eventually being siphoned off to help CNRI fuel the protest. God knows how many such CNRIs they might be funding?'

'Bhaskar,' Karan said meekly. 'This looks bigger than what I thought it would be.'

'Yes, that thought crossed my mind too. You are doing well. I will mail you the article once I am done with it. Will pass it on to Andy once you confirm. Might call you again while I am writing it.'

'Sure. Thanks Bhaskar.'

The moment he hung up, Hemant walked up to him. 'Bala wrote back.'

'Hmm. . .and what?'

'They have not done the verification for these employees. In fact, they were never asked to.'

Karan suddenly stood up. 'I expected that. By the way, did you ask him how long it would take for him to give us the reports if we send him the details right now?'

'I didn't, but there is no point. I know for sure that it will take over a week. So we won't get it before our internal deadline. Clearly, someone didn't want a background check done on these folks.'

'Holy cow,' Kavya exclaimed. 'What did Nikhil say?'

'You know Kavya, I always thought that to become a senior manager in a bank, where trust is the biggest thing for the customer, you need to be of impeccable integrity. In this case, I'm somehow beginning to believe that this trust is being compromised.'

'And why do you say that?'

'Kavya, when Nikhil was here. . .' Indrani walked in at that very instant and Karan had to cut the conversation off.

'So what has my team of Sherlock Holmes' found out for me?' While she was trying to be jovial to lighten the mood, it was clear that behind the façade was a worried person.

'Indrani, we are still at it. We've uncovered some serious issues. And it all points to the fact that someone in your organization be corrupt.'

'It's as much your organization Karan.'

'Yes. That's what I meant,' Karan snapped back. He was getting irritated that Indrani was not getting the point.

'Who are you referring to?'

'Vikram Bahl.'

'What?'

'Yes Indrani, Vikram.'

'How sure are you Karan? You cannot accuse anyone without having sufficient evidence.'

'Indrani, it's a fairly complicated story. But I will tell you everything in brief.' He told her about the Asia Logistics account, the background under which the account was opened, Vikram's involvement in the opening of the account, about sixty-eight such accounts which were sure-shot cases of money laundering, about the thirteen RMs who acquired these sixty-eight accounts. The fact that, not only had Vikram backed these RMs, but also had waived off their mandatory verifications. He also told her about the involvement of CNRI and the anti nuclear protestors in the laundering of money, about the Cochin cash withdrawal caught on video.

Indrani was stunned. 'Vikram!! I can't believe this. I hope you are wrong.'

'That's not it Indrani, there's more. And this is what kind of corroborates the entire story. I met one of your Cluster Managers, Nikhil. When he moved to Mumbai, he was coerced into taking on rent, a property owned by Vikram, that too at a rent significantly higher than market rentals. Not only that, to make sure that he was able to afford it, Vikram increased his salary by nearly a hundred per cent.'

'Who, Nikhil Suri told you this?'

'Yes Indrani, though not directly. We got to discussing compensation, which was when he mentioned this to me. No one talks to the media directly Indrani. We are trained to get them to speak.'

'Hmm,' Indrani nodded.

'And Indrani, the word in the branch banking team is that Vikram paid an event management company over a crore as fees for an event, which would have cost, not more than forty-five lakh. Anecdotal though the latter may be, it shows the kind of reputation a person has. And when that reputation gets juxtaposed with these money laundering issues, even circumstantial evidence begins to make sense.'

'I never knew that Vikram has this side to him.' She was shattered. Vikram was one of her favourites in the senior management team of GB2.

'There is a hundred per cent correlation between the tainted RMs, Vikram's referrals and the benami accounts Indrani.'

'Okay this proves Vikram is a person with suspect integrity, but what about Pranesh, Harshita and Raymond? What does all this have to do with their deaths?'

'Indrani, Raymond was investigating the Asia Logistics account. He obviously had stumbled upon something dramatic, which led to him being killed. I have a very strong feeling that this has got to do with the killing of the others too. Vikram will be able to throw more light on this, but we can't interrogate him. It will be far too dangerous to do so at this stage.'

'I think we need to get HR in the loop. And the cops as well. We need Francis Jobai to come in on this too.' Francis was the security head of GB2.

'Indrani if you don't mind, let's do that tomorrow. In any case, it's too late right now. We will close our leg of the investigation and bring it to a stage where you can share it with the others.'

'Karan, if what you are saying is true, I don't think we can wait any longer. I'll ask Jacqueline to call Tanuja and Francis Jobai tomorrow morning at 10.30 a.m. I want to discuss our future course at that time. I'm really worried now.' She let out a sigh and added, 'I am anyway leaving now. Will see you tomorrow morning.'

'Sure. In any case Tanuja and Francis sit out of this office. We can summon them tomorrow morning. We will be around for some more time today. I have requested Jacqueline to let us know when the last person leaves. We would like to scan Raymond's desk.'

'Hmm. . .I can see a few lights still on. Maybe you should wait a while.'

'And do you think I can speak to anyone to get some details on expense vouchers and reimbursements?'

'At this hour? What exactly do you want?'

'I want to see the telephone bills of these thirteen RMs that have been reimbursed. I want to see if there is anyone who all these guys are calling. It'll help me. I also need to see Vikram's bills.'

A sleepy-eyed Jacqueline walked into the room. 'I will get it for you. It will take some time, but I'll get it for you by tomorrow morning.'

'Ask for the bills of all my direct reports. You know how word leaks out? I don't want anyone to wonder why we are asking for only Vikram's bills.'

'Yes Indrani.'

'Thanks Jacqueline.'

'And by the way, Vienna police has released a statement on Harshita and Siddhartha Lele's murder. They have said that they are now officially calling it a homicide.' Jacqueline handed over a print out to Indrani, who went through it and gave it to Karan.

'Where did you get it?'

'Tanuja sent it to me. She asked me to give it to you. Apparently it's on the Police Department's website.'

Indrani went through the press-release carefully.

Office of the Commissioner of Police
Wien

Enclosed is the brief update on the death of two Indian tourists in Wien on the night of the 29th of January 2012.

It has now been established that the death of the two tourists was a result of drug overdose and not in an accident as was believed earlier. Consequently the status of the investigation has been changed from that of accidental death to homicide. The post-mortem report puts the time of their death between 1.40 and 2.00 a.m., though the accident took place at 3.05 a.m. on the 30th of January. The driver of the dumper truck, who had been taken into custody, has been released.

Siddhartha Lele and Harshita Lele were last seen at the Café Coffee Day outlet on Ringstrasse, between 1.25 and 1.30 a.m. They called out for help to the staff at the café, who was busy winding up operations for the day and uploading their daily reports to their headquarters in Bengaluru, India. The staff recognized the Indian couple, as earlier in the evening they had spent considerable amount of time at the same café. By the time the staff could open the grill to let them in, they disappeared. The police are questioning the Café Coffee Day employees for any information that may help in this investigation.

The Wien Police is also probing the possible involvement of a crime syndicate in this regard. The police have some vital clues and hope to solve this case very soon.

The Wien police in 2011 have a hundred per cent success rate in solving homicide cases and bringing the accused to book. We expect to keep that record intact and once again make Wien the safest tourist destination, not only in Europe, but the entire world.

You may visit the Wien Police website for further details. In case you have any information which may be of use to the police, you can contact Johann Schroeder's office at the numbers given below or email at info@viennapolice.com.

'You were right Karan. I'm really beginning to feel worried now. We will have to being in the cops tomorrow. This is getting dangerous now.'

Karan nodded. 'Yes Indrani, that'll be wise.'

'And Jacqueline, is Tanuja around? I need to speak to her. Can you ask her to come up?'

'She has just left Indrani. She was going to the airport to drop her husband. He came in this morning and is off again.'

'Oh. The amount he travels! Poor Tanuja, she just keeps shuttling between home and the airport,' said Indrani, earning weak smiles from everyone.

42

By the time Karan left for home, it was around 2.30 a.m. The sweep of Raymond's workstation had given them some insights, though many questions still remained unanswered. A tired Karan had dropped Kavya home and then headed back to his house. Hemant had left on his own.

In the morning, while on his way in, he called Kavya on her mobile. 'I will join you there. Dad will drop me. Will see you in the boardroom,' she said. He was the first of the three to come in that day. Kavya was next.

'Morning guys. Coffee?'

'Good morning Jacks!' suddenly Karan's face lit up. A glare from Kavya muted his smile.

'Guys the expense reimbursement claims of Indrani's direct reports and the telephone bills of those thirteen RMs have come. You want to see it now?'

'Yes of course.'

The two of them got down to work once Jacqueline printed out the bills and gave it to them. GB2 was a well organized, technology oriented bank. Almost everything that Karan required was available online. They sifted through the bills of the RMs one by one. There was no trend that they could make out. All the numbers that were common between the thirteen sets of bills were those of the bank staff, staff they would regularly deal with in normal course of work. Nothing suspicious.

'Where's Hemant?' Kavya asked all of a sudden as she was putting one bill down and picking up another.

'Must be sleeping.'

'What the hell? He should have been here by now.'

'Call him Kavya? Ask him where he is and how long he will take.'

Kavya tried calling him. His phone was not reachable. Keeping the phone back on the table, she looked at Karan. Her face went pale.

'Is everything okay?' asked Karan.

'His phone is not reachable.'

'Oh fuck. Hope he's alright.' Karan picked up his phone and started frantically calling him. He too couldn't reach him. 'Do you have his residence number?'

'No.' Kavya shook her head.

'Ask Jacqueline. Shit. Hope he is safe.' There was panic in his voice.

Kavya was back in ten seconds. 'No she too doesn't have.'

'Oh my God. . .Shit. Shit. I should have dropped him home. If something happens to him, I will hold myself responsible for it.'

'Don't say that Karan, nothing will happen to him.' At that very instant the door flew open and Hemant walked in. 'Where the fuck were you? And why is your phone not reachable?'

'Chill Karan. My phone is fine. . .I was in the lift.'

Karan heaved a sigh of relief. 'Sorry Hemant. I got really worried.' Hemant went and patted him on his back. 'It's okay. Bad times.'

Indrani came in around 9.30 a.m. 'Guys, any progress?'

'Indrani, the telephone bills don't throw up anything. I am a bit stuck, wondering what to do.'

'By the way, did you pass on information to *The Times of India*?' She had read Bhaskar's article that morning.

'Nothing that is derogatory to GB2 Indrani. The story talks about the fact that CNRI could have been funded through dubious means and that their motive could go beyond TNPP. Something which even Krishna Menon had alluded to in a conversation with Times Today.'

'I noticed. Thanks for being sensitive to GB2.' She turned her back towards all of them, 'I will be back in five minutes. Let's figure out the next course of action then. We don't have too much time.' She turned towards Jacqueline, 'The 10.30 a.m. meeting is on today. . .right?' Jacqueline nodded.

Like many others, it was a daily routine for Indrani to head to the restroom to freshen up and touch up her face before settling down into her work. She headed to the washroom. The touch-up took only two minutes. Standing in front of the mirror, she admired herself. She looked young for her age, although a few wrinkles were beginning to show up—there was only so much that a compact could hide. 'Time for Botox,' she thought as she pulled out a tissue and wiped her face.

With her right hand she cranked the handle and opened the door to head out when she ran into a sullen-looking Malvika.

'Hi Malvika.'

'Good morning Indrani.'

Indrani stepped closer to her and hugged her. The warm hug from Indrani made Malvika lose her composure, one that she was struggling so hard to maintain. She started sobbing uncontrollably.

'Oh my baby. You should have stayed at home till everything settled down. What a brave girl you are! We all admire you and your resolve.' Indrani tried her best to give solace to Malvika and get her to calm down. It had surprised every one when Malvika turned up for work the previous day.

'Come. Come to my room,' and Indrani led her to her room. 'Jacqueline, a glass of water,' she said as she passed her secretary.

'You are a brave girl. You should not be crying. If you lose your balance, who will take care of your parents sweetheart?' Indrani reasoned with Malvika. 'We are all with you my girl.'

'Thanks Indrani.' Indrani hugged her again. 'I'm sorry Indrani, I don't know how I lost control. I will try not to.'

'I know what you are going through Malvika. If I can be of any help, please let me know. I'm there for you.'

'Thanks Indrani.'

Hearing all the commotion, Karan came out of the room. 'Is someone crying?' he asked Jacqueline.

'Malvika.'

'Who's Malvika?'

'Harshita's sister.'

Karan was surprised. 'Harshita's sister? She works for GB2?'

'Yes Karan. She used to report to Raymond.'

'Why the hell didn't anyone tell us? She could throw some fresh light on all of this.'

'Indrani felt that we should keep her out of the investigation till she comes out of the trauma.'

'Hmm. . .okay let's not rule out that option. If we have to, then we will keep that as the last resort.'

At that very instant Malvika came out of Indrani's room and went past Karan and Jacqueline.

'Malvika,' Jacqueline called out. When she turned, Jacqueline added, 'Do you have a nice picture of Harshita? Need it for the e-magazine. If you have it, then I'll put it up in the article we're carrying about her. The magazine will come out day after.'

'I have a few. I'll show them to you. You take your pick.'

'Thanks love. Are you bringing them now?'

'Yup. Will be back in two minutes.' And she disappeared. She didn't smile or acknowledge the presence of Karan.

After she left, Karan looked at her, 'Magazine? E-magazine?'

'Yes my friend. I am the editor of the e-magazine apart from being Indrani's secretary. Multifaceted you see.' And she smiled.

In no time, Malvika was back with her iPad. 'Here. There are a lot of photographs of Harshita in this. Select the one you want and I'll email it to you,' she said to Jacqueline.

Jacqueline looked at the white iPad and smiled. 'New one?'

'Harshita's last gift to me. She bought it for me on my birthday. When she bought it for me, little did I know that this would be her last.' And she turned and rushed back to her desk. It looked as if she was about to burst into tears again.

'Poor Malvika. I would hate to go through what she is going through.' Jacqueline moved back to her seat with the iPad in hand. Karan stood there, wondering how it would be to lose one's sister and boss within twenty-four hours.

'Come. Let's go,' Indrani's voice pulled him out of his reverie. He turned and followed her into the boardroom.

'One sec Karan.' When Karan heard Jacqueline call out, he stopped.

'Where do I see the pictures in this?'

'There is an icon at the bottom. Touch it and the photos will open up on screen.'

'Where?' Jacqueline was struggling. 'Can't find it.'

'Is the iPad password protected?'

'No. It doesn't ask for a passcode.'

'Okay wait.' He turned towards Indrani who was standing at the door to the board room, 'Indrani, I'll be with you in a minute. I'll just show her how to find images on the iPad and come.' Indrani continued walking towards the board room.

'Give,' he held out his hand to take the iPad from Jacqueline. Jacqueline was more than happy to hand it over to him.

'Look,' he said. 'This is the photo icon. Click on this one and the photos will open up.' Once the albums open up, you touch the photo you want and it opens up on the screen. To move from one photo to the other, just swipe your finger like this.' He swiped his finger from right to left to move from one picture to the other.

'That's cool.'

'And if you want to go back to the albums, just press this tab on top. Simple.'

'Got it.' She took the iPad from him. 'Wait, let me try it once.' This time Jacqueline was successful and she smiled at Karan. She looked back at the picture and smiled. 'What a pretty picture!'

Karan looked at the picture Jacqueline had pulled up on screen. 'She was quite pretty. Aging, but pretty.' And he smiled at Jacqueline. 'Okay, I have to go. Indrani will scream.'

'Just one minute Karan. Help me select the picture and go na.'

'Fine, give me the iPad quickly.' He took the iPad from her and went through the photos. 'Let's see if there are other albums,' he said, looking at Jacqueline for a minute before returning his gaze to the iPad. He pressed the tab on top of the screen, which said 'Albums'. The photo went off the screen and in its place, five photo albums appeared. On top of the screen, right in the middle, were four buttons: 'Photos', 'Photo stream', 'Albums' and 'Events'. Curiosity took over Karan. He pressed the button which had 'Events' written on it. The photographs appeared on screen, batched up according to the dates on which they had been imported into the iPad. He clicked on the 'back' button and went back to the main screen. This time he pressed the 'Photo Stream' button.

'What's Photo Stream?' Jacqueline asked him. She was closely observing everything he was doing.

'You have two minutes Karan,' Indrani walked past talking on her mobile. Jacqueline smiled. 'It's okay Karan. I don't think she will finish in two minutes. Tell me. What's Photo Stream?'

'How do I explain?' and Karan started thinking. 'Alright, I'll try. Photo Stream is a feature on iCloud.'

'iCloud?'

'Oh my God, I didn't know you were so technologically-inept. . .and you claim to be an editor of the e-magazine.'

'Fine fine. Tell me.'

'iCloud is Apple's own cloud computing technology. It stores applications, photos, contacts, pictures etc. across multiple Apple devices. So if you have a MacBook, iPhone, iPad and iPod, and you are logged onto the same iCloud ID on all of them, then documents that you create or save on one will automatically get pushed onto the other devices, pictures that you take from one will appear on the others seamlessly, provided the devices are connected to the Internet.'

'Okay, then what's Photo Stream?'

'Is this some technology lesson or what?' Kavya had come out of the boardroom where she was tired waiting for all of them. She didn't like Jacqueline flirting with Karan.

Karan ignored what Kavya had said and looked at Jacqueline. 'With iCloud, if you take a photo on your iPhone or iPad, then it automatically appears on all devices logged on to the same iCloud ID. For thirty days, they reside in an album called Photo Stream.'

'I'm still confused.'

'Dumbo. If I have an iPhone here and an iPad at home, and I have logged on to both using the same iCloud ID and I take your picture with my iPhone, then almost instantaneously, the photo will appear on my iPad at home, provided the iPad is connected to the Internet. In the iPad and the iPhone, it will by default, reside in a photo album, which is called Photo Stream. Anyone using my iPad can see the photo instantaneously.'

'Oh that's so cool.'

'Tell Indrani to buy you an iPad for all that you do for her then.'

'I will, but only after you care to come in and finish our discussion.' Indrani had just overheard what he had said. She was standing at the entrance to the conference room, hands on her hips. 'Shall we?'

'Yes Indrani.' Karan said hurriedly. He looked at the iPad, and pressed the 'home' button to get out of the pictures menu and was about to hand over the iPad to Jacqueline when he stopped. His face took on a look of stunned disbelief. Jacqueline tried to take the iPad from his hand, but he didn't let go of it.

'Call Malvika,' he said softly

'What?' Jacqueline hadn't heard him clearly.

'I said, call Malvika. Damn it,' he swore. He sat down next to Jacqueline's workstation, looking shell-shocked. 'Are you alright Karan?' Indrani asked. By that time Hemant had come out into Jacqueline's area. 'What happened?'

Karan didn't respond to the question; instead he just looked at them and involuntarily whispered, 'Let's get back into the boardroom?' He was not trying to whisper butwords were struggling to come out. Karan tapped the 'Photos' icon on the iPad as they walked into the boardroom.

When the menu came up, he pressed the 'Photo Stream' option and then stopped. The iPad was in his left hand. Using the index finger of his right hand, he moved from picture to picture, before finally stopping on one. He sank to the carpeted floor and rested his back against the wall. His hands came up to cover his face as he let out a deep sigh and rubbed his palms against his cheeks.

'Karan?' Indrani placed her hand on his shoulder. 'Are you feeling alright?' Karan didn't respond. By that time, Malvika had come into the room. Feeling a bit confused, she asked, 'Did someone call me?'

'Yes, I did!' Karan finally spoke. 'Whose ID have you used to log on to iCloud on your iPad?'

'iCloud? I've never used it.'

'You have an iPad and haven't heard of iCloud?' Jacqueline asked Malvika. Kavya glared at her.

'I know what it is. But I've never used it. I don't think I even have an iCloud ID. But why do you ask?' Malvika asked curiously.

'But it seems to be active on your iPad. And you don't have an iPhone?' Karan pointed to the Nokia handset that she was carrying. iCloud was a popular feature with anyone using multiple Apple devices.

'I use a Nokia Lumia. I've always used a Nokia.'

'But your iPad is synced with other devices on iCloud. Whose ID is it?' and Karan started looking at the settings to see whose ID had been used to log in to the iCloud services.

'It must be Harshita's. She had given me a detailed demo on my iPad when she gifted it to me. Guess she wouldn't have logged off. I use my iPad largely for reading books and so never realized that it would still be active. In fact, she was the one who loaded hundreds of books, pictures etc. onto it when she gave it to me.'

'Did she send you any messages, emails or pictures from her vacation?'

'No. Not really. She was very particular about what she spent money on. She was telling me before she went that she would be turning off the data roaming feature on her iPhone while on vacation. Her friends had told her that it costs a fortune if you keep it on. Data charges on roaming are prohibitively expensive, particularly while travelling overseas. Hence she would normally send emails or Skype with me whenever she had access to free Wi-Fi.'

'Did you notice anything suspicious or worrisome?'

'In fact, nothing at all. The last email she sent me was from Vienna. She sent me a short email from there, stating that they found a Café Coffee Day in Vienna, and how she was very excited about it. She made such a big deal about a free twelve-hour Wi-Fi deal that CCD had in Vienna. Mom and me were laughing about it when we spoke on the phone that night—about how she exploited it to the fullest—skyped with Raymond, Mom and a couple of other friends. She was in CCD for over an hour, only because she was thrilled at the free Wi-Fi.'

'She told you that she was there for an hour?'

'No. She tried to Skype with me a few times. I was in Kolkata and not free when she called. So couldn't speak to her. Finally she sent me a mail, saying that she is leaving and will call me later. From the time the first Skype call came to the time she sent the email, the gap was over an hour.'

'Oh understood. Was there anything out of the ordinary about her phone call to your mom? No, nothing,' Malvika replied patiently. Just normal mother-daughter talk. She told her that she was planning to go to some place Raymond wanted her to and was looking forward to coming back home. Have you seen the photos in Photo Stream?'

'What's Photo Stream?'

'Never mind.' Karan was in no mood to explain all over again. 'Can we keep this iPad for some time, if you don't mind?'

'Yes of course. Why? Is there a problem?'

'No Malvika. Thanks a ton for your help.'

As she walked out of the boardroom, Malvika turned back and looked at Karan. 'Please be careful. It's Harshita's last gift to me.' The confused look was still on her face. Karan smiled and nodded, 'Of course.'

'Indrani', Karan spoke after the door shut behind Malvika, 'Harshita was killed. And it was definitely because of something to do with Asia Logistics and the Union of Jews Foundation.'

Neither of them spoke. Both had a questioning look on their faces.

'Look at this,' and Karan stood up and walked up to Indrani with the iPad. Kavya and Hemant clustered around him. 'There are four photos in the Photo Stream of this iPad.'

He brought up the first one on the screen.

'First one. The address plate of the Union of Jews Foundation. The address as per this plate is the same as the address on the remittance certificate from the boutique bank in Liechtenstein. This means Harshita did go there. How else could she have taken this picture?'

'Oh my God!' exclaimed Indrani.

'Wait, it's not over yet.' He brought up the second picture on the screen. 'The second photograph shows the address plate with the interiors of UJF's office. It shows three people standing.' Indrani glanced at it. The picture had been taken from a distance. The images of people standing inside the office were tiny. 'Jacqueline, can you please get my reading glasses. They are on my table.' When Indrani said this, Jacqueline started walking towards Indrani's room.

In the interim, Karan flipped to the third photograph. 'The third photograph has the three guys looking at the main door with guns in their hands.'

'Oh my God!' Indrani exclaimed again. 'You were so right Karan.' She could see the men holding a shining object in their hand, which she presumed was a gun.

'Wait Indrani. There is more to it. The fourth one has Siddhartha being dragged into the office.'

'Is this Siddhartha?' Indrani queried.

'Yes Indrani. I could recognize him because I just saw his picture in the other pictures of Harshita, which Jacks showed me.' Indrani looked at the picture. All the other men in the picture had guns and one of them was holding the gun to Siddhartha's head.

'So they were here till 12.46 a.m.,' Hemant butted in.

'How do you know?' Kavya was curious to know how Hemant figured out something that she had missed.

'That's what the clock in the background suggests.' Looking at Karan, he added, 'As per the Vienna Police's press release, they were last seen at Café Coffee Day at 1.30 a.m. This would mean that from 12.46 to 1.30 when they reached Café Coffee Day, they were alive.'

'Yes,' said Karan, who was lost in deep thought.

Indrani took the iPad from his hands and flipped through the pictures again. The images were small and hence it was difficult for Indrani to see the faces of the three people apart from Siddhartha. Jacqueline hadn't brought her reading glasses yet. 'Jacqueline!' Indrani called. 'Can't find them Indrani, they're not on your table,' Jacqueline replied, walking back into the room.

'Never mind. It might be in my bag. I'll find them myself.' Indrani was very possessive about her bag and would not let anyone, including her secretary, touch it.

Karan went on, 'Raymond had asked Harshita to check out the address, without realizing its implications. And Harshita, too, obliged. That's what Malvika also said, right?' and he looked at the others. 'She landed at UJF and saw something she was not supposed to. Her husband and she were obviously a threat to someone and hence got eliminated. Raymond too knew too much and he was murdered.'

'But tell me Karan. . .' Kavya began.

'Will you just hold on, I'm also thinking this through,' he snapped. He immediately realized his mistake. 'I'm sorry sweetheart. I'm just really worked up now. Really sorry. What were you saying?' and he went around and hugged her. Hemant managed a wry smile.

'I am only playing the devil's advocate here Karan.'

'I said sorry na.'

Kavya smiled. 'Okay. As I was saying, if Harshita was on the run, and her data roaming was off, how did the photos manage to get uploaded to iCloud and sync with the iPad?'

'I was thinking about it after Malvika told me that her data roaming was turned off.'

'Maybe Harshita turned her data roaming on, just so that others could see the pictures that she had clicked,' Hemant suggested.

'Unlikely,' argued Karan. 'When someone is in duress, it is highly unlikely that he or she would have the presence of mind to turn data roaming on so that her pictures could be seen on some other device. In fact, I doubt if Harshita would have even known that her iCloud ID was active on Malvika's iPad.'

'The question then is, how did the pictures appear on the iPad?' When Hemant said this, everyone in the room went silent. The same question was on everyone's mind. For a good two minutes, no one spoke.

'The only way this could have been possible was if they got connected to a Wi-Fi network purely by chance, and the pictures got uploaded to iCloud on their own. Right?' said Kavya hesitantly, breaking the deafening silence that had gripped the room.

'Bingo!' yelled Hemant. 'Fabulous! Remember Café Coffee Day?'

'Café Coffee Day?' Indrani didn't understand what he was talking about. Neither did the others, not even Kavya, who had suggested the possibility.

'Café Coffee Day, Indrani,' Hemant continued. 'Remember what the press release said? That they were last seen at Café Coffee Day at around 1.30 that night. They were there earlier in the day from where they spoke to Raymond. Harshita had called him on Skype from her iPhone, after logging on to the Wi-Fi network there. She even sent a mail to Malvika from Café Coffee Day. It's highly likely that at night when she and her husband stopped at CCD asking for help while trying to escape, her iPhone would have got automatically connected to the Wi-Fi at CCD and the photos would have got uploaded to iCloud and that's how it would have appeared on the iPad's Photo Stream.'

'Wow. That's brilliant Hemant,' Karan said. 'This is exactly what would have happened. According to the Vienna Police's press release, the staff at CCD was uploading their data for the day to the company servers in Bangalore. In other words, their network would have still been up and running.'

'And she had a twelve-hour free Wi-Fi deal with Café Coffee Day,' Hemant continued, 'Remember? Malvika just told us how she and her mother laughed about how excited Harshita was about the twelve-hour free Wi-Fi. So the twelve-hour connection would have been active when they passed through Café Coffee Day. The iPhone would have reconnected and in an instant uploaded everything to iCloud, which would have sync-ed to the iPad the next time Malvika connected it to the Internet.'

'Indrani,' said Karan, 'I think you should bring Vikram in. I'm at loss to see how we will question him. But it's very clear now. His involvement as a deal swinger is what has caused this for all of us. It's clear—the Union of Jews Foundation in some way or the other was responsible for the killing of Harshita. Raymond got to know and that's why he is also dead. Now we all know this. Before anything happens to us, we need to make sure that this is in safe hands.'

'I am not sure how to take this forward. Should we speak to Vikram first? Or should we first speak to HR, involve the regional office and then involve the cops?'

When Indrani said this, Karan got thinking.

'If we strongly believe that Vikram is the cause for all this, and we now have enough reasons to do so, I think we should only speak to him, but only after covering ourselves. We should not let him know that we know about this unless we have adequate protection. However, I am sure of one thing. I don't think we can keep it among ourselves now. It's gotten too big. We will have to inform everyone about this breach.'

'I think you're right Karan. We don't have time.' Indrani turned to Jacqueline, 'Can you call Vikram and tell him to be around and that I want to meet him. Karan in the interim, either you head down and brief Tanuja, or call her here.'

'I will head down and speak to Tanuja about it. Will be back in ten minutes. It will be a bit embarrassing if Vikram lands up while we're briefing her.'

'Sounds good.' Indrani turned to Hemant, 'Let's talk to Internal Security and use them to call the cops. Ask Francis to come and see me.' Indrani wanted to make sure that the Head of Internal Security was around when they spoke to Vikram. It was now getting far too big for the three novices to handle. And now they had enough evidence to question Vikram on his involvement.

Karan in the interim, walked out to meet Tanuja. As he opened the door of the conference room, he looked back. 'Kavya, come with me. And Hemant, Can you lend me your access card? Security will not stop me if I have the access card.' He turned, looked at Jacqueline, 'And Jacqueline, a small request. Can you please tell Tanuja that Kavya and I are coming down to see her?'

The second floor was relatively crowded—a floor that was occupied by the HR, Commercial Banking and the SME teams.

Tanuja was waiting for them. 'Hi Karan. How have you been? How is the article on GB2 coming? Found some juice for your story? Meri bhi koi achchisi photo chaap dena yaar.'

'Sure Tanuja.' Karan had a wry smile on his face. 'In fact, I came to talk to you about something important and sensitive.'

'Jacqueline told me. Come, come,' she said, leading them to a plush sofa in the corner of her room. 'And Kavya, how come you are on this project?' On seeing Kavya squirm, she added, 'Well having a boyfriend in the media surely helps the organization,' and she winked at Kavya who smiled in return.

Karan and Kavya made themselves comfortable. Kavya scanned the room out of curiosity. It was a large cabin. Tanuja's desk was in a corner, which was away from the door. Next to the door, to the left of where they were sitting, was a display cabinet which proudly showed off all the awards that GB2 had won over the years. When Tanuja saw Karan staring at the trophies, she walked up to the cabinet and said, 'This year we won the *Business Today* best employer award. We are a great organization to work for.' She pulled out the *Business Today* trophy and proudly held it out for Karan to see. 'Some day, you must come back, Karan. This organization can do wonders with a few good people like you.'

Karan managed a smile. Kavya looked at Karan from the side of her eyes. 'She really thinks that you are here to do the article,' she whispered as Tanuja turned to keep the trophy back on the top shelf of the glass cabinet.

On their right hung a bright red Persian rug. 'Nice,' said Karan, trying to indulge her with some small talk, while his mind weighed different ways in which he could talk to her about the core issue. 'Thanks! Bought it in Hong Kong when I was there on a holiday.'

'Looks quite exotic,' commented Karan, eyebrows raised admiringly.

'Chinese imitation. Cheap stuff. I bought it off the pavement.'

His eyes roamed the room from the door past the glass cabinet, skimming over her table, on to the rug. And stopped abruptly.

'Tell me. How can I help you?' Tanuja asked, settling into her chair.

Karan didn't even hear what she said. Something in the room caught his attention and he was focused on that. As the realization hit him, he was stunned into silence, sweat breaking out on his forehead. Kavya didn't notice what he was going through.

'You know Tanuja. Over the last few days. . .' the moment she began, she felt Karan's cold and sweaty hand cover hers. The chillness surprised her. Karan's hand pressed hers firmly, asking her to remain silent. Quickly, Karan stood up. 'Kavya, can you please come with me? I think I've left the list of questions we were to ask Tanuja back in the boardroom. Let's get it before we talk to Tanuja.' He looked at Tanuja and added, 'Sorry Tanuja, I will be back shortly.'

'Is everything okay? Why are you sweating so much?'

'I guess it's just the exertion, Tanuja. I will be fine.' And he stepped out.

'Call me if you need any help,' was the last thing Tanuja said before the two of them closed the door. If she followed it up with something else, which she probably did, neither of them heard it.

Kavya was wondering what went wrong. 'What's the problem Karan? Are you alright?'

'Not here,' and Karan walked briskly towards the door—as fast as he could walk without attracting any undue attention. Kavya had a tough time keeping pace with him. They reached the lift lobby but the lift was on the fifth floor. 'Come let's walk,' said Karan moving towards the stairs.

'Karan is everything okay? What the hell is the problem?' Karan didn't respond. On reaching the fifth floor, Karan made a dash for the boardroom. He pulled the door open and ran in. He sat down on the chair, elbows on the table and held his head in his hands as his fingers ruffled through his hair. 'What the fuck? I just can't believe this.'

'What happened Karan? Will you please stop going around in circles and tell us now?' Kavya was getting impatient.

'I will. I will. But let me gather myself. This is very strange.'

He got up, walked to the door, and opened it just a bit to stick his head out, 'Jacks!'

'Yes sweetheart,' Jacqueline promptly responded.

'Is Francis Jobai here?'

'Not yet. He will take about forty-five minutes to reach here. He's somewhere in Powai. There was an issue in the branch and he had gone to meet the cops there. But he's on his way back.'

'Great. We will need to be with Indrani and Vikram only when he comes here. Right?'

'Hmm. . .' Jacqueline nodded. 'In any case, she has told me to make sure you get access to her when you want to. So it's not a problem. How was the meeting with Tanuja?'

'Will let you know soon.' And he went back into the conference room.

'Kavya and Hemant, the next forty-five minutes are the most critical. We have time till Francis Jobai reaches here. Post that, we will be out of the investigation and they will take over. We need to focus and make sure we only look for what we are trying to find out. I want you to look for certain specific things.' And he went on to outline everything that he wanted them to do. 'And I want all of this to be closed out now. So guys better start moving.'

After giving them instructions, Karan walked to the corner of the room, where his mobile phone was lying. He picked it up and dialled a number. 'Is this a recorded line?'

'No asshole. You called my cell phone. Unless someone is tapping my phone,' Karan started laughing. 'I need some help.'

In fifteen minutes, Karan got off the call. He had got what he wanted.

In about an hour, Kavya and Hemant were nearly through with what they were doing. 'Nearly done Karan,' said Hemant.

'Thanks Hemant. There are two things left to be done.' The other two in the room looked at each other. 'Jacks!' he said, snapping his fingers. 'Jacks can help us with that.'

He walked out of the room and he saw Vikram there. 'Karan?' Vikram was surprised to see him there. 'Yes Vikram. How are you?'

'I'm good. What brings you here? You're still with the Times?'

'Yes yes. Very much so. Enjoying my stint there. People there atleast have a spine.' He took a dig at Vikram. They didn't get along when Karan was in GB2, but he didn't have much time to carry on the banter.

'Jacqueline. Need your help. Can you please come into the conference room for a minute?' She followed Karan, leaving Vikram alone at her workstation. Vikram, finding himself alone at Jacqueline's table started taking mental notes about things lying there. He always did that when he was around Indrani's room. When he saw an old mobile bill of his lying on Jacqueline's table, he picked it up and started going through it. When Jacqueline came back, he asked her, 'What's going on Jacqueline?'

'Nothing. And will you please stop going through my things? It's rude to do so without my permission.' She had never liked him. 'Indrani is slightly tied up now. She will only see you in an hour. Please be around. I'll call you.'

'Sure. I will be in my cabin.' Vikram turned away, a strange look on his face. Jacqueline had always been nice to him, mainly because he was seen as Indrani's pet boy. What had changed all of a sudden?

Francis Jobai arrived a little over an hour and a half from the time Jacqueline had called him. The slow traffic on the Eastern

Express highway, particularly on the Sion-Matunga belt, had delayed him. He was ushered into Indrani's cabin where he was briefed. After giving him the background, Indrani asked Jacqueline to call Karan and his team.

As he strode into Indrani's room, Karan had a smile on his lips, and deep concern in his mind. In the heart of hearts, he was worried—worried about the manner in which things had changed abruptly.

'Come on in, guys,' Indrani smiled. It was a smile that hid the pain and the sorrow that she was feeling. Three of her officers had been killed over the past few days. And there was a cloud over one of her favourite officers in the bank. Francis Jobai was standing to her left, talking to someone on the phone.

'Hi Karan, good to see you again, though not in the best of circumstances, I must say. And Indrani, they will be here in twenty minutes,' said Francis, as soon as he hung up.

Indrani looked at Karan and Kavya. 'The cops,' she explained, 'I have requested Francis to make sure that we have adequate security before we talk to anyone. He has requested them to be around, just in case we need help. On an informal basis.'

'Thanks Indrani. I think, by the time we finish, we will surely need the cops to come in.'

'Where's Hemant?'

'He's checking on one last detail. He'll be here in ten minutes.'

'Okay. Vikram had come. I asked Jacqueline to ask him to wait, so that we complete our discussion before I confront him.'

'That will not be required until later, Indrani.'

'What? And why do you say that, Karan?' Indrani asked, confused.

'Let me call the person we need to speak to first.' He stepped out of the room, walked up to Jacqueline, said something to her and then he walked back into the room.

'Two minutes Indrani.' Indrani looked at Francis, trying to make sense of what Karan was doing. There was pin-drop silence in the room. No one spoke. Indrani wanted all this to get over quickly. It was turning out to be one long nightmare for her.

Finally the silence was broken by a knock on the door of Indrani's cabin. 'Come in,' Indrani called out. The door opened and two people walked in. One of them was Jacqueline.

43

After the Times Today debacle, Krishna Menon was a very distraught old man. All his efforts over the last ten years had come to naught. For someone who hadn't ever taken a dishonest step in his life, this one wrong, albeit critical association with a powerful man had proved to be his undoing.

The call from Mumbai woke him up that morning. It was the third time in twelve hours that a telephone call had disturbed his fragile state of calm. The anger he felt from within had prevented him from sleeping peacefully. Jayakumar had turned out a miserable opportunist—a guy who rocked the boat and also gave out life jackets. Not only had Jayakumar taken him for a ride, he had compromised the position of hundreds of thousands of innocent civilians residing in the vicinity of the TNPP. In a fit of anger, he had mentioned to the person calling from GB2 that he was withdrawing from the protest, but if someone had to go, it was Jayakumar. He was not going to compromise on that. If he did, it would be a disservice to the entire community of Devikulam. The community that had given him everything. His son, Arvind, who died a torturous death in the aftermath of Chernobyl, in Ukraine—hadn't he promised him in his last days that he would dedicate his life to make sure that the people of Devikulam wouldn't meet that fate? It was around the same time Devikulam was being considered as a possible site for an Indo-Russian collaboration for a nuclear plant. If he backed out now, what would happen to that promise made to his dying son?

He was tossing around in bed restlessly when the call had come. This time, unlike last night, the caller didn't seem to be in a hurry.

Karan introduced himself and talked to him about not taking a decision in a hurry. Devikulam needed him. Karan also told him about the possible money-laundering angle. When he heard about the likelihood of CNRI being funded through an organization based in Vienna, which in all probability was a conduit for pumping in money by the American and German nuclear bodies, to stall the commissioning of TNPP, he was a bit surprised. Krishna Menon told Karan about the CBI interrogation in detail. When he told Karan about the discussion with the defence secretary about the arms deal with Israel, Karan was not shocked. Bhaskar had mentioned it to him the previous night. When Krishna Menon told him about the conversation with Dr Heldrich and the French nuclear scientist, matters became clear to him.

'Jayakumar is a double agent. It is clear that he is working undercover for the Americans and Germans and maybe some others who do not want India to be a nuclear power, in their quest to stall the commissioning of the TNPP. I am sure they have multiple Jayakumars floating in the system to further their cause. Not only that, from what you are saying, and from what I have seen in the last twenty-four hours, Jayakumar is also working for the Israeli ammunition lobby, as a deal-maker. In the process, he is arm-twisting the people in the government who are on his payroll. He will succeed in one of the objectives. The government might succumb to the kickbacks and the pressure and end up buying from the Israelis. They might buy peace and save their three billion dollar investment. Or the government may procrastinate and delay the commissioning of the project, which suits the other nuclear powers. Either way, Jayakumar succeeds. And in the process, he will make his money.'

'What a criminal mastermind!'

'He is a criminal sir. He must be dealt with as a criminal.' And Karan spoke to him at length, trying to talk Krishna Menon through the confusion and depression in his mind.

'Thanks for the conversation friend. You have helped me see things more clearly.'

'Have a good day sir. The TV anchor might not know the true story, and that's why they would have succumbed to wrong information. Once they get to know the truth, they will back you sir. I know them very well. And that's why I called back to tell you sir, that you must not back out. If you back out now, the anti-Indian forces will win. We would rather die losing than back out. It will be a shame on this nation if people like you are brow-beaten into submission. I will make sure my newspaper supports you.'

For the first time in thirty six-hours, Krishna smiled. 'Yes my son. God bless.' Karan bid him luck and hung up.

After this discussion, Krishna got up and walked to the washroom, where he splashed a few drops of water on his face. The call from Mumbai had rejuvenated his thoughts, his dreams, and had made his desire to fight even fiercer. By the time he walked out, Sulochana was also trying to get out of bed to make him some coffee.

'It's okay. Sleep for some more time. I will make the coffee for you today.'

'What?' She couldn't even remember the last time Krishna had made coffee for her. Something was different. When she saw a changed Krishna, she began to wonder what was wrong. Or rather, what was right. Whatever it was, it had pepped up Krishna and made him happy.

'I'm not going to give up. Jayakumar can do what he wants. I have the people supporting me. I will not give up. I will live my remaining life on my terms,' said Krishna, when he saw her puzzled look and he poured a glass of water into the percolator and switched it on. A pleasant aroma of coffee filled the room as Krishna walked out through the connecting passage and opened the door and stepped out into the verandah. A new day had begun.

44

Indrani stared at the two people who had walked into her room.

'Tanuja!' a shocked Indrani exclaimed as she turned and looked at Karan. To Jacqueline's right, with a big smile on her face was Tanuja. When she saw the grim looks on everyone's face, her smile vanished.

'Is everything alright Indrani?'

Indrani was confused. She didn't know what to say. 'Karan, do you know what you are doing? You'd better be sure.'

'I am Indrani.'

Indrani was extremely unhappy that Karan had brought Tanuja into the picture. 'Hope you have a plausible explanation for this. It's disgusting.'

'What is this about Indrani? I'm a bit confused. Is this something to do with the story that the Times is doing on GB2?'

'There is no story Tanuja,' Indrani responded.

'Then? What is Karan doing here?'

'Dilip Singh Rajput,' Karan began his story without waiting for Indrani to respond to Tanuja's query. 'Heard of him?' he asked, eyes firmly riveted on Tanuja.

'I think Dilip works in our Jaipur Branch,' Tanuja casually responded.

'Yes Tanuja. He does. In fact, he is the Branch Manager of the Jaipur branch.'

'Okay?'

'Yogesh Bhargav was paid three hundred thousand rupees for having referred Dilip's CV to GB2 for hiring.' When Karan made this statement, Indrani wondered what the connection was.

'That's normal. We pay sixteen per cent of CTC for all the hiring we do through recruitment consultants.'

'That's fair,' and he looked at Indrani. 'Only if. . .'

'Only if?' Tanuja enquired.

'Only if the candidate was referred by a recruitment consultant.'

'What do you mean?' Tanuja was getting increasingly agitated.

'23rd September 2011, 2.46 p.m., Dilip Singh Rajput sends you a mail enclosing his CV. Same day at 4.52p.m., the CV gets forwarded to Yogesh Bhargav, who resends the same CV to you on 24th September at 9.45 a.m., with his stamp on it. Dilip Singh Rajput becomes a Yogesh Bhargav referred candidate, overnight. The funny thing is that as per Dilip Singh Rajput's confession this morning, he doesn't even know who Yogesh Bhargav is and hasn't even spoken to him once.'

'Are you insinuating that we are a corrupt bunch of HR professionals?' Tanuja took him head-on.

'Don't get me wrong Tanuja. I am not insinuating anything. In fact, I'm stating it outright.'

Tanuja looked at Indrani, anger flashing in her eyes. 'Indrani we can't have an outsider passing judgments on all of us in your presence. I am answerable to you—not to him.'

Indrani was silent. She wanted to hear the whole story. Tanuja had questioned Karan's intent, but she had not denied whatever he had said. 'Let's hear him and then we will decide Tanuja. There is no smoke without fire.' Indrani was sitting at her desk, elbows on the table and her chin propped up by her palms.

'Of the fifty personnel files we asked for, Indrani, twenty-nine were hired in the last two years through Yogesh Bhargav. Between the three of us, we spoke to fourteen of them this morning. I was shocked to know that none of them had sent their résumés to Yogesh Bhargav or had ever spoken to him. All fourteen of them had sent their résumés to either Tanuja or Vikram directly. Each RM is in the salary range of around ten lakh per annum, which means that we have paid around a lakh and half to recruit each of these guys. In the twenty minute check that we have done, it comes out that Yogesh Bhargav has been paid over twenty-one lakh extra for work that he's never done.'

'This is utter nonsense. You can't corner me like this. I have no means of validating anything that you are saying. If I have the data, I can respond. My conscience is clear.' It was irking Tanuja that Indrani was quiet and not saying a word. 'I can go down and get the details right away in case you need it Indrani.'

'I am fine as of now. I suggest you wait. And Karan. . .this was not in the remit. What is the relevance of Yogesh Bhargav in what we were trying to do?'

'Indrani I was just trying to set the context. It only suggests that over the years, lakhs of rupees could have been siphoned off from the bank under the guise of vendor payments. It shows the mindset of the people in your management team.'

'Point made. Move on Karan. I'm getting impatient. And don't pass value judgments about people in the team. One bad apple does not mean the entire basket is rotten.'

'Sure Indrani. I mentioned this to you earlier, but I will bring it up again. For the sake of Francis and our guest here, Tanuja,' he said sarcastically, 'when we examined all the accounts opened in the last year, we saw that in sixty-eight of these accounts, money came in from overseas and was withdrawn in cash in almost immediately. These transactions, particularly repeated instances of such transactions, confirms the presence of money laundering of some kind.'

'Hmm. . .I am aware of that.'

'All these accounts have been opened by a group of thirteen relationship managers. All these RMs have been hired with Vikram's reference. There are mails from Vikram to Tanuja, which are on file which confirm Vikram's comfort with the candidate and his approval to hire them. In all these mails he explicitly states that he knows the candidate, the reference checks have been done by him and he would like the candidate to be hired as a RM in a particular branch.'

'Shouldn't you be having this discussion with Vikram then?' Tanuja seemed quite hurt by the accusations.

'Yes. We can. Let's call him in.' He opened the door to Indrani's cabin, stretched his neck and called out, 'Jacqueline, can you please get Vikram?'

'Sure.'

'And also please ask Hemant how long he'll be.'

In no time Vikram was in the cabin. Karan quickly handed him a list of thirteen RMs.

'Do you know any of these RMs?'

Vikram looked at the names. He smiled as he saw Zinaida Gomes' name there. 'Yes. I know some of them. Not all. Why?'

'If you don't know all of them, how have you referred them for hiring, saying that you know them personally and are convinced of their capabilities?'

'Rubbish.' Vikram defended himself strongly. 'In fact, I don't even get involved in that process. And I haven't recommended any of these for hiring. All of them have been hired following proper procedure.'

'What's this then?' Karan asked, handing him a piece of paper. 'As per this mail, you have recommended all of these RMs and have stated that you know them well. This has also been treated by HR as a tacit approval to waive off mandatory verifications.'

Vikram perused the mail. He had a surprised look on his face. 'I need to check, because I don't recollect having sent this mail.' He looked at the piece of paper again. It was a mail from Tanuja to one of her direct reports, forwarding Vikram Bahl's mail recommending the candidate. For a minute he was confused. Did it have anything to do with the deal with Yogesh Bhargav that he and Tanuja had? He didn't know what to say and what not to. 'Can I check and get back to you?'

'See? It's not my doing. Indrani, you unnecessarily insulted me in front of an outsider. If I don't take it up with the region, it will only be because of our relationship and the respect that I have for you,' Tanuja chimed in, sounding indignant.

'We'll see who takes it up with whom.' The door flew open and Hemant walked in. 'Before you go to the regional office and complain, just let us know why you hired these thirteen guys in the bank.'

'Hemant you were not here when we discussed this issue. Vikram is going to check and get back to Indrani.'

'That may not be necessary,' Hemant barked. He seldom got upset, but when he did, no one could stand in front of him.

'Why? May I ask?' Tanuja mocked with a drawl.

'Because, Tanuja, while those mails are on record, Vikram never sent them to you.'

'What do you mean?' Her voice was shaky now. Hemant observed that her phone was being passed on from one hand to the other and back again. . .a sure sign of nervousness. *Time to move in for the kill,* he thought.

'You doctored those mails. You modified some other mails from Vikram and made them look like Vikram's recommendations and forwarded them to your team to be printed out and included in the personnel file. You knew that no one from your team would dare to get back to Vikram on any of those candidates, knowing the two of you were close.'

Tanuja was indignant. 'Are you out of your mind Hemant? Do you even know what you are saying?'

'Yes madam, maybe while doing this, you forgot that there is a permanent imprint—a shadow copy—of every mail on the company server. A quick check run by IT confirmed that Vikram did not send those mails to you. We checked all thirteen cases for a match on time, date and content. And Tanuja, I am happy to confirm that these mails are fabricated. They just confirmed a minute ago.' Karan had an evil grin on his face when Hemant said this, a grin which Tanuja hated. She had begun to despise him. 'Hemant does this for a living. It took him all of fifteen minutes to figure out that these mails were fabricated. He was actually on a call with IT which is why he didn't come in with me and Kavya,' Karan looked at Indrani and offered an explanation.

'And Indrani, I even spoke to a few branch managers,' Hemant continued. 'They don't have the courage to check these RMs because of the perception that these RMs are close to Vikram. And using that to their advantage, these RMs opened sixty-eight fraudulent accounts which have been used as a conduit for laundering over two hundred crore rupees. And worse, none of the Branch Managers want to confront these account holders and classify these accounts as a suspicious transaction monitored account because in the branch-banking world there is a perception created by these RM's that these are Vikram's references.'

Vikram was aghast. He didn't know any of those relationship managers. How could Tanuja double-cross him? He was not ready to believe that Tanuja could have fabricated those mails.

'My email ID is accessed by multiple people, including my secretary and a few people in the department. They have the right to send and receive emails from my ID. We need to investigate this further to get to the bottom of this before we affix the blame on one individual.' Tanuja's defence was a good one. But she was not prepared for what came next.

'We can do that Tanuja, but before that, can you take a look at this list and see if any name rings a bell?' Karan handed her the same list he had given Vikram earlier.

Tanuja refused to be drawn into a conversation with Karan. In what she considered a direct snub to Karan, she looked at Indrani and answered Karan's question. 'I don't remember these cases Indrani. I will check and get back to you.'

'Do you know these guys at all?' Karan ignored the snub and handed her the list with thirteen names.

'No, I don't think I know them.'

'Are you sure you don't know them?'

'I may know *of* one or two of them but I don't know any of them well enough.'

'Then how do you explain this?' Karan handed her the mobile bill reimbursements for the last few months.

'What is this?'

'According to this bill, there are fifteen people you call every day. One I presume is your husband, one is Vikram and the other thirteen are these thirteen RMs. If you don't know them, why do you call them every day?'

'I don't know what you are talking about.'

'Indrani,' Karan continued, 'these are the last three months' telephone bills claimed by Tanuja, which you have approved. I have marked the numbers I was talking about. I can't figure out why she calls them every day, when there are members in her team that she doesn't talk to for days together. I guess she has the responsibility to herd them together and make sure they do what she wants them to do. Right?'

'Karan!' cried Tanuja. 'This is a serious invasion of privacy. And Indrani, I don't think you should keep quiet. I can take shit from you, but not from an outsider. . .and that too in front of junior colleagues,' she pointed at Kavya and Hemant while stating this.

'Maybe privacy will be a bit too much to expect after we finish whatever we have to say,' Hemant too joined in. He was extremely pissed at the way Tanuja had exploited the system to her advantage.

'Shut the fuck up Hemant.' Tanuja was close to tears. She had never been put in such a position in her career. She was being pushed into a corner and she was trying to fight back.

'Karan,' said Indrani. 'You are really worrying me. Can you please stop being dramatic and tell me what the real story is?'

'Indrani, pardon me for this long preamble. It was necessary in order to reveal to you the character of someone who is held in such high esteem within GB2.'

'So? Now what?'

'Indrani, humour me for some time. I won't take too long. Please let me do it my way.' He turned to Tanuja, 'Raymond Saldanah was found hanging from a bridge, yesterday morning. Why did he call you the previous night?'

'I didn't speak to him.'

'Are you sure Tanuja?'

'Yes.'

'Great. Can you please give me a print out of Tanuja's telephone extension?' Karan extended his hand towards Kavya, who gave him a piece of paper. 'Thanks. There you go Tanuja. Day before yesterday night, the night Raymond was killed, he spoke to you once for twelve minutes at 6.48 p.m. The detailed print out of the call records, that you have in your hand now, prove that. Thank God for technology Indrani. EPABXs these days register the incoming numbers too.'

'The mobile service provider too confirmed the calls, when I spoke with them this morning,' Hemant added.

'Also after this call Tanuja, Raymond tried your number nine times and each time it went to voice mail. What was it that Raymond was trying to tell you? What was the conversation that you had with him?' Karan was unrelenting.

Tanuja was dumbstruck. She had not expected this. 'I don't know where this is heading. You guys have pre-conceived notions about me. I am not answering any more questions. I need to talk to my lawyer.' She flung the print out of the call records of her extension at Karan and turned towards the door.

'Tanuja, please stay. Else you will be forcing us to take action against you.' By then, Indrani had realized that Karan was not entirely wrong in his hypothesis. At the same time, Jacqueline walked into the room. 'Indrani, ACP Vishnu Shome is here. He is asking for Francis.'

Everyone in the room, with the exception of Kavya, knew that ACP Vishnu Shome was the Assistant Commissioner of Police for South Mumbai and was one of the most influential officers in Mumbai's Police department.

Francis got up from where he had been silently sitting and watching the entire saga unfold. 'I'll go bring him.'

The colour of Tanuja's face changed when she saw the ACP walk in with Francis. She knew that she was cornered. 'I need to speak to my lawyer before saying anything else.' Her voice had sobered down a bit, thanks to the ACP's presence.

'Okay. If she does not want to answer any questions let me brief you.' When Karan said this, Indrani nodded, 'Go on.' By then, pleasantries had been exchanged between the top cop of South Mumbai and Francis.

'Before we get to Raymond, let me start with Pranesh. One fine day Pranesh meets with an accident. . .or rather something that looked like an accident. It was, in fact, cold-blooded murder. Pranesh had a history Indrani. He was earlier in the Thane branch. He had been accused of being negligent while accepting cash from the customers. Counterfeit notes were pumped into the banking system through him. On a daily basis, two specific account-holders of other branches would come and exchange amounts in the range of tens of lakhs in cash for smaller denomination notes. That was what everyone believed. The fact was that they were exchanging counterfeit notes for genuine ones. They would deposit lakhs of rupees in counterfeit currency and Pranesh would happily exchange it and give them genuine currency. Two to three crores of counterfeit notes came into circulation in the banking system every month. Everything was fine till one day, Raymond, who was posted in the Thane branch, saw him meet the same guys outside the branch and he decided to look into it. Around the same time, some Thane branch customers complained about counterfeit notes being found in their thousand rupee bundles.

Raymond did a surprise check and found out that twenty per cent of the cash in Pranesh's cash box was counterfeit. Pranesh's defence was that the cash came in through a large customer who had deposited thirty lakhs that day. It created quite a ruckus. The issue was hushed up because GB2 was scared about its reputation and brand image. Even a single counterfeit note found needs to be reported to the RBI, let alone such a huge haul. The counterfeit notes found in Pranesh's cash box were destroyed, and the amount was somehow adjusted. The issue was hushed up. The customer was asked to shut his account and Pranesh was moved to the Bandra branch. They did not have enough evidence of Pranesh's involvement in the counterfeit currency scandal. Had the bank taken action against him, the bank staff union would have got involved and the issue would have come into focus and blown into a media scandal, or so everyone thought. But what people don't know is that it was Tanuja who dangled this staff union issue blowing up as a sword on the heads of Vikram and Juliana and used it as a tool to defend Pranesh in these investigations and orchestrated his move to Bandra. He got a fresh lease of life. Why did Tanuja support him? She could have got rid of him and the union would not have even created a whimper. They have never supported anyone caught in an integrity trap.'

'Yes. There is a mail that Tanuja had sent me. I think it was marked to Juliana as well,' Vikram volunteered. 'She was categorical that we will get into issues with the union and the entire counterfeit issue will come out in the open if we took action against Pranesh. That was the key reason we dropped all action and just cautioned him for his negligence in accepting counterfeit notes.' He was simmering at the thought of Tanuja having taken him for a ride. 'I will have a copy of that mail on file.'

Indrani looked at Vikram and then at Karan. 'So are you saying that Tanuja orchestrated his move to Bandra? And how did you get to know this in one day?'

'We did a sweep of Raymond's desk last night. We saw the full note on this in one of his drawers. In the note he does not suspect Tanuja of any wrongdoing; he only says that she might have been worried of the union's response, which led to her supporting Pranesh. Here's the note. Raymond had sent this to Juliana, but she chose to ignore it.'

'Then why are you blaming Tanuja for it?'

'Because I haven't yet told you the entire story yet.'

'Go on. . .'

'What Raymond didn't know is that Tanuja saved Pranesh because if she hadn't, he would have exposed her.'

'As in?'

'The account that was involved in this counterfeit business was opened by one of the RMs brought in by Tanuja who was intricately involved with the money laundering business and counterfeit trade.'

'Are you sure?' Indrani asked, sounding dazed.

'Yes Indrani.' Karan was sure of every word coming out of his mouth. 'Tanuja hired these thirteen RMs who then opened the sixty-eight fraudulent accounts, which were then used to launder money both from within the country and overseas. Pranesh was roped in to help them in the counterfeit business. Whether Pranesh was a part of an elaborate strategy or just stumbled into this plan, I don't know.'

'Okay.' Creases appeared on Indrani's face.

'At some point in time, Pranesh became greedy and turned rogue. He started blackmailing Tanuja.'

'And how do you know this? I am sure the note that Raymond left behind does not cover this.'

'At about 4.00 p.m. on the day he died, Nikhil had overheard Pranesh speak to someone about a cash transaction. Pranesh was on his phone, oblivious of the fact that Nikhil could hear him. He was saying that if he didn't get the cash, then he would speak to others in the bank and that would prove to be embarrassing for the individual on the other side of the call. Nikhil told me this when I met him last evening. I checked with my contacts at Vodafone this morning. The only call Pranesh has made between 3.00 and 5.00 p.m. from his mobile was to Tanuja. And the call went on for eighteen minutes. He was blackmailing Tanuja and she chose to eliminate him. There were no incoming calls to his mobile during that period.'

'I must say, you're a great script writer,' Tanuja said sarcastically.

'Oh yes. Wait till you hear the remainder of the story. It's a blockbuster.'

'With Pranesh out of the way, she had everything working for her. Complete control over the RMs who danced to her tunes. She became smarter after the Pranesh episode and would be in touch with them every single day to make sure that they didn't go the Pranesh way. She kept a tab on what they did, who they met, what they spoke. She needed an update on everything they did.'

'Hmm. . .' Indrani was all ears.

'All was fine till Raymond got wind of Asia Logistics. His intuition told him that something was not right. He tried to investigate the account but met with resistance at every level. His boss was too scared to take on anyone who was close to you. She was happy being in Vikram's and your good books. Raymond didn't get any support from her. This is anecdotal though. Raymond then tried to ask the branch some uncomfortable questions, but Zinaida, who was one of Tanuja's thirteen RMs, was up to the task. She managed the queries quite well. In fact, these RMs were trained to make every account opening appear perfect and genuine. If one were to go by the documents and memos which have been attached to the account opening form, no one can point a finger at her—the documents are impeccable. She has done a great job covering her back. In fact, the account opening documentation of all the sixty eight accounts is flawless.'

Tanuja was getting fidgety. Her nervousness showed as she restlessly shifted from one leg to the other.

Karan didn't pay any heed to her frame of mind and went on, 'This phase too would have passed had Harshita not been close to Raymond. As luck would have it, she landed in Vienna.'

'I know this angle.' Indrani referred to the discussions earlier that day.

'The remittances into the account of Asia Logistics came from a boutique bank in Liechtenstein. The remitter, Union of Jews Foundation, had a Vienna address. Raymond had figured out that these sixty-eight accounts were benami accounts, which were being used to launder money and would also have figured out the UJF angle. The reputation of Liechtenstein as a tax haven also increased his suspicions. In fact Indrani, Raymond had asked for the same data that we asked for. So I am reasonably confident that he would have arrived at the same conclusion. Raymond asked Harshita to check out the veracity of the organization—whether it existed and if the address was correct.'

'How can you be so sure? Both Raymond and Harshita are dead.' Francis asked Karan. He had not been a party to the discussion with Malvika and hence was not aware. Karan and Hemant took turns in taking Francis and Vishnu Shome through their findings about Harshita, her Skype with Raymond, Raymond's request to check out the address, the morning discussion with Malvika etc.

'Harshita went to visit the address that night, found it, and got killed.' Karan looked at Vishnu Shome and then at Tanuja.

'It was an accident,' Tanuja intervened.

'Not if one were to go by the press release Tanuja.' So over-confident was Tanuja that she had missed reading the contents of the press release that she herself had forwarded to Indrani the night before.

'We don't even know if they found the address of UJF.'

'Of course we know. They did find the address. They even went to the office.'

'How the fuck do you know this? Please make sure you have your facts in place before spinning tales and accusing someone,' Tanuja was beginning to get hysterical.

'Here, take this,' and he gave both Tanuja and Indrani a sheet. 'This is a picture Harshita had clicked outside the office of UJF the night that she died.'

'I have seen these. It proves that Harshita went there and was killed as a consequence. But still does not prove Tanuja's involvement. I refuse to believe that Tanuja could have played a part in killing someone.' Indrani still wasn't completely convinced.

'Indrani you will, once I'm done.'

'I hope not.' Indrani turned her face away from Karan. She was praying that what Karan was insinuating wasn't true. ACP Vishnu Shome who was standing next to Indrani's table, took the picture from Indrani and looked at it intently.

'How did you manage to get this image?'

'Harshita had clicked this and a few other photos that night, before they got caught. When on the run, she happened to pass by the same Café Coffee Day outlet that they had visited in the evening. When she was calling out to them for help, which is what the press release says, her iPhone automatically connected to the store's Wi-Fi, and all the photos that she had taken got uploaded to iCloud. She was logged on to iCloud on Malvika's iPad, which she had configured while gifting it to Malvika. And bingo, all the photos taken on the iPhone appeared on the iPad.' He turned to stare at Tanuja. 'The photo you have in your hand Tanuja, is the first of the pictures taken outside the office of UJF.'

'I feel so sorry for her.'

'Here are the other pictures Indrani.' Tanuja strained her neck to see what those pictures were but Indrani was reasonably far from her and she couldn't make it out.

'Why are you showing this to me again?' Indrani's expression changed as she saw the photos again, one by one. Her face betrayed her anxiety, which quickly turned to frustration, followed by horror and finally, anger. The pictures had been taken from a distance and hence all objects appeared to be small. However, this time she had her reading glasses on and hence could see what was going on, though the faces were still not clear.

'Jacks!' Karan shouted loudly.

Jacqueline walked in. She had a packet in her hand which she gave Karan. The latter opened it, pulled something out and handed it over to Indrani.

45

'Sir,' a voice reverberated over the speaker phone, when an irritated Johann Schroeder pressed the button on the instrument lying on the table in front of him. The phone had disturbed his preoccupied thoughts about the two Indian tourists.

'Yes', he snarled into the speakerphone. 'Yes Karl. What is it?' Karlis Simanis was the head of the Forensics division of Vienna police.

'You need to get down here to see something Johann.'

'What is it Karl?'

'The team's found something.' Karl was personally leading the forensic sweep of the Union of Jews Foundation apartment, given the sensitive nature of the case. 'I wanted you to see it before we did anything about it.'

'How many people do you have on site?'

'Three. We have been as discrete as we possibly could. We've sent in a small tactical team, that's it. No one has noticed us so far.'

'Great. I'll be there in fifteen,' and Johann hung up. Jumping up from his seat, he instinctively reached out and patted the Smith and Wesson 1911, which was firmly holstered on the right side of his trousers. Taking it out of the holster, he admired its scandium alloy frame momentarily as he caressed its 4.25" barrel. He turned it around and performed the customary checks, making sure it was loaded with its usual two eight round magazines. 'Hope I don't have to use these,' he said to himself as he put it back into the holster and rushed to his car. Wanting to keep it a low-key operation, he drove on his own. No pilot cars. No howling sirens.

In twelve minutes he was in Odeongasse. After driving round and surveying the neighbourhood, he chose a nondescript location to park his car. Johann was glad that he was in plain clothes. He had been invited to give a talk at his son's school that afternoon. Not wanting to intimidate the kids by wearing a police uniform, he had chosen to wear a normal suit that day. No one noticed him as he parked two blocks away from the UJF and stepped out. There weren't too many people around in any case. He patted his holster again to check for the S&W 1911.

He walked as fast as he could without attracting attention and reached the façade of the Jewish Towers. Vienna had encountered mild snowfall the night before which accounted for the wet pavements. He scanned the area to see if he was being watched. It took him just two seconds to realize that the old lady walking down the street was only a harmless morning walker. In any case, she was at a distance and was preoccupied with adjusting her muffler around her neck and wouldn't have been able to clearly make out what he was doing there. Sprinting across the road, he entered the ground floor of the building. It was much warmer in there.

The lobby was empty. Even the day he had led a search party there, it had been empty. He quickly ducked behind the pillar to his right, towards the staircase and away from the lift. He waited there for a minute and a half. Despite his fitness levels, Johann was panting. It was the excitement. What had Karl found that he wanted Johann to see? In any case he was now only two floors away—not too far.

Stealthily he made his way up the stairs, trying not to make any sound. In no time he was standing in front of the door. Pulling out his mobile phone, he dialled Karl's number. 'I am outside,' he whispered and turned around, only to see Karl standing at the door. 'Welcome sir,' Karl said and led him inside.

'What's this about Karl?'

'Let me quickly update you on what we have done so far. Isaac, Nelson and I have taken this place apart over the last fourteen hours. We have scanned every inch. We haven't found anything. They have scrubbed this place clean.'

'Any neighbours? Spoken to anyone around?'

'This building is surprisingly silent. There hasn't been any movement whatsoever since yesterday. We haven't spoken to people in neighbouring buildings yet. You wanted this to be as low key as possible, right?'

'Then why did you call me here?' There was a touch of irritation in Johann Schroeder's tone.

'Sir, we were about to call off the entire operation when we found something intriguing. A bit strange. I wanted to show it to you, before we moved forward. In fact that is the only thing we have got to show for this entire operation. Nothing else. No fingerprints. No clues. No nothing.'

'What is it?'

'Why don't you come on in sir? Let me show it to you,' and he walked further into the apartment, heading towards the far end that was closer to the exterior wall. Schroeder followed him wondering what was in store. Enroute, Karl stopped near a black box lying on the floor. He bent down, fiddled with the contents and within a couple of minutes was back on his feet. However, this time around he had something in his hand, which Schroeder recognized as a thermal scanner.

Karl walked a few more step still he was standing right adjacent to the washbasin fixed on the wall outside the bathroom. To the right of the washbasin was the door of the apartment bathroom. To its left was the wall, which had a small four feet by three feet window, which overlooked the street below.

'See this?' Karl said, pointing towards the washbasin. Schroeder nodded his head and looked towards the basin. It was a normal white basin, with a fancy faucet on top. A white plastic pipe was connected at the bottom of the basin which drained out the water. 'This white pipe connects to a secondary pipe, which is concealed here under the flooring,' and he tapped the floor below the basin, 'inside the floor here.'

'Hmm,' nodded Schroeder.

'This secondary pipe is short, three feet long, and runs beneath the floor and exits the building through this wall,' and he pointed to the wall which had the small four feet by three feet window. Outside the building, it connects to the primary drain pipe, through a T-joint. And by the way, the secondary pipe is exclusively for draining water from this washbasin.'

Schroeder stepped up to the window, stretched himself, pulled the curtain aside just a bit, and looked outside the building through the window. 'Hmm. Yes, I can see it. The primary pipe connects the secondary pipes from all the apartments and goes straight down to the ground.'

'Yes', said Karl. 'It goes about thirty-five feet vertically down and connects to the underground sewage system of the city.'

As Schroeder drew the curtain back and turned towards Karl to listen to the rest of the story, he could see a Wien Sewers Authority (WSA) service van pull up into the road adjoining the building from the corner of his eyes. It was not too difficult for him to figure out that it belonged to the WSA—its logo and the colour combination were distinctive enough to make it recognizable from a distance. 'The city has woken up,' he said to himself as Karl went on. Schroeder curtailed his impatience and decided to allow Karl to proceed unhindered. Karl was one of the best forensic experts they had; Johann had trained him himself.

Karl saw the questioning look on Schroeder's face and volunteered, 'The thermal scan of this area confirmed all that I just told you. We pulled data from the WSA network. It revalidated what the scan told us.'

'Alright. What then?' When Schroeder said this, Karl stepped closer to the washbasin and brought his hand up to the knob on the right of the faucet.

Instantly Johann moved his gaze to Karl's hands only to see that Karl was wearing his gloves. 'Standard operating procedure. I learnt it from you, remember? Don't be paranoid.' Johann smiled.

Karl pressed the knob and water started flowing into the basin. 'Wait for a second,' said Karl and didn't move his gaze from the basin. Within five seconds, water started to accumulate, indicating a back flow from the drainpipe into the basin. Hurriedly Karl pressed the knob again and the flow of water stopped.

'A drainage problem? Is that what you are here to check son?' Johann asked him.

'Come on Johann. Give me some credit. It's the second floor. This white pipe, then three feet of the secondary pipe and then a thirty-five feet drop to ground. The pipe from this basin is the only pipe that feeds into the secondary pipe. Nothing can get stuck in that thirty-five feet. It's very unlikely that there is a drainage problem. In fact it is definitely not a drainage problem.'

Schroeder looked outside. Karl was right. 'But if it's not a drainage problem, what is Wien Sewer Authority's truck doing here?' His eyes were riveted on the WSA service vehicle that had just driven in.

'Must be here for some other apartment or building.'

'Possibly. But what is the relevance of the water and drain pipes to what you called me here for?'

'Let me show you.' Karl picked up the thermal scanner and moved some dials on it, presumably to adjust it and looked at Schroeder. The screen of the thermal scanner lit up in shades of red, orange and black. He pointed the scanner towards the 250 watt bulb hanging in one corner of the room, and a portion of the scanner screen, which in any normal camera would have been occupied by the image of the bulb, became red, indicating the presence of a heat generating substance. 'I know Karl that the thermal scanner measures the differences in temperature, which cannot be normally perceived by any normal human being. Can you please move on?' Schroeder couldn't contain his impatience. If he could go straight to the result, he would have. But he was the one who had taught Karl that, in forensic analysis, it's always helpful if one goes through the process of deduction while presenting it to anyone, else the veracity of the end result would always be questioned.

'You are the boss,' said Karl and he adjusted the thermal scanner in such a way that it pointed towards the white pipe. Schroeder could trace the path taken by the water through the pipe, the flow of which had generated a miniscule variation in temperature, which the scanner had registered. A feeble orange glow on the scanner in an L-shaped cylinder indicated the flow of water through the white and secondary pipes. Once the water flowed outside the building, the external chill made it too difficult for the scanner to register any variations in the temperature and hence the screen was largely black in the area, which would have corresponded to the T-joint on the primary drainpipe.

'It's not clear,' said Schroeder.

In response, Karl just lifted his hand and moved it to the knob on the left of the faucet. Schroeder was focused on the screen of the scanner. Karl pressed the knob. Hot water rushed into the basin and thereon into the white pipe, onto the concealed secondary pipe and out of the building into the primary pipe. And as it did so, the image on the thermal scanner underwent an intriguing transformation. In no time, the scanner recorded the dramatic variation of temperature on account of hot water flowing through an otherwise cold pipe. An L-shaped cylindrical image in orange appeared on the screen of the scanner almost instantaneously, tracing the entire route of the water, till it disappeared into the main pipe. He looked at Karl, who pressed the knob to stop the water flow and joined Schroeder. This time the thermal image right up to the T-joint was visible. The outside chill and the hot water inside the secondary pipe had caused a definitive variance in temperature, thereby aiding the thermal scanner in recording the same.

'Well, clearly the water flow is fine. There's no drainage problem. But what the hell is the damn issue?'

'This is the issue sir, which I haven't been able to figure out,' said Karl pointing at the T-joint on the screen. Schroeder could not figure out what he was referring to.

'Sir, look at the flow of water. When it flows through the first tube from the basin to the pipe below the floor, it flows in a straight line. An orange vertical cylinder is all that you see corresponding to the water flowing through the white pipe.' Schroeder nodded.

'Now this is where the water hits the horizontal concealed secondary pipe which leads water through the building wall to the external pipe here,' Karl traced the entire orange cylinder on the screen, from the source to the external drainpipe. 'At first sight, everything seems normal. But when you look closely at the T-joint, something is not right here.'

Schroeder strained his eyes and looked at the image on the thermal scanner. 'Yes, the point where the water flows from the secondary pipe into the main pipe is uncharacteristically different from the remaining path of water. The water flow here is not a steady stream of orange.' Karl nodded.

'Why is it peppered with dots of black?' Schroeder looked at Karl with raised eyebrows. There was silence for a moment and then Schroeder exclaimed, 'A filter!' His eyes were wide open.

'A filter with very minute holes sir. Thermally speaking, such an image of orange peppered with black spots would mean that at the T-junction, despite the hot water flowing through it, there are spots which are cold, i.e. not at the same temperature. Which can only mean that there is something else there. And the pattern of these black spots within the orange suggests that there is a metallic filter there. Surely that's why the flow of water is being blocked.'

'No one puts in such a filter, particularly in drain pipes.'

'Yes sir. But that's not it. Look at this.' Schroeder's eyes followed Karl's fingers as they moved to spot on the screen, just before the T-Junction and the filter

'Look here. Before the two pipes meet, there is a ball of orange.'

Schroeder looked at the image closely. A horizontal rod-like cylindrical stretch of orange colour marked the image of the water flowing in the secondary pipe till the T-junction, except at one point. Just before the T-junction, the red colour seemed to momentarily dip into a small abyss and then recover its trajectory before heading straight into the filter marking the intersection of the two pipes. The trajectory followed by the red at that point seemed to be like an inverted omega symbol (Ω). 'The hot water is accumulating at a point before the filter. Looks like a niche,' Johann Schroeder noted, surprised.

'This means, sir, that there is a chamber there, in the drain pipe. The hot water flows out of the apartment, and accumulates in the niche. This accumulation of water is what caused a back flow, which resulted in clogging of water when I opened the knob earlier. Only water that escapes the niche goes out through the filter into the external pipe.'

'Why would someone design a pipe like that? Is this in the Wien Sewer Authority master layout?'

'We checked. It's not there. The master plan, which we pulled out, showed a normal pipe. Nothing out of the ordinary.'

'So is this a secret storage for something? If so, what could that be?' Schroeder pulled back the curtains and looked out again.

'Karl,' he called out and even before Karl could respond, 'trouble,' he added. Karl quickly ran up to the window and looked out in the direction towards which Schroeder was intently staring. 'What is it?'

'Why is the Wien Sewer Authority truck backing up into this building and extending its telescopic turntable ladder towards this apartment? As far as I know, this building has been empty for some time now.'

Karl looked out again. Johann too, silently observed what the WSA truck was doing. A mid-ship, like the ones used by firemen to rescue people stranded on higher floors in case of a fire, was affixed to the ladder being raised. Two men were standing on the road adjacent to the WSA van and were looking at their colleague who was inside the mid-ship. From a distance, the man on the mid-ship looked too polished to be a WSA employee.

'Ask for back-up', whispered Schroeder, turning towards Karl. 'Quick! We have a team stationed at Nestroy,' and looking at the other two men who were with Karl, but had stayed quiet all this while, he added, 'You two watch the door. If anyone walks up, and you don't get answers, shoot. And use silencers. We don't want the entire neighbourhood rushing in here.'

Karl immediately got away from the window, and made a call. In no time, he was back to give Schroeder company. Schroeder took out his S&W 1911 from the holster and brought his hand up to the stainless steel slider. He cranked it back, and took position. 'How long?' he asked. 'ETA, seven minutes,' Karl responded.

'They're clearly not WSA employees. It's a façade. If they are not what they are pretending to be, then I presume they are the ones who killed the Indians.' The wind was strong. The jacket that the intruder in the mid-ship was wearing moved just a bit, but it was enough for the razor sharp eye of the deputy chief of police to catch the outline of a revolver tucked inside the trousers. 'The bastard's armed.' Schroeder did a quick calculation and whispered, 'It will take him three minutes to get the ladder down, so if he takes at least four minutes at the drain pipe, we will get them. Murderers. Bastards.' Johann Schroeder was furious. Vienna was his city, and crime of any sort was unacceptable.

By this time, the mid-ship had come to a halt just below the window. Through a gap in the curtain, Karl and Schroeder observed what the visitor was up to. There was no way the man in the mid-ship could have seen Schroeder and Karl unless they exposed themselves to him. On reaching the drainpipe, the intruder took some tools out and got to work. He unscrewed a small portion of the secondary pipe, just next to the T-Joint. 'He's opening up the niche,' whispered Karl. Schroeder nodded, but he didn't remove his gaze from the intruder.

The intruder lifted the piece of the pipe which had come loose and carefully placed it next to him. When Johann saw what was below the piece that the intruder had lifted off, he was shocked. Concealed below the cover pipe that had come off, was a keypad. The intruder keyed in a six-digit code and the layer came free. He carefully removed that layer and one could see water in the pipe below. The suspect pulled out a pair of latex gloves from his pocket and wore them in a jiffy, post which he put his hands inside the pipe, into the niche and pulled out four tiny packets. Each packet was of the size of a pouch containing about ten Hershey's kisses. The packets quickly disappeared into some secret compartment in his clothing. The intruder placed the keypad back, locked it with a code, and screwed on the top of the pipe back. Schroeder looked at his watch. Two minutes and the back-up would be there. He would be covered on the ground level and could take his chances. He drew back the curtain and threw open the window. Cold breeze caressed his face as he took aim and screamed, 'Freeze!'

The intruder looked up and was shocked to see someone in the apartment, that too with a gun in his hand. Instinctively he reached out for his revolver with his right hand. Johann Schroeder fired. The bullet ricocheted off the railing of the mid-ship and disappeared somewhere in the thirty-five feet abyss down below. 'Next time I will not miss. Put your hands on your head, where I can see them,' cried Schroeder. The hands came up, in an indication of submission, and snaked their way up to the head, where they finally came to rest. The intruder looked down. For a minute he contemplated jumping. But it was too high, too risky. Chances of survival were limited. He dismissed that as a bad idea. Suddenly three police patrol cars with sirens blazing raced into the street and came to a screeching halt near the WSA van. Eight men jumped out of the cars and took positions, ready to fire at the two accomplices of the intruder, on the ground, just in case they tried to flee. They were hiding behind the WSA van.

Schroeder looked down. He was glad that he had things under control. The case was close to getting solved—almost.

At that very instant, one of the accomplices from behind the van hurled a low intensity grenade at the cops. There was a minor blast followed by lots of dust and smoke. The cops ducked for cover. Sensing an opportunity, the two men turned away and started running, leaving the intruder behind. They were running towards an alley hoping that, by the time the cops would regain composure, they would have disappeared into the alley and thereon into the complex maze of lanes and by-lanes. Schroeder was watching. The men were approaching the alley. He couldn't let them get away. Something had to be done. The S&W was put to use. He took aim and fired. It hit one of the men, who tumbled to the ground. Egged by what Schroeder did, Karl too took aim and fired. The first one missed but the second bullet hit his target on the ankle. He too crashed, holding his ankle in pain. Karl and Schroeder looked at each other and smiled. It was a mistake. This momentary lapse of concentration gave the window of opportunity to the intruder to pull out his gun and shoot in their direction. The bullet brushed past Karl's left shoulder, knocking him down. Blood started oozing from of his shoulder. When Schroeder saw his protégé injured, he was furious. Looking out of the window, he took aim. The intruder had stepped out of the mid-ship and was hastily climbing down the ladder. It was a stupid move, as a posse of police officers was waiting for him near the WSA van.

Schroeder considered his options. He wanted some leverage. If his men accosted the intruder and took him into custody, it would take him ages to interrogate him and get to the bottom of the murder investigation. Once taken into custody, protocol had to be followed, which would prevent him from using certain techniques the cops normally liked to use. He needed quick answers.

Schroeder waited for about fifteen seconds. The intruder was now only ten feet from the ground. A few more steps and he would be a jump away. Carefully, he took aim and muttered something as he pulled the trigger. The bullet hit the intruder on his thigh. He fell off the ladder and landed on the ground with a thud. He tried to get up but couldn't. Schroeder, followed by Karl, who was clutching his profusely bleeding left shoulder in his hand, rushed to the ground floor right and out of the building, to the place where the intruder lay bleeding.

By then, the back-up team had surrounded the intruder and disarmed him. Schroeder walked up to him and said, 'What were you doing up there?'

'I was repairing the sewage lines. We had received a complaint. . .aaaah,' the suspect writhed in pain. It was becoming unbearable.

'Since when did WSA employees start carrying firearms?' he thundered. 'And crude bombs?' Karl added pointing towards his accomplices lying a few feet away.

'What was it that you came for? Out with it!' Schroeder demanded. The suspect kept moaning and didn't respond. Schroeder bent down, caught hold of him and patted him down. He felt something midway between his chest and abdomen on the right. One of the cops gave him a small knife. He cut open the clothing to find the secret compartment, and out tumbled four packets that the intruder had pulled out from the niche in the drainpipe. He opened one of the packets and emptied the contents on his palm. He was shocked.

'Raw uncut diamonds!' Schroeder exclaimed. 'Diamonds!' Karl exclaimed. 'Blood diamonds! Here in Vienna?'

Schroeder systematically checked the other three packets. They contained diamonds as well. 'What the hell is this?' exclaimed Schroeder. 'Is this what you killed the Indians for?' He was shocked to see raw uncut diamonds, the kind found in the mines of Africa. He didn't know what or rather who he was dealing with.

'I didn't kill anyone,' the intruder protested weakly. It was not without reason that Schroeder had shot him. Schroeder turned and looked at the eight cops who were a part of the back-up team. They were a team of hand-picked loyalists. He turned back. The intruder was still lying flat on the road, writhing in pain. Nonchalantly, Schroeder took aim. This time it was the other leg. The bullet pierced the thigh and burnt its way through, right up to the bone where it firmly embedded itself. A shrill scream erupted and shattered the calm of the neighbourhood. The intruder was in desperate pain. Schroeder was unmoved. He was not willing to hand him over to the medics till he gave them the whole story. Who was he? Where did he get the diamonds? Why did they kill the Indians? It was not too difficult, given the tremendous pain that the intruder was in. It was only a matter of time before he started to sing like a bird. The leverage that Schroeder had bargained for when he shot at the intruder was working. After getting all the information he required, Schroeder let him be taken away by the medics. He walked to his car, accompanied by Karl, who by then had been administered first aid. The bleeding had stopped.

As they were driving back, Schroeder asked Karl, 'How did you figure out the secret of the niche in the drain?'

'Quite by accident. In fact, we were checking the faucet for fingerprints when we accidentally pushed the knob. Water started flowing. Quite a fancy faucet it was. We didn't know how to shut it off. In the interim, the water started filling up in the basin. That was quite a surprise because, given the proximity to the main drain and the height, water should not have clogged. That was the warning sign. And now when I look back at it, it was a very smart place to hide these diamonds from everyone. Smuggle uncut diamonds, drop them into the basin. The flow of water will take them to the filter connected at junction with the main pipe. The filter will stop them from going any further and they would collect in the reverse omega shaped niche, which is then accessed using the security passcodes, which our friend David Kosinski knew. No one else in their wildest dreams would have imagined that the drainpipe would contain diamonds. But I still have one question in my mind—why did they not take the diamonds when they hurriedly evacuated the building, the night the Indians went there?'

'This question crossed my mind too. The only rational argument for this could be that the way the diamonds were stored in the niche in the pipe, made them difficult to access, particularly at that time of the night. Hence they fled the site on the night of the 30th leaving the diamonds behind, extremely confident that no one would be able to locate them. After the situation cooled off, and when they were convinced that there was no surveillance and it was safe to come back for the diamonds, they sent David Kosinski, their most trusted aide, who also knew the passcode, to recover the booty. They did not expect us to be there in the apartment. I guess they underestimated the Vienna police in general and Karlis Simanis in particular,' Johann remarked, giving Karl an admiring look.

'Yes sir. You're right. There could be no other explanation for this. By the way, when is Purtsi retiring? Time for you to take over the Vienna Police,' Karl smiled.

'This gesture of sucking up is both unnecessary and appreciated,' Schroeder winked at Karl. The car turned right off the main road into the building, which housed the Vienna Police Headquarters. 'Time to get back to work,' he said as he opened his car door and got out. Someone hurriedly collected the keys from him to safely park the car in the designated slot.

'Yes sir!' said Karl and followed him dutifully. Both of them walked into the building. They both knew they were close to busting the murders which had soiled their impeccable record.

'And Karl, now that we know how the Leles were killed and who killed them, we must alert Interpol on what Kosinski told us. Will you call them and also the Israeli police right away and let them know that Joseph Braganza is scheduled to arrive into Tel Aviv airport this morning? In fact, he would have already arrived,' Schroeder said to Karl as they entered Schroeder's cabin. 'David Kosinski gave us the name of the hotel. Pass it on to them and tell them that they will have to pick him up and extradite him to Vienna. He has to be tried for homicide in this country. I also have to brief Purtsi on the latest developments. We will work out an acceptable story for the media.'

'Will do.'

'Thanks Karl. You were great today. I am proud that you work with me.'

'Thanks sir. But you were the one who inducted me into all this.'

Schroeder smiled as he turned towards his computer screen and started scanning his inbox. After clicking on a few mails, he looked up. Karl was still standing there. 'That will be it, Karl. Just let me know once you have informed Interpol.'

'I will have the information passed on to them. But we still have a problem Johann. We only have a name. We don't even know what he looks like. What will Interpol do with just a name?' He paused. Thought for a couple of seconds and added, 'It's unlikely that Joseph Braganza is his real name.'

'Agreed. But that's all we have.'

'Well, I suppose some information is better than no information at all,' muttered Karl as he turned to exit the room. He knew that the information would not be sufficient to nail

Joseph Braganza. He was a smart operative. Faked nationalities, multiple identities etc, would be a part of the game for someone running an operation of this nature. They had recovered uncut diamonds worth at least twenty million dollars. Once polished, they would be worth at least five times that value. He knew that anyone who operated at this level would not be alone. However, a name was all that they had, and it was necessary that he pass on the information to the Israeli police.

'Wait,' exclaimed Schroeder. 'We might have something here.' Karl turned, only to see an excited Johann Schroeder furiously clicking away on his computer. He got up, walked to his photo printer, picked up the print that he had just fired and walked up to Karl. 'Here, take this.' He waited until Karl had seen the picture. 'Change of plan. Let's not talk to anyone about what David Kosinski told us. Let's do it ourselves.' Karl nodded. 'Send a covert team to Israel. Take him out.'

46

When Karan handed over the contents of the packet, which Jacqueline had brought in, Indrani was both intrigued and irritated. 'Why are you showing me this?' She first looked at Karan and then at Tanuja.

'Indrani you haven't looked closely at the pictures that I gave you earlier.' When Karan said this, Indrani picked up the pictures and looked at them again. She reached out to her reading glasses lying on the table.

'Jacqueline, do you still have Malvika's iPad?' Karan asked Jacqueline who was still in the room.

'Yes I do,' and she dashed out and was back in a jiffy. 'There you go, Karan,' she said, handing over the iPad to him. With a few deft moves of his fingers, Karan manoeuvred the iPad and the pictures appeared on the screen. He went closer to Indrani and tilted the iPad towards her. He zoomed into the picture with his thumb and index finger.

Indrani was now staring at a close-up of the man holding a gun against Siddhartha's head. She was also wearing her reading glasses. The man in the picture was looking around, possibly to see if Siddhartha was alone or if he had anyone else with him.

The fact that Harshita was able to take this picture pointed to the fact that she had not been captured yet. Indrani was shocked when she saw the zoomed-in version. There was unmistakable fear in Siddhartha's eyes. And then she saw the guy holding the gun. The gash on his forehead stood out. Smart, in his late thirties, the guy had stubble, which indicated he had not shaved for a few days. Had Indrani not known him, she would have mistaken him for an Israeli. She looked at the picture and then at Tanuja. Slowly she lifted the photo frame she had pulled out of the packet that Jacqueline had given her and brought it next to the iPad. The person in the photo and the iPad were the same. She knew him; she recognized the cut on the forehead very clearly.

'Abhishek?' she exclaimed.

When Tanuja heard that name, she freaked. 'What? What are you looking at?' Tanuja was suddenly very anxious. She ventured closer to Indrani, but Karan quickly took both the iPad and the photo away. He didn't want Tanuja to have access to the iPad.

'Karan? What is Abhishek doing there?' For the first time that afternoon, Indrani sounded weak. It looked as though she was about to collapse.

'Indrani, what are you talking about? Why are you bringing Abhishek into all this?' Tanuja demanded hysterically. She had started sweating the moment Abhishek's name had come up.

'Abhishek is as involved in this as Tanuja is. Indrani, till the time I walked into Tanuja's room, to keep her in the loop, I was under the impression that all this was done by Vikram. When we sat down in Tanuja's room, I saw her wedding photo on her table and it immediately struck me that the guy in the picture was the same guy I had seen in the photos on Malvika's iPad. The gash on the forehead is so distinctive, I couldn't have missed it.'

'Yes it is,' was all Indrani could say. 'I couldn't see clearly at that time. I didn't have my reading glasses.'

'Since you couldn't recognize him when I showed you the picture earlier today, I asked Jacqueline to get the photo frame from Tanuja's room. It's clear Indrani. Harshita checked out the address of Union of Jews Foundation. She found the place, and then who did she find there? Our very own Abhishek Mathur. She recognizes Abhishek but in the process gets caught. Somehow both of them escape from there and run. Abhishek fears identification and the resultant consequences. The best thing for him to do is to get rid of them. They run, cross Café Coffee Day, the photos get uploaded to iCloud by chance, and the rest is history. While running, Harshita calls Raymond, but in the melee, calls his direct line at work, instead of his mobile. The phone goes to voice mail, since it's late at night and no one picks up her call. She leaves a voice mail for him. All that she manages to scream into the phone is, "Raymond. . .Raymond. . .we found the address of UJF. It's correct. . .and Raymond, it's Abhishek. It's Abhishek, Raymond. It's Abhishek. He's after us now."'

'Hmm. . .and how did you get to know what she said?' Indrani was curious.

'After I saw Abhishek's picture on Tanuja's table, I ran back upstairs. I was too shocked to react. In that blank state, I suddenly realized that while running away from Abhishek, Harshita would have tried to reach out to someone. And that someone would have to be Raymond. . .no one else. So I ran up, and went to his desk. I got lucky. Harshita had indeed called him. I don't know how and why we forgot to check his office phone's voicemail last night. We checked everything. . .even the redialled numbers on his direct line, but we didn't check the voice mail.'

'Raymond had heard the voice mail; it did not show up as a new message. The communication system records too show that the last time Raymond accessed his voicemail and heard this message was at 6.47 p.m. yesterday. He called from his mobile phone and used his password to access it. At 6.48p.m. he called Tanuja. Poor fellow. He would have called her to figure out who was the Abhishek that Harshita was referring to. His big mistake was to take Tanuja into confidence. That proved to be his undoing. He too was eliminated before he could share what he knew with anybody else. Obviously Tanuja was not alone; there were people working for her, who carried out these tasks under her instructions. Who these operators are, is not for us to say. Hon. DCP Vishnu Shome and his team will be able to figure that out,' said Karan looking at the DCP.

Indrani looked at Tanuja, shocked. 'Tanuja, is this true?'

'Indrani, we have enough hard evidence to nail the two of them.' Karan butted in.

Indrani ignored Karan. 'Tanuja?' Indrani asked her again. 'What is all this? I need to know if this is true.'

'I need to talk to my lawyer first.' She just turned around, opened the door and walked out. She couldn't go much further. The entire security team of GB2 and a small team of police constables were waiting outside Indrani's cabin.

When Tanuja saw them, she was furious. 'Anyone touches me, mark my words, he is dead!' she screamed. There was only one female security officer and she was quite scared to take on the fury of Tanuja, who just pushed her aside and ran towards the lift.

Francis couldn't do anything. He was worried that if any male security guard touched her, it would become a case of sexual assault and criminal intimidation, which could work against the organization. 'Stop her!' Karan shouted as he saw her dashing away from them.

'Go. Get her,' Vishnu Shome hurriedly instructed his team, which was waiting for his orders.

'She can't be allowed to leave the premises. Jacqueline, please tell security at the main gate not to allow her to get out of the building. At any cost,' Francis instructed and ran after Tanuja. 'Restrain her. Close down the main gate,' he yelled to his team as he blindly followed Karan who was going after Tanuja towards the lift lobby.

As Karan entered the lift lobby to stop Tanuja from running out of the building, he saw her waiting anxiously. The lift was on sixth floor and was on its way down. Seeing Karan enter the lobby, Tanuja darted left, opened the door and headed into the fire exit. Karan and Francis followed suit. They were surprised when Tanuja, instead of running down, started running up towards the terrace. In no time, she flung open the door at the top of the stairs and ran onto the terrace. For a moment, she stopped and checked if she could bolt the terrace door from outside, but there was no latch on the metal door.

She walked up to the edge to see if there was any way she could jump across the buildings and escape, at least for the time being. She would live to fight another day. There was some commotion at the entrance to the terrace. She turned. She could hear footsteps and voices heading towards her. There was no escape; they would get her soon. One last look at the terrace door and she had made up her mind.

The windscreen of the Mercedes parked beneath the building was blown to smithereens, and the roof caved in to kiss the leather of the seat as Tanuja's body crashed onto it with a big thud. Colleagues and others standing nearby rushed towards the Merc, but were only able to pull the lifeless and limp body of Tanuja out from the car.

47

The headline of *The Times of India* next day was a very poignant one: *'Father–Daughter duo meet tragic end in money laundering scam.'*

In a startling turn of events, two people died under tragic circumstances. Tanuja, the Head of Human Resources at a global bank, jumped from the terrace of the bank building at MG road in the busy Fort area of Mumbai. She is alleged to have been one of the key perpetrators of a massive money-laundering scam spread across the country. In an operation, which lasted till late in the night, the Central Bureau of Investigation, acting under specific instructions from the Government of India, and in tandem with Greater Boston Global Bank, arrested Zinaida Gomes, the Bandra-based relationship manager and twelve other relationship managers of the bank, from their residences.

In what seems to be linked to the money-laundering scam, the bank has fired its Head of Retail Banking, Vikram Bahl, even though the bank claims that it was on account of some irregularities and misappropriation of bank funds. Bahl too has been taken into custody by the CBI.

In Devikulam Kerala, the Trikakulam Nuclear Power Plant (TNPP) protests took a really ugly turn when, around the same time as Tanuja's death, Jayakumar, one of the founders of CNRI, an NGO supporting the anti-TNPP movement, was shot dead by 75-year-old Krishna Menon, using his licensed revolver at his resort about ten kilometres from TNPP.

It might be worth noting that Krishna Menon had gone public with his allegations against Jayakumar being an arms lobbyist and having access to dirty money, in a television interview only a day earlier. This had soured the relationships between the two and had led to a power struggle based on who would champion the movement.

Addressing assembled reporters outside the Devikulam police station, Krishna Menon said that his conscience was clear and that what he had done was to make sure that the anti-TNPP struggle remains a struggle of the people of the region and that too for genuine reasons. Krishna added that people like Jayakumar were manipulating the locals for their own gains and on behalf of certain foreign forces and nations opposed to the TNPP.

What lends credibility to the claims of Krishna Menon is the fact that Tanuja, the foreign bank's HR head, involved in the same money laundering scandal, is the youngest daughter of Jayakumar.

A red-corner notice has been issued by the Interpol for the arrest of Abhishek Mathur, Tanuja's husband, whose whereabouts are unknown. A search of Abhishek and Tanuja's residence revealed that Abhishek used different names and identities to travel out of the country. Multiple passports in the names of Joseph Braganza, Mir Zawawi and Suresh Ramamurthy were recovered from the Mathurs' residence. Visiting cards in the name of Abhishek Mathur, McKinsey Consultants were also recovered. McKinsey has denied that anyone by that name ever worked there. Raw uncut diamonds valued at over twenty-two crore were also recovered from the Mathur residence leading one to believe that the Mathurs were a part of a larger global money laundering syndicate. (Detailed report on page four.)

This tale brings into focus the changing aspirations of urban India, and the saga of greed which prevails in most corporates in India, where

morally bankrupt managers are willing to go to any extent to fulfil their
materialistic desires. Has the end become more important than the
means? (Detailed report on page three.)

Karan was sitting at home that morning, reading the morning
edition of *The Times of India*. He had just returned from work a
few hours ago. It had been very difficult for him to convince
Andy and Bhaskar that their cover story should not be derogatory
of GB2 or its management. Hadn't he given his word to Indrani?
Kavya walked into the dining room—she had just woken up. It
was the first time she had stayed back with him for the night.
Karan disappeared into the kitchen and reappeared in three
minutes with a cup of freshly brewed filter coffee and placed it
delicately in front of her on the table.

Kavya smiled. 'If you promise to make me a cup of coffee
every morning, then I might consider allowing you to meet my
parents.' Karan smiled and hugged her. 'I don't need to meet
your parents sweetheart. As long as you are there to savour it, it's
in my own interest to brew it for you,' he winked.

EPILOGUE

The Next Nine Months

Vikram Bahl had to face intense media and legal scrutiny for his alleged involvement in the money laundering scam. After six months of trial by media, which was quick to pronounce him guilty, the courts found no evidence against him and he was acquitted. But the stigma of his association with Tanuja and his brashly corrupt practices became the talk of an industry where trust and integrity were increasingly being seen as the most important personality traits. No financial services firm was willing to hire him. He had to give up his banking career and now relies on his wife's fledgling business as a painter. His career as a banker was doomed the day Tanuja found in him an able ally and more so the day he had met Chandrasekhar at a party at Tanuja's house.

Indrani, the only CEO to have ever had the courage to allow someone from the media investigate an internal scam, was initially touted as a hero, a leader with a vision, as someone who had the courage to take an unprecedented step in corporate history. However, it was not lost on the organization that she had committed a cardinal sin in breaching customer confidentiality and passed on detailed customer and employee information to someone who was not authorised to have access to them. Some would argue that she was left with no other choice. Had she not done what she did, she faced the prospect of GB2 being hauled over coals by the same media which had ended up praising her after the revelations. It could even have been accused of being an accomplice in money laundering. That could have been disastrous for GB2's brand image. A few CEOs, in private, even acknowledged the fact that they too might have done what Indrani did. This argument, however, didn't cut ice with the board of GB2, which in a sweeping gesture, banished her to Mauritius to handle GB2's miniscule operations there, in what was largely seen as a punishment posting. However, given her resilience and the goodwill she enjoyed, she is expected to bounce back strongly in the coming years.

A badly mutilated body of an Indian, said to be Abhishek Mathur was found in a hotel in Israel. It is suspected that after the exposé related to the involvement of the German and American nuclear agencies and the CIA in the laundering of money, which made its way to the TNPP protests, he was disavowed by the agencies backing him. It was widely speculated that in order to prevent any damage to their reputation resulting from any leakage of information—had Abhishek Mathur been taken into custody, he might have been taken out by the very same agencies that he worked for. Though not many know that moments before he died, armed with revelations of an injured David Kosinski, a tactical team of the Vienna police had clandestinely raided the hotel and knocked on the doors of the room in which an unsuspecting Abhishek Mathur was holed up.

Mumbai police reclassified the Raymond Saldanah suicide case as a homicide and began investigations into the murder of the compliance head. Not much is expected to come of it as the brains behind the murder were already dead.

The TNPP protests continued as usual. With Krishna Menon in jail for the killing of Jayakumar, his wife Sulochana is leading the battle for the citizen's rights. Though she is not expected to win the battle, and TNPP is closer to commissioning than it ever was, the events that took place in the cusp of January and February surely turned the attention of the local and international media on the quaint town of Devikulam in the Western Ghats. It forced the government to come clean on a number of issues related to the site selection and rehabilitation, which was what Krishna Menon was fighting for in the first place.

Johann Schroeder took over as the President of Vienna Police in five months. No one ever got to know about the covert operation in Israel, which Karlis Simanis, on explicit instructions from Schroeder had staged. Johann Schroeder had, at the last minute, changed his mind about passing on the information about Joseph Braganza aka Abhishek Mathur to Interpol and the Israeli police, when he had seen the images which had been mailed to him by Karan Panjabi, who had got his email id from the Vienna Police's press releases. Karlis Simanis was rewarded for his loyalty to Schroeder and made the Deputy Head of Vienna Police, in line to succeed Schroeder in three years—the second consecutive time that someone from the forensics team had made it to that post.

Karan and Kavya got married within the next three months. Karan quit the media and moved back to GB2 as the Head of Retail Banking. There was little he could do when the board of GB2, under specific joint recommendation from Ronald McCain, the erstwhile CEO of Indian operations and Indrani, had insisted on his return. The money was just too good to refuse. Karan diligently went about strengthening GB2's retail franchise in India. The first thing he had to rebuild was in fact, the most difficult—the trust that GB2's employees, customer and regulators had on the bank. And there was no one else who was more equipped to handle this task than him.